Praise for

THE WAYS OF WATER

". . . Engrossing and unsettling, this riveting and beautifully told story held my attention from the first vivid page to the last. *The Ways of Water* is a stunning debut!"

—ANNA QUINN, author of *The Night Child* and *Angeline*

". . . The authentic voice, rich sensory imagery, and often lyrical, poetic language create an emotional and descriptive feast."

—*CHANTICLEER BOOK REVIEWS*, 5/5 STARS

" . . . immersive . . . . A precarious life is limned with great care and great heart—and with prose that often verges on the poetic."

—LAUREL DAVIS HUBER, author of *The Velveteen Daughter*

"Building on family lore and deep research, Teresa H. Janssen's *The Ways of Water* is a young woman's poignant coming-of-age story that reveals a fascinating slice of early 20th-century life in the American West."

—MARGARET RODENBERG,
author of *Finding Napoleon: A Novel*

". . . riveting . . . . reminiscent of Jeannette Walls's *Half Broke Horses* and Kristin Hannah's *The Four Winds*. The prose is exceptional. . . . The imagery is breathtakingly vivid. . . . But it is the fully fleshed-out characters that will grab the reader and refuse to release them, even long after the reading is complete . . . ."

—ADELE HOLMES, M.D., author of *Winter's Reckoning*

"From its captivating beginning to its redemptive end, Teresa H. Janssen's immersive debut, *The Ways of Water*, weaves a tale of heartache and joy based on family history set in the American Southwest in the early 20th century . . . . A five-star debut."

—ASHLEY E. SWEENEY, author of *Hardland*

". . . captures your heart. With its vivid description, sensuous and poetic detail, you are at one with Josie Belle on every curve and dip of her path. You feel the sting of desert sand on your face and smell the sweet lavender in a baby's bath. But mostly, you are touched by the strength of Josie's family and their bond of love which holds them close, if not always in space but in heart. This is a breathtaking story, exquisitely told, that you will not forget."

—ANNE BROOKER JAMES, author of *The Marsh Bird*

"Teresa H. Janssen's lyrical writing style, narrative voice, and impressive powers of description offer a slice-of-life history lesson that, like all good story-telling, never feels like a lesson. Though faced with daunting hardship, the novel's protagonist, Josie, never loses her determination or sense of self, offering a character worth rooting for. A compelling read for anyone who enjoys thoughtful, well-researched historical fiction."

—SUZANNE MOYERS, award-winning author of
'Til All These Things Be Done

THE
WAYS
OF
WATER

A Novel

TERESA H. JANSSEN

SHE WRITES PRESS

Published 2023
Printed in the United States of America
Print ISBN: 978-1-64742-583-8
E-ISBN: 978-1-64742-584-5
Library of Congress Control Number: 2023913603

For information, address:
She Writes Press
1569 Solano Ave #546
Berkeley, CA 94707

Original cover photo by Teal Smith
Interior design by Stacey Aaronson

She Writes Press is a division of SparkPoint Studio, LLC.

Dedicated to my foremothers, humble women of courage:
Josie Belle Gore Healy, Nannie Belle Lightsey Gore,
Louzaney Edwards Lightsey, Elizabeth Bass Edwards

—✦—

"I might be silent, while you spoke for me and the rest, but for the accident that I was born with a pen in my hand. . . . We love to read the lives of the great, yet what a broken history of mankind they give, unless supplemented by the lives of the humble. . . . The man or woman thus endowed must speak, will speak, though there are only the grasses in the field to hear, and none but the wind to carry the tale."

—MARY ANTIN, *The Promised Land* (1912)

CONTENTS

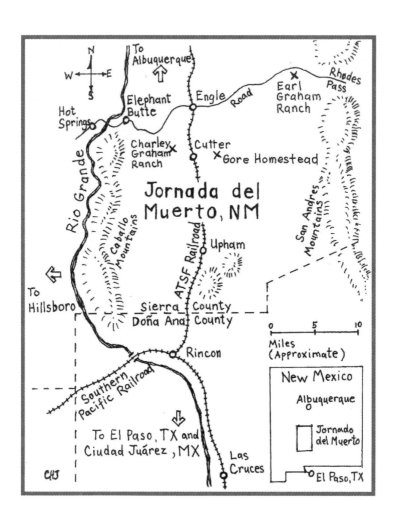

I

THE DESERT

My story is twined, like rope, with that of my kin. The first strand began to fray when Mama, a city girl from Austin, fell in love with a Louisiana railroad man. As Papa ran the steam locomotives across the great deserts of the West, Mama followed him. Steam engines always follow water, and we did too.

_-4-_

When Papa came home, he stalked out to the well, drew up a bucketful, smelled it, and leaned over for a look.

"There's something fouling the water." He let down the bucket again. "I can't get to it. I've a mind to send somebody down."

He scanned the clump of family until his eyes settled on me.

"Josie Belle, you're the one."

I hid behind Mama's skirt.

"I can do it," Charlie said.

"You're too little. Josie's just right."

I poked my head out and glared at Charlie. This was his fault. We'd been sick as dogs for a week. A critter had gotten into the well or been thrown in. When I'd accused my brother, he'd shook his head, spit on his palm, and swore he hadn't done it.

"Sakes alive, Harry, Josie's only six," Mama said. "Can't you send down one of the section crew?"

"Too big and too heavy." Papa took my arm and led me to the well. "I'm going to tie you to the bucket. The rope's plenty strong. I'll let you down nice and easy. When you hit the water, shout and I'll hold you there. Grab onto whatever varmint's floating, and I'll bring you up."

I stared down into the shaft. I wasn't sure Papa was strong enough to pull me back up. What if the rope broke? I couldn't swim.

I shook my head and looked down at my toes. "I don't want to."

Papa bent down, lifted my chin, and looked me in the eyes. "Child, nothing on this earth comes easy. You just got to do what needs doing."

Mama leaned over the opening and peered down the well. "How deep is it?"

"Dunno. Thirty or forty feet."

"Shouldn't we get help?"

"No, I can handle this."

I wished he'd call for Shorty, the railroad crew leader, who was as strong as a steer. Mama sighed. Water was everything to us.

"Take off your shoes and your dress. Your undershirt and drawers are all you need. You don't want to get tangled up."

She pulled me to her belly, nuzzled her face in my hair, and turned me away.

"Now be sure to hold on tight and call out if something's not right."

Then I was straddling the wooden bucket, had a rope securely tied around my waist, and Papa was letting me down into the dark. The bucket jerked. I swung from side to side, and my shoulders, back, and knees bumped against the hand-dug walls. As I went lower, a foul smell rose up to meet me. I wanted to cover my nose but was afraid to let go of the rope. It was so black I could hardly make out the water, and then I saw a reflection of light.

"Stop!" My cry bounced off the walls.

The bucket jolted. I peered into the inky water. I held on to the rope with one hand, leaned forward, and skimmed the top of the water until I felt a lump. Something sank and came up on the other side. It was a bloated animal. I grabbed for it but only pushed it back under. The stench was overwhelming. I wanted to retch.

"Are you all right, Josie?" Mama's voice echoed in the chamber.

I glanced up. I could see her head in the opening, blocking what light I had.

"I need to go down more!" I yelled.

I was jerked lower, and my feet were in the black water.

"Stop!"

Now I was frightened. I let out a sob.

Mama's head blocked the light again. "Hold on, Josie Belle."

She pulled back, and the bit of light returned. I felt for the knot that held the rope around my waist. I leaned over and reached deep into the water. I caught a slimy leg and lifted it into the air. It was a little jackrabbit, swollen to twice its size, its ears wilted, mouth open, tongue stiff and extended. I closed my eyes.

"Pull me up!" I shouted.

I heard the creak of the rope, felt a shudder, moved up a foot, and tilted sideways. I felt another yank, swayed in the opposite direction, and stopped, my back against the clammy wall. What was taking them so long? The rabbit was dangling from my hand by one scrawny leg. Its skin was peeling off. I mustn't drop it. I gripped it tighter. My hand ached.

The rope stayed still. Something was wrong. Maybe the crank was broken, and they'd never be able to pull me up. Maybe the rope was fraying, and I'd fall into the water to drown. I was going to die in this watery tomb.

"Get me out!" My voice sounded hollow, as if I were already half ghost. Then I heard voices above—men's voices.

"Oh, hurry, hurry," I whispered.

"Don't let go," Papa called down.

I was shaking, afraid I hadn't the strength to hold on. Then I felt a tug on the rope, and I was being lifted in steady jerks. The light came closer. The air freshened. Arms reached out and pulled me clear of the well—Papa's arms and Shorty's.

I dropped the rabbit onto the ground and gulped the clean desert air, and it was too much. My stomach cramped, and I vomited onto the dirt. I looked up into Mama's soft eyes. She cupped my cheek and wiped my face with her handkerchief that smelled of roses.

I turned to Shorty. "You're here."

"I run and got him," Charlie piped up.

Oh, my dear brother. I would never be mean to him again.

Papa patted me on the back. "You've done the job of a man, Josie Belle."

I looked up into his grin and beamed.

From that spring day in 1908, I cherished my role as savior of the family.

As we walked back to the house, Mama pulled me close. "I was afraid we might lose you, Lamb."

But it was Mama the desert would claim first.

⚜

There was a time in our family when all was good, like the sixth day of creation in Mama's favorite book of Genesis, when the earth's deserts were still grassland, its precious metals lay undisturbed beneath the soil, and its rivers flowed free. Our days were full of hope. We dreamed of the Promised Land, and I was the lamb, willing to sacrifice myself for the family. That was before our fall from grace and before I decided I couldn't stay as meek as a sheep all my life.

I'm telling my story for Mama. She would want to know about the ones she left behind and what happened in the end. The places have disappeared under a cover of sand, the people have gone to ghosts, and Mama's grave is vanished and unvisited. I'm the only one left who remembers.

Life, like a river, can take some sharp twists and turns. People can shift as much as a water's course. I want to tell the reasons I broke my promises. I want them to be known.

2

We didn't always live in the desert. We'd arrived there years earlier by rail. Mama said we started out in the grasslands of Texas, where the water was plenty, but Papa's trains kept moving west, and we followed them from tank town to whistle stop. My first solid memory is of that almighty train.

I knew Papa ran the train—all the way across Texas and New Mexico. And now he was going to run a different one in Arizona. I was four years old in 1906 and giddy with excitement to be lifted onto the iron machine to go to our new home.

As I sat on the edge of the leather seat, the train began to vibrate. It groaned louder than any creature I'd ever heard, belched great guttural burps, snorted, jerked, and shook to life. I grabbed at the seat. I was trapped in the bowels of a monster sure to send us crashing into the earth. I tried to call for help, but my heart jumped to my throat and cut off my breath. I closed my eyes and covered my ears. The train hissed like a demon and, with a last spasm, stopped.

"Is it over?" I said, only to be thrust into motion again as we shimmied, snarled, and screamed our way out of the station.

Beside me on the seat, my big sister Irene, already eight years old and wise in the ways of the world, held my arm to steady me.

"Don't fret, Josie. You'll get used to it." Clouds flecked with ash curled in through the open window and rushed at our faces.

My eyes stung. I covered my nose. Irene coughed, reached across me, and shut the window with a clack. The din lessened.

Across the aisle, Ida May balanced, her hands folded, already self-contained at six years of age. Mama held little Charlie on her lap, lifting a hand to brush bits of cinder off his tousled head.

As we gained momentum and exploded our way west, I surrendered to the reckless speed of the train and abandoned myself to the unknown. I don't remember the rest of the ride.

Memories of the months that followed have fused into a blur: playing with Charlie under a sawbuck table beneath the skirt of a red-checked tablecloth, feeling the shake of the wide-planked floor as a monster train roared past, falling asleep to the creak of the rocker and Mama's low purr.

An open cabin doorway framed a rectangle of sand, cacti, and sunshine. The white heat of the bare yard seemed somehow perilous. Safety lay in the cooler, somber indoors. I had my hand slapped for picking the leaves off Mama's potted jade plant whose plump petals tempted me beyond reason. The words *Nacozari*, *Douglas*, and *Bisbee* glided from the lips of Mama and Papa to hover above me in dry air.

A man in a white jacket came to our cabin one day. In his hand was a suede suitcase. He told us he was a missionary recently returned from China. Mama let the stranger in. When he removed his straw hat, his head was as bare as an egg. I laughed at Humpty Dumpty come to call.

Mama gave me a frown. "Excuse the children, Minister. They don't see strangers often."

She served him coffee. He opened his suitcase, filled with

leather Bibles. Mama gasped, picked one up, and caressed it.

"I'm a student of the holy book."

To prove it, she bought one. I watched the man walk out the door, his bare-naked head mercifully covered by his hat. He leaned from the weight of his suitcase like a wind-bent tree. As his figure receded down the dusty road, a haze of desert heat rose between us. His legs and torso wavered in the shimmering air, and then he disappeared into the rippled light.

I thought perhaps he'd been a dream, but Mama was sitting at the table with the opened book. She took a pen, dipped it in a squat bottle of India ink, and in loopy script wrote, "Naco, Arizona, 1906" on the inside cover. On the crisp white page that followed, she slowly penned the names of her parents and grandparents, their dates and locations of birth. Then she wrote her own name and Papa's, blotting each line carefully before moving on. On the last two pages she listed her four children. I held my breath as she scribed my name beneath that of my two older sisters: "Josie Belle Gore, born 1901." I'd been given a part in history.

A short time after, Mama's stomach grew big, and she told me a baby was coming to join our family tree. A woman came and helped her have the baby, but he died before I got to meet him. When we were allowed to see Mama, she lay on a white sheet and cried without making a sound.

"Did he have a name?" I whispered as I stroked her arm.

"I named him Gabriel," she whispered back. She said our baby was God's cherub now, and even though he didn't survive, his spirit would always be with us. She didn't smile for a long time.

Sometimes I'd stop what I was doing and quickly look up to see whether I could catch my cherub brother fluttering above, but he was faster than I.

Not long after the baby died, Mama announced we were moving again. Papa had a new train to run. We were heading to New Mexico.

"Will Gabriel come?"

Mama pulled in her breath and gave me a look. "He'll always be with us, Lamb."

We took trunks and bags, the rocker, the sewing box, and Mama's jade plant, since recovered from my ravages. I rode the train with apprehension but no longer feared we were on the verge of exploding.

─✍─

For a time, we lived in a boardinghouse near the tracks in El Paso, several blocks from a Harvey House where travelers could get a room and a meal. Mama watched several of the children of the women who served the food. I remember the constant *clop* of horses bringing passengers to and from the depot.

But soon Papa found us a house so far away we took another train to get there. The air in the crowded coach lay heavy and stagnant. Irene opened her window, and a gust of wind scattered a passenger's newspaper. Mama made us gather and return the pages to the red-nosed man, who rewarded us each with a caramel candy.

Mama pointed to the parched land as we hurtled north. "This is the country Coronado traveled in search of the seven golden cities of Cíbola."

I scanned the blanket of brown. Golden cities? Could that be?

"He never found them."

Disillusioned, I returned to the candy wrapper I was folding into a fan. We stopped briefly at the red-roofed, white stucco depot in Las Cruces, New Mexico Territory, and continued north to the Jornada del Muerto.

"It's a Spanish name. It means 'route of the dead man,'" Mama said. "This is where our new home will be. Oh, don't wrinkle your nose, Josie Belle; it isn't becoming. There's a tale behind the name."

Irene, Ida May, and I scooted to the edge of our seats. Mama leaned across the aisle and spoke above the din of the train.

"Through this desert valley ran the Camino Real, the Royal Road, built for a Spanish king over 250 years ago so he could carry his gold, silver, and jewels between Mexico City and Santa Fe. The road followed the Rio Grande until the river curved to the west."

I searched the old trail running alongside the tracks, to see whether, by chance, a few gold coins had been left behind.

"A river takes the easiest way to the sea, but people cannot always follow such a path. The route along the Rio Grande became too difficult for oxcarts, so they took a shortcut across this waterless land—and many lost their lives."

I got worried. "How'd they die?"

"Some were attacked by robbers or Indians, and others died of thirst."

I scanned the horizon for men on horseback, for a watering hole or dry riverbed, but saw nothing but rock, dry grass, and sand extending to ruddy, far-off mountains.

"I'd just turn around. I wouldn't die of thirst."

Mama gave me a solemn look. "Sometimes you must pass through the desert to get to the Promised Land."

I turned back to the dry sands. "But if there's no water, what'll we drink?"

A shadow crossed her face. "Now we dig wells."

She leaned back in her seat, pulled sleeping Charlie close, and kissed his moist forehead. My belly felt queasy for the rest of the ride.

As we neared our destination, a fleeting rain speckled the dirty window, and I begged to open it again. My first sensations of the Jornada del Muerto were the smell of creosote, like medicine after the scant shower, the whirl of dust, and the glint of rails flanked by telegraph lines dipping between tall poles stretching into eternity. From that day, it was as though I'd stepped out of a dream and started my real life.

II

JORNADA DEL MUERTO, NEW MEXICO

(1907–1909)

The train jolted to a halt, and we clambered off. Mama counted our bags as the handler tossed them onto the hard-packed dirt. I stood close to my sisters. A boy offered us oranges from a cart. A man asked whether we needed our bags carted to the hotel. Mama said no, thank you, we were meeting our party at the depot.

As we stood waiting, the train growled, hissed, and chugged away. I was glad to see it go. I swatted at coal cinders floating in the air and stomped on the ground—so solid, so firm. As the sound of the train died, the travelers and vendors dispersed, leaving us alone.

Sand scratched across the tracks. The wind lisped through the desert grass. A rooster crowed. Someone slammed a door. Mama squinted toward the lot next to the station. A man limped toward us. At his heel loped a lanky dog, fawn-colored with black streaks.

The man approached and stopped, leaning to one side. One of his legs appeared to be shorter than the other. He put his hand to his worn Stetson, cocked his head, and flashed a tobacco-stained grin.

"Good afternoon, ma'am. You must be Mrs. Gore. Marv Fenton's my name. Welcome to Cutter."

I stepped closer to our bags, keeping an eye on the dog.

"Your husband done told me to show you to the house. Said his train would be by on Thursday."

Mama turned to us. "We'll leave the bags here, children."

She took Charlie's hand. Ida and Irene trailed after her, but I didn't want to abandon our belongings. They were all we had.

"Come along, Josie Belle. Our things are plenty safe."

Mama's rocker creaked in the breeze. Her jade plant drooped in the heat. I knelt in the dirt and pushed the plant into the rectangle of shade beneath the chair. I set Mama's drum-sized hatbox on its side to block the wind. Brown-kneed, I hurried after Mama as she kept time with Marv Fenton's crab-like gait.

We followed the cowboy, staying clear of his jetsam of tobacco spittle and the dog that slunk behind him. I glanced up to see whether our cherub brother was following, but as usual, he wasn't to be seen.

"This way, Gabriel," I whispered.

Mr. Fenton led us past the depot, the water tank, the cement block section crew bunkhouse, the stationmaster's house painted Santa Fe yellow and green, and the railroad warehouse. We veered past the livery barn, with its bittersweet smell of urine and manure, and filed by the railroad commissary and the saloon. I spied a cowboy inside, slumped over a plank bar, his face hidden in his bent arms. Ahead was a cluster of shacks sun-bleached gray, and farther on, a real house.

The house stood alone, surrounded by clumps of tall grasses, with a tin roof perched at odd angles over its square walls. We climbed to the porch. The breeze wheezed around us like a tired asthmatic.

"You wait here," Mama said. "No telling what's moved in."

I smashed my nose against a dust-frosted window to peek in and listened to the echo of her heels on wood flooring as she made her way through the sparsely furnished house. Doors creaked as she advanced from room to room. She came out and clapped her gloved hands together, making a puff of dust. "The place is crying for a coat of paint and a roof repair . . . and the dust. Oh, the dust."

She frowned at the dirt on the palms and fingertips of her gloves.

"Mr. Fenton, could you have our bags delivered? And thank you for showing us to our new home."

She put a hand to her moist forehead, leaving a brown bruise.

"By the way, where is everyone?" She glanced at the cluster of nearby shacks. They looked deserted.

"Oh, it's mostly miners stay there." Mr. Fenton tossed his head toward the mountains to our west. "They live up at the mine and come down to spend their pay. The company carts the vanadium, copper, and lead down here by mule, and it gets processed at the Victoria Chief mill." He pointed toward the other side of the depot. "The mill workers live over that way."

Mama nodded and turned to us. "Girls, break off some branches of creosote for brooms. It's time to clean up."

Irene and Ida jumped to it. Charlie whooped, clomped off the porch, and galloped in tight circles in the yard until a larger cloud of dust encased him and blew away. The dog crawled out from beneath the stairs to trail its master from the yard. I went inside and helped Mama air out the house and sweep it clean.

As soon as the baggage arrived, Mama found an old fruit crate, turned it on its side, covered the rough boards with a linen cloth, and set the jade plant upon it like a princess on a throne. It was still deemed an adventure, the settling in.

I wandered out to the porch, where Charlie was rolling marbles down the cracks between the planks. I dropped onto the splintered boards beside him and was pierced in the back of my thigh by a barrage of slivers.

2

Papa had rented the drafty house from a railroad man he'd met in El Paso whose wife had refused to leave Topeka.

"He finally gave up on her," Papa said. "Good thing your mama loves adventure."

I looked at Mama to see whether it was true. She shook her head.

"Don't you believe your papa's tommyrot. One day, we're going to stay put."

From the set of her jaw, I knew she meant it.

A chicken coop, outhouse, and wash stone stood in the dirt yard. Next to the house was the well—the one I would later descend. To the southeast were the buildings of Cutter and, in every direction, a carpet of brown sand and coarse grass with jumbles of spiny branches.

Our days in the gray house were quiet but for the train. Charlie and I spun tops, shot marbles, and skipped rope in the shade of the narrow, covered porch. To the east, we could see the wrinkled ridge of the San Andres Mountains, and to the west, the peaks of the Caballos, the horse mountains. At sunset, when the slopes darkened and were backlit by brilliant shades of orange and red, Charlie and I picked forms out of the peaks and ridges, as other children find images in clouds. We saw the outline of a colossal lizard clinging to the rock, a witch's hat, and the silhouette of a sleeping giant with a lumpy belly. Although I knew he was made of stone, I kept an eye on the ogre, lest he awaken, rise, and trample our valley. Once I thought I saw our angel brother, Gabriel, fluttering near the line of horizon, but Charlie scoffed and said it was a bat going after bugs.

Each morning, after drying the breakfast dishes, it was our job to carry out the stove ash, sweep, and dust. After a day and night of desert wind, the interior of the house was coated with a layer of grit Mama called devil's snow. My last task was to wipe the dust from Mama's jade plant. She told me it had come from China and was as old as she was. I whispered words of encouragement to our exotic guest as I washed its waxen leaves.

After chores, it was our school time. Engle, eight miles north, had a one-room school, but Mama wouldn't send us so far. Irene, Ida, and I sat at the round kitchen table while Mama taught us Mother Goose rhymes and sayings from Poor Richard. We learned our numbers and letters and traced the flowery cursive of the day. I loved to watch the chalk shapes appear on my gray slate and learned to copy the words I used most: *Mama*, *Papa*, *wind*, *sand*, *sun*, and *rain*, and two of the most important—*water* and *train*.

We looked at pictures from an old Sunday school book. My favorite was of Noah ushering the last animals—a pair of elephants with long tusks—aboard a tub of an ark surrounded by rising water. I wondered how water, like gold to us, could be so frightful. Mama said too much of anything could lead to ruin, but that was hard to imagine in a land where everything but sun, sand, and wind seemed scarce.

Mama read the story of Exodus from her Bible. I was haunted by the tale of the Egyptians who had ridden their horses into the dry seabed to be drowned by the waters of the Red Sea. One summer afternoon, as the land baked in a great blue oven, I watched the hens gobble bits of corn and looked up to see two cowhands ride off over the heated sands of the Jornada toward a distant shimmering sea. I feared for their lives should the rippling waters overcome them. I found Mama in the kitchen and told her of their peril. She laughed and said not to worry. Then she caught her breath and gave me a strange look, put down her rolling pin, bent down to the level of my face, and put her floured hands on my shoulders.

"You must never walk toward that water, child, no matter how thirsty you are. It's a mirage . . . a vision of water made by heat waves over sand."

She walked me to the porch, and we followed the progress of the men on horseback as they headed south, trailed by a tawny plume of dust.

"'When thou passest through the waters, I will be with thee, and through the rivers, they shall not overflow thee.'"

From the dreamy tone of her voice, I knew this to be one of the Bible passages she kept ready in her head to sum up a situation.

She broke her reverie.

"Those cowboys won't drown in the desert. Water here is scarcer than a hen's tooth."

She withdrew her hand and went back to her piecrust.

I sat on the gray boards of the porch and mouthed the new word for distant water—*mirage*—as I listened to the soft cluck of hens in their dust baths, contented after having chewed up the last of the corn. I sobbed quietly as the cowboys disappeared beneath the quivering sea.

Later in the Bible story, when Moses led his people into a great desert, God gave them quail at night and manna in the morning. From our porch, I searched the horizon, hoping a flock would appear for suppertime. I ran out on winter mornings to see whether the snow or hoarfrost might be tiny flakes of bread. I believed the Jornada was our mighty desert and that someday we, too, would move on to a land of milk and honey. I believed in miracles.

—❦—

In the lazy heat of the afternoon, the gray planks of the porch became our children's world. Charlie and I lined up the kitchen chairs to play "passenger train." Irene served us pearl tea—warm water with a teaspoon of evaporated milk and a sprinkle of sugar. She looked like a lady in Mama's old apron. Irene was one of those girls who seemed born wise, as if they'd figured out life while in the womb. Mama told her everything.

Ida May joined us for make-believe—but only if she got to be Annie Oakley. Ida, who Mama called "petite," had Papa's gray eyes and golden hair. She was fine and ladylike, and so clever she nearly always got what she wanted.

With her daring shooting skills, Annie Oakley tried to capture Billy the Kid or Geronimo. They, in turn, robbed stagecoaches and took captives. Mama had told us stories of the Kid, who'd been killed twenty-six years earlier at nearby Fort Sumner. Papa told us tales of Geronimo, the fearless warrior who'd been the chief of the local Apache. We knew he'd been captured and sent to prison far away, never to return, but on the bare boards of our porch, the local legends entwined for exciting play.

—❦—

A girl who lived nearby, Guadalupe, came to our house to do the washing. I liked to stay in the yard with her while she squatted over the worn wash stone. Her black braid hung like a fat snake down her back. As her muscular arms beat the stubborn dirt from our clothes, her braid would creep toward her shoulder and leap into her work. She'd pause, grab the thick rope of hair with her free hand, and toss it high through the air to flop on the square of her back.

I played in the dust next to Guadalupe's sturdy legs just to hear the plop of the braid, the slap of wet laundry against stone, and the squelch of water as she squeezed it out. I handed her the wet spindled clothes from the washtub and watched as she hung them to dry over the line of rope running the length of the yard. She chatted to me in Spanish. Although I couldn't understand her words, their melody was sweet to my ears: "*Cariña chiquita, angelita, florecita, mi corazoncito.*"

She let me play with the beads she kept in the pocket of her skirt. They were brown seeds, strung together with coarse thread and knotted to make a circle. From the knot hung five more beads and a tarnished cross. When I held them in my cupped hands and shook them, they rattled like rain hitting our corrugated roof.

When it came time for the midday meal, Guadalupe shared her tortillas, and I returned the gift with johnnycake or a slice of pandowdy, if we had them. Once she brought me a jar of cactus jelly. Mama let me keep it for myself.

"Something sweet, to cover up the bitterness. It's what you need to get by in this place."

I was surprised. I didn't know what was so harsh about our Jornada, except for the wind that chapped my lips and blew sand in my eyes. But Guadalupe and Mama knew the desert better than I.

3

Besides the everlasting wind, the constant of our lives was the train. Cutter was on the track of the Atchison, Topeka, and Santa Fe Railroad. Papa ran its freight between Albuquerque and El Paso. Cutter was a water stop and headquarters for the section crew.

In the beginning, the roar of an engine, screech of brakes, hiss of steam, and piercing whistle were beacons. Charlie and I ran to greet the engineer, always looking to see whether it was Papa. We watched the crew dump cinders, jerk water into the engine, oil up the wheels, fill the headlamp with coal oil, or clean the glass, and we waved to the conductor in the red caboose as the snorting giant thundered out of town.

After a time, the thrill lessened. The din of the trains went unremarked, like the pulse of our veins. Even at night, we hardly woke to the whistle and rumble of locomotives coming down the valley. We sighed, rolled over, and dreamed on. The noise, the smoke, the ash, and the coal smut that littered the ground and blackened our feet weren't merely endured—they were lauded as evidence of progress. The train was our source of income, our lifeline to the greater world, and the vehicle that delivered and carried away our papa.

Mama warned us about strangers who came in on the rails. We weren't to talk to them. Charlie and I minced through prickly weeds to the depot to gawk at the strangers. Prospectors disembarked to head into the Caballos or Black Range. Mr. Fenton kept his livery for those who needed to hire a horse or buy a mule. Ranch hands came to town on payday, while others rode north to Engle's saloons or to Palomas Hot Springs, where ranchers had built a room over one of the sulfur springs. I eyed the miners and cowboys with a mix of curiosity and caution. They were from different worlds.

Salesmen disembarked at Cutter and came by the house to sell their wares. One sold Mama a tattered McGuffey's Reader and an old blue-backed speller. She paid a dentist a dollar to pull Irene's rotten tooth. Sometimes Mama bought an item just to send the peddler on his way.

"Some are poorer than Job's turkey. They make me nervous, so footloose and desperate for company."

I gave the shifty men wide berth when I met them in town.

Aside from the transients, we came to know the local farmers and ranchers—the Jacobs family, who owned a few milk cows and raised Angora goats, and the Grahams, who had a horse ranch west of town and would one day play a key role in our lives.

4

Papa had two days off a month, but they rarely coincided with a birthday or holiday. He was nearly always gone. Mr. Fenton was the only man, aside from Papa, that Mama wanted in her kitchen.

Shortly after we arrived, Mr. Fenton brought over a basket of vegetables.

"Did my husband ask you to bring these vittles, Mr. Fenton?"

"No, ma'am."

"What do I owe you?"

"Nothin', ma'am. I reckon it's the neighborly thing."

He turned scarlet, pivoted, and hobbled off.

Other days, especially near the end of the month when money was scarce, he came by with a sack of flour, a slab of beef, or a bag of Arbuckle's coffee. Mama invited him in to sit for biscuits and a coffee. His dog followed him like a shadow.

Mama took in the hound's sharp canines. "I take it he's good with children."

"I'd trust him with my life. He was left by a Swiss miner who pulled foot."

"What's his name?" I said.

"Angel." He said it the Mexican way, with an *h* in the middle.

I wrinkled my nose and scrunched an eye in disbelief. "I ain't never heard a dog called that."

"*Haven't* heard of *any* dog. And it seems a fitting name for a watchdog," Mama said.

I contemplated how a wolf of a dog could be considered an angel.

I believe Mr. Fenton first came by for Mama's coffee. It was the custom in the valley to reuse the grounds, adding new to the old, and boil them long. Folks joked that if you threw in a horseshoe and it floated, the coffee was ready. It was always drunk black. But Mama bucked the tradition, making her coffee fresh, scattering the old grounds around her potted plants. She never let it boil more than five minutes, and she served it with a sprinkle of sugar.

"Don't that beat the Dutch," Mr. Fenton said. "I never figured java could taste so fine."

Mr. Fenton had run his hitch stable for many years, with some time away as farrier for the cavalry horses in the Spanish–American War. He made his real money breaking mustangs for the Bar Cross Ranch. He'd go anywhere there was a wild horse, break it, and sell it. His short leg didn't interfere. He simply cinched the stirrup higher on one side. Ida once remarked that our "pillar of the community," as Mama called him, was leaning. Mama admonished her.

"What makes you think you're a huckleberry above a persimmon, young lady? Everybody's given a handful of gifts and a peck of troubles. What marks the quality of a person is how he uses his gifts and the manner in which he gets past his burdens."

Mr. Fenton never talked much, but from the glint in his eye, we children knew he enjoyed our company. He sat on the porch, Angel sprawled at his side, and taught us to play songs on his harmonica.

"He's got the patience of Job," Mama said after he'd played a tune for the fifth or sixth time so we could learn it. He taught Charlie marble games—ringer, hot scramble, and Spanish bowl—

and how to plait narrow leather strips into lariats. He showed me how to braid mecates from different-colored horsehairs he'd saved from his brushings and how to twine them into belts and make tassels.

We pointed out the silhouettes in the far mountains—the lizard, a dragon, the sleeping giant.

"Some years back," he said, "a fellow calling himself a geologist come to Cutter. Borrowed a horse and went snooping around. Claimed the reds and browns of these mountains are layers of an ancient sea bottom." He shook his head. "Can you fancy that?"

We couldn't believe it.

"The man declared it was ice that carved out the valley. Now it's filling up with sand from the mountains."

Mr. Fenton said it was rain and wind wearing away the solid ridges until they became the peaks, crags, and saddles we saw from our porch.

"It's a puzzle what centuries of wind and water can do."

We gazed at those mountains and wondered at the work of a patient God.

The day we were over at the neighbor's goat farm petting the kids, and Charlie fell into the pen and sliced his leg open with barbed wire, Mr. Fenton carried him home. He held screaming Charlie while Mama poured iodine the length of the wound. Afterward, we gathered around our brother, now pale and quiet, and Angel touched his cheek with a wet muzzle.

"Now you know why the Apache call barbed wire 'devil's rope,'" Mr. Fenton said as he examined the tear in Charlie's flesh.

His voice was like the armored pads of prickly pear, tender and tough at the same time. He offered to ride for the doctor in Las Cruces but warned it could take a day or more to bring him back.

"I'm no surgeon, ma'am, but I did learn to stitch folks up in the war with Spain. It's best to sew it right quick, while he's still numb. And it'd save you a bundle of money."

Mama studied Charlie, who lay strangely still.

"Yes, it's deep and will need repairing. I'll prepare a needle."

She made Charlie take some gulps of whiskey.

For a work-hardened man, Marv Fenton's touch was gentle, and the way Mama nodded, I could tell she was impressed with his handiwork. Charlie, still in shock, whimpered but endured the stitching. Then, drugged by the alcohol, he fell asleep. Afterward, over a strong cup of coffee, Mr. Fenton told Mama how he'd broken his leg some years ago when a rascally bronco slammed him against a fence post. It had never been set and was reinjured many times before it eventually healed, in the end, an inch and a half shorter than his left. Since then, he liked to see things taken care of in a timely fashion.

"By the way, ma'am," he finished, "you can call me Marv."

He checked Charlie's leg every day until it healed as it should, with a welt running down one side like a lumpy pink snake. We found comfort in Marv Fenton's permanent sun-grin, his bristled face, the wart on his left temple, and his horsey aroma. Even Angel became a close friend, greeting us with a wag of his bushy tail, allowing us to pet his brindle back as he sought relief from the heat in the porch's shade. When our well ran dry during the winter drought of 1909, Marv Fenton brought us buckets of water from his deeper well. When the train derailed outside of Albuquerque, he delivered word about the fatal crash, and later, when Mama was frantic with worry, brought the message that Papa was safe in El Paso. Marv Fenton was as good as family.

~

One frigid December afternoon, Marv Fenton brought us a bag of coal for the stove, and he and Angel came in to warm up. He eased into the chair next to Charlie, who was sorting marbles. Mama ground beans and boiled up a pot of coffee. While Ida and I cleaned the oil lamps, he told us the local history.

"Cutter was one of the campsites along the Camino Real where pools of water collected in the low spots."

He leaned closer to the fire to rub warmth into his leathery hands.

"Back in sixty-eight, they dug a well and found water, and the ranchers came. Mostly from Texas."

He stopped talking and limped to the back door. As he pulled it open and spat into the blowing sand, a gust of bitter cold rushed in. I shivered and inched closer to the stove. He settled in his chair and Mama handed him a spittle jar. He took a swig of coffee and talked on.

"The cattle business is only good if there's water. You missed the drought three years ago. A third of the cattle on the Jornada died. It's a killing place as much as it's a place for living."

Mama cringed and reached for another rag for the rug she was braiding with Irene. "What was here before the ranchers?"

"It's the Apache homeland. But quite a number got killed from smallpox or consumption or captured and run out."

I began to worry. What if our well ran dry in a drought? What if we got sick? Was this still a killing place, true to its name?

Marv Fenton took another gulp. "Then they found gold and

silver in the Black Range, and the miners come in. Things was different then. Heck, they had bear hunts up in the range and shot wild horses in the Caballos for sport. Lots of ridge runners then."

I gasped. I thought horses were the most beautiful of creatures. "Why'd they shoot 'em?"

"Shipped the meat off for feed. Wanted the grazing land for cattle." He glanced up at me. "Plenty survived. They're still up there."

He leaned down to scratch Angel behind the ears.

"Wasn't much here but cattle till the railroad plunked down rails and a water tank. Now we got the mill and quite a town. And there's more change coming." He spat into the jar and shook his head as if it were all bad news. "All a man can do is try to stay in the saddle, no matter how the bronco twists and turns."

He leaned back and gnawed off another corner of a plug of tobacco. He was done.

"Try to stay in the saddle," Charlie repeated to his marbles.

We laughed. Mr. Fenton finished his coffee, nodded to Mama, patted Charlie on the head, and went back to his horse shed.

"He sure pays us a lot of social calls," Ida said as she set her polished lamp back on the table.

"He helps us out," Mama said. "If there's one law of the land, it's hospitality."

I believe Mr. Fenton was sweet on Mama. We all were, for she was charming and pretty. Her dark hair, parted down the middle and pulled back in a loose bun, formed a wispy frame around her face. She had a turned-up nose that made her look younger than she was. Her eyes were the color of milky coffee.

Mama was a softener, like the powder you add to the wash. A lace trim stitched over a severe dress, a linen cloth spread on a rough table, a melody hummed during a tedious wait, a touch, a tender look. She had her ways of rounding off the edges, of filling in the emptiness. She read her Bible and trusted in the good of the world.

I know she liked Mr. Fenton. She may have loved him as much as we children did. But with Papa gone, I heard her tell Irene, encouraging a lonely man was like playing with fire. "And we all know a mere spark can burn down a house."

Although we took our friend up on his offer and called him "Marvfenton," like one long name, Mama refused to address him by anything but "Mister" Fenton.

5

Papa's life was spent on the rails. In that sense, he belonged to the railroad more than he belonged to us. He was gone for weeks at a time.

He was a Horny Toad man, and we were proud of it. The Horny Toad line, also called the Rio Grande Division, was the run between Albuquerque and El Paso. Mama said it took its name from the horny toad lizards that came out after a rain. When they got squished on the tracks, it made the metal rails so slick that the trains lost traction. The firemen and brakemen who swept off the lizards and threw sand on the tracks were called Horny Toad men, and so the division earned its name.

The trip took twelve hours if all went well, and Marv Fenton claimed it was one of the toughest in railroading. In the open gangway, Papa was exposed to the firebox and oven-like summer heat, icy winter winds, and spring dust storms. When I indicated to Guadalupe that my papa ran those trains, she nodded. "*Mucho hombre, tu padre.*" And I believed there could be no finer man.

Papa arrived for his first visit home on the northbound four o'clock. Mama made us wait for him at the house, dressed in our best and dust-free for the moment. He walked through the door, tall and lean, in grimy engineer overalls, neckerchief, and denim cap, gloves tucked into his back pocket, his toolbox and torch in one arm. He tossed a catch of fish in the washbasin. He smelled of engine grease, coal smoke, perspiration, tobacco, and the faint mist of whiskey.

Mama handed him a bar of soap, a towel, and his "home clothes." Irene gave him his china shaving mug, his straight-edged razor with its leather strop, and Mama's hand mirror. He carried these to the pump and doused himself with water. As he scrubbed, he sang "Clementine" in his lazy Louisiana drawl:

Light she was and like a fairy,
And her shoes were number nine,
Herring boxes without topses,
Sandals were for Clementine.

Mama combed her hair, got out her atomizer, and misted her neck and wrists with rose water.

Ruby lips above the water,
Blowing bubbles soft and fine.
But alas! I was no swimmer,
So I lost my Clementine.

He boomed his railroad favorites—"The Lightning Express," "Wreck of the Old 97"—and new songs he'd picked up at the flophouse. Cleaned and shaved, in striped slacks, a collarless shirt, and suspenders, Papa joined us. This time he radiated the sharp scent of lye soap. Even after the hard times when liquor was his balm, it's what I liked to remember about Papa—that tang of soap.

While Mama finished preparing supper, Papa sat with Charlie on one knee and lucky me on his other. He handed his Waltham pocket watch to Ida May to polish. She examined the bold, practical numbers on the open face and rubbed a cloth over the smudged back.

"Did you have the time checked, Papa?"

"It was fifteen seconds off. Not bad, considering I dropped it."

Irene took his engineer's torch that looked like a teapot, polished the brass, trimmed the wick, and filled it with coal oil. Ida wiped the glass of the lantern until it was so clean it squeaked.

Papa related the news from Albuquerque, Las Cruces, El Paso, and places between. I gripped his arm as he described the herd of stampeding Herefords at milepost ten-seventy, and the wagon driver outside of Socorro who'd raced the train to the crossing, forcing Papa to brake and lose time on the run.

"He barely got away with his life. It was that Westinghouse air brake that saved the fool."

He brought news of a boiler explosion in the mountains north of Santa Fe. "It was Gus Bright running that train."

Mama made a funny sound, turned from the stove, and stared at Papa.

"Did . . . did he get off in time?"

Papa shook his head. She got a sad look on her face and went back to her cooking. Papa fiddled with his mustache and stayed quiet for a minute, and then he told us a story about a very slow train winding through the mountains of Colorado.

"An old man with a long white beard tramped up and down the aisles selling popcorn and candy. 'Hey,' called one of the passengers, 'I thought only young boys were supposed to do the selling.' 'That's right,' the old geezer replied. 'I was a boy when this train started.'"

We giggled.

Mama asked what engine he'd run last.

"It was Old Myrtle. She's my favorite gal, strong and steady. A good steamer, and oh, such a pretty whistle." His gray eyes shone.

Mama laughed. "I've never been a jealous woman, but children, I think Myrtle's stolen your papa's heart."

We got to know every engine's name and personality, like that of a horse or a dog. Each was a little different in the amount of steam needed to keep up speed, in the peculiarities of her valve settings, and in the way she'd pull up a hill.

"You run your engine by sound," Papa instructed. "You listen, and she'll help you out. Change your valve setting, and she changes her tone. I nurse my engines along—keep the water and coal just right."

I stayed silent, basking in his smell, the deep timbre of his voice, and the foreign cadence of his speech. We children, having taken on Mama's flatter Texas drawl, were intrigued by his relaxed Louisiana consonants and grandiose vowel lengthening. I believed I was Papa's favorite, but perhaps we all did. That was his charm.

Conversation at the table was between Mama and Papa. They discussed the Brotherhood—Papa's union—the merits of the gold versus the silver standard for currency, and President Roosevelt, whom Papa respected for his military prowess and Square Deal, even if he wasn't a Democrat. I remember talk of cattle rustlers and water disputes, and of coming elections in Sierra County.

That first visit home, Papa cleared his throat and told us about the murder of Pat Garrett in Las Cruces, for no good reason. Garrett was the sheriff who'd killed Billy the Kid.

"Someone's finally settled his hash."

I thought long about that vendetta and added another episode to our back-porch serial.

While Irene washed the dishes, and Ida and I dried, Papa poured himself a glass of whiskey, pulled Mama's rocker up to the stove, and got out his bag of Bull Durham. He set a rectangle of paper on his thigh, took out a pinch of tobacco, and lined it up. Both hands engaged, he closed the drawstrings of the bag with his teeth. He rolled the paper into a pencil-thin cigarette, touched the tip to a hot coal, leaned back, spread his legs, lifted his chin, and inhaled deeply. I stopped drying to watch him exhale white rings that floated up like wavy lassos. They wobbled, came undone, and disappeared into the yellow light of the coal oil lamp.

The dishes done, we sat around the stove. I leaned against his knee and asked him to tell us how he got to be a hogger—a railroad engineer.

"Oh, you know the story."

"Tell it again," I begged.

He took a drag on the last of his cigarette and blew out a little row of smoke rings. Charlie jumped up and tried to catch one but wiped out the whole row. Papa stamped out the butt and began.

"I fell in love with the train when I was a boy. I used to race the Baton Rouge express from the edge of town, then hurry to be the first to bring cold water to the engineer and fireman. I wanted to wear my own striped overalls and carry around a long-necked oil can." He chuckled. "When I was fourteen, I hitched a ride to New Orleans and got a job collecting fares on the streetcars."

"That's when your papa developed his distaste for cities," Mama said. "You lived in an alley for a year, didn't you, dear?"

Papa nodded and regarded the wall for a minute, a hard look in his eye.

"By luck, I got on with the Southern Pacific as a caller. My job was to find the workers called to their trains. I got to know every flophouse, saloon, and brothel within a mile of the depot."

"Harry, please."

Papa cleared his throat. "A year later, I became a shunter. Now, that's mighty dangerous work—crawling beneath the coaches to couple them together. Before I lost a finger, I managed to get a job as wiper, swabbing the caked oil from the engines."

As he rolled another cigarette, he described his climb up the railroad ladder. As hostler's helper, he dumped out the ash pans at night and prepared the trains for the morning run with a new fire, a full tank of water, and a load of coal and sand. Next, he worked as hostler, running the engines and cars in the yard. Finally, he was promoted to fireman.

"I built my muscles shoveling sugar beets in the depot. On one run alone, I shoveled thirty tons."

"That's when I met your papa," Mama added. "He was working the run from Austin to Fort Worth. It was in Austin we met, at the Fourth of July celebration. In ninety-five. Papa offered to hold my hat while I bobbed for apples. He wouldn't give it back until I told him my name. Then he said he'd buy me a slice of cherry pie if I'd talk to him. I always have been partial to cherry pie." She laughed. "It was my undoing."

"And my good fortune." Papa grinned. "Now, to fire a hog, you need a strong back and a weak mind. After I married your mama, my back got tired and my mind got wise."

After years of coal shoveling and studying the railroading manual, Papa passed the test and was promoted to freight engineer.

"We lived in Galveston, Estancia, then El Paso," Mama said. "After that, he took a job with the Southwestern in Naco. You girls remember Naco."

"And then we moved to Cutter," I said.

Moving from place to place seemed as natural as the motion of the sun and the wind.

"And now it's time for sleep. Come give a kiss, then skedaddle off to bed. Your papa's tuckered out."

It was an early bedtime those evenings, with none of the usual complaints. We knelt next to the bed and said our evening prayer as Mama had taught us. We wanted Papa to think of us as good children, for the truth was, he hardly knew us. On nights when he wasn't too tired, Papa set down the stub of his smoke to sing to us through the cracked door of our room. Peace was falling asleep to his mellow bass crooning my favorite, "Daisies Won't Tell."

> *Sweet bunch of daisies,*
> *Fresh from the dell.*
> *Come and kiss me, darling,*
> *Daisies won't tell.*

I couldn't imagine wanting to kiss a boy, but if I did someday, I hoped there'd be daisies.

A day and a half later, the sky a chill blue, the tips of the mountains aglow with embers of sunrise pink, Papa put on his railroad garb and gathered his gear and lunch pail. We stood sleep-warm in our rumpled nightgowns and kissed him goodbye. Soon we heard his train rumble in, and he was gone for another month.

Before leaving, he gave Mama money to pay for the next

month's expenses. I could tell by the purse of her lips whether it was more or less. The amount varied, depending on how many buddies he'd run into in the saloon or how well he'd done at craps. Mama said Papa had too much time between runs. He stayed in a dismal twenty-five-cent room in El Paso and worked on the board, meaning he was put on the list for freight runs. When his name came to the top, he ran the next train going out. For many railroad men waiting to be called up, the saloons became second homes where they found company, card games, and liquor.

On the months when cash was scarce, it was always the same: Mama's stiff embrace and Papa's escape toward the train like the cat who'd swallowed the canary. Yet by the time he arrived home a month later, it seemed Mama had forgotten it all. But I had not. I treasured his arrival, but over the months, as I became aware of how little he left for Mama, I began to begrudge his leaving.

6

To help make ends meet, Mama took up her trade as a modiste. Her reputation as a seamstress spread through the valley, and some women hired her to sew. Papa approved but complained that she looked tired and thin.

"Ours are among the best-dressed children in the county," she reminded him, and perhaps we were. Despite the dust, smoke, and desolation of our ever-changing homes, an unforgiving climate, prowling disease, the whims of the railroad, and the wiles of an absent father, we were always well clothed.

As we grew older, we did what we could to help out.

"Be a good boy, Charlie," Mama said, "and gather some fuel. You go too, Josie."

With Irene and Ida to help in the house, she let me wander with Charlie, though she cautioned us about snakes and forbade us to play on the tracks.

"The trains are plumb dangerous," she warned. "If the wind's blowing from the other direction, you can't hear the whistle." She leered at the shifting sand out our door and shook her head.

"But it's fun to walk the rail," I said. "If you go sixteen ties without falling off, you get your wish. The rails always sing when a train's coming. We'll be careful."

"Stay off those tracks," she repeated.

I was glad to grab a burlap sack and gather cow chips, mesquite, and coal. They were easy enough to find. Coal would blow off the cars as the trains passed, or Papa would have his fireman toss off a couple good lumps just north of town. The company knew of the practice but looked the other way. The railroad could afford it, Mama assured us. When our sacks were full, we stashed them and headed to the depot to check for mail or to stare in the windows of a fancy Pullman.

If the track was empty, we went in search of the section crew whose job was to make sure the rails lay smooth and were clear of hazards. The section around Cutter was straight, but the wind piled sand and debris over the tracks, flash floods destroyed bridges over washes, and cattle had to be chased off the rails before a train was due. The railroad had to pay for every cow it killed.

Charlie and I stood by as the crew gathered up their tools from the supply house. We followed them to the section to be worked, sometimes tracing the ruts made by the iron wheels of the old Spanish oxcarts. We crouched in the sand to watch as they repaired a rail, replaced a tie, or shoveled away blow sand. The crew was mostly "boomers"—single men who moved from job to job with the railroads, mines, or ranches. There were Mexicans, Anglos, Southern Blacks, and men from Europe who hardly spoke English.

The crew leader and quickest spike driver was Shorty, a brick of a man from a place called Memphis. He taught us to play checkers during his dinner breaks, saying we reminded him of his little sisters and brothers.

Back in town, we avoided the hotel and the saloons Mama warned were full of strangers and stopped by the livery to sit on scratchy bales of straw to watch Marv Fenton curry or shoe a horse. After our outings, brown grit clung to our hair and brows, invaded our ears, lodged under our nails, and crept beneath our clothes. Mama gently scolded us as she gave us cat licks on our faces, ears, and necks, but she tolerated our dusty adventures for the fuel we brought home.

-~-

One gusty afternoon, Charlie and I followed Shorty and a new crew member down the tracks and watched them wedge a jack under a rail in the center of a low spot. They grunted as they pumped a five-foot aligning bar used as a jack handle to raise the track, shoveled and tamped crushed rock beneath the rail. They were gathering up their tools when I heard a whistle, like the trill of a bird—but it wasn't a bird.

"A train's coming," I announced.

The men hadn't heard it.

"Off schedule," Shorty said. He and his partner threw their shovels in the wheelbarrows and started wheeling them north toward the depot.

I looked for Charlie, but he was gone. The rail began to hum, and to the north I saw a line of smoke. I scanned the horizon. Then I saw Charlie, upwind, squatting over the track. He couldn't hear the train.

"Charlie!" I shouted, but the wind tore the words from my mouth and shredded them. "Charlie, move!" I screamed.

I ran toward him, fighting against the wind that pushed me back like a fence. I could hear the train behind me now, a tornado of sound. Why didn't he move? He was crouching like a little toad in his brown shirt, his head down. Shorty shot past me, his legs pumping hard over the uneven ground. I stopped. The train roared in my ears. Ahead of the locomotive, Shorty reached Charlie, grabbed an arm, and flung him from the track. The two of them hit the ground on the side of the rails. I caught up to them, and the three of us lay sprawled on the sand as the train barreled by.

They both looked dazed. When the noise faded, I asked Charlie why he hadn't moved. He said he'd been picking at a dead lizard and was surprised when Shorty threw him off the track. He rubbed his shoulder and said it felt like it'd been yanked half out.

"It was Josie who saved you as much as me," Shorty said. "If she hadn't hollered and gone after you, I wouldn't have seen you there."

I looked up to see if my cherub brother was nearby. Maybe he'd been the one to help me hear the whistle. But he was staying hidden.

Charlie and I kept quiet about his close call, but Shorty was a talker. It didn't take long for Mama to hear about it. She came home from the commissary sorer than I'd ever seen her. She pressed her lips into a hard line and stuck her face right up to Charlie's.

"If I ever hear of you on that track again, I'll be meaner than a peeled snake. And after I finish, you'll have your papa to answer to. Lucky for us all your sister was there." She turned to me and managed a half smile. "You are your brother's keeper, to be sure, Josie Belle."

Mama's cheeks were pink and splotchy, she was so worked up. She reached around, grabbed the leather Bible, and held it in front of Charlie.

"Swear, Son, you'll stay off those tracks."

He stared at the holy book but didn't budge. Mama waited, staring daggers at him. Then she set it down.

"You'll have no supper until you swear to God." She turned away. "Now I've work to do."

I followed Charlie out to the porch. He was looking more and more like Papa—tall for his age, handsome, with light brown hair, a nice straight nose, an earnest look—and getting smarter every day. So why was he being so stubborn? It was because our Charlie was an honest Abe. If he couldn't swear to the truth, he'd say nothing.

He went to bed hungry and ate no breakfast or dinner the next day. I looked for a glimmer of sympathy from Mama, but she was as firm as rock. That evening Charlie, half-starved, took hold of the Bible, placed a trembling hand across it, and swore to God and Mama he'd stay off the tracks. And I, always intimidated by the train's power and roar, stayed clear as well.

7

When I was seven and a half, my brother Stephen Talmadge was born. When Mama was so big with child that I feared her belly would burst, she awoke one morning, frightened.

"I had a nightmare," she told Irene. "I dreamed I had a baby and I died. I don't want to frighten you, but dreams are warnings. I'm going to have your papa take me to a doctor for this birth. Just to be safe."

A week later, Papa took her to El Paso. Irene took care of us, and Marv Fenton checked in once a day. Guadalupe did the wash while she mumbled prayers to San Ramón for a safe birth. I was afraid I'd never see Mama again or that I'd have another cherub brother. I could tell Irene was scared too, because she pressed her lips tight, like Mama. But we didn't talk about our worries. Saying the words aloud might make them happen.

Three weeks later, a nurse brought Mama and the baby home. As she left, she turned to Irene.

"Your mother's weak. She's lost a lot of blood. You tell your father that this is the last child your mother should bear."

Irene winced.

Later, as Mama was sitting in bed nursing little Stevie, she told us to enjoy this baby, since it would be our last. I was glad to hear the news. I didn't want her to go away again.

Stevie was a beautiful baby, and I fell in love with him. His head was round as a plum, with soft tufts of black hair, russet skin, and a little white nursing blister on the tip of his upper lip that Mama assured me caused him no pain. Mama found it fitting that he was so pretty. Stephen, the martyr, she reminded us, also had the face of an angel.

I held Stevie in my arms, gazed into his large eyes, still the nebulous blue of a newborn, and wondered what shade they'd turn. There were rainbows of color over his iris, like oil in a puddle. In his eye, I could see the reflection of my face, surrounded by pink and violet. I marveled that my infant brother could see those colors like a halo around me and felt sorry that, as the oil of the womb departed, the hues would be replaced by flat planes of standard color.

Charlie adored Stevie too.

"Thank you for bringing me home a brother."

Mama laughed. "You're welcome, Charlie."

She winked at me. It made me feel grown up.

After Stevie was born, I didn't look for my cherub brother, Gabriel, anymore. I figured that Stevie might be Gabriel come back to live on Earth.

Mama was too weak to nurse for long, so we gave him cow's milk, but it made him colicky. His face went from plump to pinched. I circled the kitchen table with my squalling brother, trying to be extra patient, nervous he'd decide to return to heaven. After a few weeks, Mama was up and about, though peaked. She never had much milk, but she could usually calm our angel baby.

8

I t was during the late summer of 1909 that things changed. Papa lost his job and moved home. He wasn't sick, so I figured it had to do with the railroad. We were seven in the house with no regular income but sporadic amounts from Mama's sewing and the sale of our eggs. Papa got irritated when we made noise and was unnerved by Stevie's crying. He picked on Charlie for small failings and took over Mama's rocking chair. Marv Fenton stopped coming by, so Charlie and I sought him out at the livery.

Papa started leaving the house to socialize with the section crew. Late at night I heard him come back home singing melancholic love songs, "Red River Valley" and "Daisies Won't Tell." I listened as he fumbled with the door latch, tripped over the sill, shut the door loudly, and bumped his way through the darkened house to the back bedroom. Some mornings I woke early to find him snoring on the sofa next to the stove. To give him peace, Mama shooed Charlie and me outside, where we played buckaroo, trying to lasso hens with our homemade lariats.

I was disappointed. All I'd ever wanted was for Papa to be home, and now that he was with us, I wished he'd go back to work.

One morning, when Irene and I were making bread, she told me the truth about Papa.

"He got fired," she whispered as she leaned over her ball of dough. "He broke the rules and got caught drunk running a train.

Mama says there's no second chance for an engineer who drinks."

I pulled my hands out of my dough and stood up straight. "Our papa?"

She nodded. "Somebody turned him in. Mama says it was bound to catch up with him sooner or later. She says it's just as well somebody snitched before there was a crash, but Papa says it would never have come to that."

Irene gave me a long, hard look, making me feel as old as she was. "He's been blacklisted. Means he can't run the hogs anymore."

She began to pummel her dough with clenched fists.

My hands went limp. "What will he do now?"

"Dunno." She flipped the round of dough and kept on kneading.

I was embarrassed for Papa and for our family. For a time, I couldn't look at him without seeing the image of a black blotch. It was then that my stomach aches began, like coals smoldering in my gut. At first Mama told me it was indigestion and gave me chamomile or ginger tea to drink. When it didn't go away, she said I needed to stop worrying. Everything would be all right.

After a few weeks at home, Papa got a job with the Diamond A north of town, driving cattle to the stockyard in Engle. The ranch provided a mount and a saddle, but he had to spend ten precious dollars on a pair of store-bought boots. He left us for several weeks, and my stomachaches went away.

His first night back, Papa looked like another man, his clothes, skin, mustache and eyebrows brown as Mama's pie meringue.

"I was stuck riding drag. It's nothing but dust in the back of the herd." He coughed and spat out a wad of brown phlegm. "If

I don't fall out of my saddle and get trampled or dragged from my stirrup, I'll probably get bit by a snake or suffocate from the dust. I'm too old for this, Nannie. It's like starting over."

He peeled off his hat. His hair was matted, his forehead pale above the hat line. He looked beat.

"It's no safer than running trains. We nearly had a stampede a night I was riding watch. A pack of coyotes started yapping nearby and spooked the cows with calves. Good thing Charley Graham and Elias Gomez were there to head 'em off."

Irene brought Papa soap and a towel, and Mama took his hat to be scrubbed.

"About all I'm good for is swearing and singing."

Papa untied his soiled kerchief and removed it from around his neck.

"Singing?" Mama said.

"We swear all day to keep the cattle moving and sing to calm them at night."

To think that my papa, who used to stand so proudly in the open door of a locomotive, was riding drag, the lowest position in the drive, and singing to cows.

He brought home a registry book he'd borrowed from the trail boss and studied the brands and earmarks of the local herds. The cattle drive over, he left again to help with a fencing project on the Graham horse ranch, but it was a move of desperation. He was no cowboy, although he rode well enough. We all knew a wrangler made chicken feed—not enough to support a family.

***

In early October, just after my eighth birthday, Mama received a letter from her sister Lucy in Austin. Grandmother Louzaney was gravely ill. Aunt Lucy urged Mama to come to Austin to pay her last respects. She enclosed twenty dollars. With Lady Liberty gazing from that bill, Mama announced that she'd like to go back to Texas.

"I'll not step into the same room as your sister," Papa said. "Not since her tirade the last time we left Austin. She's hotter than a branding iron." He shoved his hands in his pockets. "No, Nannie Belle, I'd as soon stay here."

"I've a hankering to go, Harry. With you out of work, there's no reason for us to stay."

Mama stood with her hands on her hips, her lips pursed so tightly that a ring of white encircled her mouth. I felt tense. It was unusual for the two of them to speak so forcefully in front of us children.

"Now, don't get huffy. I reckon I can find a train to run if you could be patient. I hear they're hiring in Mexico."

Mama cut him a look, then bent to the floor, plucked up Stevie, and pressed him to her breast.

"It's my duty to see my dying mother. And I won't leave the children here."

"Go then. We'll need to move sooner or later. Give your father my regards and your poor mother."

Papa stalked out the door, leaving Mama standing.

Years later, I read the other part of Aunt Lucy's letter: *How can you manage, Nannie Belle, living in the wilderness with five children and a husband who's never home? And now he's out of a job, as I predicted. Come to Austin where Brother Stephen can find Harry work, and you can raise your children to know the comforts of civilized society.*

⚓

The next morning, Papa left for El Paso to look for work. Saying goodbye to him in the chill dawn seemed like old times, but I clung to his neck longer than usual. I didn't know when I would see him again, and it would surely be in some new place.

That afternoon, Mama packed up everything—our clothing, a box of photographs and letters saved, the Bible, the bag of medicines, toys, linens, kitchen supplies, her sewing box, her spindle-back rocking chair, and our jade plant. We sold our chickens to the Jacobs family.

I was sorry to leave Shorty, Marv Fenton, and Angel, who'd lived up to his name. Guadalupe, who'd become my friend, gave me a jar of my favorite prickly pear jelly. Marv Fenton came by with food for our dinner basket—bread, sausage, and cheese—delicacies. He was quiet as always. He reached into the pocket of his work vest and handed Charlie his Hohner harmonica. "That's to share." Then he searched in another pocket and brought out a small black rock for me. "It's called Apache tear. I got it up at the lava bed. It's so you'll remember this place. Angel's going to miss you something frightful."

The rock was as dark as jet, but when I held it up to the sky, it was as if I were looking through smoke-stained glass. The whole world looked cloudy.

Marv Fenton placed a five-dollar bill in Mama's hand "to buy fixings for the children." When she tried to give it back, he wrapped his calloused hand over her small fist, held it for a long minute, and shook his head. She probed his face and didn't argue.

Before we headed toward the train, I turned around for a last look at the house. Its warped boards had seen no new paint. The tin roof was as awkward as ever. Above its peak, a V of honking geese winged by on its way to other lands. I couldn't help thinking that something better lay ahead, maybe that land of milk and honey.

As we neared the depot, black smoke, like a bloated snake slugging through the sky, signaled the locomotive's approach. Marv Fenton saw us aboard, touched the brim of his hat, and returned to his horses. I was glad he didn't watch us go. We all knew that if you watched a train out of sight, you wouldn't see those travelers again.

I sat calmly on my cracked leather seat, no longer bothered by the clamor and speed of the machine that had become a primary player in my life. The train was our safety line, rescuing us from our troubles, carrying us back to our roots. That blue-sky afternoon, as we roared south through the Jornada del Muerto, Irene and Ida chattered, Mama hummed a husky lullaby to Stevie, and Charlie knelt next to me, pretending to run the train. I clutched my jelly jar, feeling as sweet and sour as its contents.

—≈—

I suppose that's when the flow of our lives took a swerve, like a river run up against a boulder. Papa took one course and we another. Yes, I sensed it as a girl, but I see it clearly now. That was the first deviation.

III

AUSTIN

(1909)

My sisters sat across from me for most of the train ride to Austin. Irene crocheted a lace collar to beautify the first simple dress she'd sewn herself. Ida stitched the hem of an apron. I pushed aside the dusty brown curtain and pressed my forehead to the window.

Outside, over the copper earth, flaxen grasses bent to the breeze. Clumps of mesquite and saltbush, bunches of spear-leaved yucca, and stands of evergreen creosote flew by. Most of the desert creatures knew to hide at the first vibrations of the rail, but I saw a javelina snuffling in the flat-jointed leaves of a prickly pear, and a mother quail and her four tiny babies scurrying for shelter behind an agave.

My eyes grew sore from the glare of sun on sand. I lifted my head from the window and turned to my sisters. They laughed.

"You look like you've been kissed by the devil, Josie Belle," Ida said. "It's a big red mark on your head."

I fingered my forehead.

"And your hair's mussed up and your ribbon's fallen out."

I found my crumpled bow on the floor, tried to tie it back on, but gave up. I wished that I could be as composed as Ida. Unlike the rest of us children who'd been named for members of Mama's and Papa's families, Ida May was given her name because Mama thought it was beautiful. I figured that was what made her so self-assured. She could live for herself. I watched her fingers fly as her dainty foot tapped to some internal rhythm. I was two years younger than Ida, but I was already an inch taller and wore a size-6 shoe. Papa joked that if my feet kept growing, he was going to have to order me herring boxes for shoes, like poor Clementine. I was built strong and long-limbed, like Papa, but I favored Mama in looks, with my dark hair and hazel eyes. I hoped I might be as pretty one day.

My other special feature was my hearing.

"Josie has ears like a coyote," Ida announced. I was offended until I realized that she was referring to how well they listened, rather than their size. I could hear a train or horse before anyone else. Papa said to pay attention for the first crack of the shells of the mourning dove chicks in the nest on our roof. That made me laugh, and I did try to hear their pecking. I began to keep an ear out for birds and learned to distinguish their calls.

※

"You may have been marked by events around your birth," Mama told me one day. "You came into the world early and alert. A fortnight before you were due, we received news that President McKinley had been shot. The nation was shocked and I was desolate, as I had high regard for our peace-loving president."

"Even if he did wage a campaign against free silver?" Papa interrupted.

Mama nodded. "I was staying with my sister JoJane in St. Louis so I could have the care of a doctor for your birth. After the shooting, she invited the neighbor women to the house. They collapsed into hysteria, and I was drawn in. Not eight hours later, on the ninth of September, my labor pains began, and you arrived before midnight. You were a quiet baby, as if you were born listening for the news we were all waiting for. And just five days after your debut, we received word that our president had passed away."

She shook her head. "The year of your birth, 1901, signaled the end for so many. In January, Queen Victoria died, and her daughter, Empress Frederick of Germany, passed on the same day as our president. And sadly, my dear brother Johnnie died two months before your arrival."

"Wait a minute," Papa said. "A mighty fine thing happened that year. Teddy Roosevelt became president."

Mama nodded again. "Now, our Charlie was born in a year of beginnings. In 1903, the Wright brothers flew their airplane, Mr. Ford started his motor company, and the government leased the Canal Zone, a progressive move."

She scrutinized me. "I wonder what it means to begin life in a year of death."

"It means she's got big shoes to fill," Papa said. He glanced down at my feet. "And she seems to be growing into them already."

"Oh, don't tease." Mama suppressed a giggle. "She's doing a fine job. Twice now Josie's saved our family from harm."

I treasured my story.

2

The trip to Austin took a day and a night and involved two transfers. We slept fitfully beneath thin blankets in the tourist-class day coach. By morning, the cramped restrooms stank, the aisles were strewn with orange peels and peanut shells, and the car smelled of the coal oil gas lamps. I woke with a headache. Baby Stevie cried, so Mama carried him from carriage to rocking carriage, until the train jerked and threw Mama and the baby against the back of a seat, and she bruised her hip. It was safer to stay seated. We passed Stevie among us to keep him amused.

As we neared Austin, clouds began to congregate on the horizon. In the heavy dawn, church steeples and tall buildings sprouted like weeds from its bluffs. Irene and Ida opened their window to better see. Mama handed us our good dresses, and we changed in the cramped restroom. I perked up when I returned to my seat and saw Mama's face, flushed with excitement.

Then, in the humid air, lightning flashed. I whiffed its acrid scent. A crash of thunder followed. Stevie wailed in Mama's arms, and Charlie held on to her like a clingstone. More bursts lit up the city. Colors came out—red roofs, white belfries, green shade trees. A blast of wind broadsided us, and Irene jumped up to shut our window. As we neared the station, the clouds burst. Torrents of water poured onto the train, beating the roof like a herd of frenzied horses. The train slowed.

Mama peered out the window and let out a sob. Alarmed, I looked into the sideways rain. Gray water slipped down the glass, and I could see nothing but blobs of color. When she spotted her family in front of the depot, I watched her features contort. Her eyes became slits, her nose crinkled into a red ball, her mouth trembled in an upside-down smile, and she started to weep. I got up to comfort her. She shrugged me off and struggled to pull herself together. As we inched along the track, she wiped Stevie's face, tucked in Charlie's shirt, and righted the jade plant that had spilled dirt onto the floor. I craned my neck to see what she'd seen. Somewhere behind that wall of rain was a force so powerful as to make my grown-up mother cry. I wanted to go back home.

We lurched to a stop, gathered our belongings, and descended the giant steps of the train. Mama pushed us forward toward a clump of strangers huddled beneath the covered area outside the station doors. A woman emerged. She wore a hat with a rain-spattered brim and a drooping feather. She lunged toward Mama, blubbering, embracing her, kissing her, and nearly smothering little Stevie. Then she turned and gathered the four of us children into a jumbled hug. I held Mama's plant, turning my shoulder to protect its leaves. This must be Aunt Lucy. Behind her stood a smiling man in a bowler that dripped water from its center. He had a waxed mustache that turned up at the ends. He asked us our names and then pulled us into his frock coat for a wet embrace. This was Uncle Stephen.

"Your grandparents are at home. Neither is well enough to leave the house." He linked his arm in the crook of Mama's elbow. "Nannie Belle, let's go find the redcap who's got your luggage."

Mama smiled, handed Stevie to Irene, and walked off with Uncle Stephen. Aunt Lucy ushered us into the station.

"Let's look at you now." She stepped back. "Have you ever

seen more handsome children?" she boomed in the vaulted hall.

Some people paused and looked our way.

"So you've finally left that dreadful desert and come home to us." Her feather, drier now, bobbed as she spoke. "Your aunt JoJane will be coming from St. Louis in another week. Won't it be grand to have the family together?"

We stood, unsure of what to say. Aunt Lucy thundered on about the ghastly hot summer that had finally ended. Irene bounced Stevie in her arms and nodded politely. Charlie stood pigeon-toed, staring up at the ornate ceiling. I tried to pat down the loose soil around Mama's plant.

Uncle Stephen appeared at the station door and motioned for us to come. We followed him out to the street, where two buggies stood waiting. Mama was already seated in the hired Rockaway carriage. Uncle Stephen took Irene, Stevie, and Charlie and made a dash to join her. Aunt Lucy, Ida, and I ducked out of the deluge into the smaller runabout. As we moved away from the station, I could see little but rain and blurred lights, and then nothing, as the small oval window was fogged by my warm and rapid breathing.

My grandparents' house on Weslyn Avenue was the finest place I'd ever seen. The permanence of the brick exterior (each brick laid by Grandfather), the generous, high-ceilinged rooms, the heavy mahogany furnishings and rich decor—all exuded a rightness of being that I'd never imagined. I felt safe.

"Now, where's your grandfather? It seems he dozes every time he sits down. Father," Aunt Lucy shouted, "come greet your grandchildren!"

An old man with a pale face and wispy white beard shuffled into the hall, leaning hard on a cane.

"I heard you come in."

He began to cough. The hacking shook his frail frame, and he struggled to breathe. His chest crackled. I feared he'd pass out. Mama went to him and held his free arm.

"Father, you're unwell. Should he go to bed, Lucy?"

"No, he does better upright."

"I'm fine now," he rasped.

Mama gently embraced him and then turned to us.

"Children, meet your grandfather Joel."

The withered man looked lost in his baggy suit. His cane was of glossy wood with a yellowed ivory handle that I knew came from an elephant. I remembered the picture of Noah's ark and the long-tusked creatures in our Sunday school book. How uncanny that one of those tusks should have found its way into my grandfather's hand.

I stepped forward in my turn and embraced him. He smelled piney and sharp, like Mama's bag of medicines. He placed his hand on my shoulder and regarded me directly. Milky circles rimmed his colorless eyes.

"I finally meet my namesake. Josie, you're most welcome."

His chest rumbled, and a deep cough stopped his breath again. He leaned over like a wind-battered bush, finally pulled in a breath, and straightened up. He looked all worn out. Aunt Lucy clucked and led him back to the parlor.

Then she ushered us upstairs. I felt like a princess ascending the wide staircase to the second-floor bedroom where Irene, Ida, and I were to share a canopied bed. Aunt Lucy told us to keep our voices low because Grandmother Louzaney was in the room at the end of the hall and was terribly ill.

3

Grandmother Louzaney was dying of cancer, and nothing could be done. I met her one afternoon when Mama whispered for me to follow her upstairs. Mama pushed open the heavy bedroom door as the nurse, a small woman with a white wimple, slunk out. I swiveled to stare at her retreating figure. As I turned back, a sour odor overwhelmed me. Heavy curtains covered the window. A gas lamp across the room burned low, throwing more shadow than light.

I followed Mama's gaze, almost missing Grandmother's alabaster face amid a mound of pillows. I shrank back, but Mama took my elbow, and we approached the bed.

The old woman turned to us. Her cheekbones protruded beneath tissue-thin skin. Her dark eyes gleamed, as if all the life she had left were concentrated there.

"This is Josie Belle, Mother."

Grandmother held her hand out to me. It felt like a dried leaf, withered and weightless.

"Josie Belle," she croaked, "be a good girl. Help your mother take care of your brothers and sisters." She struggled for breath. "God keep you."

She let go of my hand and closed her eyes.

I glanced up at Mama.

"Give your grandmother a kiss."

I felt too sick to kiss her. The stale air, rank with the smell of laudanum, was smothering. I sent Mama a panicked look. She nodded sternly. I bent close to Grandmother's face. Blue veins stood out from her transparent skin. Her eyebrows were gone.

I kissed her forehead. She didn't stir. I peered up at Mama, pleading to leave.

Entering the hallway, I felt my stomach draw into a tight knot, somersault, and I was afraid I would retch. I looked at Mama. Her face was pale.

"I can hardly bear this myself." Her hands shook as she smoothed her skirt. "When you pull yourself together, you may join the others below."

She turned and walked downstairs. I stood in the center of the hall and recalled Grandmother's pallid skull and the stench of her breath. My stomach flip-flopped, and I ran to my room where I vomited into the washbowl. When I felt better, I dumped the contents of the bowl into the garden below, washed my face, and descended the stairway.

4

After the first week of novelty in my grandparents' home, a weight settled on me. Perhaps it was the shadow of Grandmother's impending death, or the paucity of light in the dim, curtained rooms, or the humidity of the Texan air. I longed for the open sky, pure light, and freedom of New Mexico.

The house was crowded. Aunt Lucy, who wasn't used to having children underfoot, scolded us when we played tag around her skirts or hide-and-seek behind the furniture, blew tunes on our new harmonica, or called to one another in voices that were too shrill. And she was unnerved by Stevie's crying. She was quick to instruct Mama on ways to calm him: a soak in lavender water, tincture of oregano, tummy massage, a new type of bottle with a nipple that prevented air bubbles. Mama tried them all. Stevie continued to fuss.

Aunt JoJane's arrival on a Saturday afternoon in mid-November brought a dose of relief. She breezed in the door in a billowing travel duster.

"I'll stay until the end," she promised her sisters. "We'll get through this together."

I wasn't sure what this meant. The end of her stay? The end of winter? And then I knew. The end of Grandmother.

I was always a light sleeper. Several nights after Aunt JoJane's arrival, I lay awake for a long while, then went into Mama's room to cuddle in, but she wasn't in bed. I padded downstairs. Grandfather was snoring in the parlor. From the dining room I heard voices. I stood outside the doorway.

"It's a crying shame," Aunt Lucy boomed. "Stephen has a lovely house, you've yours, JoJane, but Nannie Belle has nothing of her own."

"Father is traditional," Aunt JoJane said. "Our family home will go to Brother Stephen."

I peeked around the doorframe to see Mama and her two sisters sitting around a table spread with fabric. Mama held sleeping Stevie in her arms, and my aunts were pinning pattern pieces to the beige material. I pulled my legs into my nightgown and huddled in a ball outside the door.

"Now tell me about this nurse, Lucy," Aunt JoJane said. "Why in heaven's name, this being a Baptist home, have you hired a Catholic sister to nurse Mother?"

"There's a whole flock of nuns from Germany living at the mission," Aunt Lucy said. "They need to raise money to build a convent and hire out for nursing. Please pass the pincushion. She gives excellent care, even if she can't speak English. And as you know, we Baptists excel at new beginnings, but Catholics do death the best."

Aunt JoJane snickered. "Well, as long as Mother doesn't mind, and Father never did worry much about religion."

I heard the metallic slice of sewing shears as someone began cutting, the crinkle of the paper pattern, and a murmur that the fabric cut well, and that the girls' dresses should turn out nicely. Then a pair of scissors hit the table with a clank.

"I won't beat around the bush any longer. Nannie Belle, what are you going to do?" It was Aunt Lucy. "Of all your suitors, you chose the least promising. Harry charmed you into marrying him. I told you that years ago."

"Nannie married for love," Aunt JoJane said. "And I don't intend to be harsh, Lucy, but I'm not sure you did better."

No one ever talked about Aunt Lucy's first marriage, which had ended unhappily.

"We can't all marry staid bankers," Aunt Lucy said.

"I chose the middle path, some love and some security," murmured Aunt JoJane. "But we are on the subject of Nannie's future."

Why didn't Mama speak up in support of Papa? Then I remembered how it felt when my two older sisters discussed me—as if my views were of little importance. I felt a slow ache begin in my stomach.

"We're simply trying to help, Nannie," Aunt Lucy said.

"Yes, always trying to help! Your opinions are the reason Harry doesn't want to return to Austin."

"Whatever Lucy thinks of Harry, the fat's in the fire," Aunt JoJane said. "You're here, Nannie, and homeless, while your husband's out roping cattle without a proper means to support you." She pounded her fist onto the table. The shears rattled. "And your dire situation is because of that cursed alcohol."

"Are you still involved in that cause?" asked Aunt Lucy.

"I am indeed. Prohibition will help women like Nannie. What's the future for you and your precious children, Sister? You need to think of their education. Now, let me hold that baby."

Skirts rustled. Chairs creaked. Aunt JoJane cooed, "What an angel."

"I doubted he ever slept," Aunt Lucy said.

"I received a letter from Harry yesterday," Mama said. "He's been offered a job as freight engineer in Old Mexico. On the run from Juárez to Chihuahua City. He's gone to appraise the living situation in Chihuahua."

"Goodness, now he's dragging you to live in another country?" said Aunt Lucy. "You're a city girl, Nannie. You've no business in the desert."

"You don't know anything about life in Mexico."

"Oh, maybe I'm jealous. I was the one who dreamed of travel and have rarely been out of Austin. And you who were content to sit home and sew have been dragged all over the West."

"What do you want, Nannie Belle?" Aunt JoJane asked.

I held my breath. The clock in the parlor ticked loudly. Grandfather coughed in the parlor.

"I want my children to be healthy and happy. You know I live for my children." Mama's voice lowered. I strained to hear above Grandfather's hacking. ". . . Harry home more." She paused. "And I want him to stop drinking."

The sisters were quiet.

"Harry will never want to live in Austin. Not only because of Lucy. He hates cities." Mama's voice broke. "I'll always have to live far from home."

"It looks as if you're stuck between the devil and the deep blue sea," Aunt JoJane said. "If you stay in Austin, it will be the end of your marriage, and I pity a woman alone with five children. I've heard that Chihuahua has a growing American community."

"I think she should stay in Austin," Aunt Lucy said. "Harry can ride the rails to Timbuktu, if he pleases, but if he cares about his family, he'll find work in Texas. We all know he'll never stop drinking. They never do." She slowed her words. "Nannie would do fine without him. She could open up a dress shop. Stephen could help her get established. Nannie's as talented a seamstress as Mother was, bless her."

My mind reeled. Never see Papa again?

"Gentlemen are sure to come courting. You're still pretty as a peach, Nannie."

"Oh, Lucy. Have you never been in love?"

"You're too sentimental. You need to get angry as a hornet at Harry. Scare him into behaving—"

"Oh, help gather the pins, Lucy, and stop badgering your sister." Aunt JoJane sounded cross. "It's for her to decide."

I could hear Mama crying. My throat tightened. I wanted to go to her but couldn't give myself away. I rested my forehead on my knees and smelled the scent of soapy flesh in flannel. Inside my scrubbed skin, I could hear the pounding of my heart.

"Here. Take my handkerchief, Nannie."

Mama blew her nose.

"We only want what's best for you," Aunt JoJane said. "What I've learned from my years in St. Louis is that your home is where you make it. I'm sure you'll come to the right decision. Now, wipe your tears, Little Sister, and let's head to bed. It's late, and this baby has gotten heavy."

Stevie woke during the transfer of arms and began to whimper. Aunt Lucy mumbled some kind of apology. I heard the scrape of chairs and the sound of the table being cleared.

I jumped up from my cocoon. My lower limbs had fallen asleep. As I mounted the stairs, my feet pricked, like the sting of burrs in the Jornada. I suddenly missed my home, and Marv Fenton and Angel, and Guadalupe and Shorty. Most of all, I missed Papa.

I tiptoed back to bed, careful not to wake my sisters. I heard my aunts' slow steps up the stairway. One of them opened our bedroom door and peeked in. I played possum, and she moved on to her room.

I curled my legs around Ida's limp body. New thoughts spun in my head like little whirlwinds kicking up dust from corners of my life—Papa's drinking, Mama's loneliness, and our rootless, transient life. And now talk of Mexico? What would become of us? When would we see Papa again? And in what new part of the desert? I lay thinking for a long while. As long as Grandmother was still alive, our place was here in Austin. After that, I didn't know. I hoped that Grandmother would live forever.

W e children were scolded for making noise in the house, but Weslyn Avenue had enough buggies and erratic motorcars passing to make it hazardous for play. Charlie and I stood at the window, lured by the rattle and roar of those new machines on wheels, but after a time, they lost their pull. Sympathetic to our confinement, Aunt JoJane commandeered Uncle Stephen's runabout buggy and driver and organized tours to get us older children out of the house.

She took us to city parks and once to see the pink granite capitol building that stood like a palace with its magnificent metal dome and Goddess of Liberty statue. I gawked at the marble memorials to Sam Houston and Stephen Austin and wondered whether they were always so stern.

"It's the largest state capitol in these United States," Aunt JoJane said. "Makes you feel proud to be a Texan."

Was I a Texan? I wasn't sure what I was—born in St. Louis, lived in Texas and Arizona, but most recently in New Mexico. I'd have to ask Mama.

One afternoon Aunt JoJane tried to teach us to swim under the shade of a row of pecan trees lining Barton Springs. I stripped down to my bloomers and splashed around in the warm, spring-fed pool, but I couldn't manage to keep above the water. I wanted to stay longer to figure out this thing called swimming, but Aunt JoJane feared we would be late for supper. I left disappointed, determined to learn to float another day.

6

Three weeks later, Mama received a telegram from Papa, then locked herself in her bedroom for an entire afternoon. Aunt Lucy relayed its message.

"Your father's in Chihuahua. He wants you all to come to him. I suppose your mother's trying to decide whether her affection for your father warrants risking your lives. She never was quick about making up her mind. Of course, she knows my opinion." She stood and made as if to wash her hands.

I crept up the stairs and stood outside the door. What was Mama doing? Was she trying to decide whether she still loved Papa? Should I tell her that I still loved him and wanted our family to be together and didn't mind where—Mexico, Austin, or Timbuktu? No, I mustn't disturb her. I left to find Charlie who always cheered me.

The next morning at breakfast, Mama lowered her head to lead the blessing, but instead she announced, "We're moving to Old Mexico, children. Your papa's waiting."

Aunt Lucy dropped her fork and left the table. Ida scowled. She wanted to stay in a fancy house in Austin. Irene smiled. I jumped from my chair and hugged Mama.

When a river comes upon a large impediment, it splits. When safely past, its branches often reconvene, and it resumes its course. But the river has been altered and has surely picked up sediment along the way.

Our murky path decided, we enjoyed that Austin Christmas, more festive than our simple holidays at home. Uncle Stephen had a tall pine delivered. Mama and her sisters decorated it with red-and-white ribbons and silver balls.

They gave us girls beige dresses with extra-wide hems. I feigned surprise. For baby Stevie, a wooden train with a bobbing smokestack sat beneath the tree. Charlie received a real bow and arrow from Uncle Stephen, the quivers made by a Comanche Indian, and from the aunts, a pair of rawhide cowboy boots with scalloped edges, mule ears, and his initials embroidered on the sides. He slept in them that night. I wanted a pair of boots with my initials, not a boring dress.

Papa sent Mama a gift he'd bought in Albuquerque—a silver brooch of Cerrillos turquoise and red coral. Mama sent Aunt Lucy a look I recognized as the kind that shoots like lightning between sisters and crackles with "I told you so." Mama pinned on the brooch.

We stayed two weeks beyond New Year's. I suppose we were all waiting for Grandmother to die. Finally, the aunts told Mama she needn't stay longer. Their mother wouldn't go until she was ready. We packed our bags.

Grandmother was asleep when we filed in to kiss her cheek. I could just make out the rise and fall of the sheet from her shallow breaths. With her veined lids cloaking the light of her eyes, it seemed that nothing much was left. Amid Stevie's cries, we went into the parlor to say goodbye to Grandfather. Tucked into his large leather chair, he reminded me of a pod of yucca, slowly drying up at the end of the season. He appeared to be dozing but opened his creamy eyes, and they were wet with tears. Mama ushered us out and spent a few moments alone with him. I felt melancholy as we descended the front stairs. Perhaps I sensed that none of us were to see Austin or that solid brick house again.

We left early for the afternoon train. Uncle Stephen went ahead to check in our baggage. The rest of us stopped at the park for a picnic dinner. My last memory of Austin was from the height of a Winesap apple tree. My view was punctuated by a riotous chirping of birds after the recent downpour and an ardent, humid breeze that scoured the leaves, filled my skirt, and promised more rain. Stevie sat below on the damp blanket, gumming a peeled apple, finally quiet.

I can still see Mama and her sisters, neatly circled around the baby and the carefully arranged picnic, too desolate to enjoy their final meal. Like a still life they huddled, frozen in time on the green grass. Only the birds sang.

IV

CHIHUAHUA

(1910–1911)

At the roar of the approaching train, the pinto lifted its muzzle, flared its nostrils, rolled its eyes, pulled back its lips to show square yellow teeth, and whinnied its terror. As our train exploded past, it strained against the rope that secured it to the hitching bar in front of an adobe house. I pitied the panicked creature, wishing I could give it comfort, but the horse quickly receded into the distance.

I rested my cheek against the dirty window. Across the scrubby plain spread thickets of thorny green mesquite, clumps of spiky agave, yucca shagged in last year's dead leaves, and gangly bushes of sticklike ocotillo. Nearer the train, slender stalks of gray-green lechuguilla reached to the sky like fingers pointing to the single wisp of cloud.

We were in Old Mexico, though it looked no different to me than the New Mexico I knew. To the west and east, bare brown mountains crowned the wide valley. In the distance, a broad-winged hawk circled.

We neared a scattering of adobes. In the dirt yard next to a hut, a barefoot boy jumped up from his play when he heard our whistle. He picked up a ball of sorts, a pig's bladder, and raced toward the train, his legs pumping to cover the distance. With all his strength, he hurled the bloated skin at the locomotive, but it burst just short. We roared on. Deflated, the boy turned his back and trudged away. I craned my neck and followed him until he became as small as an insect. His home shrank to a dot and disappeared. How long had he waited for our train to pass for his moment of glee? I felt sad for the boy who'd missed his mark. I turned from the window, closed my eyes, and slept.

—✺—

We rented a house in a barrio outside of Chihuahua City on a narrow dirt road that eventually meandered west to the towering peaks of the Sierra Madre. Our casita, in a row of small houses not far from the roundhouse, was an adobe rectangle with thick walls, a red-tiled roof, and a dirt floor. In the middle of the main room stood a heavy table flanked by high-backed Spanish chairs. Above it hung an iron lamp, like a spider ready to drop. The adobe stove that filled one corner was lit on cold nights and kept stoked until the nippy mornings warmed to noon heat. Mama's rocker and sewing table sat below a deep window, and next to it, her jade plant.

An open kitchen with a beehive oven and fire pit stood across the yard. Blackened pots and oversized wooden spoons dangled from square-headed iron nails in the supporting beam. A table with shelves stored brown-and-yellow pottery bowls, a *mortero* for grinding seasonings, and a larger stone for grinding corn. A barrel-shaped olla stored our water. The area was enclosed by a mesquite fence. We children were free to play in the weedy yard, as long as we could tolerate the wind, as constant as the sun.

The Mexico that greeted our arrival appeared tranquil, like a lazy river wending through a peaceable land. But turbulent waters were just around the bend. We didn't see the revolution coming.

2

Mariana appeared the day after we arrived, asking for work. Mama hired her to cook and wash. She lived on a nearby farm she called *el rancho*. She was quiet and somber, but when she broke into a smile, her face lit up like a bright moon appearing from behind a cloud. Enchanted by Stevie, she gave him goat's milk to drink and rawhide to teethe on, and he stopped crying.

"Well, I'll be. All that time he couldn't tolerate cow's milk," Mama said, and she relaxed.

Stevie took on a peculiar goaty scent, thrived, and became sweet and serene. He cut his teeth and began to crawl like a desert tarantula, quickly and silently, already an athlete. It took all of us to keep track of him.

Mariana served us tortillas, fried cactus leaves, chiles rellenos, and our favorite, sopaipillas steeped in honey. She teased us by calling us *pochos,* meaning "washed out," because we weakened culinary traditions by spreading jam on her tortillas and ladling her frijoles over biscuits. She eagerly learned to make biscuits, chicken pot pie, and Mama's recipe for prickly pear marmalade with thinly sliced lemons and oranges. She sang us Mexican folk songs, taught us to say things in Spanish, and learned more English. We loved to be at Mariana's side because she took pleasure in our childish ways. She smiled at our mistakes and loved us as we were.

Mama loved us in a bigger way. She encouraged us to improve. Mama cried when she learned that the American school near our home had closed. A week after our arrival, the teacher departed due to politics. We couldn't understand how distant troubles in Mexico City could make a teacher leave. When a replacement couldn't be found, the other American families near the barrio relocated to the city. Mama thought the American school in Chihuahua City was too far and wouldn't consider a Mexican school.

I took hold of her sleeve. "I don't mind learning at home."

"Well, of course not. It's all you've known."

"You're the best teacher in the world," Irene said.

Mama smiled.

Ida sat stabbing needles into her strawberry pincushion. She always wanted more.

—☙—

The next week, Mama received a telegram from Aunt JoJane. Grandmother had died in her sleep.

"That does take the cake," Mama murmured. "She passed away the day after her seventy-second birthday. She must have wanted to count another year. Doesn't that just sound like your grandmother?"

I couldn't answer.

Mama didn't go back for the funeral, having just left. In February, Aunt JoJane telegrammed that Grandfather had pneumonia and was now confined to Grandmother's four-poster bed. The German nun had been called back to care for him. Mama moped for days. She stopped in the middle of her work to stare at nothing. She picked at her food.

"My father's dying, and I'm so far away."

Eight days later, we received the telegram that Grandfather

had passed. Mama was swollen-eyed for a week, often pulling Charlie or wiggly Stevie up onto her lap to rock. One morning I caught her standing at the door gazing out at the dry plain.

"Are you well, Mama?"

"There's a raven on the fence post. Do you see him? He's there every morning. Look at the satin luster of his feathers. He's so black, he's blue. Do you see his pretty fan-shaped tail? He sits and looks at our house. He makes the oddest cry, like the wail of a child. Then after a time, he flies away, cawing so mournfully."

I was surprised I hadn't noticed him. I always kept an ear out for birds.

She pulled me in and hugged me tightly. "He was such a dear man. Now that he's gone, we've no home to go back to. All we've got is each other."

Grandfather's death changed something in Mama.

"Growing up near the Hill Country, I was always partial to green." She surveyed the blanket of sand extending toward the Sierra Madre. "Now I've taken a cotton to brown. All shades. It's more subtle than green, mellower, but no less beautiful."

She took to wearing a brown-striped rebozo.

"Are you still a Texan, Mama?"

"Oh, I'll always be a Texan. Born and raised. Texas is a part of my very fabric. It's the lens from which I'll always view the rest of creation."

"Am I a Texan?"

She drew in her breath.

"Fancy that. You weren't even born there, were you?" She paused for a moment. "You're a child of the West, Josie. I suppose you'll always compare the rest of the world to this great brown desert. Every place will look lush to you, but crowded, by comparison."

She would pause in her work to remark on the splendor of the mountains and beauty of a desert flower. She explained that every desert was different—each with its own special plants and animals. She pointed out the scarlet bloom of ocotillo, dark yellow of prickly pear, and pale pink of sand verbena, which colored the spring desert like dabs of paint on a brown canvas. She stepped outside to take in the burnt-orange sunsets or to savor the perfumed air of the starry evenings. She took pleasure in what was around her: her children, her sewing, and her potted plants.

Mama didn't grow practical things like corn, beans, or squash. Blossoms meant more to her than vegetables. She planted cornflowers, sunflowers, and herbs—aloe vera, mint, and chamomile in earthen pots that she set around the house or on the porch and cared for as needed, as she nurtured her children. Potted plants were the surest things for a family on the move.

A yucca grew next to the fence of our adobe. We called it Spanish dagger for its long pointed leaves. Once Charlie sawed off two broad leaves with a knife, handed me one, and challenged me to a duel. The needle-sharp tip of his dagger pierced my arm. I cried when I saw the blood.

Mama came out to the yard. "Put that down, Son. It could take out an eye. The only weapon we need is your father's rifle."

Frustrated, Charlie sat on the back step and separated the leaves into coarse fibers that he spread around him. Later, as Mariana gathered the shredded pieces to toss over the fence, she showed us how they could be woven to make cords and lariats. The yucca stalk made good firewood, and the roots were used for soap.

"Don't harm the plant," Mama said. "It blossoms only once."

3

Papa was running freight trains between Ciudad Juárez and Chihuahua City for the Ferrocarriles Nacionales, but within a month he threatened to quit because the fireman assigned to him, a slight Mexican teen, wasn't up to the work. Over supper in our adobe, he explained that a fireman had to be as strong as an ox to keep up the steam. He might have to shovel as much as thirty tons of coal in a twelve-hour trip.

"And he's gotta be tough. The firebox is as close to hell as a man can get."

"Your language, Harry," Mama said.

"It's the bottom fact, Nannie. By the time he's tossed in a couple shovels of coal, his overalls are smoking." He turned to Charlie and stretched out his arms to demonstrate. "He's got to reach into that blazing box with a long rake to spread the coals to the back and into every corner to keep the fire even. And he's got to be a mechanic. If he hears a clanking in the firebox, it means a piece of steel's been thrown in with the coal. If it isn't removed, it can tear up the gear." Papa picked up the pitcher and poured molasses over his pork and biscuits. "If the engine isn't steaming right, he's got to make sure the flues aren't plugged and make repairs if a valve's out of square, a stay bolt's loose, or a wedge needs aligning."

Charlie nodded.

"Sometimes we trade places to give each other a break. My

coalie's got to be able to read the pressure gauge and know how to work the safety valves. Too much pressure can cause a boiler explosion, but if he lets the water fall below the boiling point, we'll have a slowdown." Papa paused to shovel a forkful into his mouth, chew, and gulp it down. "I don't want to get behind schedule if I don't have to—if you got a signalman taking a siesta, you risk a head-on collision. I'll never forget the Santa Fe wreck of oh-six. Telegraph operator fell asleep after three straight days on. Failed to give new orders to a passenger train running a half hour late. The head-on killed thirty-five."

"Yes, sir." He reached for another biscuit. "The driver and coalie are a team. I need a fireman who knows an engine and can make a repair with fence wire if he has to."

--✦--

The railway company reluctantly permitted Papa to send back to El Paso for an experienced fireman, though wages for foreigners were often twice what they paid the Mexicans. As soon as his old friend Bernie Sommers started firing for him, Papa was content to be running the train again. Mama was pleased that Bernie's wife and son might be our neighbors but disappointed when they decided to stay in El Paso.

Papa's visits home were rare but pleasurable. He taught us some Mexican songs he'd learned, and Charlie and I took turns playing along on our Hohner. When he departed, we walked with him to the roundhouse where he lifted us beside him in the engine, and we rode with him for a thrilling mile or two. Then he braked the train, helped us down the big steps, and after ardent goodbyes, we began the walk back home to the fading *chug* and final whistle of his train.

That spring, clusters of fat buds grew on our yucca, hanging from the plant's ten-foot central stalk like Mexican church bells. Mama told us that the flowers would open only after dark because they couldn't endure the desert heat. One warm night she called me to the door to show me the full moon over a saddle of the far mountains. Then she pointed to the yucca. The buds had opened. In the light of the moon, the blossoms gleamed like creamy flames. She said she preferred the Mexican term for the yucca, "our Lord's candle." The Mexicans knew the holiness of such illumination.

4

I n April, Papa told us about the comet.

"It's a fiery ball that shoots through the sky, with a long, wispy tail like a kite. They say it will be passing over next month."

I frowned. This must be another of his tales.

He laughed. "I'm not pulling your leg, Josie Belle. It's going to be flying right through the sky. It's all folks are talking about."

He reached into his pocket, brought out a section of the *El Paso Herald*, and read to us about the comet mania that had gripped the country. I scrutinized his shining eyes and could see he'd caught the fever too.

"Folks are saying all sorts of things. They believe the tail contains poisonous gases. Some claim it might hit the earth, but an article from the observatory up in Flagstaff says that's a crazy rumor. Bernie Sommers knows something about the stars. He tells me the comet will be millions of miles away and not to worry."

"There's nothing we can do," Mama said, "save put our lives in order. That done, I'd love to see the comet."

"Oh, we'll be able to see it all right. Right above our heads. You wouldn't believe it, Nannie. Some say looking at the comet will make you blind or insane. They're selling goggles and nose masks at the mercantile in El Paso, even comet pills to protect against the gases. Back East, there's downright hysteria."

"I think it's a crime taking advantage of people's fears. Do you remember, Harry, how in ninety-nine so many were predicting the end of the world? They were certain that civilization wouldn't survive the turn of the century. And pranksters made money from people's fright. And we're ten years into the twentieth century, and doomsday has not yet come."

My parents made the courageous decision to ignore the warnings and observe the passing of Halley's Comet in May of 1910. But while we waited, I dreamed of being pursued by a cloud of poisonous gas, as deadly as a swarm of bees. And of holding baby Stevie with a cloth over his face until the poison overcame me, and I dropped him and fainted. I envisioned us watching the comet skim across the sky, then scattering in panic as it fell to the earth in an Armageddon-like ball of fire. I didn't share my worries, but my stomach ached. And I slept fitfully.

Papa somehow was able to schedule his night home for the appearance of the comet in our skies. He invited his fireman, Bernie Sommers, and an American train conductor to our house to watch the comet. Mama made a squash casserole, corn pone, cabbage and pepper relish, and pecan spice cake. Papa brought home several jugs of root beer and his usual whiskey, set up an iron grill to roast beefsteaks, and moved the heavy dining table and chairs to the yard. Mama spread linen over the table.

The conductor, a tall man with a lordly air, arrived in his neat uniform with a spyglass that had belonged to his father, a sea captain. The fireman brought his sixteen-year-old son, also an enthusiastic stargazer.

The adults sat at the table, while we children sprawled on a blanket on the ground. We didn't need to travel to see a dark sky. The desert always afforded a breathtaking view of the heavens. The wind picked up, and we put rocks on the cloths to keep them from blowing away. It was odd to be outside in the dirt, waiting for sunset so that we could see a passing fireball with strangers.

As the sun spun gold over the Sierra Madres, the adults drank coffee, ate cake, and talked. Then Papa and his fireman drank whiskey while his son tinkered with the new binoculars he'd bought for the occasion. As the sky took on a peachy hue, Charlie and I stationed ourselves outside the fence, determined to be the first to spot the comet. Charlie took out the harmonica, and as we lay waiting, we took turns playing.

The sun dropped below the peaks and the sky turned to orange. And then we saw a white light against the sienna backdrop, bigger and brighter than any star.

"It's the comet! It's here!"

All heads turned to the heavens. The conductor put his spyglass to his eye while Bernie scanned the sky with the binoculars. It was agreed—it must be the comet. As the mantle of night gradually darkened the sky, the head of the comet grew bright. The tail was a long wisp, like the train of a wedding gown flowing behind a radiant bride.

"But it's standing still," said Charlie. "It was going to shoot across the sky."

"It's moving very fast," Bernie said. "It's so far away, it appears to be still. If you watch every night, you'll see it cross a vast distance, and in a month or two it will have gone by."

"When will we pass through the tail?" I asked.

"Of that I'm not sure. You'll never notice a thing."

I sniffed the air and smelled only sagebrush and the smoke of our fire. Not a trace of poison.

We were silent for a long time watching the fuzzy ball of light and its trail of stardust above. Bernie Sommers examined our upturned faces, taking note of baby Stevie asleep in Mama's arms.

Then he fairly whispered in the night, "Mark this moment,

my good people. Except for the youngest in our party, we'll never set our eyes on such a sight again. It will be seventy-six years until this comet returns. Look well and remember."

—≈—

I was the only one in that party to see the comet again. Bernie Sommers's boy was killed in World War I, and my siblings preceded me in death. It seemed dimmer the second time around, but perhaps nothing could match the splendor of that Chihuahua night.

Our visitors, including Papa, left the next morning, talking and laughing as they departed, leaving us to our quiet routine. Mama sighed as she cleaned up from the evening. Like the comet, Papa had appeared out of nowhere, dazzled us, and gone away again. I didn't want another comet in my life. I wanted a father who would stay put.

5

That spring, Mama hired Manuel, Mariana's brother, to haul wood to our place, deliver food from the market, and serve as Mama's driver and escort when she ventured into Chihuahua City. He took Charlie with him to gather wood, where he taught him to use his new bow and arrow and make snares to catch quail, doves, and the jackrabbits that were a nuisance in the campesinos' gardens. Once or twice, he and Charlie trapped roadrunners basking in the sun—not for game but to sell to the curanderos in Chihuahua City, who used them to cure lesions, boils, and tuberculosis. Charlie learned Spanish from Manuel in that natural way a child picks up a language, as effortlessly as drinking water. And Manuel taught Charlie to ride bareback.

One afternoon, as Ida and I were drying the dishes, the two rode up to the house, whooping and hollering. Manuel, his black eyes glittering, his pearly teeth gleaming from a wide smile, sat easily upon a marble Appaloosa. Charlie rode a stocky mare, a pretty overo with a brown coat and patches of white. He dangled a puny rabbit from one hand. I wanted to ride a horse too.

"Can I go with them, Mama? I can help get wood."

"You have chores and need to watch Stevie."

I stomped off, grabbed the pan of dirty dishwater, and threw it sloppily over Mama's potted plants.

"Don't waste water, Josie."

I badgered her again that evening.

—✢—

The next morning when Manuel arrived and collected Charlie, I begged to go again. And Mama said yes.

I untied my apron, laced my boots, and pulled on my hat. Manuel lifted me onto his Appaloosa, and we trotted into the mesquite. I felt as though I'd been loosened from a tether.

Gathering wood was work. From a distance, a grove of mesquite looked like low spiny apple trees with delicate leaves, but close-up the sharp thorns made the thickets impenetrable. Manuel whacked at the solid wood with his machete. As we pulled out broken branches, the spines scratched our hands and arms. Sometimes we heard the clear *quink, quink* and *what cheer* of the desert cardinal that nested in the branches. When we got hungry, we munched on the trees' tender pods.

Another morning we rode to Manuel's rancho where his mother sat weaving in the shade of their adobe. She was squat with deeply wrinkled skin and kind eyes above broad cheekbones. Her long name reminded me of the earth around us, the consonants grating like sand against rock, unlike other Mexican women's names, where the vowels counted for more and the syllables rippled like water over pebbles. When Manuel introduced us, she curled her lips into a grin and caressed my cheek. Manuel said something. She laughed, dipped a gourd into a barrel, and offered me water. She smiled as I drank, and her eyes were full of love.

I wondered how she could love me without even knowing me. I hoped that someday I could love in such a way.

When I was done drinking, Manuel led me to the yard and helped me onto his Appaloosa.

"*Se llama el Cohete.*"

"Fast as a skyrocket," Charlie said.

Manuel led me around the yard, first walking, then trotting. Then he handed me the reins and I was on my own. The pulse of the animal beneath me, the horsey smell, the warmth of the sweat-drenched blanket against my thighs, and the freedom of having my dress hitched above my parted knees was intoxicating. From the wind in my hair to the tips of my boots, I felt alive.

―⚜―

We often went to ride at the rancho, where Manuel's mother greeted me with a gourd of cool water and her warm smile. When I rode well enough, Manuel let us take the ponies to the open desert, where Charlie and I rode bareback through the seared grasses. The wind tore at my hair and lashed at my face. My skirt whipped behind me as we whooped, raced, and ate dust. I felt as free as a hawk.

Returning home after our rides, I headed for the washbasin, where I brushed my tangled hair, washed the dirt and sweat off my body, cleaned my shoes, and put aloe on my cracked lips. I liked the feel of the newly discovered muscles in my arms, thighs, and buttocks. My newfound independence made me feel brash and as gritty as the dust. I coveted Charlie's cowboy boots, and I wished I were a boy. I tried out several manly expressions, but Irene and Ida weren't impressed.

Mama knew I'd learned to ride and was proud when Charlie told her I rode bareback as well as a boy. So I wouldn't chafe my thighs, she made me knickers to wear under my skirt.

"Riding's a life skill, like learning to cook and sew, read and write," she mumbled from lips full of pins as she made me turn so she could measure the length of my knickers. "Like learning to swim." She took the pins from her mouth. "I swam as a girl at Barton Springs. Now turn, Josie. I do hope you children will have the opportunity to learn someday. You never know if sometime in your life you'll find yourself in a small boat on rough waters."

"Or down a well."

She looked up at me. "Oh, yes. That too."

She stood and laughed. "If darling Clementine and her sweetheart had known how to swim, it would've saved them all that sorrow. But then there wouldn't be a song."

Papa approved of my riding too.

What they didn't know was the manner in which I rode or the spirit that was now a part of my nature—and how it changed me. Only Charlie shared the fervor and recklessness of those bareback runs. It was my first experience of a man's world—the intense physical exertion and rash abandon to sport, with no excuse or apology. I didn't want to be a lady. I wanted the pursuit of happiness to be a part of my life forever.

Pay for an engineer was less in Mexico. If we'd eaten like the locals, Papa's wages would have been enough, but we liked our coffee, white flour and sugar, cow's milk, and butter, which cost more south of the border. And Mama, so often alone, found Mariana and Manuel's company a comfort and necessity. To stretch Papa's pay to the end of the month, she returned to her sewing. One morning, Manuel took her into Chihuahua City to meet with a woman, Mrs. Mildred Winston, wife of an American mining engineer, who had a reputation as a gossip but knew everyone in the American community. She promised to send dress customers Mama's way.

Women came to our home and paged through the book of Butterick patterns Mama had brought from Austin, eager to wear the latest Yankee fashions. Mama showed them the new hobbled skirts and the shorter, looser "walking skirts." When the women decided on their style, Mama measured them, took a deposit, and later went to town with Manuel to buy fabric and notions. Irene and Ida, who were careful with their handwork, helped Mama with the sewing. Since she had two able assistants, I never learned to sew.

One day, Mrs. Winston came to our house to be measured for a dress. She was homesick, as were many of the American women, and wanted a chance to speak English and visit over a cup of coffee as much as she needed a new garment. She had a head of copper hair, was as round as a butterball, and had the smoothest skin I'd ever seen. She confided that she rubbed it every day with a mixture of lemon, borax, and sage, slathered it with cold cream at night, and made great efforts to never let a ray of sun touch it. She wore a voluminous blue shawl and a matching silk hat with an eight-inch brim and a fine mesh veil to keep out the dust.

By the time Mrs. Winston left our home, Mexico had changed for us.

I sat in the corner entertaining Stevie with his train and listened to her talk, while Mama served her coffee. Mrs. Winston thought it odd that American families were still moving south, what with the economic downturn, labor strikes, food riots, and radical ideas circulating.

Mama said she'd heard mention of problems.

Mrs. Winston continued in a confidential tone. "I know about this because I'm privy to information that isn't generally known."

She explained that since many Mexican farmers had lost their lands to the huge haciendas growing cash crops for export, they had to import the food they used to grow. Some could hardly afford staples.

She paged through the pattern book, made her selection of pattern, fabric, buttons, and trim, and chattered on.

"There are all stripes of talk. Some Mexicans are calling for the ouster of foreign interests. Do you know what they say?" Her eyes brightened. "That their country has become the mother of foreigners and the stepmother of Mexicans. And perhaps they're right." She lowered her voice. "Everyone's got their fingers in the pie. The British are profiting from the oil, the French from their textile mills, the Germans from the banks, and the Americans from the mines and railroads. The Hearst company alone owns more than six million acres of land in the state of Chihuahua."

Mama's eyes widened. She got out her measuring tape and asked Mrs. Winston to stand on a low stool.

"A man named Madero is in San Antonio gathering weapons and an army of Mexican rebels and American mercenaries. He's organizing to overthrow the president."

"What does this mean for us, Mildred?"

"It means there's rebellion in the making, Nannie."

I looked up. What was this woman saying? Foreigners in Mexico and Mexican fighters in Texas?

While Mama measured the woman's generous curves and read out numbers in a low voice that Irene copied onto a piece of paper, Mrs. Winston talked on. Farther north in Chihuahua, a man named Pancho Villa had become leader of a band of insurgents, as well as another man, Orozco, and his rebel fighters. Some ranch foremen had joined their brigades.

Mama's cheeks flushed. "Are we safe here?"

"This might fizzle out, but only time will tell." Mrs. Winston shifted her weight on the stool. "Have you heard about Zapata?"

Mama shook her head.

Mrs. Winston said there were insurgents in the south, led by a man called Zapata, that wanted the land redistributed to the peasants.

"Well, isn't it only right?" Mama said. "The people are poor. But an uprising would wreak havoc on us all."

"Their lives are already in shambles. They have nothing to lose. My husband says they're out for blood."

Mama cringed.

I was confused by those names and places that our visitor was so worked up about. I listened hard but could make no sense of her talk.

The woman smirked as she stepped down from the stool,

wrapped her shawl over her broad bosom, and stepped out the door. She seemed to relish her role as purveyor of fear.

Mama put away her measuring tape and pattern book.

"She could talk the hind legs off a donkey. I pray that this talk of insurrection is mostly rumor."

I asked Mama whether we were going to get to stay in Mexico.

She sighed. "These troubles are complicated and far away. Don't worry, Lamb."

7

By summer, the flowers on our yucca plant had shriveled and dried. At the base of each flower, a hard kernel had formed. Mariana said the kernel would grow into a fruit because a little white moth had pollinated the flower during the night. The small four-winged creature had laid her eggs in its center, and its babies would live on the seeds of the fruit until they turned into moths. I gained a new respect for the lowly moths that found their way into the house at night to flutter around our oil lamps. I didn't know which were the yucca moths, but I wouldn't let Charlie kill them. I caught them in my cupped hands and released them into the night.

Mama liked Mexico. As a girl in Austin, she'd learned Spanish from their maid, a spinster who was like family. Mama began to teach us grammar and how to conjugate verbs. She was putting together a plan to have one of her dress customers teach a group of us children in the former schoolhouse, now taken over by bats.

Midsummer brought long days of white heat. When the temperatures rose to unbearable levels, the storms of July and August arrived. Above us, dark clouds congregated, jagged branches of lightning crackled, thunder rumbled, and brief torrential rains made water holes in shallow dips of the land—greening up the desert overnight. The day's heat brought back the world of yellow and blue, the desert drank up its windfall, and the pools went away.

Fall blew up the valley, warm but drier. Shadows grew longer. Dust pervaded everything. One morning, Manuel came to fetch Charlie and held out his open palm. In it lay several cylindrical fruits, the gift of the yucca.

A growing uneasiness marred Papa's visits. Over supper, he told Mama about the growing revolt.

"Madero's calling for the people to rise up against President Díaz. If I read the situation correctly, he has a strong following."

He wiped sauce from his mustache.

"He's set the twentieth of November for his insurrection. The Federales will put it down, but there will be violence."

Mama stopped chewing. "That's but two weeks away, Harry. Is it safe for us to stay?"

"The government's their enemy, not us. But I want you to go to Chihuahua tomorrow and stock up on supplies. Have Manuel do your errands after that. You'll need to stay put until we see what comes of this."

He went back to his meat and said no more.

The next day, Mama returned from the city shaking her head. There were too many soldiers. Too many guns. It made her nervous.

Two weeks later, Papa arrived home late. He threw his toolbox and goggles onto the table. He was quiet, his face pale, his eyes underscored with puffy bags. He'd stayed awake the last two nights on the train, keeping watch for bandits. On his run four days before, the insurgents had attacked the train about fifty miles south of Juárez. They'd forced the Mexican soldiers off, tied their hands, gagged them, and sent the train on.

Mama sucked in a breath. "Will they be killed?"

"They'll probably keep them captive for bargaining with the central government. This is serious. I'm hoping it doesn't last long."

Papa went back to the train. Manuel brought us our news. I was puzzled at how our relaxed days had become so tense.

—≈—

As I try to reconstruct the events that followed, the timeline goes awry and incidents compress. I remember it as a child might—disordered and askew. Or perhaps I recall what was told to me years later or the way Mama remembered it.

A group of revolutionaries took over a town in the north called San Andrés, and when Díaz sent soldiers, they were shot as they left the train. We prayed it wasn't Papa's. The newspaper *El Correo* reported that thousands of federal soldiers had been moved into Chihuahua. Pancho Villa and Orozco had thousands in their armies too, pledged to Madero. Battles were breaking out—but far away in another part of Chihuahua, Mama assured us. The newspaper told of federal victories. Mama was edgy, and I was baffled. My stomach began to burn.

The night temperatures plunged. Fires in the hearth kept us warm. The yucca leaves dried up and formed a shaggy brown necklace around the tall stalk. The uneaten fruits split into open pods—their tiny seeds scattered into the wind. The seed jackets became stiff soldiers on a high lookout, stoically enduring winter's cold blasts. Mama and I stood in the yard, listening to the rustle of its leaves.

"Isn't it a pity? It grows all these years to flower once, spread its seeds, and die."

"It's not fair."

"This world's not fair." She got her faraway look. "'Blessed are the poor in spirit, for theirs is the kingdom of heaven.' How could we endure without the Beatitudes?"

I wasn't sure.

That February of 1911 news came that Madero had left San Antonio and was moving south. Mama said she was glad to be living near Chihuahua City, where there was a stronghold of soldiers, and to be living in a bit of a house with no livestock. She'd heard that some rebels were stealing cattle to trade for guns.

Americans were fleeing to the United States in droves. It was the first question asked when Mama's customers came by. Staying or leaving?

Mama looked up from her sewing. "Your father's due home soon. He'll know what to do."

I noted the familiar white line over her pursed lips and her trembling hand as she tried to thread a needle, gave up, and set down the garment to help Mariana prepare supper.

"Josie," she called to me. "Come peel the onions. And while you're at it, please conjugate the Spanish verb *luchar*. It's a regular verb—'to struggle.'"

"*Lucho, luchas, lucha, luchamos . . .*" I began.

Reports came that Orozco had captured a military convoy and that Madero had led his men in an attack in northern Chihuahua but was crushed. In southern Mexico, Zapata had a following of peasants fighting against the Federales.

Papa came home and said that President Taft had mobilized

twenty thousand American soldiers on the US–Mexico border, in the Gulf of Mexico, and in the Pacific.

"What should we do, Harry?" Mama demanded. "I can hardly stand to be here alone with the children."

"I wish I knew how this will end. If things get worse up north, we're going to have to leave. You should be safe enough for now. Chihuahua's well garrisoned."

More strange names and places I couldn't sort out. What I knew was that Mama was worried. She took to sitting up at night in her rocker. I watched her through the open door of my room, my petite soldier of a mother, chin set, facing the bolted door, the Bible lying open over one knee, our Winchester upon the other. She rocked and read as I dozed. When Stevie woke up, she put down her gun, bundled him in her arms, and rocked him long and steady, as if the simple act of rocking a child might calm the world.

8

The insurrectionists attacked another train. This time they'd stolen rifles being shipped north to supply troops in Juárez.

"Harry, are you in danger running that train?" Mama said.

"It's getting riskier." Papa slumped on a kitchen chair in his grimy pants and collarless shirt. His suspenders hung loose over his shoulders. "It's not unknown for them to shoot in order to stop a train, but Madero's no fool. He'll still need men to run the train, come hell or high water. It's a supply line for Federales now, but he knows it'll be vital if things turn in his favor."

Papa had new worry lines. He didn't bother to wash or shave until after he'd talked to Mama. He was hoping that Madero would be successful.

"Things will calm down, and we can get on with our lives."

Mama shook her head. "I don't know. I used to think that you were a courageous man, running those trains with all that danger and responsibility. Now I wonder if you're not just foolish." Her voice cracked. "Harry, I want you to quit your job. I don't feel safe here anymore. I worry about the children. I want to move to El Paso."

Papa didn't speak for a long time. "All right, Nannie. I'll give my month notice."

I was relieved. We'd already had to end our carefree days gathering wood, visits to Manuel and Mariana's, our horse rides, and were now confined to our small home. Everyone was antsy. I'd be willing to go anywhere that Mama could relax again.

In May, when Papa was due home, his train was two days

late. When he finally arrived, he was tired and hungry. While he wolfed down grits and gravy, he told us what had happened.

"Two days ago, Orozco and Villa's forces took Juárez. They shot up the town, took over the garrison, captured the federal commander, and now control the customhouse. Madero's set up a provisional government there."

Mama set down Papa's coffee.

"But why Juárez?" Her face had gone gray.

"It's a port of entry to ship in supplies for the revolutionary forces—guns, gunpowder, cannons, dynamite . . . and mercenaries. Food for their fighters too. Before long, the train may be carrying supplies to the renegades. The civil war's here."

Papa began unbuttoning his soiled shirt.

"Oh, Harry, what shall we do?" Mama paced next to the kitchen table. "We have to leave right now. Can we get back to El Paso?"

"Not without going through Juárez. I don't want you anywhere near there now."

He lifted his chin and rubbed the bristle on his neck. "Plenty of federal soldiers have been shot. Government troops could organize an offensive at any time. You're safer here."

"We waited too long," Mama wailed. "We should've left months ago."

Papa removed his shirt. He stank of sweat and grease. He stretched his legs, then bent a lanky limb, pulled the garter from the top of a sock, and peeled it off his foot. The smell was foul. He sat and stared at the wall, one sock in his hand. Then he turned a grave face toward Mama.

"You need to be ready to leave at a moment's notice. Keep some bags packed under the beds. If things get worse, I'll come for you or send a message."

In the following days, Mama was short-tempered. Some days Mariana stayed home with her mother. Mama's dress customers stopped coming. Only Manuel came to deliver food. Mama hid our rifle during the day because she'd heard stories of rebels ransacking houses, demanding food, guns, horses, and saddles.

I no longer felt safe in our snug adobe and was scared to go to the outhouse after dark. I assumed Juárez was close, not 230 miles away. I imagined Pancho Villa beyond the nearest ridge, planning his next attack. I lay awake at night, wishing that Papa were home, listening to the creak of Mama's rocker as she sat on guard with her holy book and rifle. To keep awake, she set a tin pail on the floor and held a ring of keys. If she dozed off, the clatter of keys in the pail woke her. She napped in the daytime when she believed we were safer.

One morning while Mama was sleeping, Charlie and I went into the yard with our list of spelling words. Charlie found a horny toad lizard hunkered flat to the ground. We poked at the harmless creature with a stick until it hissed and blew up its skin.

Then we heard the pounding of hooves. We looked up to see a pack of men on horseback armed to the hilt, bands of bullets around their torsos, rifles at their saddles, revolvers on their hips. Scarves covered their faces. Their horses were thin and travel-worn. They cantered past, then were obscured by their dust. Mama flew out the door, grabbed our arms, and pulled us into the house.

"If ever they pass again, you run inside, do you hear? We've nothing they need, but I don't want to tempt them." Her hands shook. "You're to stay in the house for the rest of the day."

Mama couldn't sleep anymore. She stayed up and quizzed us

on words we couldn't spell. I worried that the desperados had gone to Manuel and Mariana's to steal the ponies for fresh mounts. But our friends were left alone that day. As I lay in bed that night, I was comforted by one good thing—Papa was hardly drinking.

―⋇―

In late May of 1911, we woke to the sounds of guns in Chihuahua. Mama held us close as cannons boomed. When they let up, she made us get dressed. She pulled our bags out from under the beds.

"When Manuel comes he can tell us what's happened."

Manuel was late. When he walked in with firewood and a basket of peppers, his eyes danced.

"*Arriba* Madero!" he announced. "*El presidente dimitió ayer.*" The president had resigned, and the federal government had signed a treaty with Madero. New elections would be held. Madero was as good as in. The fighting was over.

―⋇―

After Madero's celebrated entry into Mexico City in June, Chihuahua quieted down. Pancho Villa put down his arms and set up a butcher shop. Manuel and Mariana were optimistic. The American community was split. More businesses moved out. More families returned north. Papa was pleased Madero had won. Mrs. Winston ordered a new dress.

My hours were filled with sweeping and dusting, husking corn, shelling beans, and quartering squash with Ida on the back step as we recited times tables, Bible verses, or the names of the presidents of the United States. I worked out sums on a fragment of slate until my sweaty fist blotched the gray surface. I sang nursery rhymes, played clapping games, and showed little Stevie how to tap rocks with the hammer he'd fallen in love with and carried everywhere. I entertained my siblings with the songs Mariana had taught me that I'd learned to play on the harmonica. Some days I went riding with Charlie. The mockingbirds still sang in the pure morning light, the sun followed the same fiery arc from mountain to distant mountain, and Mama's jade plant thrived.

9

That year the American community had a Fourth of July picnic
for those who'd stayed, and we attended, even Papa. A pig
rotated on a spit over an open fire next to a side of beef, both
served with a spicy sauce. We feasted on white bread and molasses cakes. Women brought cold potato, parsnip, sweet carrot,
and string bean salads, mashed turnips, buttered squash, relishes,
and iced watermelon. Charlie ate four helpings of mince apple
pie as a crowd of smiling women watched, impressed by both his
enormous appetite and his head of bushy hair that, after our
windy ride to the picnic, looked like a tuft of scruffy grama
grass.

Mama pointed out a group of Americans I hadn't seen before—Mormons who lived in a colony nearby. Some had lived in
Mexico for more than thirty years. Irene whispered that their
men had come south so they could have more than one wife. In
Mexico, the law against it wasn't enforced. They'd come to discuss the political situation.

Mama visited with several of her dress customers. Mrs.
Winston wore a new pink hat, more widely brimmed than her
last.

"The men are worried," I overheard her tell another woman.
"The conservatives are planning a coup. And down south the
anarchists want radical reforms—unions, all the land given to the
peasants." She shook her head like the coiled wire whistle on

Stevie's toy train. "My husband says Mexico's a box of dynamite, with little sparks everywhere. Things could blow any moment. Oh, I'm a bundle of nerves."

I walked as far from the woman as I could. At the dessert table, I stepped in line for a slice of peach pie.

Papa joined the men's tug-of-war and got second place in the men's footrace. Later, under a sprawling oak, between rounds of cigars and bourbon, he talked politics with the men. The Mormon men didn't drink or smoke but conversed with the others from their own piece of shade.

We children had egg-and-spoon races, three-legged races, and a long game of blindman's bluff. The day ended with fireworks, the rockets speeding upward to burst into flowers of fire. I recalled Mrs. Winston's predictions of the coming explosion and had to close my eyes.

We bumped our way home in Manuel's wagon, cuddled in the straw. Sleeping Stevie lay like a warm dumpling on my lap. Charlie dozed against my shoulder.

Madero became president that fall. Mama resumed plans for the school to open in January.

⁓

One quiet November morning, Mrs. Winston rushed through our open door, stood in the middle of the room, and flapped her shawl like a bird in a puddle.

"Did you hear? They want us out." She pulled a newspaper from her handbag and waved it in Mama's face. "Zapata has broken off from Madero. He's issued his own plan. Orozco and Villa may follow. No one knows. The revolutionaries have vowed to continue fighting until the land is given to the people. They want foreigners out." Her chins jiggled. "All over the country they're blowing up bridges . . . striking at the mines."

Her eyes filled with tears. Red blotches the size of strawberries mottled her perfect complexion.

"I came to say goodbye, Nannie. I'm going back to Kentucky," she blubbered. "I can't live here anymore." She buried her face in Mama's shoulder. "Oh, I need my nerve tonic."

"Now, don't have a conniption fit, Mildred." Mama led her to the bench and gave her a dose of salts. She sent us children out to play.

After Mrs. Winston left, we drifted back into the house. Mama was packing. She didn't want to talk.

"Your papa comes home tomorrow. We'll know more then."

I stepped into the backyard and stood next to the beehive oven as Mariana, unusually sober, took the long wooden spatula and shoved in two rounds of dough. Then she sat me on her lap and sang me a new, sad song, as though I were a baby. Nothing appeared different, but I sensed a change in the air, like the first whiff of a new season. East of the house, half a dozen turkey buzzards hovered over something in the sand. I shivered in the oven's heat.

Papa came home the next night, long after dark, his unshaven face haggard. He didn't greet us children.

"Another rebel group's gearing up to take over Juárez. Madero's refused to support land reform. They say he's betrayed the people. They've threatened to attack the train again."

He removed a pillow from a chair, sat down in his soiled overalls, and told Mama about Zapata's rebellion in Morelos, the uprisings in Oaxaca, Chiapas, and Sonora, and now a new revolt in western Chihuahua. Madero was being attacked from all sides.

"Oh, Harry, how's it going to end?"

"It's a crapshoot. There are at least a thousand rebels roaming the countryside of Chihuahua with their wives and children in tow. They're hungry and desperate. Nothing's changed for them. Now a conservative named Reyes is in San Antonio planning a counter-insurrection."

My mind spun. I couldn't keep track of who was who and what side they were on.

Papa removed his cap and rubbed an ear. "I figured they'd done well to get rid of Díaz. I thought we had a future here." He sunk his head in his hands. "I haven't gotten paid in months. There's no guarantee I'll ever be compensated. Running the train's too risky. Even for me."

"Can we discuss this later? The children . . ."

"Of course." His eyes were vacant. He gave us each a peck on the cheek and clomped out back to wash up.

"It's bedtime, and your papa's safe at home. There's nothing to worry about."

We knew better but didn't argue. I suppose the others slept. I stared at the rough wall next to my bed and strained my ears. Through the thick adobe it was impossible to eavesdrop. But the partially opened door let in the smell of frying pork and the clatter of dishes as Papa was served a late meal. I heard the scuff of chair legs when Papa finished, the whine of the back door as he went to get firewood, the clump of sticks dropped onto the floor, and the shuffle of boots as he moved toward the chair by the fire.

My parents talked late into the night. It was as if the organic, sentient walls of adobe were protecting me from the grievous particulars of their conversation. All that came through the arch of my doorway was a wash of sound: Papa's deep muttering, Mama's murmur, a rustle of response. I heard a ripple of laughter, then a pause. A grumble from Papa. A purl from Mama's throat. Then another silence. The chair creaked as Papa rose to throw more sticks on the fire. A sizzle as dry wood hit burning logs, a cough from Papa when the smoke billowed, the groan of his chair as it absorbed his weight again, Papa's monotone monologue, a short ring of reply, a hiss of a whisper from their lips or from the fire. And I slept.

⁂

A tapping woke me the next morning. I sat up, scared that Zapata was knocking at our door, and was relieved when I recognized the fast, familiar rhythm of a woodpecker searching for insects on the mesquite outside my room.

Papa had already gone back to the train. As we gathered for breakfast, Mama told us we were going back to America, so everyone was to please help Mariana and Irene pack up.

"While you fold the linen, Ida May," she added, "please conjugate the verb *salir*. It's an irregular verb. You know the meaning."

"To leave," and Ida began to recite.

Mama worked two days finishing up a dress order, and at night she resumed her watch. I lay awake in my bed, keeping vigil with her, fearful that the fighters would come bursting through our door.

The following Sunday, I heard the thudding of horse hooves, and our door was thrown open. I whirled around to see who it was. Papa strode in.

"The time is now, Nannie . . . children. I got my pay. The train north leaves in two hours."

Mama spun around. "Charlie—no, Josie. Take that horse and ride to Manuel's. Tell him to bring their wagon."

Before Charlie could argue, I flew out the door. Papa helped me onto the saddle, and I trotted out of the yard.

"Be careful, Josie Belle," I heard Mama cry as I galloped beyond earshot.

I didn't have to say much to Manuel. He knew why I'd come. He hitched his wagon, Mariana climbed in, and we returned to our casita together. As we pulled close to the house, Mariana jumped from the cart and lunged at Mama.

"*Lléveme, por favor, señora.*" Mariana pulled Stevie up off the floor and held him tightly, his hammer dangling from his hand. "*Lléveme con ustedes.*" She wanted to come with us. She could take care of Stevie in America.

"No, Mariana. Manuel and your mother need you."

Mama removed her brown-striped rebozo, wrapped it around Mariana's shoulders, and handed her their final pay.

"*Espero que puedan encontrar otro trabajo,*" Mama said. "Be safe, dear. I hope these troubles end soon."

Mariana fell into the arms of Manuel, who held her while she wept. Irene, Ida, and I ran to her and wrapped our arms around her waist. She kissed the tops of our heads. Then, overwhelmed with my tangle of feelings, I pulled away.

I stood apart, numbly watching, as if severed from the scene. Papa, Manuel, and Charlie loaded our bags. Mama instructed us to climb into the wagon. A flock of crows flew in from the north and thronged a grove of spindly mesquite like cutouts of black filigree. They made a terrible racket, repeating and repeating the same eerie wail, as if preparing for battle. What is it about the squall of crows that makes one feel as if the end of the world is at hand?

At the depot, Papa herded us past heavily armed soldiers to board our car. As the train thundered north, Papa stood guard at the window, his rifle against his hip. I sat next to Mama.

"Thank you for getting Manuel so quickly, Lamb. I can always count on you."

She squeezed my hand, then pulled Stevie onto her lap and tried to distract us all with a game of knock-knock on the forehead, eyes, and mouth of his angel face.

I scanned the speeding sands, helping Papa watch for horsemen with guns. Once, Papa tensed as he squinted at some figures in the distance. I stared too. A group of men with horses, dogs, and rifles stood amid a copse of trees several hundred yards from the track. They watched our train go by, but none pursued.

Papa glanced at Mama. "They're waiting for a different train."

She frowned and pursed her lips, then took Stevie's pudgy fingers in her own to start him on a game of Johnny-oops.

At Juárez, Mexican soldiers swarmed aboard the train as we hustled off. We walked across the tracks, where customs officers checked Papa's papers, and then we boarded an American train that slowly chugged across the border into Texas, where soldiers inspected it again. When we boarded the next train at Union Depot, Mama finally relaxed. Papa set down his gun and took a seat next to Charlie, and we rumbled north to the Jornada del Muerto, the valley we'd left two years before.

I stuck my head out the open window. The wind stung my eyes, chafed my cheeks, and ripped at my hair, sweetly reminding me of Manuel and his Appaloosa, and my golden rides.

"I learned something in Mexico," Mama said after Stevie had fallen asleep. "*Jornada* has several meanings. It can be a journey, an opportunity, an act in a longer drama, or a passage from life to eternity. Oh, to be a fortune teller with a crystal ball . . ."

—❦—

Had I known what we were heading for a few years down the line, I'd have begged the brakeman to stop, so we could switch tracks and seek a different destination. But, as a river flows faster when it approaches a falls, our train took on speed and barreled ahead.

V

ENGLE AND CUTTER

(1911–1916)

Dry stalks of yucca shook in the gusts, their pods rattling like castanets, while dust devils spun across the powdery desert. I looked east to the frigid peaks of the San Andres and to the Caballos to the west. It was bitter cold, but I was warmed to be returning to a familiar place. We'd come back to Cutter, where they needed engineers for the mine trains. This time, Mama promised, we were staying for good. She and Papa were going to file a homestead claim. There would be no more moving around.

We descended the train and stood on the platform while waiting for our trunks. Bowlegged cowboys lounged against the posts of the depot, mouthing the sharp *r*'s of English, spitting watery chew onto the stained boards below. Vendors sold sandwiches, hard-boiled eggs, and fruit to hurried passengers at rates that undercut the prices on the train. The smells of coffee and fried bacon wafted from a house next to the depot. The baggage crew unloaded bags, crates, and barrels, and put aboard the local shipment.

We followed Papa down the street, where he checked us into two rooms at the Victoria Hotel. It was the finest place I'd ever seen. The rooms were furnished with high brass beds, mahogany and marble commodes, and thick carpets. A restaurant, store, post office, and bank shared space under the same roof.

That afternoon, Papa took Charlie, Ida, and me for a walk. No mere water stop now, Cutter was a town of three thousand people. Three hundred men from all kinds of places were working at the mill to process vanadium ore from the mines in the Caballos that Papa would be carting by train.

"And they'll be putting up a school next year for you kids."

I clapped my hands.

The town had new stores, a lumberyard for all the building going on, and a real livery and coach station. I wondered whether Marv Fenton was working there—his hitch stable was gone. I counted five saloons. Charlie was thrilled that several locals owned motorcars that rattled by, kicking up dirt.

"The boom's mostly due to the dam," Papa said. "The government's building one to stop up the Rio Grande."

It was being built about twenty miles northwest at a place called Elephant Butte to provide irrigation for the farmers. All the supplies for the dam came north from El Paso by rail, and to the dam site on a spur from Engle. Most of the workers and their families lived at the government settlement near the dam.

"But they do their business here."

Ida grabbed my hand and squeezed it. We were going to live in a genuine town.

Mama gave us permission to sit on the cane chairs in the lobby to watch the comings and goings of the hotel. We collected the foil cigar wrappers that had been discarded into a wooden waste bin and took sideways looks at the folk coming in— prospectors in wide-brimmed hats, a government inspector in a pressed uniform, a pair of slow-talking ranchers who looked as though they owned the place, a well-dressed businessman from some faraway city, and ordinary travelers.

Two days after we arrived, Papa took the coach to the assay office in Hillsboro, the county seat, to file a claim for a half section of land three miles east of town—a quarter section for him and one for Mama. He came home the next day, smiling and waving the papers for our acres. We walked to the edge of town. "Straight out that-a-way our claim begins," Papa said. "Prime grazing land. And there's water to be found too."

I studied my papa standing straight and tall against the southeaster pulling at his coat and trousers. I turned to where he pointed and squinted into the sun. All I could see was an expanse of pale yellow grasses, creosote, black brush, sage, and shaggy yucca being pushed about by the ceaseless wind. In the distance rose the purple peaks of the San Andres. Mama stood next to Papa, her lips pursed, her skirt flapping, a hand over her hat to keep it from flying away. She scrutinized the horizon as if to decipher her destiny. I don't know what she saw, for she said nothing as she scooped up Stevie and carried him back to the hotel. I took a last look and scurried after her.

2

We had no money to build a house or dig a well on our claim. The wages Papa had managed to collect before he left Mexico had gone to pay off debts and buy our tickets north. With the boom in Cutter, there was a shortage of housing. While Papa searched for a place to rent, we would stay a few more days at the hotel.

That Friday night there was a Thanksgiving dance in the dining room. I was ten years old and thrilled to attend.

The room was crowded with the families of local businessmen and ranchers, and cowhands who'd ridden twenty miles for the dance. Their boots were polished, their dungarees and Stetsons cleaned, their brown leather faces shaved bare, save for the nearly uniform mustache. Their spurs, Colts, and Winchesters had been set aside for the dance.

Charley Graham, the rotund horse rancher from Cutter, and his hand, Elias, tuned their fiddles. Marv Fenton was there, accompanied by his wife of five months, the widow Dora Middlestone, whose husband, we learned, had been killed several years before by cattle rustlers. Marv Fenton was working at the new livery. He wore a pressed shirt and bolo and was closely shaved. It seemed he'd been scrubbed into another man.

Mama walked over to the two of them, huddled together like turtledoves on a bench with Angel, the dog, curled beneath. When Marv Fenton stood up to make introductions, Mama took

Dora's hand and the two commenced a warm friendship. I felt shy as I shook his outstretched hand. After two years and a new wife, he was like a stranger. But Angel was the same. I scratched his belly and fondled his ears until it felt like old times.

The fiddlers broke into the first song, and couples rushed to the floor. We watched Mama and Papa dance the fandango like a sparking couple, all smiles and eyes on each other. When the fiddlers needed a break, Cephus, the Grahams' hired man, who'd once been a slave in the South, played the harmonica, and a woman led us children in singing games—Skip to My Lou, Pig in the Parlor, and Bounce Around. When the fiddles started again, Papa asked me to dance. I was graceless, and he laughed when I tried to go backward under his outstretched arm. Ida wanted to dance too, but Papa went back to Mama.

"He's partial to you, Josie," Ida said.

"I don't know why."

"It's because you're pretty like Mama, but you're brave like a boy."

I couldn't deny it. Papa often favored me.

Irene danced every dance with a poise that surprised me. When she took a lemonade at the refreshment table, she was surrounded by young cowboys.

"When did Irene learn to dance?" I asked Ida.

"She's been practicing with Mama at night."

I'd heard bumps coming from Mama's room but thought she'd been moving bags. Ida was always in the know.

Mama leaned over to Papa. "I believe Irene may have a beau come courting soon. There must be four men to every lady here."

"What's she now . . . soon fourteen? Too young."

He surveyed the clumps of eager men bordering the dance hall, and I looked too. There were a few of the hardened types—

wild, breakneck cowboys in battered hats who drank, gambled, and swore enough to make you blush. Desperados, Mama called them—short-timers, for the most part. Several of the more prosperous Anglo and Mexican ranchers and their longtime hands stood along the wall. Papa called them the noblemen of the West. He went outside to have a smoke.

Over wedges of pumpkin, mincemeat, and sweet potato pie, folks talked about local concerns: the dry spell we were having—no rain for thirty-five days—wells being drilled for a new ranching syndicate, the price of beef back East, a mine cave-in near Hillsboro, and rumors of gold in the San Mateo Mountains. Adults discussed the progress on the dam, results of the sweepstakes race in Mesilla, and New Mexico's approaching statehood. Around eleven, we filed up to our rooms, but the dancing went on. Papa stayed downstairs to talk with the men.

Mama's eyes shined as she helped us undress. "Oh, doesn't that Charley Graham play the fiddle well? Emma Graham says he doesn't dance or drink. Imagine that. It's so nice to see Mr. Fenton married, and his wife's as plump as a partridge."

I'd never seen her so happy. Irene too. Her cheeks were flushed from all her dancing. She had Mama's dreamy look on her face.

Mama put out the lamps but didn't go to bed. She sat at the window. I tossed and turned as I listened to the whine of fiddles and waves of laughter below. Finally, the music stopped, and I heard bright goodbyes, creaking wagons, and the clomping of hooves. Papa didn't come upstairs. He was probably at the bar.

I crawled out of bed and joined Mama at the window. A creamy half-moon glowed above the mountains. Stars twinkled like gold dust.

"Look at that Milky Way," Mama said softly. "The Mexicans say it's a path to heaven. It looks solid enough to walk on tonight."

In the moonlight, the spiny branches of an ocotillo flailed in invisible gusts, reminding me of a giant spider raking the valley floor. The moon shadows of creosote looked like nets of black lace. Fierce yaps and yelps came from somewhere nearby. The coyotes had a kill. Then we heard the frail wild whistle of a train.

"Must be the late train from Las Cruces. I remember that whistle."

We heard the clump of Papa's boots in the hall outside. He was singing "Betsy Brown."

Oh, I love a little girl, she lives in town,
Her father is a butcher and her name is Brown.
Her father is a rich old man, he's the richest man in town.
He's going to give me a house and a lot, along with Betsy
Brown.

Mama laughed. "It's time for bed, Lamb. Your feet must be cold."

The scent of rose water filled my nostrils as she bent to tuck the blanket about my neck and kiss me good night, and then she joined Papa in the other room.

I snuggled close to Ida's warm back. The past year's fears seemed to have blown away into the moonlit night. It was good to have our family together in this place where we felt we belonged.

3

At the dance, Papa met a man who'd filed a claim northwest of Cutter on the route to Elephant Butte. He'd dug a well and built a twelve-by-fifteen-foot homestead dwelling above mountain rock. Now he was going back to Michigan to bring out his family. We were welcome to live in his place until he returned. For Papa, a home for no rent, away from the bustle of town, seemed an offer too good to refuse. But Mama claimed it was too isolated. In the end, our education decided it. The town of Engle east of it had a schoolhouse.

Three days later, we rented a wagon and moved. The homestead was set on land littered with rough boulders and loose rock, speckled with juniper, piñon, and sagebrush. All it was good for was cattle, if that. We were connected to Engle by the dam railroad that followed the ridge above the cabin and the dirt road that ran to its south.

It wasn't a cabin but a barn, with two beds at one end. A cast-iron stove stood in the center of the dirt floor, a cottonwood table beside it. Mama hung canvas to separate the space into rooms, spread a linen cloth over the rough boards of the table, and hung the ristra of dried chili peppers Mariana had made her. We placed Mama's rocking chair in a corner and set her jade plant on a flat rock brought in from the hillside.

Papa spent our last dollars to buy a buckboard wagon and a strawberry roan gelding we called Blaze, for the milk-white stripe down his face. To make a team, the seller threw in a swayback, short-legged bay I named Duchess. She was ornery but healthy for her age. I was thrilled to finally own a mare and spent hours brushing her creamy mane. If I didn't hurry her, she'd let me ride.

As soon as we moved in, Papa went to work for the Victoria Mining Company. He ran the five-car narrow-gauge train from the Cutter depot over the ridge of the Caballos, through Palomas Gap to the vanadium and copper mines, and back to the processing mill. Ore was in demand back East. Vanadium was needed for steel alloys, and copper for electrical wiring. He spent his nights in Cutter.

We were alone again, our nearest neighbor a mile away. Papa came home on Sundays, the only day the train didn't run. I asked Mama why we couldn't be like the families of the section crew or the dam workers, whose papas went to work in the morning and came home every night.

"It's the way he knows to make a living. He gets respect for how he runs his engines." She described the treacherous grades of zigzagging track Papa's train had to climb, the bed so poorly maintained that he was limited to ten miles per hour, all the time hanging his head out the window to watch for washed-out track, fallen boulders, or slides of scree over the track.

She twisted her wedding band around her finger and laughed sharply. "You could say the steam locomotive is his second love, though a difficult one. We wouldn't want to take that away from him."

⁂

After Christmas, Irene, Ida, Charlie, and I started school in a square adobe, a block back from the tracks in Engle. Our teacher was Miss Marietta Stanley. She was only eighteen, with white-blond hair and pink freckled skin. She didn't like boys. She made them work harder than the girls and punished them more often, even the tender little boys who sat in the front row, wiggling their legs over the edge of their bench like pollywogs caught between worlds. Irene won our first spelling bee, and Ida's penmanship was the prettiest in the class, which earned them the privilege of arranging the readers, clapping the chalk erasers, and washing the blackboard after school.

While waiting for our sisters, Charlie and I wandered over to the tracks. Every train stopped in Engle to dump ash and take on water pumped from the Ojo del Muerto spring. The dam trains took the spur to Elephant Butte. Sometimes we moseyed by the Hickock Hotel to eye the men who smoked, spat, and gossiped from chairs on its narrow porch, then passed through the lobby to pick up cigar foils for our collection. Since liquor wasn't allowed at the government dam settlement, workers came to Engle for its saloons. The town served locals' needs with a post office, bank, stores, and a Methodist church. The Catholics took the train to St. Genevieve in Las Cruces, and others attended service in the schoolhouse when a circuit-riding preacher came to town.

A few months after our move, Mama told us she was expecting a baby. Charlie and Stevie were thrilled at the prospect of another brother. That evening, as Irene and I bathed Stevie in the tin tub behind the stove, I whispered my concern.

"Mama wasn't supposed to have another baby."

Irene looked at me and pursed her lips, like Mama.

"Oh, Sister. Things don't always turn out the way we plan."

4

In her will, Grandmother had left Mama her sewing machine and a small sum of money. The Singer arrived at the depot on the morning train, and Mama paid two young men to cart it to our home. She and Irene worked for half an hour to loosen the nails of its pine crate, while Stevie tried to help by tapping the boards with his beloved hammer.

Mama lifted its cloth cover, caught her breath, and ran her hand over the machine's oak top. Recently polished, it smelled of sun and beeswax. The iron filigree of the legs, treadle, and cross-piece curled and twisted like pea vines.

"This Singer was the first item my family ordered from Montgomery Ward. What a treasure, that catalog. It weighed two pounds and was over five hundred pages."

We opened and closed the small cabinet drawers and traced their decorative woodwork with our fingertips. Charlie and I crouched to move the foot treadle with our hands.

"Wait, you two. I'll show you how it operates."

Mama lifted the edge of the tabletop, and out of the belly of the cabinet a sewing machine was born. Stevie squealed. Across its voluptuous middle, SINGER was painted in gold Gothic letters, embellished with flowery scrolls. She pulled up a chair, threaded the needle, inserted fabric under the foot, and turned the wheel with her right hand to show us how the needle went up and down to make a small, even stitch. She warned us never to put a curious finger near the fast-moving needle, lest we get a hole through it, then she pressed her foot to the treadle and the machine whirred, stitching faster than our eyes could follow.

Mama told us that she'd made dresses for an Austin department store before she married Papa. Her mother had been a well-regarded seamstress, sewing gowns for debutantes.

"Those girls were so fickle, if they didn't like a dress, they'd tear it off, and Mother would have to begin again. She spent hours at this table."

Mama caressed the machine's wheel.

"These Singers provide a livelihood for countless women. Many around these parts buy their machines on time, paying for them in monthly installments."

"What happens if they can't pay?" Ida said.

"The company takes it back."

I gasped at the cruelty.

"Sewing is about hope," Mama explained. "A seamstress believes that with skill and patience, the scraps of life can be stitched together to make something lasting. A thing of beauty and worth."

"Oh, Mama, will you teach me to sew?" Irene asked.

"Me too?" said Ida.

"Of course. Now, where should we place this miracle, children?"

We decided on the wall next to Mama's jade plant. As we pushed the machine toward its new home, its tiny metal wheels squeaked, as if to protest its demotion from a carpeted room in Austin to our humble dirt floor. With the arrival of the Singer, our lives settled into a new rhythm. Weekdays we commuted to school in Engle. Nights we slept, cradled by the steady tap of Mama's treadle, like a heartbeat.

5

Irene learned to operate the Singer nearly as well as Mama, and then my once-placid sister began to argue with her about little things—dress style and the right length hem.

Irene got a job cleaning the hotel on Saturdays and promised to bring us the cigar wrappers. I watched amazed while she ironed every wrinkle from her clothes, scrubbed and polished her shoes, and fastened her hair in a pile on the top of her head before leaving.

One Saturday, I rode Duchess to the hotel to give Irene a ride home. She stood at the end of the porch talking to a cowboy. I saw it was Earl Graham, the son of the fiddler who owned the HG horse ranch. As they spoke, Earl stepped closer and took Irene's hand. She lifted her chin to look into his eyes. I noticed the graceful curve of her neck and how pretty she looked in profile. She looked my way, let go, and said a quick goodbye.

We rode home nestled close on the back of the plodding mare. She and Earl had met at the dance. He had business in Engle on Saturdays and often stopped by the hotel to chat. And yes, she was sweet on him.

"Does Mama know?"

"Some of it." She smiled a secret smile.

A month later, on a Sunday when Papa was home, Irene announced that Earl Graham was on his way over to speak to Papa and Mama about something important. They shot glances at each other over our hush puppies and glazed carrots. We finished the meal and hurried to clean up. Papa put on a clean shirt. Mama removed her apron, reknotted her bun, and sprayed rose water on her wrists. Then we heard the clop of hooves of Earl's palomino.

Earl knocked loudly, and Irene skipped to the door to let him in. He looked handsome in his polished dress boots, black denim dungarees that looked stiff and new, a pressed shirt, and a dress Stetson that was as white as milk. The kids at school claimed he could break a mustang quicker than anybody in the county.

He removed his hat to reveal a lily-white forehead. The muscles of his clamped jaw twitched, and his voice sounded hoarse. Mama and Papa asked how his family was doing and made small talk about the weather. Earl's voice went back to normal, but he kept looking at Irene across the room. She'd changed her dress.

Then Mama sent us outside, including Irene, who headed to the corral to feed oats to Earl's palomino.

I sat between Ida and Charlie on the narrow bench against the rock wall of the barn and tried to eavesdrop, but Stevie was chasing the hens, throwing his hoop over as many as he could. Between his squeals and the chickens' squawking, we couldn't hear a word.

"Stop that, Stevie," Ida said. "Mama's told you a hundred times it makes the hens too nervous to lay."

Stevie found a whiptail lizard and sat in the dust of the yard, urging it to crawl up his pant leg. But the hens were unsettled, and the banty rooster had begun to crow.

We sat on the bench, raking the dirt with our bare toes, while we watched the light fade. A cool breeze brought the smell of sage. In the mauve sky, the first star appeared, like a shiny glass button. Then we heard the clap of the door and Earl joined Irene at the corral. They stood together speaking quietly while stroking his horse's coat and mane. They looked like charcoal cutouts against the graying horizon. Then Earl kissed the back of Irene's hand, mounted his horse, and rode off.

Irene strolled back to the house. I herded the last hen into the coop, latched the door, and followed.

"Charley Graham's one of the more prosperous ranchers in the Jornada," Papa said to Mama. "Been here since ninety-six. And a fair man too."

"Yes, they're an upstanding family, but she's not marrying Charley Graham—she's marrying his son. She's too young."

"Earl's been to the agricultural college. He'll be able to provide for her."

"I believe he'd be good to her," Mama said. "But she's only fourteen. Sixteen is more reasonable. They'll have to wait."

Irene's face was red. "Mama, if I may speak for myself, I can't wait until I'm sixteen. It's too long." Her voice shook. "If you don't let us marry soon, Earl and I will run away—"

Papa burst in, "You'll do no such thing, young lady."

Irene began to cry. She put her face in her hands, and her shoulders shook. I stood and put an arm over her crumpled back.

Papa pulled a bag of tobacco from his pocket and fiddled with it. Irene wasn't the type to make idle threats. We believed her.

"Do you feel so strongly, dear?" Mama said.

Irene lifted her blotchy face.

"Yes, Mama. And Earl feels the same."

Her eyes blazed with a queer kind of light. I never imagined that mild, agreeable Irene could be so defiant, or that love could be so strong.

Mama looked at Papa. "I know we told Earl that Irene would have to wait, but perhaps we could reconsider." Her voice softened. "We were married within a year of when we met."

Papa put his tobacco away. "She could do plenty worse."

"A bird in the hand is worth two in the bush. Maybe Earl isn't willing to wait."

"Papa," Irene pleaded, "Earl already has title to three hundred sixty acres, with grazing rights on top of that. And he has his own rig. Maybe he can drill us a well."

Mama fixed a long gaze on Papa. Irene watched him too.

"All right, you may marry within the year. Your mother and I will sign the papers, since you're underage. I'll talk to Charley Graham."

Irene rushed across the room and dropped a kiss on Papa's cheek. She held Mama in a long, tight embrace. She was crying again but smiling between sobs. Then she ran outside to be alone with her joy.

Papa and Charlie went out to check on the horses. Ida and I found each other's hands and beamed at one another with smiles as wide as our Jornada.

"How old were you when you got married, Mama?" Ida said.

"I was twenty years old. And that felt young."

Papa and Mr. Graham met that next week. In the end, they agreed to the marriage that summer when the preacher came to town. Earl would be twenty-five, and Irene fourteen and a half.

Irene spent her hotel earnings on a pair of kid leather slippers from the Sears, Roebuck catalog. When they arrived, she put them on and waltzed across our dirt floor. I wanted to try them, but my feet were too large to fit. I imagined those pretty slippers carrying her away from the rocks and ruts of our lives to some finer place.

Irene and Mama took a trip to El Paso to buy her first corset, taffeta for a petticoat, and the fabric for a new dress to get married in. In El Paso they heard the Sousa Band perform, and Mama took Irene to the Baptist church. Irene spoke to the preacher and was baptized.

I looked her over to see whether she'd changed. "What was it like?"

"I told the preacher how much I loved Jesus, and he said a prayer and poured a pitcher of water over my head." She laughed. "I'm glad I wasn't wearing my best dress."

Mama smiled. "When I was baptized at the age of twelve in an eddy of the Colorado River, it was a horse of another color. The preacher was such a frail old man that when I leaned back into his arms, he stumbled, and we both ended up underwater. I must say, I've never felt so clean in my life."

"What about you, Papa?" Irene said. "Were you baptized?"

"I suppose I was," he said. "But the water must not have been hot enough."

Mama laughed. "You're hopeless, Harry Gore."

Papa grinned.

Earl called on Sundays, and he and Irene took walks. I didn't get to know him well, but he made her happy. Irene was back to her old guileless self since she'd gotten her way, or maybe it was the baptism that pacified her.

6

Mama got ill carrying the baby. One Saturday, Dora, Marv Fenton's wife, showed up at our door with a basket of chipped beef, stewed tomatoes, and a chess pie.

"I heard your mother was doing poorly."

She'd come by before to visit. The first time she'd brought Marv Fenton, but he'd looked so uncomfortable sitting at the table between Mama and Dora that she didn't bring him back.

I let her in. She took in Mama's sallow skin and the circles beneath her eyes. "I'll watch the children, Nannie. You have a rest."

Mama thanked her and lay down. Dora gave Stevie some wooden spools to play with; then she pulled a book from her bag, sat on the sofa, and started reading. I waited for her to share a passage, as Mama did when she read her Bible. Finally, she looked up.

"Do you like to read, Josie?"

"Yes, but the school reader's dull."

"Reading can take you many interesting places."

She placed the book on her lap. Her hands were plump and pretty.

"I used to live in San Francisco. My first husband suffered from consumption, so we moved here for the dry air. But things didn't go as intended." She smiled sadly. "I've a good life now with Mr. Fenton, but there are times I'm homesick. I pick up a book then and imagine I'm in another place." She laughed. "That's why your mama and I get on so well—we're both city girls at heart. I've some books you'd like."

The next week, Dora brought a baker's dozen of squash muffins and a stack of books. She said I could keep them until I'd read them. I could see why Marv Fenton married dear, generous Dora. At night, while Mama sewed and Ida and Irene crocheted the lace for Irene's wedding dress, I sat before the fire and journeyed twenty thousand leagues under the sea and to Treasure Island. When Mama finally started to feel like herself again, Dora stopped coming, and I missed her.

That spring, Earl drilled a two-hundred-foot well on our claim and built a windmill to pump the water. By the time it was finished, Papa had saved enough for a house.

He hired a Mexican mason-carpenter who constructed an adobe brick cabin with a cottonwood plank floor, a porch, and an outhouse. Little Stevie followed the builder around, hammer in hand, ready to pound in a nail when the patient man let him. Earl helped Papa put up fencing and offered him several steer he could pay for when they'd sold.

Mama took the inheritance money she'd hidden away and paid the carpenter to build a cupboard, a kitchen table and chairs, and the frame for our sofa. She spent eighteen dollars on a new cast-iron stove with embossed nickel trimming, rolls of paper for the walls, and a blue enameled teakettle that sang when the water boiled.

Our new home was completed in June, and the following week we moved in. It smelled of clean dirt, freshly cut cottonwood, and paper glue. It was the first home that was truly ours. Mama stood on the porch and looked out over our own square of desert, began to hum a tune, and went into the house to unpack the last boxes.

"It's good to be settled," she said that night as she waddled around the new table, patted the Singer in its new corner, and bent to wipe the dust from the leaves of the jade plant. "Isn't it curious, though? We're living closer to town, but I feel more alone. There's no train whistle and no passing wagons." She wiped her moist brow, sat heavily in her rocker, and patted her round belly. "Lord willing, this baby will give our place the housewarming it deserves."

Living near Cutter meant that Papa could be home, but it was odd having him with us each night—like having a lodger. He got cross when we children squabbled, expected silence at the supper table, and took up residence in Mama's rocking chair.

7

One afternoon in late June, as Mama was placing the corn flour in the cupboard, a queer look crossed her face. I saw a ragged stain on the back of her skirt.

"My water's broken, though it's early to have this baby."

Irene helped her to a chair. "Is the baby coming right away?"

"It's just a trickle and I've no pains so far. I'll have your papa ride over to the Grahams' this evening, so Earl can fetch the midwife. He'll know where to find her."

The next morning, Earl arrived with Luisa Riseau and a basket of food from his mother. Luisa checked on Mama and told us the birth would be soon, but there was time to prepare. Irene went to be with Mama, and Charlie disappeared in the brush with Stevie, while Luisa boiled water and took bundles of dried herbs from her saddlebag.

Half Mexican and half French, Luisa lived in a garden spot in a slip of a valley in the Caballos, northwest of Cutter. Mama called her a grass widow—separated from the husband she'd once had, though no one knew why. The Mexican women and many of the Anglo ranch wives called her in to help bring in their babies.

She had wavy black hair she wore long down her back, tied with a cord to keep it out of her work. Her nose was narrow and crooked like a ridge of the San Andres, and her eyes were dark crescents. Her hands were slender, her fingers tapered. Strength was in them. And knowing. Mama was in good hands.

"This is *cardo santo*," she told me. "You call it thistle. It will strengthen your mother's labor."

She explained that *canela* lessened the bleeding and another herb, called *inmortal*, helped remove the afterbirth. *Yerba buena* was good for everything.

Luisa didn't speak Mexican or Texan, like most of the people in the Jornada. She didn't have Papa's languid Louisiana diction or sound like the circuit-riding preacher from Boston, who spoke with a fast city clip and couldn't say his *r*'s. She spoke in a slow, careful way, as if every word mattered.

She told me that she'd learned about herbs from her Mexican mother, who'd been a *partera* too. Her mother had learned from the Indians. Other secrets of herbs, weeds, and roots had been passed down from the Spanish, who'd learned them from the Moors.

She pulled scissors, a ball of string, and a flask of oil from her bag.

"What size are your mother's feet?"

"She wears a size-five shoe," Ida said.

Luisa nodded. "I like to know that when I come to catch a baby. The size of a woman's foot indicates the size of the pelvis the newborn must pass through."

I began to worry.

The kettle was singing on the stove.

"I need flour browned in the oven. And have you some quart jars?"

Ida took care of the flour, and I got some Masons out of the cupboard. We washed out the cobwebs, and Luisa filled them with boiled water. In each she placed a different herb to steep.

"Your mother doesn't have to worry this time. It's a small baby. I hope not too small."

She stirred grape powder and sugar into cold water. It turned a rich purple. Then she took out an aloe leaf as long as my forearm and scraped the gel into the jars.

"My father used to tell me the story of *la Cendrillon*. I think you call her Cinderella. I longed for such dainty slippers. Later I learned that a woman with such undersized feet would have had difficult childbirth." She looked up from her work. "She might not have survived."

I gasped.

Luisa looked down at my bare toes and chuckled. "I can tell by the size of yours that you won't have a problem when your time comes."

It was a relief to know that my large feet might one day serve me well.

She glanced down at Ida May's. "You've got small feet, like your mother."

"I'm not going to have any babies," Ida said. "I have different plans."

Luisa stopped stirring. "I made other plans too."

She screwed on the lids of the jars and shook them until the liquid resembled runny pectin. She held them up to the window to see their colors.

Irene came out of Mama's room. "She's thirsty."

I helped Luisa set the jars and her birthing tools on a tray. She went to Mama then, carrying the luminous herbals, like jewels for our queen.

Mama had a tiny girl she named Bethel. Irene told us she'd come out too soon and was as blue as Indian corn. Luisa had rubbed her all over to get her breathing, patted her with oil, and sprinkled flour on her navel.

Bethel was too frail to nurse long. Luisa taught Mama how

to coax milk from her breasts if the baby couldn't suck. She made us a milk tit with a diaper and showed us how to use it to feed her.

Then she buried the placenta in the hole Papa had dug, left us more herbs, and packed up her saddlebag.

"Your mother will need to eat beef liver, molasses, and greens to gain her strength back."

I opened the door to see her out and pointed. "Look. On the creosote."

She nodded. "Doves. A good sign." And she rode off.

The white-winged doves remained there, their shiny eyes staring above black beaks. Their soft cooing sounded like wind through hollow reeds. Then, in a whistle of wings, they burst into flight.

I went in to see Mama, found the baby's miniature hand, and gently squeezed her cool fingers. They were the same blue gray of my fingernails when I washed clothes in the winter.

Then she awoke and let out that inhuman newborn cry, like the bleat of a goat.

"At least she has strength enough to complain," Mama said.

After a few weeks of Mama's milk, Bethel took on weight. She seldom cried. Perhaps she was simply grateful to occupy her small place on Earth.

Irene and Earl's wedding was set for July when the circuit preacher was due, but then we got word that there'd been a death in his family, and he wouldn't be returning until September. They would go to El Paso to be married, but we would celebrate their marriage at the Grahams' annual picnic and dance.

That day, we rode our wagon the seven miles to their ranch, going slowly to avoid jostling tiny Bethel and the layered cake Mama had packed in ice.

"Oh, isn't this lovely," Mama said to Papa as we pulled in. "This is what I want our place to look like someday."

Around the ranch house, rows of cottonwoods, acacias, and fruit trees made shade for our picnic, a rare pleasure in our nearly treeless valley. A wide porch ran the length of the house, and next to it, grapes climbed an arbor. Roses bloomed in Emma Graham's garden, her flowers and vegetables enclosed by a stone wall. Three wells, a barn, bunkhouses for ranch hands and guests, Elias's and Cephus's small houses, and various sheds flanked the adobe.

Emma Graham had set out a fine spread. We filled our plates, grabbed leafy switches to ward off flies, and settled in chairs in the shade. After supper, Earl's twelve-year-old brother, Neil, passed out Prince Albert cigars, and Mrs. Graham poured glasses of red currant wine, letting slide her rule against alcohol on the ranch.

Charley Graham stood up. At five feet four and more than two hundred pounds, he was nearly as wide as he was tall. He wore a ten-gallon hat that stood up high with no crimp. Since he rarely spoke, the crowd hushed to listen.

"With all creation here, it's time for a toast. We welcome Irene, Harry, Nannie, and all the Gores to our family." He lifted his glass. "Earl and Irene, here's wishing you a happy life together."

The adults cheered and drank their sweet wine. Then Papa waxed elegant about the strong ties that bind family and community. Folks toasted again and drained their glasses. Cigar smoke curled around the tables. Someone brought out whiskey, but Emma Graham made the man put it away.

Earl's married sister, Leslie, owned a Brownie camera. She herded our families over to the grape arbor and had us bunch up in the middle. Mama fussed because Charlie couldn't find his shoes and she couldn't coax Stevie, sad to have left his hammer at home, off the porch. Leslie told us to freeze like statues, but just then, her girl stepped in front of me and her big bow blocked my view. Leslie snapped our picture, and it was too late to move.

Charley Graham headed to the dirt yard next to the house and nestled his fiddle under his chin. Elias took up his own, Cephus put his harmonica to his lips, and the music began. The Grahams' ranch hands, always treated like family, moved the tables out of the way, and folks danced. Emma Graham set up a dessert table with Mama's cake, pies, and lemonade. Charley Graham had ordered two hundred pounds of ice from El Paso, and we children took turns turning the crank to make ice cream.

After sunset, oil lamps were set on the tables. A breeze cooled the dancers and loosened the last cottonwood fluffs, which floated over the crowd.

"Look, Josie." Charlie nudged me, pointing into the air. "It looks like snow."

He jumped up and darted among the dancers, trying to catch the cottony seeds in his cupped hands. They hardly missed a step, unaware of the flurry around them. One fluff came to rest on Earl's broad shoulder, and another landed in Irene's dark hair. She looked ready to be a bride. Mama chatted with Leslie and Emma Graham. Papa talked with the men. It felt as though our whole family was getting married to the people of the Jornada.

Eventually, guests headed home or to the bunkhouse. Tired Mama, Ida, who always liked her sleep, Emma Graham, and Leslie rounded up the younger children and put them to bed. Irene and Earl had disappeared. Charley and Neil Graham, Elias, Papa, Charlie, and I were left. Charley Graham brought out a lantern, led us to the porch, and fetched the last of the pies.

"Don't think Emma would mind if we finished these off. Ladies first. Would you like a slice, Josie?"

"Yes, Mr. Graham."

"You can call me Daddy Graham, like my grandchildren do."

He handed me a piece, then served the others. Elias brought out his guitar, coughed his permanent dust hawk, and sang a couple Mexican love ballads, "El venadito," and my favorite sad song, "El abandonado." Papa sang "Call Me Up Some Rainy Afternoon" in his fine deep voice. I giggled at the spicy lyrics about lovers stealing away and thought of Irene and Earl alone somewhere. Charlie pulled out our Hohner, and we passed it back and forth to play, wiping it on our sleeves between turns. Then Papa brought out a flask of whiskey.

"Here's something to wet the throat." He took a swig and passed it to Elias.

Papa rolled himself a cigarette and took short puffs until it lit up orange on the end. Daddy Graham pulled tobacco out of his vest pocket, studied the plug, and carved off a piece. The men smoked, chewed, and talked about all kinds of things—mean weather, unforgettable horses, runaway trains, and satisfying food. I perked up when they got to the topic of mine closures.

"The government hasn't been buying enough silver, since the repeal of the Sherman Act," Daddy Graham said. "First the mines in the Black Range closed, and now they're talking about the mines here. When the dam's finished, if the motor route goes in west of the Rio Grande, Cutter's bound to suffer. Engle too."

I wondered how stopping up a river could change so much.

The men were quiet then, listening to the rustle of leaves in the breeze, lost in private thoughts. Elias leaned close to the lamp and shaved a callous off his palm with the small blade of his pocketknife. Daddy Graham spit a dark wad into the night. I dozed off and then jerked awake.

"Josie Belle," Papa said, "it's time for bed. You too, Charlie. Y'all get along."

Neil was already snoring on one of the cots on the porch. I forced myself to rise, and Charlie and I stumbled toward the bunkhouse, pushed along by the wind.

─╬─

In August, Earl and Irene took the train to El Paso and got married. When they returned, they lived in one of the cabins on the Graham ranch. Earl repaired windmills, dug wells, and helped with the fall cattle drive for cash to build a house on his land east of Engle. When it came time to dig a well for himself, Irene told us, he had to drill down four hundred feet for water. Frustrated, he dropped a half a case of dynamite into the hole. The explosion opened up so many seams that the water came to within one hundred feet of the surface, providing enough for several hundred head of cattle. Then he built a two-room cabin out of railroad ties and mud.

Mama cried when Irene moved to their ranch. She was so far away and so alone. They wrote postcards to each other to keep in touch. I was struck by the finality of it all. Irene was Earl's wife first, and our sister second.

A family is like a fabric. When someone's missing, it leaves a tear that needs repairing. I grieved our loss but knew that my sister was weaving her own pattern with Earl, a man committed to his family. I was happy for Irene, knowing that hers would be more resilient than ours.

9

That fall, the Victoria Mining Company closed most of its mines in the Caballos. They cut back operations at the mill by two-thirds. The company stopped running the mine train and hauled the ore by mule team. Papa lost his job.

Hundreds of men were out of work. The first to act found employment at the dam site. Some stayed to prospect for silver. A few found jobs on ranches. Most packed up their families and took the train in search of another boomtown.

Papa returned from looking for work in El Paso with sober news. The city was filled with refugees. In late July, the Mormons in Mexico, victimized by Orozco's men, had crossed the border for safety. Thousands, both Mexican and Anglo, had fled north and were looking for jobs.

Cutter shrank to a few hundred citizens. Charlie and I wandered among the empty shacks looking for treasures left behind, but the most we found were a few marbles and a broken dollhouse. Locals pulled apart the buildings to salvage the wood for other projects. I helped Papa and Charlie rip off planks to fortify the chicken coop and build a lean-to for the horses. Earl took wagonloads of boards back to his ranch to build a real house for Irene.

Papa got work at the Engle stockyard during the fall roundup and came home with cash from the sale of several of our cattle. Then, by luck, one of the engineers running the freight train for the dam left his job. Papa took his place hauling cement, heavy equipment, and construction supplies from El Paso to Engle, and on the spur line the twelve miles to the dam. Things were looking up. Papa was delighted that we had a Democrat in the White House for the first time in fifteen years. He believed Wilson to be a clever man and liked his adviser, Colonel House, a soft-spoken Texan who understood issues in the West.

For his new job, Papa was required to spend his nights away. Just as I'd gotten used to having him around, he left us again.

That fall, Charlie and I started at the new Cutter school, built by the mining company two years late. With so many families gone, the room was half empty. We were disappointed that the school board hired mean Miss Stanley to be our teacher. Ida didn't think she had much more to learn from her, and Mama agreed. When she turned thirteen, Ida got a job as a maid at the Hickock Hotel in Engle, rooming in the quarters on the top floor. We'd become closer since Irene had gone, and I missed her. She gave some of her earnings to Mama but saved the rest. I was sure Ida had a plan.

Blaze had broken his leg in a prairie dog hole that summer and had to be shot, so Papa sold the wagon since an old nag couldn't pull it alone. Charlie and I rode the three miles to school on glue-footed Duchess. The afternoons were warm, and we grew languid on the way home. We took turns on the Hohner and talked about what we would be when we grew up—I, a teacher, and Charlie, a sailor, the most exotic thing he could imagine. We dismounted and let Duchess mosey after us as we snailed home. Ever watchful of snakes, we lingered over rodent holes to see what might happen when we probed them with sticks. We dawdled to watch iridescent black beetles and other armored insects carry seeds twice their size to hidden nests.

One afternoon I heard the *bok, bok, bok* that reminded me of a deep-voiced chicken. I kept my eyes open for movement, and then I saw it: a bronzy roadrunner scurrying through the brush, a lizard in its mouth.

Marv Fenton had told me that roadrunners mate for life and stay settled in the same place in the desert for most of their existence. "Like me," he'd said. "I'll be staying in this corner of creation till the end of my days."

I wished Papa could be more like Marv Fenton, who was steady and sober and attached to his home. Even a roadrunner never left its mate for long.

The crisp winds of late fall blew through the valley as if to sweep it clean. On winter nights when snow brought bitter cold, we lit a fire in the stove and sat close, wrapped in wool shawls and Indian blankets. We popped corn, toasted bread, or passed around a jar of piñon nuts. I'd learned to crochet and made scarves, while Charlie played the harmonica to the even beat of Mama's Singer. We passed Bethel from lap to lap. She was always happy to be held.

That Christmas, Charlie cut us a piñon. We strung popcorn, wrapped cotton balls with our collection of cigar foil, and hung them on the branches. Irene and Earl joined us for supper. Over Rio Grande duck with orange sauce, Irene announced that she was pregnant. The baby would arrive in early summer. Mama looked stunned and then walked around the table to kiss her and congratulate Earl. The corners of her mouth turned up, but her eyes didn't smile.

"My baby having a baby," was all that she could say.

⁂

Papa began drinking again in El Paso. He came home only every few months. When he'd imbibed, his speech got slower, his stories got longer, and sometimes he'd tell a joke and forget the punch line. When he kissed us good night, the bouquet of whiskey laced his breath like the nip of an autumn breeze. I feared he'd be fired again.

I found Mama on the porch bench one evening, Bethel in her arms. She held one of the baby's tiny fingers in her mouth.

"What are you doing, Mama?"

"I'm cutting her nails. Even my finest scissors might nick a finger. Her nails are so delicate, I can trim them with my teeth."

Bethel was still bald. Though her cheeks had filled out, she still had the squinty eyes of a preemie.

"Who do you think she'll look like when she gets bigger?"

Mama picked the slivers of nail from her tongue and flicked them onto the porch.

"Oh, she takes after your papa, to be sure." She held up the pearly nails of Bethel's small hand and examined her trimming. "I hope she doesn't inherit his weakness."

"You mean the drink?"

She nodded.

"Why don't he stop?"

"Why *doesn't* he stop? You must speak proper English."

"Why does he drink so much?"

"I suppose he drinks to forget."

I stayed quiet.

"Your papa was born six years after the end of the Civil War in a poor section of northern Louisiana. The South was filled with war-damaged men. His own father lost his leg at Vicksburg. Things got so bad, they had to sell off their land for a pittance."

Mama caressed Bethel's soft head. I stroked it too.

"He left home when he was fourteen. Life was always hard for your papa."

The sun had disappeared behind the ridge. Mama gazed at the dark spine of mountains against the apricot sky. Bethel stared there too, mesmerized by a beauty she couldn't fathom.

"Your papa's handsome, intelligent, charming . . . but in his soul lives the sorrow of the South."

Bethel whimpered. Mama unbuttoned her blouse and attached the baby to her breast.

"I suppose that's why he loves the rails. He's afraid that if he stays in one place too long, the melancholia will overtake him."

She patted the back of my hand.

"I'm telling you this because I want you to understand your papa. He wants to be happy. That's why he sings and tells jokes. And drinks." She shook her head. "And just can't stop."

Bethel had fallen asleep, a trickle of milk dribbling from the corner of her flaccid mouth. Mama lifted her and tickled her awake, then turned her around and placed her on the other breast.

"He loves us but won't change."

She looked out into the lonely desert and sighed.

Bethel was asleep again. Mama shifted the baby and buttoned her blouse. Bethel's thin arms dangled, as slack as a rag doll. The nails on her tiny left hand were five circles of shell pink. The uncut nails of her other, like feathered rice paper.

That spring, Mama went to help Irene have her baby. Mother Graham went too, and Luisa the midwife.

"It was nip and tuck," Mama told us when she came home. "Thank goodness Luisa Riseau knows her art. The cord was wrapped around the baby's neck. She took forever to take her first breath. She's doing fine now. And Irene's up and about."

As she wiped the dust from her face with a damp handkerchief, I noticed how tired she looked.

"That's the bright side of having children so young," she told Ida, her oldest girl now. "You don't know enough to be fearful."

I spent two weeks with Irene and baby Mona on their ranch that summer, helping her with chores and picking the beans and corn she'd planted. Irene was a cheerful, caring mother. A girl herself, it seemed as though she were still playing dolls on our porch in Cutter.

⚜

That fall, I turned twelve, and Charlie and I went back to school.

"Miss Stanley's as tiresome as mush. And she still doesn't like boys," Charlie said.

He asked Mama whether he could get a job instead. She wouldn't hear of it.

"You stay in school, Son. Your education and your faith are the only things they can't take away from you."

"Who's 'they'?" he asked me.

I shrugged.

"It's fine for you to go because your dream's to be a teacher. A nice one. But sailors don't need school."

He said he hoped Miss Stanley would quit, so we could stay home. That winter, he got his wish when she married a dam engineer and moved to Elephant Butte. The school board couldn't find a replacement, so they closed school for the rest of the year.

That was the last year I attended school. I could not have imagined then how events on the horizon would conspire to take me from my dream.

Early June of 1914 was scorching hot, wearing us down. Ida was bored with her job at the hotel, and when she was home, she wrangled with Mama. One morning while we were pickling watermelon rinds, Ida told us of her plan to move to St. Louis. She'd been accepted at a school of secretarial studies.

I nearly dropped my knife. Mama stopped pouring the vinegar.

"Is this a jest? How will you pay for it?"

Ida said she'd already saved enough for the first part of the year, and Aunt JoJane had offered to pay the rest if Ida would stay with her family and help out.

"I'll be fifteen in the fall, Mama. You know there's no future for me here."

"What makes you think you won't sour on it after a spell?"

"Because ever since Austin, all I've wanted is to live in a city."

"I'll have to talk to your papa." Mama led Ida to the sofa to discuss it more.

I dropped the last of the cut rinds into jars and drowned them in vinegar. I knew Ida would leave us, just as Irene had.

The heat spell broke with a vivid lightning storm followed by a June monsoon. We got more rain in one week than in most of the previous year. Water holes filled in the old *parajes*. Lago Engle reappeared. Hillsboro flooded. One person died, and many of the town's buildings collapsed.

⚜

At the end of that fateful month, Ida brought the *Rio Grande Republican* home from the hotel, and we read that Archduke Ferdinand and his wife, Duchess Sophie, had been shot in a place called Bosnia. I was impressed by their fine names, but royalty had little to do with us. Folks in our valley talked of tensions in Europe, but Mama and Papa believed it was a problem for the Europeans. The troubles in Mexico took more of our attention. Victoriano Huerta had led a coup and taken control of the government. President Madero had been assassinated. The country was still in turmoil.

Through July the paper brought news of continuing troubles in Europe, but in Mexico, Venustiano Carranza overthrew President Huerta. More Mexican refugees flooded the border towns. I wondered what had happened to Mariana and Manuel and their loving mother. Mama had written them several letters but hadn't heard back. I wandered out into the scrub with the harmonica and played the melodies that Mariana had sung to me. Our friends were lost to us, like the many that disappear during years of revolution and turmoil.

In August, Mama read to us that Germany, Russia, France, England, and Austria-Hungary had all gone to war. The adults in town talked of nothing but warmongering Europe.

At the height of August's searing heat, the last of the Victoria mines in the Caballos shut down. The Cutter mill closed for good. Papa said it was foolish to close the mines with a war on. Plenty of ore remained, and prices would only go up, but the decision had been made months earlier back East by company shareholders, and there was nothing to be done. The last of the workers and their families scattered to other parts of the West. The Elephant

Butte dam was scheduled for completion the following year; men were being let go there too.

In September, we studied newspaper maps to locate the battles at the Marne and Flanders, but they seemed a universe away. The progress of the dam, the price of beef, and the misfortunes of our neighbors concerned us more.

Cutter shriveled like a dried squash, with nothing left but the rind. The depot was the only place with any vigor. The Santa Fe trains still rumbled through, and Papa's supply train for the dam. Only two of the saloons, two stores, and the Victoria Hotel remained in business. The bank had already shut its doors when the manager left town after his baby daughter died from whooping cough. Each time I walked into Cutter, I heard the rip and crash of abandoned buildings being pulled apart. Earl took down two dwellings for boards to build an extension on Irene's house and sheets of tin for its roof.

The storekeeper who owned the last motorcar in town closed up his mercantile and reopened in Palomas Hot Springs, the town on the other side of the Rio Grande where a graded road for motorcars was to be built. The day he rattled down the old Camino Real, trailed by a pillow of dust, we waved goodbye. I felt as though we'd been left to fall back in time.

12

Before Ida's move to St. Louis, Mama took her on the train to El Paso. She had her fitted for a corset, purchased sturdy gray and navy gabardine to make two practical dresses, and took her to see an animal circus. At the Baptist church, Ida was baptized. "The preacher insisted on a river baptism. Can you imagine? In that muddy Rio Grande? But when Mama explained how little time we had, he agreed to do it at the church."

I knew that one day it would be my turn to go to El Paso with Mama and be blessed with water.

Ida talked Mama into letting her raise the hem of her dresses and sew on outside pockets, the new fashion. Mama stitched her a lovely corset cover. She'd need a warm coat and new shoes too. The winters could be cold in St. Louis. The two of them were busy sewing and planning—and finally getting along.

In late September, Ida packed up her single bag, and she and Papa caught the train to Denver, from where she would continue on to St. Louis. I hugged her hard, scared that I might not see her again.

First Irene and now Ida—our family was dividing like forks of a river.

⁓

In January, Mama told me she was pregnant again. She informed Papa after she told me. He was half drunk that night.

"You've heard the saying," he said. "As if things aren't bad enough, Granny has to go and have a baby!"

All I heard from Mama was the slam of the bedroom door. I realized that this pregnancy wasn't wanted, and my stomach began to ache.

13

Mama got discouraged with her two oldest daughters so far away and the town dying. One April evening when Papa was home and the little ones in bed, Mama abruptly stopped the treadle of her Singer. I looked up from the beans I was sorting.

"I've been thinking of Texas, Harry. I want to go back to Austin to live near Lucy and Stephen."

Papa looked up from his paper and stilled the rocker.

"We've got our land, Nannie. In a year and a half, this place will belong to us. That's something to stay for."

"It's not enough. I can't endure this isolation for the rest of my days."

Papa tossed the paper to the floor and stood up.

"How was I to know the other homesteaders near our section would sell out to the syndicate? That they'd fence it and that the range rights would go to them too? Ranching may be out, but we can still make a life here."

"Oh, let's not whitewash the truth." Mama spoke in a low voice without a shred of hope. "A homestead in Louisiana or Ohio or Oregon might mean something. But here? We can't grow anything to speak of, and it's too costly to irrigate. There's only enough grass for a dozen or so steer and a few wormy calves, not a family. You can't make a silk purse out of a sow's ear, Harry. Cutter's dying. The homestead was a mistake. This patch of desert means heartache to me."

Papa began to pace. "Who could know the mines would close and the town would clear out like it has? Who would've guessed that building the dam would make everyone want to move to the water? Damn the Rio Grande. Damn the dam."

Mama didn't complain about his cussing.

Papa stopped in front of Mama's machine and crossed his arms. "I thought you didn't want to leave Irene."

"Oh, I can hardly tolerate the notion. But I have to think of the rest of the children. Josie and Charlie need an education. Irene has her home and her own family now. Earl and his kin will take care of her."

"What about me?"

"Your job will end when the dam's finished. You can join us in Texas."

"There are no mine trains near Austin. That's my work now."

"You'll have to find another kind of train to run."

Both were quiet for a bit.

Papa let his arms drop. "Seems like I'm beating a dead horse."

Mama rubbed her swollen belly. "I'll leave after the baby comes."

"Do you want to go to El Paso for the birth?"

"No, I've had an easy time so far." She let out a sharp little laugh. "I have more faith in Luisa than any doctor for this eighth time around."

Papa turned his back and went outside.

"So we're moving to Austin, Mama?" I said after the door closed.

"Yes, Josie, my little pitcher with big ears. I've made my decision. I'm relieved, but I feel so . . . so . . ." She shrugged her shoulders and fiddled with the fabric lying across the machine. "Something happens to you when you discover that you've shot the moon and missed. Don't tell the others we're leaving. Especially Irene. She'll take it hard. Wait until the time gets nearer."

She adjusted the needle, repositioned her belly behind the oak table, and began to beat her foot against the treadle. I returned to the beans and tried to match my sorting to her rhythm. I remembered that child in Mexico who'd thrown his precious balloon at our passing train but had fallen short. Like him, we had no recourse but to turn and walk away. Charlie was the only one I told. I could trust him with a secret.

Ida sent a typed letter on thin paper saying that her term had gone well. She'd won some money in a typewriting contest and was saving to buy her own Underwood. The school had found her a summer job in a lawyer's office. My lucky sister.

In May of 1915, news arrived that the Germans had sunk the *Lusitania*. Dora Fenton's second cousin drowned, along with a thousand others. The war was coming closer. I wondered how many of the victims had known how to swim. Had they had any chance to save themselves?

Some folks in the Jornada called President Wilson a coward. They said we should jump into the war and smash the German menace before it got any stronger. If we were in, the demand for horses and the price of beef were sure to rise. But others didn't want to get dragged into the fight. They believed the president should stand up to the munitions makers and other Eastern interests that stood to profit from war.

South of the border, the US had recognized Carranza's government, but Pancho Villa was leading a new rebellion in Chihuahua. We heard stories of foreigners who were attacked and trains that were ambushed. Papa complained that arms dealers, mercenaries, and other unsavory types were coming to New Mexico and Texas to smuggle guns across the border or join Villa in his fight. Rumors flew that Villa had begun raids across the border to steal cattle and collect arms. The safety of our border was a bigger worry than the security of the North Atlantic.

14

On a torrid morning in late July, I set to polishing the range
with stove black. Its sharp odor gave me a headache, so I
stepped out for air. Stevie and Bethel were playing on the porch
with the wooden Tink set he'd gotten for his birthday. Mama
called for me. I went to her room, where she was lying on the
bed, her face flushed.

"I believe I'm going to have this baby soon. Ride to Cutter,
will you, Lamb? You can pay a fast-rider at the livery to carry a
note to Emma Graham to send Luisa here. Take money out of
the ironstone jar in the cupboard."

I untied my apron.

"If Emma can't reach Luisa, tell her to send someone else.
But not the doctor in Las Cruces. He won't get here in time."
She arched her back and grimaced.

I scrubbed the worst of the polish from my hands, grabbed
my hat, a canteen, and the money. Charlie helped me with the
saddle and gave me a leg up.

"Hurry back, Sis."

The road west to Cutter wasn't much more than a track. It
was always a lonesome ride. After a while, I could see the buildings of Cutter on the horizon, and somewhere beyond, in a valley
in the Caballos, was Luisa Riseau.

I put my head down and pushed Duchess through heat that
pressed in like a metal cage. A white lather of sweat ringed her

neck. My dress stuck to my back and thighs. As I entered town, I saw Marv Fenton on his buckboard and waved.

He leaned down from the wagon bench. His hair had gone gray, and his hands, holding loose reins, had grown gnarled.

"I'm just back from the hot springs," he said. "What do ya need, Josie?"

I told him about Mama and asked if he could send for Luisa.

"I'll do that straightaway. You go home and take care of your ma. Help will come soon."

I urged Duchess home. Charlie met me at the gate. He'd just checked on Mama. She'd gone to sleep.

Duchess was beat. I took time to give her water and oats and rub her down. The dear old mare, my best friend—she had done us well.

Charlie took the kitchen chairs out to the back porch so Stevie and Bethel could play passenger train. Mama woke up, and I sat with her as she tried to manage the waves of pain. We waited all afternoon. Luisa didn't come.

As Mama's spasms started coming closer, she held her distended belly and moaned. Sweat collected on her brow and on the curve of her lip. I wiped her face with a damp cloth. I was scared I might have to be her midwife, and I didn't know what to do.

"Josie, I'm as dry as a stick. Bring me water, please," she rasped.

I brought her a glass and she relaxed.

"Watch over the little ones, dear. I still have time."

I fired up the stove and fed them eggs and grits.

"Oh, Luisa," I whispered. "Save us. Come, Irene, Mother Graham, Mrs. Lyons. Someone."

I walked into the yard, willing Luisa to appear. A wasp zeroed in on a half-eaten plum that Stevie had left in the dirt. Thirsty flies circled Duchess's head. The chickens cackled from the shady side of the coop, where they'd scratched out shallow dust baths. I looked out over the parched sands but saw only fluid waves of heat. In the distance, a pack of gray clouds huddled. I could see rain falling, but it was a ghost rain. The heat near the ground swallowed the drops before they could land. I went back inside.

I cleared the table, straining my ears for the sound of horse hooves, but heard only the slam of the door when the boys went out, the high-pitched drift of Stevie's voice, and the thin whisper of the hot breeze. I rinsed the dinner plates and checked on Mama. She was breathing fast.

"Go boil water, Josie. Then throw in a knife to clean it."

I hurried into the kitchen, tossed in more coal, and set a pot on the stove. My hands shook. Then the door flew open and a woman I'd never seen walked in.

"Is this the Gore place?"

"Yes."

"I'm here to catch the baby. I walked from the depot. It's hot as a furnace out there."

"Where's Luisa?"

"She's in Santa Fe getting herbs or something. An old man came into Lyons' store asking for a midwife. He sent me here."

She didn't carry a bundle of herbs, like Luisa. Her dress was filthy, her face and hands streaked with dust. She removed her crumpled hat from a rat's nest of hair. Still, I was relieved to see her.

When I took her to Mama, I could smell the stench of her unwashed body. Bethel began to cry, so I left the woman to her work.

I held Bethel and waited for the water to boil. Time slowed to the crawl of a lizard. Finally, bubbles rose from the bottom of the pot and multiplied. I cleaned the knife.

As I was lifting a bowl of steaming water to take in to Mama, I heard a groan and then the loud, long grunt of Mama pushing the baby out. I heard the muffled wail of a newborn. I went to the bedroom, carrying the water, knife, and a clean blanket. When I pushed the door open with my foot and stood in the doorway, Mama looked up and gave me a tired smile. A bloody sheet covered her body, and she was holding a bundle in her arms.

"Easy as pie," the stranger told me. "The baby nearly popped out. Had the cord around her neck, but it was loose enough. She's a healthy one."

She looked at the water I was carrying.

"We don't need that."

She shut the door on me.

I sat on a kitchen chair and waited. I stared at my hands, still stained with stove black. I used the boiled water to make coffee. It was quiet in the bedroom. Finally, the woman came out. She sat down at the table.

"I don't mean to scare you, but there's still a piece of afterbirth in your ma. I pulled and pulled, but I couldn't get it all out."

I knew this wasn't good. "What should we do?"

She slurped her coffee. "There's nothing to do. She may bleed it out."

"Are you a midwife?"

"Any woman who's had seven babies can catch one. I help out where I'm needed."

She got up. I thanked her and handed her the money that Papa had left for Luisa. With a nod, she set her hat on her disheveled head and left. I leaned on the doorframe and watched as she walked toward Cutter. I didn't even know her name.

The sun was already on its downward arc. Thin clouds hung in the sky, like shreds of paper on a blue backdrop. The sands pulsed white heat. I looked at the creosote on the other side of the corral and searched for a dove, a bird, a sign, but the tree was empty.

I peeked in at Mama. She and the baby were sleeping. I tiptoed to the kitchen. The woman's cup and saucer sat on the table. Brown smudges dirtied the handle and side. I scrubbed the tarnished china until every trace of her was gone.

I went into Mama's room and pulled back the sheet to see the baby's face. She was round and hearty, with a mop of hair like Stevie's. I kissed her dark head and tucked the sheet back around her.

"Isn't she beautiful?" Mama raised her eyelids the smallest amount. "I've named her Sally, after your papa's mother. Can you change the cloths between my legs and put on a clean sheet?"

I removed a bloodied wad and replaced it with clean diapers.

"I'm so tired," she said, and floated back into sleep. I changed the sheet and carried out the chamber pot that held a long gray cord attached to a spongy purple mass I knew to be a part of the placenta. I tossed them down the outhouse hole.

Irene came over the next day with little Mona.

"I'm so sorry I wasn't here to help. I went with Earl to Las Cruces to order a sofa and a Kitchen Queen, and Mother Graham was away at the Sewell Ranch for a few days. And, oh, the woman that came to catch the baby . . . she has a bad reputation. But how could Marv Fenton have known?" She put her arm around me. "Poor Mama. Poor you. But the baby's healthy, and that's the most important thing. You've taken good care of them."

I told her about the piece of afterbirth still inside Mama. Irene didn't know what to think.

"I'll ask Mother Graham about it when I see her."

She set Charlie and Stevie to pumping water and washed Mama and the baby. She helped me scrub the bloodstained cloths and sheets. While we were pinning them to the line, she sidled up next to me.

"I'm going to have another baby. In February, I think."

A white sheet flashed in the sun, blinding me for a moment. I looked down at her waist. It was surely thicker.

"Will you come help me out for a few weeks afterward?"

Of course, I agreed to help.

Irene went home, and Dora Fenton came by. She said Mama looked drained.

"She must have lost a lot of blood, and she's still bleeding. She'll need rest. Do you remember what Luisa told you to give her to build up strength?"

"Liver and molasses and greens, but we're out of greens."

"I'll bring some tomorrow. Can you manage the children and the newborn?"

"I'll be fine."

"You're a good girl, Josie." She kissed me on the cheek.

The following afternoon she showed me how to make a rich chicken broth with bits of liver seasoned with herbs and garlic. As we chopped the cloves, she told me that she and Marv Fenton would be moving away in the fall.

"But Marv Fenton told me he'd never leave the Jornada."

"His rheumatism has gotten worse." She avoided my eye. "He can hardly bend his bad leg. We considered moving up to

Hot Springs, but even the baths don't help anymore. We're going to San Francisco. They have good doctors there who will surely have a treatment."

It seemed that no one wanted to stay in our valley, not even Marv Fenton.

"My daughter lives there. I miss her and the city. And the sea." She tossed slivers of garlic into the pot. "Have you ever been to the sea, Josie? No, I don't imagine you have."

"I've seen the Rio Grande."

"The sea is different. It sparkles and changes with the tides. It leaves you gifts of shells and bleached driftwood, polished rocks and bits of salty seaweed." Her eyes were bright. "It smells tangy. And of birth and decay at the same time. I hope one day you can see it."

She dumped some salt into the broth and stirred.

I wiped a stray hair from my face. The zest of garlic filled my nostrils. I wondered whether it was like the nip of the ocean. Out of the blue, I had a vision of myself sitting on a bench in a city by the sea. White-bellied birds wheeled above. I didn't know whether it was wishful thinking or an apparition.

I washed my hands with Mama's Palmolive and handed Dora the books she'd lent me.

"Thank you, dear. I'll bring them to my granddaughter in San Francisco. She's nearly old enough to read."

How could I be envious of a girl I didn't even know?

15

I fed her beef broth and liver and cared for her as well as I could, but Mama got childbed fever. I asked whether I should go for a doctor, but she said she'd had it once before and had recovered on her own. I slept in the rocker next to her bed, fed Sally cow's milk with a milk tit, and changed the rags beneath Mama. I sent Papa a telegram.

When he came home, he looked worried.

"If your mama's not better tomorrow, we'll send for the doctor."

That night, Mama's face glowed with a ghostly sheen and the fever broke. She said she must have bled out the last of the placenta because she felt like herself again. She didn't look well, but I was relieved she was feeling better.

After Papa left, she called me into her room.

"We'll stay until Irene's baby arrives this winter, and then we'll move to Austin. It can't be soon enough."

She stayed in bed and rested, and her milk came back. Sally was a robust baby who thrived despite her chancy arrival. In another week, Mama was up and about, though thin and pale.

It rained well and started grass, and then the heat came back, and the grass dried up again.

That September, I turned fourteen. They still hadn't found a teacher for the Cutter school, so Mama allowed me to work three days a week for George and Martha Curry, the managers at the

Victoria Hotel. I made beds, scrubbed, swept, helped in the kitchen, and slept in the maids' quarters. I picked up the discarded newspapers from the lobby and read accounts of battles in Europe. Mr. Curry predicted we'd join the war within the year.

─⚹─

I dreaded saying goodbye to the Fentons when the time came. At the Cutter depot, Mama gave Dora a lavender sachet embroidered with pink hearts. Marv Fenton held Mama's hand, touched each of us children on the cheek, mumbled something about it being time to sell his saddle, and hobbled to the train where the porter had to boost him up the stairs. Their gray heads bobbed as the locomotive lurched into motion. The black smoke plumed around us, stung our eyes, and filled our lungs, but we stayed to wave them off. When the train had dwindled to a thin line, we headed home.

─⚹─

Ida wrote that she was at the top of her class. With plenty of jobs for secretaries in St. Louis, she was sure to find one when she finished in seven months. I tried to stop the surge of jealousy that swelled like water from a spring.

"If only we had the money, Josie, I'd send you to the Loretto Academy in Socorro or Las Cruces," Mama said. "They teach courtesy and etiquette, housekeeping and thrift—subjects I learned in school in Austin. I'm sorry we can't do better for you. You're going to have to make your own way when it's time."

I didn't know what way that might be. Everyone had a plan— Ida and Irene, even Charlie. I wished I had one too.

16

One Sunday after my hotel shift, Charlie fetched me on Duchess. As we neared home, Stevie ran to meet us.

"Mama's sick," he puffed.

The breakfast dishes were still on the table, the mush had hardened in the pot, and Mama was in bed with a fever. Her face and hands were swollen. I brought damp cloths for her head and cold chamomile tea. Papa came home and talked about going for the doctor, but the next day, her fever dropped, and Mama figured she was on the mend.

Papa told me I needed to stay home until she recovered her strength. He'd explain to the Currys at the hotel. I took care of baby Sally and kept Bethel and Stevie occupied so they wouldn't bother Mama. I tried to teach Stevie his letters and his numbers, but he wouldn't try. I read him stories from the Bible as Mama had done, and he drew pictures of the sheep, cows, and horses on Noah's ark.

A few weeks later, Irene was ready to have her baby. Mama was worried because it was early. "I want to go to her."

"Are you sure you should?" I didn't tell her how poorly she looked. She had permanent circles under her eyes. Her lips were gray.

"I need to be with her."

She packed up Sally and a bag and took the train up to Engle. Luisa was already there.

After a long birthing, Irene's healthy boy was born. She

named him Joe. Mama had planned to stay on to help, but Luisa sent her home.

"She gave me these herbs." Mama plunked a packet on the table. "Alfalfa, rose hips, and juniper berry. She said I must rest and drink tonics to get my strength back."

"Should I call the doctor?"

"I trust Luisa more."

Mama continued to swell. She couldn't breathe lying down, so she slept in her rocker. On good days she swept the house and cooked. Most days she only had strength enough to sit, hold the baby, or sew. Her milk dried up. She complained of a dull headache that wouldn't leave. She became fretful and got irritated when Sally cried or Bethel whined, so she handed them off to me. Then she turned apologetic.

"I feel so light-headed. I'm not myself. I can no longer fasten my skirts."

She leaned her head back and closed her eyes, and I could see a flush ascend her pallid cheeks. She'd lost her spunk. She no longer talked about Austin. She stopped sewing. The Singer went silent.

One afternoon as I folded diapers and she sewed a button on Charlie's coat, Mama cleared her throat. I looked up. Her eyes were dull, her face ruddy. She laid the coat onto her lap and studied it as if the weave of cotton spelled a message.

"I try and try, and it seems to make no difference. I'm too dog-tired to even think about moving."

She looked up to the ceiling and exhaled a terrible sigh.

"I wish we'd left sooner. Remember, Lamb, regret comes mostly from what you neglect to do. It's the largest part of our sins on Earth."

She let the coat fall to the seat of her chair, wandered into her bedroom, and gently closed the door. The button dangled from a thread. I didn't know how to help, except to complete her last stitch and do the work that had once occupied her days.

On the first of February, Mama's fever soared. I sent Charlie to telegram Papa and send for the doctor.

"Tell him it's urgent."

Papa and the doctor arrived the next morning. Mama had dropsy. Her heart was failing. The doctor left medicine and told Papa that if she wasn't better in three days, to send for him again. Papa sent for Luisa. She felt Mama's head, chest, and back and got busy in the kitchen, strangely silent. She boiled water and soaked herbs until the liquids took on colors.

"You must make her drink," she told me in her slow, exacting way. "The infection's spread. I don't know if I can help her."

She'd said what I most dreaded to hear.

The next morning, Luisa had to leave to deliver a baby near the dam. I scanned the winter sky as she headed to the corral. A Chihuahua raven circled in the cool morning air. Its feathers glinted in the sun, looking as brittle as glass.

Mama wouldn't eat. She only wanted to suck limes. Charlie found some at the Cutter store. She asked for more, but we'd bought them all.

I sent for Irene. She came with baby Joe. She helped me with the housework and spent all afternoon with Mama.

"I'd no idea how ill she was. I've been no help these past weeks. I was so tired after Joe's birth. And there's so much work on the ranch. And now I have to get back home to Mona. She's got the chicken pox."

I didn't blame her. I knew the load she carried. Her hot tears stung my neck as she hugged me goodbye.

On the third day, Papa sent for the doctor. After examining Mama, the man looked grim and gave us a stronger medicine.

"If this doesn't help, there's no more I can do."

He looked around our home. A pile of dirty clothes lay next to the kitchen table. The floor was gritty with dust. The unwashed dinner dishes sat next to the sink.

He refused his pay.

We did what we could. We moved her rocker to her bedroom where she could have quiet. Papa gave her the medicine and emptied the chamber pot of foul liquid. Though I washed her, her skin smelled sour. She slept and asked for limes. Once she sat up with a jolt and told me she needed to do the mending. I had to plead with her to stay in her rocker. She looked at me with the eyes of a child, whimpered, and stayed put.

On that final day, Papa carried a kitchen chair to Mama's side, sat down, and laid his head in his hands. All day he stayed with her. Through the closed door, I could hear the drone of Papa's voice. Once I walked in to hear Mama stumbling through a Bible verse. "They that dwell . . . in the land of the shadow of death . . . hath the light shined." She drew a short breath and coughed.

I returned to the kitchen to wash the dishes. I longed for that light Mama was so sure of and cursed our valley of death. That afternoon Papa took a break to check on the cattle. As I sat with Mama, she opened her eyes.

"I don't know if I'm going to get through this, Lamb." Her lips were cracked, her voice thick. She took some quick, shallow breaths, and ran a dry tongue over her lips. "And you . . . you need to sew on the buttons."

I supposed she must be addled by fever, talking about buttons. Her lungs crackled. A tremor shook her body, and a look of fear came into her eyes.

"I told your papa . . . he needs to keep the family together. You must help him."

I leaned closer to hear her better. Her breath smelled like rotting potatoes. The whites of her eyes had gone yellow. I held her hand.

"Tell me you'll take care of our babies."

"I swear, Mama."

"Don't forget the buttons."

"I sewed on Charlie's button, Mama."

Her eyes held mine with a look of love that shook me, and then she closed them. My vision clouded. I had to leave the room. I poured myself a glass of water and slow tears ran down my face. I wiped my eyes with a corner of my apron and took a glass of water to Mama. She was asleep. I picked up her hand. It burned.

Papa came back and sat with her, and I went out and did the wash. Though the wind blew sand over the wet clothes, it no longer mattered. I fried up beef and onions and made biscuits. We sat down at the table, but I couldn't eat.

"Is Mama getting better?" Charlie said.

"I don't think so."

Our eyes met. He looked away. Papa looked at his plate and picked at his meat. Stevie regarded me with eyes as round as marbles but said nothing.

In the middle of the night, I was awakened by a coyote howling near the house. My head cleared. It was a human cry. Someone was in pain. I crossed the cold floor to Mama's room. A single candle burned on the table. Papa knelt next to her rocker, wailing like a beast in agony. He looked up at me, his features contorted.

"She's gone," he cried, collapsing into sobs.

He leaned forward and laid his head on her lap. The candle threw grotesque shapes onto the wall. I turned in the dark and bumped into Charlie, close behind me. I closed the door to Mama's bedroom, and Charlie and I sat on the sofa. He leaned into me and cried steamy tears on the shoulder of my nightgown. Behind the bedroom door, Papa wept in choking spasms, and then got quiet.

I felt too numb to cry. Charlie's head grew heavy, and he slept. I thought about Stevie and Bethel waking up and wondered how to tell them about Mama.

I dozed, and when I awoke, the darkness had begun to fade. The furniture emerged from the shadows. In the ghostly light, Grandmother's sewing machine, draped with fabric, looked like a bloated monster. The heap of Papa's coat on the chair resembled a crouching coyote; Bethel's crumpled rag doll was a rat.

Slowly, the room filled with gritty light and the furnishings regained their old characters. Charlie shifted and groaned. Light filtered in through the kitchen window, and the walls took on a pale yellow glow. A mockingbird called, and the pinky-gray sky turned blue. Mama was dead.

I don't remember that morning. Papa must have gone to Cutter to send word to Irene. Someone must have contacted Ida and Aunt JoJane and Aunt Lucy. I fell asleep in the afternoon with Sally and Bethel.

I awoke to the clink of dishes. Irene and Emma Graham

stood at the sink. It took me a minute to figure out why they were there. Sally, Bethel, and another baby—Irene's newborn, Joe—were asleep on the sofa. Stevie slept on the floor in front of the stove. Through the half-open door of Mama's bedroom, I could see Papa sprawled on the bare floor, snoring. Someone had thrown a blanket over him.

When I got up, Irene dropped the plate she was drying. It shattered on the floor, but she ignored it and rushed toward me. I stood still as she held me tight and wept. My mind was too sluggish to speak. Emma Graham crouched, picked up the shards, and watched us with wet, sympathetic eyes.

I made my way into Mama's room. Someone had laid her on the bed and covered her with a white sheet. She looked small, like a child. An odor clung to her that repelled me. I took the bottle of rose water, removed the atomizer, poured some in my hand, and pulled the sheet from her face. A silver dime lay on each closed eyelid. Her lashes were black against her yellow skin, her face blank. No one was there.

I patted the skin of her waxen forehead with the perfumed water. It ran down her temples onto the pillow. I massaged more rose water onto her stiff neck and pulled back more of the sheet to wet her yellow wrists. Now the smell of roses overpowered the stench of death. That was what I wanted to remember. Only the sweetness.

Sally awakened and began to whine. I went to her, moving in a frozen kind of way. I picked her up and sat in the kitchen, watching Irene wipe the dishes. Emma Graham had found burnt mush on the back porch and was scrubbing the blackened pot, grateful for an arduous task.

17

We couldn't afford to have her embalmed, and so Mama had to be buried the next day. A man arrived in a wagon with a coffin. Irene and Emma Graham prepared her body, then wrapped the coffin in calico and tied a white ribbon around it. Stevie was in the yard with his hammer when the cart with the coffin pulled away. He wailed as he watched his mama go, and I couldn't console him.

The memorial service was delayed because Ida and Aunt JoJane were on their way from St. Louis. In the days of waiting, nothing was real. I changed and bathed Sally, brushed the tangles from Bethel's hair, swept the house, and helped prepare meals.

Ida and Aunt JoJane arrived the same day as Aunt Lucy and Uncle Stephen's bouquet of white gladiolas, which, after its long journey, sprawled listlessly in its purple wrap. Ida and I hugged, wordless. There was nothing to say. Aunt JoJane cooed as she embraced me and broke into sobs when she saw Papa. Grief marred the beauty I'd once admired.

The morning of the funeral, Ida and I were slicing the cheese and sausage they had brought for the supper to follow. Aunt JoJane turned to me.

"I can't ask your father, he's so terribly stricken, but tell me, Josie, how did your mother's illness come on?"

I told her about the midwife and the placenta and the fevers that came and went and the swelling.

"Why, Josie," Aunt JoJane's voice soared and trembled, "if she'd been brought to St. Louis right away, before the infection set in, she might have had an operation. She might have been saved." She started wiping a serving plate in rapid circular motions. "I'd have gladly paid for the train fare and the hospital bill."

I stared at Aunt JoJane. Would Mama have lived if she'd had better care?

Suddenly, it felt as though the walls of our home were caving in. It was my fault. If I'd gotten Mama to a city doctor, she'd still be alive. Ida continued cutting the sausage into thin wedges, without an upward glance. Aunt JoJane vigorously dusted another platter. Things were turning gray. I couldn't see what I was doing. I staggered to a chair.

"Are you all right?" Ida said.

It was then that the ringing started in my ears.

"Josie, are you well?"

She sounded far away.

"I don't know."

I don't remember much about the funeral except that Aunt Lucy's limp flowers were laid on the gravesite next to daisies from Dora and Marv Fenton and a big bouquet from the dam project. Papa stood tall and pale in the black jacket, stiff collar, and bowler he'd worn for his wedding. He stared at the plot of fresh dirt in the Cutter cemetery beneath which Mama lay. Bernie Sommers was there, some other railroad men, and the Grahams and other neighbors. We children stood in a clump. The wind blew steadily, plucking up the minister's words and tossing them into the desert.

I could have saved Mama. I could have asked Luisa to care for her after Sally's birth. She might have removed the afterbirth. I could have sent for the doctor during her first fever or written to Aunt JoJane in St. Louis. I should have never believed that woman, who wasn't a midwife at all, when she said that nothing could be done. I burned with shame. Did everyone know of my part in Mama's death? Were they blaming me but too polite to say it?

The day after the funeral, Earl and Charlie built a picket fence around Mama's grave and painted it white. Two days later, Aunt JoJane sent Papa back to work. He was worthless at home.

In the following days, I felt as though I were sleepwalking.

"You need to keep up your strength," Aunt JoJane told me. "Please eat."

I was a cow chewing flavorless cud. My ears still rang.

Aunt JoJane sat next to me at the table. "It's about the operation I mentioned, isn't it? I'm sure you gave your mother good care." She shook her head. "I should never have said anything."

But it was too late.

I worked in the kitchen, took care of Sally, watered Mama's plants so often Ida warned me I'd kill them, and listened as Aunt JoJane instructed me in matters of keeping house. She gave me one of her skirts and a shirtwaist.

"Now that you're fourteen, you may need them."

I couldn't imagine where I'd ever wear such grown-up clothes.

Aunt JoJane and Ida stayed for ten days. Ida would forfeit her year of study if she stayed longer. Irene could look in on us, and Papa agreed to hire a housekeeper. They filled the shelves with food and left. I was alone in the desert with my siblings.

18

Each morning when I woke up and remembered what had happened, I was stunned by the pain. I lay in bed at night, exhausted from the work of running the house and caring for my siblings, too numb to cry. I felt as though I'd descended into the deep well of my childhood, but there was no one to pull me out.

Sally was teething and cranky from diaper rash. She woke at least once each night crying, and the only thing that soothed her was a bottle of warm milk. Bethel got clingy and developed an insatiable thirst. She followed me around the house, asking for something to drink. "Wa-wa?" she said in the baby talk she'd outgrown. She asked sweet questions about Mama. "Why did she leave us?" "Why can't she come back?" I grew short with her and then regretted it. Stevie moped, abandoned his hammer, refused to learn his letters, and started wetting his bed. Washing his sheets added to my work. Charlie grew silent. He'd take his bow and arrow and the Hohner and go out all day, I don't know where.

After waking at night to feed Sally her bottle, I couldn't get back to sleep. I listened to the wind whip around the house—and then I heard the rocker. In the quiet of the night, it began to creak. At first it was hardly noticeable. Then it quickened to a rhythmic rock. It was Mama.

I stared at the wall next to my bed and remembered our last conversation. Her fevered mind had alighted on buttons, but mine had settled on guilt that acted like a stopper against the flow of good memories. *Creak-creak.* The rocking went on and then petered out, to return the next night. In the murky dawn I stared at the chair, innocent as stone.

Papa never hired a housekeeper, though he arranged for deliveries of food staples from town. He was sure I could manage. He came home every few weeks, but he was no good. His eyes had dulled. I could smell the drink on his skin. I longed for an outrageous tale, a joke, a song, but he'd no heart for it. He sat at the table with his head in his hands and hardly touched his food.

"How am I going to take care of this family?"

It seemed we'd made a shift from living to surviving. A new theme began to govern my life—the precarious journey of motherless children.

19

I n the middle of March, Duchess stopped eating and her belly swelled. One morning I found her lying down outside the lean-to. I coaxed her with oats but couldn't get her up. I sent Charlie to telegram Earl.

"Tell him it's urgent," I told him. "He'll know what to do."

Charlie took off on foot for Cutter and sent the message. Earl came that afternoon. He'd rushed, thinking that one of the children was ill. He looked over Duchess, then stood.

"She's old, Josie. She's in pain. I can tell by her breathing." He looked past me at a spot on the fence. "We can try to get her up, but if we can't, it doesn't look good." He brought his eyes back to mine. "I've seen this before in old nags. A sudden cold night can do 'em in."

Earl put on her halter and rope and had me tug while he tried to lift from behind. Then we both pushed. It was useless.

"I'll have to shoot her. It's the kindest thing to do."

I glanced at Earl's gun on his saddle. He was right. I looked around for Charlie. He'd disappeared.

I knelt down beside my mare. She looked beautiful with the sun glinting off her red-brown coat. She nickered and looked up at me with liquid eyes. I rubbed her nose and kissed her forehead.

I couldn't watch. I took Bethel's and Stevie's hands and hurried inside. I sat in Mama's rocker with Sally in my arms and rocked steadily until I heard the shot.

I stopped the rocker with my foot. One clean shot in the still afternoon.

When Earl came in, I offered him coffee, but he declined, saying that Irene was waiting for tonic for the baby's cough. He said he'd send Slim Walters to take the horse away.

"The knacker?"

Earl nodded.

"To make her into leather and dog food?"

"It's him or the coyotes."

My throat was tight. I couldn't talk anymore. I nodded my assent.

"You going to be all right?"

I nodded.

"Goodbye. I'm awful sorry."

Earl walked out the door.

I sat in the rocker. Tears slid down my cheeks. Stevie looked up at me and went out back, and I could hear the scratch of his hoop over the sand. Finally, I got up and stoked the fire in the stove.

I decided to make corn bread. As I measured out the flour, tears dripped off my chin and pocked the yellow mound. I remembered how we used to lope though the grasses, the wind pulling at Duchess's mane. Drops fell into the pale yellow froth of eggs and milk and disappeared.

I heard Slim Walters drive into the corral with his wagon. I mixed the batter with the wooden spoon and beat it as hard as I could. I heard the pounding of Slim's axe, and I was back to the day after Mama's death, as nails were hammered into the lid of her coffin. My vision blurred as I tried to measure out salt, sugar, and baking powder.

I heard the groan of the wagon as he loaded the pieces of

carcass, the snort of his horses as they adjusted to the weight, and Slim drove away with my horse.

I sat at the kitchen table and sobbed as the corn bread baked. Bethel came up behind me and smoothed my hair with her little hand.

"Wa-wa," she whispered.

It was dusk. I changed Sally and warmed up the beans and bacon from the previous night. My tears spattered onto the iron stovetop and sizzled into nothing. By the time I took the bread from the oven, I'd cried myself out.

Stevie and Charlie smelled supper and came into the house, dirty and hungry.

"Charlie, Duchess had to be put down."

"I know."

"She was too far gone."

He looked at me dully. "I know."

I put my hand on his shoulder. He shrugged me off. I poured milk, dished up the boys' plates, and gave them each a generous square of bread. They wolfed it down, using the crusts to scoop up their beans.

"This is the best corn bread you ever made," Stevie garbled through a mouthful.

"It's good," said Charlie, reaching for another piece and crumbling it into his milk.

I laughed out loud. They stared at me. I was a lousy cook. How dear of them to compliment my bread. Was it the long beating or the tears that had made the difference? Perhaps it was the extra salt that had been missing all along.

As I lay in bed that night, I watched a tarantula climb the opposite wall. It was looking for water. I was too tired to go after it. I could feel myself falling back into that trough of despair.

Memories of Duchess and our good times together flooded back. My thoughts went to Mexico, to the red mountains, the hot winds, the joy of racing Manuel's Appaloosa, and a sweet peace settled over me. For the first time in weeks, I slept well.

I awakened to something that didn't belong—a patter on the roof, a tapping in the yard, a smell in the air. I rose from bed, careful not to jostle Sally, who always woke up crying. I opened the kitchen door to a cool rain.

The rooster had already announced the day. The chickens were clucking and scratching in the coop. I crossed the rain-pocked yard, opened the door, and threw out grain. I laughed as the silly hens stretched their scrawny legs and raced for the kernels. I gathered warm eggs in my nightgown and stopped to inhale the scent of damp creosote. I felt awake for the first time since Mama's death. The dampened dust stuck to my bare feet like talcum after a bath. I left footprints on the porch and sprinkles on the kitchen floor and didn't care.

The shower ended as swiftly as it had begun, and the sun emerged from the edge of the cloud. A pastel arc appeared overhead, a rare morning rainbow. It made me think of Duchess somewhere up there. I took it to mean she was better off now, in a place where the grass grew sweet and green.

⁂

Earl stopped by the next week with a basket of ribs and pickled onions from Irene. I stood at the door with Sally in my arms. He glanced around the room. Bethel was napping. Stevie was playing in the corner with his train. The dishes were washed, the floor swept.

"Looks like you're holding up all right here. Irene's been

worrying. Nagging me to ride over and look in on you." He stuffed his hands in the pockets of his Levi's. "You know Irene's got work enough at the ranch just now. She's cooking for our crew."

He leaned against the doorframe and concentrated on lining up the heel of one boot with the toe of the other.

"She can hardly leave the place, with all she's got to do."

I wanted to say, "No, I'm not all right. You've caught me on a good day. I'm lonely, short on sleep, and too tired to do all I need to. And I cannot forgive myself for my part in Mama's death. I need Irene." But I didn't say anything. I was too proud to admit I wasn't up to my lot in life.

I offered Earl a cup of coffee.

"Got to get back to the ranch."

I accompanied him out to his palomino, so well trained it never needed tying.

"Irene sends her love." He tapped his horse's flanks and was gone.

Watching him go, I was suddenly angry at all the men in my life—Earl, Papa, Marv Fenton, and even Charlie—who, with little remorse, just went away.

20

The greater world was floundering too. A newspaper Papa brought home reported that a German sub had sunk a French steamer. Papa said it was a done deal—we'd soon be in the war. I read about a place called Verdun, where thousands of soldiers had been killed. The news frightened me. I worried that if we went to war, Papa would go away to fight, and then what would we do?

In mid-March, Pancho Villa and his men crossed the border into Columbus, New Mexico, just a hundred miles from Las Cruces. They killed seventeen people and burned much of the town. I was afraid his gang would storm north into our valley. I scanned the horizon while pumping water and panicked when I saw a cloud of dust. At night I was agitated by little noises like the clawing of mourning doves on the roof or the gabble of hens when a rat bothered them. I strained my ears above Bethel's and Sally's breathing to listen for the sound of Villa's horses. I got up to check the bolts on the doors and kept Papa's rifle within reach beneath my bed.

I was relieved when Papa told me General Pershing and the US Cavalry were chasing after Pancho Villa. They were even using airplanes to find him. When I read that he'd escaped deep into Mexico, I relaxed and ended my watch.

One day in early April, a woman stopped by. She introduced herself as Mrs. Holbrook and said she'd moved to Cutter a month ago.

"Is your mother at home?"

I swallowed hard. "She passed away two months ago."

She asked to speak to Papa. I said he wouldn't be back for another week.

"My heavens, child, are you alone?"

She knew I wasn't alone because I had Sally in my arms. I let her in. Charlie sat in front of the cold stove playing the harmonica, his gangly legs propped on a kitchen chair, his trousers torn at the knee, his feet filthy, his nails black with dirt. Stevie and Bethel were on the floor rolling marbles. Stevie looked up at us, his eyes huge in his thin face. His skinny arms stuck out like a scarecrow's in Charlie's old shirt. Bethel sat picking her nose. I glanced down at Sally. Her chin was smeared with the squash she'd eaten for breakfast.

Beneath the table, a tub of wet diapers reeked of ammonia. Pans encrusted with grits, gravy, and beans were stacked on the sideboard. The coffee had boiled over while I was feeding the chickens, and grounds were scattered over the stove. I was ashamed we weren't cleaned up for company.

Mrs. Holbrook's face was shaped like a heart. Her protruding eyes, too big for her face, took in everything.

"Tch, tch," she clucked. "It's a sin to Moses, leaving a house full of children alone. How about y'all come home with me for a while? I've a whole side of bacon that needs to be et."

Charlie jumped to his feet at the mention.

I considered for a moment. "I think it would be all right."

"Bring a change of clothing and diapers for the baby, in case you decide to spend the night. No matter that they're not clean. We can wash them."

While Mrs. Holbrook washed the dishes, I rinsed some of Sally's diapers and put them in a burlap sack.

"While you sweep up the house moss, I'll finish straightening up, and we'll be on our way," she said.

I found everyone's stockings, shoes, and hats, and wrote a note for Papa. We shut the chickens in and began to walk.

After keeping us for a night, Mrs. Holbrook refused to let us leave, though she sent Charlie back to feed and water the chickens and collect eggs. She fed us, cured Sally's diaper rash with castor oil and zinc, insisted we all took baths, and didn't ask questions about Mama. She said she had a bone to pick with Papa.

Mr. Holbrook joined us for supper. He was a collector for the Singer Manufacturing Company. He traveled between Santa Fe and El Paso to collect overdue installments or confiscate machines from those who couldn't pay. The barn next to his house held a dozen or more dust-covered Singers. Every few months he shipped them to Denver, where they were refurbished and sold from the company store.

Mr. Holbrook ate heartily. I wondered how he could have an appetite after taking away so many women's livelihoods. How could he smile and sigh so contentedly, knowing that his income came from breaking women's hearts?

I played hide-and-seek with the children among the idle machines in the barn. We played school, using the sewing tables as desks. I found one that looked like Mama's and used it as my teacher's desk. I remembered how she'd loved her Singer, and I mourned for the women who'd lost theirs.

—❧—

Papa arrived the next week. Mrs. Holbrook met him at the door and ushered him out to the yard. I held Sally and watched from a window while she talked, her pointy chin bobbing like the beak of a bird after seed, her eyes bulging more than ever. Papa listened, leaning an elbow on the side of the barn, nodding from time to time, his face obscured by the shadow of the roof. In the end, he said something, and they returned to the house.

Papa joined us for supper. He made pleasant conversation and listened politely as the Holbrooks told how they'd come west on one of the Santa Fe Zulu trains "looking for the elephant." Sight unseen, they'd bought a cheap town plot in Cutter because the dry air and bitter creosote tea were good for Mr. Holbrook's asthma. They talked about weather, trains, the Singer Company, and the war in Europe. It was the first time in weeks I'd seen Papa lively. After supper he went home to our empty house and, the following morning, back to his train.

Mrs. Holbrook took me aside. "I told your father that something must be done. I can't abide you children living alone in the desert, but my husband won't tolerate you staying here much longer."

Her chin jutted as she spoke. "Your father needs to make decisions. He can send you to a children's home until he's able to find someone to care for you—there's an orphanage run by the sisters in Albuquerque—or you can go to relatives. Your father assured me there are enough of them to take you in."

My stomach turned. As hard as things were, they could get worse. My little brothers and sisters might be split up and sent far away, to Texas, Missouri, or Louisiana, and I might never see them again.

She put her hand on my forearm. "Don't you worry. Your father's fixed on the notion that you stay together. He's agreed to look for work that will allow him to be home at night. I told him you can stay here until he finds that work."

She looked satisfied. I was relieved that change was coming. I found Sally asleep in the bedroom, picked her up, and touched her warm, silky head.

"I'll take care of you, baby," I whispered into her delicate ear.

--

A week and a half later, Papa sent word that he'd quit his job and was looking for new work. After three days he returned. The Phelps Dodge company was hiring engineers for the mine trains near Bisbee, in the Mule Mountains of southern Arizona. We would be leaving directly for Tucson, where they did the hiring. Papa seemed pleased for the first time since Mama's death. I smiled. It felt strange to lift the corners of my mouth.

Charlie and I went home to pack our things. Dust coated the furniture and floors. I stepped from room to room in the only house that had been our own. I packed our clothing and the sewing basket, and gathered Mama's Cerrillos turquoise, silver comb, and hairpins—keepsakes for Papa. Everything else would go to Irene.

I opened Mama's Bible and wrote below the date of her birth: *Died Feb. 8, 1916, at Cutter, N. Mex. Buried at Cutter, N. Mex.* I wrapped the Bible and her jewelry in a petticoat and tucked it into the trunk.

Charlie appeared in the doorway.

"I can take the trunk out."

I gently closed the lid.

He blinked hard and looked out the window. "We're leaving Mama."

"She would want us to go."

We waited outside in the shade of the lean-to. I cradled the jade plant in my arms. The wind blew through the grasses like a relentless gossip whispering that we were going away. The chickens pecked each other, somehow knowing things had changed. I contemplated our family, as out of kilter as our flock of hens.

Papa let us stop at the cemetery. We walked out to the white picket fence where Mama lay. Aunt Lucy's funeral bouquet had dried to a brown skeleton in faded paper. I tore at the remains, tossing them onto the sand.

I looked up to see that the willow next to her grave was in bloom, a mass of white-and-purple blossoms. It took me by surprise. It was already spring.

We spent our last night at Earl and Irene's, where I gave her the jade plant. After supper Earl and Papa sat on the porch. I lay awake next to Irene and listened to their talk through the open window.

"Congress finally passed the Stock-Raising Homestead Act," Earl said. "The minimum claim of grazing land is a full section now. About time they figured out grazing's nothing like farming."

Papa grunted. "Too late for us."

"Too late for most. I've got a good spread, but I'm still hanging on by my teeth."

Earl said he'd file the final papers on our half section in six months, when our five-year occupancy would be completed.

They would try to find renters. Past midnight, I heard them stumble into the house, knock into a chair, strike a boot against a table leg, and end the evening in loud snores on bedrolls on the sitting room floor.

I could hardly stand to leave Irene.

"The clerk at the post office says Bisbee's a lively town. You can go to school." She lifted my chin and kissed me on the cheek. "Take good care of our babies. Things will be better soon."

She promised to look after Mama's grave.

I pulled her close. She reminded me so much of Mama. I kissed Mona and baby Joe, and Earl drove us to the train.

21

I awoke from a pressure on my bladder. My neck was stiff and my spine ached from how I'd slept, pushed to the edge of the plush seat against the vibrating wall of the train. Sally, curled into fetal position, snored on the other half of my seat, her chubby foot pressed to my stomach. Bethel lay under a thin train blanket next to us, open-mouthed, dreaming, her eyelashes fluttering like blinded moths.

Passengers slept, wheezing and sighing as they shifted in their narrow seats. The car was dank with odors of perspiration and sour breath. I pulled back an edge of the thick curtain. A sliver of pinky-orange sun peeked over the edge of the desert, throwing yellow rays over the shadowed sand. I slipped out of my seat, went to the toilet, and stood at the window to watch the day arrive.

We were in Arizona now, in the Sonoran desert. The sand took on hues of amber, changing to golden brown. This desert was different from the Jornada. The cacti grew larger and sturdier and took unfamiliar forms.

I turned to see a small woman standing near me.

"Isn't it divine?" she said. "The desert's in bloom for such a short while."

She was lovely too. She had yellow hair that curled around her face, and she looked as fresh as the new morning. I was groggy from my poor sleep. My hair was uncombed, my mouth gummy.

"Do you know the Sonoran?"

I shook my head.

"I believe it rained last night, so the desert's having one of its glory days." She pointed out the window. "That big cactus is the saguaro. It grows slowly, so you know that the tall-branched ones are old. It's in bloom now, but you'll only see the bud. The white flower opens after dark and blooms for only one night."

The saguaros stood like sturdy giants above the other cacti. Their thick, tubular arms reminded me of the coat tree at the Cutter hotel.

"The fat, cylindrical one is the barrel cactus. It grows curved, pointing toward the north. It can help you find your way if you're lost in the desert. Its orange bloom is my favorite to paint."

I glanced over at her. I'd never met an artist.

She sidled up next to me. I caught a hint of rose water and thought of Mama.

"And that's paloverde."

Her pale artist's hand pointed toward a lacy green-and-gold bush.

"It looks feathery, but underneath its leaves are sharp thorns. Some call it Jerusalem thorn. It would make a wicked crown, wouldn't it? It has little pealike flowers, like a yellow veil."

We passed clusters of flowered pincushion, jumping cholla in lavender bloom, and other vegetation I knew from the Jornada.

"Oh, there's the Indian paintbrush," she said. "It's brash, isn't it?"

She pointed out plants near the tracks: yellow brittlebush, blue and purple horse nettle, and orange Mexican poppy. I tried to see them as a painter might.

The sun had mounted the sky and shone a pure yellow. Passengers awoke, and a line formed at the lavatory next to where we stood. People pushed past on their way to the dining car.

"It's been nice talking with you," the woman said. "I have to get back to my Pullman. We'll be going to breakfast now. Safe travels, miss."

She passed through the vestibule to the next car. A waft of rose hovered for a moment in the space she'd vacated.

In the window, I saw Mama's reflection. Serene, she gazed into my eyes. I heard Sally's high wail from the day car, her usual siren that she was awake. Mama's face distorted into my own. I went to comfort her child.

In our car, Papa snored, immune to his daughter's cry. Charlie had picked Sally up and was pacing the aisle, trying to comfort her. Glazed-eyed fellow passengers stared at the two of them, too groggy to complain.

I took Sally and gave her a sip of flat ginger ale. She licked her lips and stopped crying. The boys started playing with a dirty piece of string they'd found in the aisle. Charlie tied knots and let Stevie unfasten them. I buttered bread and passed it around. Bethel woke up and asked for water. Stevie had discovered a shiny metal watercooler at the back of the car. He traipsed back and forth to fill the collapsible cups, spilling half their contents onto the floor, bringing Bethel all the water she could drink.

We got off the train in Tucson. Papa left us at the station and went to the Phelps Dodge office to apply for a job. I herded the children to the lunch bar and waited for a spot. When the warning gong sounded and travelers rushed to their trains, we ate chipped beef sandwiches and drank root beers in the empty hall.

I took Sally and Bethel out behind the depot to the toilet, pumped water, and washed their sticky faces and hands. Near the door, two little girls sat on a blanket selling roasted corn kernels. Their hair hung ragged, their clothing soiled. The buttons had fallen off their dresses, which were fastened with pins. Behind them, a man sprawled on the ground. As I passed, I got a whiff of alcohol. I pulled a penny from my pocket and bought a cone of corn.

As I turned into the building, I took a last look at the buttonless girls with their patient eyes and sad mouths, and it hit me like a rock that their mother was gone. They were, in that instant, like sisters. We were on the same hazardous journey of motherless girls. I wanted to hug them.

Papa strode into the depot with a grin on his face.

"I got the job. Now hurry up, y'all. The train leaves in fifteen minutes."

I looked up at my papa, betrayal far from either of our minds. He couldn't know that he was soon to sell me down the river. I couldn't guess that I'd jump ship and, in doing so, break the most important promise I'd made.

VI

BISBEE

(1916–1917)

While the children napped, Papa tried to prepare me for Bisbee. He said I'd never seen the like.

"It's the biggest mining town in the country. The busiest place between El Paso and San Francisco. Near eighteen thousand people living in the district. And with the war in Europe, it's gonna keep on growing. Everyone needs copper nowadays."

As our train pulled in, I saw for myself. Unlike Cutter, set in the center of a wide valley, Bisbee was built into two narrow canyons and onto the surrounding mountainsides. A maze of roads, most no wider than alleyways, wound up steep slopes, and stairs and twisting paths climbed stone-terraced levels hacked into the mountainsides. The tin-roofed wooden buildings, some ramshackle, others grand with gingerbread trim and wraparound porches, reminded me of Stevie's wobbly Tink towns—haphazardly stacked in defiance of gravity. The trees on the surrounding hills had been cut for fuel, except for thickets of scrub oak, juniper, and manzanita that grew from the steepest cliffs. Lean cypresses and leafy cancer trees had been planted along the main roads. It looked lush to me.

We were gathering our bags when a long whistle sounded.

"That would be the train bringing home the miners," Papa said. "Everything here goes by the whistle."

To the right of the depot stood the brick headquarters of the Copper Queen Mining Company owned by Phelps Dodge. Papa told us to sit on the bench outside the building while he checked in.

"We're hungry, Papa."

He handed me a fifty-cent piece and looked around. The street took a turn past the company headquarters. "Head up that way and get something to eat. Be back in a half hour."

We walked up Main Street. A recent rainstorm had carried soil off the hillsides and turned the cobblestone street into a muddy mess. As we picked our way over the slick, uneven sidewalk, I admired the well-dressed gentlemen and the fine ladies who passed, holding their skirts above the mire. Delivery men slipped and grunted behind overloaded carts. Two Chinese men in waist-long braids hurriedly packed up their vegetable stands. A pack of boys raced by, shouting words I couldn't understand. A shop owner locked his door, pocketed his keys, and strolled away. Stevie gawked at the buildings. Bethel cowered from the noise.

The three-story Copper Queen Hotel overlooked Main from the street above. I marveled at the red tile roof, white brick exterior, red trim, and pretty green balcony that flanked the top floor. Up the long, bent street, buildings of stone and patterned bricks stood tall on either side. The sign for the Copper Queen Hospital brought a vision of Mama's fevered face and bloated belly. What would I have given for such a place months ago?

We strolled beneath the arches of the post office building. When we got to Wallace's Pool Hall, we crossed to the tamer side of the street and stopped to look at Woolworth's display of baby dolls and toy cars.

Bethel pulled on my arm. "I want to eat."

We crossed the street again. I was shocked at the prices at the Angus Market but had enough for bread, butter, peach jam, and soda water. We picked our way back to the mining office, sat on the bench, and dipped chunks of bread into the jar.

Then, as if hit by lightning, the street lit up. Sally squealed. Electric lamps shone like round yellow moons above the streets. The passersby picked up their paces. More businesses shut. The noisy rumble of a green-and-yellow streetcar startled me as it descended the hill and passed.

We watched the mine train chug into the depot and a load of miners step off. The men trudged by, weary-eyed and silent but for the rattle of empty dinner pails against their thighs. The street quieted. Papa came out of the office holding a map and a lantern.

"Never seen such a lot of paperwork in my life."

"How's come so much in this town's named the same thing . . . Copper Queen Library, Copper Queen Hotel, Copper Queen everything?" said Charlie.

"Because it's a company town. There's a family boarding-house not far, but I need to see to our luggage."

We trailed him back to the station, where he hired a boy with a mule and cart to deliver our trunks and bags. We walked, dragging up the winding streets and steep steps. Papa had to keep looking at his map. Twice he made us backtrack and take a different set of stairs to the next level. It was a strange and beautiful walk. Looking up at the lights of the terraced houses over the canyon was like gazing at stars fallen to Earth to twinkle softly amid the black hills.

Finally, we reached the boardinghouse, a long frame building clinging to the side of Clawson Hill. At the far end, a cabin served as a dining room, with a kitchen add-on in back. The proprietor, a tired-looking woman with her own three children clinging to her skirts, gave us a choice of how many meals we wanted a day.

"Your place has a stove. Looks like your girl can cook. You can cook, can't you?"

I nodded. I got the idea she didn't want to cook for us.

"Maybe you don't be needing board."

Papa declined meals, and she showed us our quarters—one large room with a strip of threadbare carpet, a lumpy sofa, and a cook stove. A tiny bedroom in the rear contained a sagging double bed and cracked mirror. Papa assigned it to me and the little girls. The boys would sleep on the sofa. The proprietor had her boy bring over a cot for Papa, which was set next to the stove. I was too tired to think about our dismal lodging and dropped off to sleep, hoping it would improve with daylight.

2

Stepping out the next morning to shop for milk and bread, I was thrilled with the bustle of the town. The bakery carried Italian, French, Irish, and American bread, more choices than I'd ever seen. At the company mercantile, which extended credit to employees, I got the staples we'd need until Papa received his first pay. Food was costly, and it felt wrong to start out in debt, but Papa said that was how it was done.

Papa went straight to work running the company freight train that ran from the hoists at the Sacramento Workings to the smelters in Douglas. I packed meals for him in the round metal box he took to work. He told me dinner was called "lunch" because they always ate it cold. He came back tired in the evening, covered with coal dust, sweat, and grime—and I was glad to have him home.

We stayed out of school, since the term would be ending in a matter of weeks. Papa gave us strict instructions to stay away from Brewery Gulch, the rough part of town, but the rest of Bisbee was ours to explore. There were all types of stores, theaters, an opera house, private clubs, and churches. The town was teeming with horses and carts, motorcars, and people from all over. Miners came from Cornwall, Wales, Finland, Germany, and from foreign countries I'd never heard of. Strange aromas and undecipherable talk wafted from doorways at suppertime.

—✢—

After Papa received his first paycheck, I went to the merc to buy a stock of staples and shoes for Charlie, but with all the purchases, we didn't clear our debt.

"There's more than one way to skin a cat," Papa said. "You're nearly fifteen, Josie. Old enough to work this summer. It's the only way we'll get ahead."

3

I was glad to leave the dreary boardinghouse and let Charlie look after the little ones. I tried to think of what job I could do. I considered knocking at the doors of the bankers and lawyers up on Quality Hill to see whether they needed a nanny or kitchen help, but my chest tightened at the prospect. I didn't even have the nerve to climb the stairs up to Jiggerville, where the camp foremen lived.

I liked books, so I went into the library above the post office. The room smelled of furniture wax, old paper, and dust. A thin, beetle-browed man at the front desk glanced up at me, adjusted his spectacles, and returned to his book. Intimidated by the rows of silent men reading papers and foreign-language books at oak tables, I didn't dare ask for work.

I wandered up Main, inquired at several shops, but had no luck. Up a side street at a boardinghouse, I asked a woman cleaning the lobby whether they needed help with the laundry.

"Our washing goes to the Irish. And we don't need kitchen help." She lifted her feather duster. "You might ask at a hotel. Sometimes they need maids."

"Which hotel?"

"Oh, any of them. Why not start with the best? That'd be the Copper Queen."

I thanked her, hurried to the brick hotel on Howell Street, and mounted the stairs. Standing in the hiring office, I waited while the manager studied his accounting book and grumbled about a problem in the kitchen.

"Rotten fish. Wouldn't you think they'd know enough to smell it?" He looked up. "What do you want?"

I told him I was looking for work.

"Know anything about cigars?"

I told him that Papa rolled his own but smoked a Prince Albert to celebrate.

He laughed in a nervous way.

"It would help business to have a pretty face behind the counter."

I turned to go.

"Whoa there. Can you make change? If I buy three five-cent cigars and give you a dollar, how much change will you give me?"

I panicked but then did the arithmetic.

"Eighty-five cents."

"Good. Can you clean rooms?"

"I was a maid for a while at a hotel in New Mexico."

"Tell the lady at the cigar counter in the lobby that you're her replacement. Have her teach you what you need to know."

I had the job?

"Oh, go on. I'm busy."

I spotted the tobacco case at the end of the lobby desk and introduced myself to the woman there.

"You're just a girl. Did he ask how old you are?"

"No."

She shook her head. "What will they think of next? School-boys selling bourbon? I don't even want to know your age. Come here behind the counter. You don't have much time to learn this. I leave for Kansas City in two days." She opened the glass case and pointed at the boxes.

"Our most expensive cigars are Cuban. The Montecristo, the Bolivar, and the Ramon Allones are some of the finer ones."

She opened up a white box with a Spanish lady on the cover. Some of the less-expensive cigars were made in Puerto Rico and milder ones made in Manila. She said the age and blend of tobaccos made the flavor and aroma—smooth or robust, fruity or nutty. A lot of cigars were machine-made, but the *preferidos* were hand-rolled.

My head spun. How would I remember it all?

She pointed to a large wooden box behind the counter. "We keep the better cigars in the humidor—isn't this electric model nice? Everything dries out here otherwise, except during the summer rains. Then you're lucky if you don't drown." She chuckled. "Where you from, sweetie?"

I told her I was from New Mexico.

"Then you know how things dry out." She showed me the white powder on a cigar, plume from the sweating of oils in the tobacco. "Dust the white off, but if you see a bluish color, it's mold. Throw it out, then adjust the humidor."

I must have looked dazed.

She stopped talking, put her hands on her hips, and stepped back.

"I've been selling cigars for five years, and what I didn't know before, my customers taught me. You'll get the hang of it. Come back tomorrow, and I'll teach you the rest."

4

Papa didn't like the idea of me selling cigars.

"A girl like you shouldn't be working in a place like that."

I told him to go look at the fancy hotel. He went that night, and one of the bellboys gave him a tour. Papa decided I could take the job, since I'd be working in such a fine lobby.

The next afternoon, the woman had more facts to fill my head.

She said the best American cigars were made in Florida from Cuban tobacco or from tobacco grown in Virginia and the Carolinas.

"Don't worry about knowing the prices. I'll write them down. Customers know what they want, and if they don't know, they won't admit it." She snickered. "If a fellow asks for a stogie, you offer him one of the cheaper ones."

She picked up a Garcia Vega. "This's a premium cigar. You see how it's rolled so pretty? And sealed tight with squared corners at both ends? For a man to inhale, the end needs to be sliced off."

She showed me a bulky wooden object that resembled two slices of bread—a guillotine cutter. She stuck a cigar in the little hole and let the steel blade fall.

"Cut off only a dime's width."

I felt dizzy, unsure whether it was from the sharp smell of cured tobacco, the stale air of the warm lobby, or too much information.

"We're almost done, Missy. These little white ones are milder, factory-made cigarettes—Players, Camels, and the new brand, Lucky Strike."

She said I was to start the next day. Mornings, I'd clean rooms, and in the afternoons, sell cigars.

"I'm going to miss this job, though I suppose they smoke cigars in Missouri too. Good luck, girl."

—✦—

The Copper Queen was more than a fine place—it was elegant. The walls of the lobby were of warm California redwood, the floors covered with lush wool carpets. There were forty-four guest rooms on the upper two floors, which kept us morning maids busy.

The lower level housed the lobby, a ladies' parlor, a dining room buffet, and a barbershop. The bellboy said there'd been a saloon off the lobby, but when Arizona went dry in '14, it'd been converted to a men's smoking and billiard room.

At the cigar counter in the afternoons, it didn't take me long to remember the names and prices. I learned to know the cigars by how they were rolled and how they smelled. One from Mexico smelled like vanilla. A Romeo y Julieta had the smell of cocoa.

I got to know who the Phelps Dodge executives were, the local bankers and lawyers, and the cigars they liked. Although I'd complained as a little girl, I was grateful that Mama had corrected my speech. I grew comfortable talking to people staying at the hotel—investors, politicians, and mining officials. The high-class men wore suits and top hats, which I'd never seen in Cutter. Once, General Pershing spent the night. He didn't buy any cigars, but some of his party did.

When a stranger strode up to the counter, I tried to guess what he'd ask for. A cheap cigar or a pricey blend? Strong and woody, or a sweeter, smoother smoke? Sometimes I guessed right. How could I tell? By the man's stride, the lines on his face, or the clothes he wore. Like any bartender, I learned about human character by selling a product my customers craved.

When a traveling quartet played in the lobby, the guests gathered to listen before they dined at the hotel or strolled over to the Edelweiss, an expensive restaurant across from the theater. The men sucked on their cigars and exhaled gray plumes that mixed with the women's perfumes and filled the lobby with a sweet, smoky cloud.

At the Copper Queen, I was a different person in a new life.

In the early afternoons when business was slow, I daydreamed. On the inside cover of one box of cigars, a magical city of white turreted buildings rose on the shores of a blue lake that glistened like a jewel. I picked out the house where I'd like to live and pictured myself walking those sparkling streets. The cover paper of La Gloria Cubana showed a woman in loose robes sitting on a cloud with baby angels around her. I imagined Mama in heaven with my angel brother, Gabriel.

Sometimes I chatted with the hotel receptionist, who liked to talk about the war in Europe. I got to know the Black man who shined shoes in the lobby. I learned that in Bisbee, each group had its assigned "place." The Chinese could sell vegetables from their carts but weren't allowed to own a business, do laundry, or stay in town after dark. The Black men could stay in town but work only as shoeshines, porters, or barbers. The Mexicans could do any job on the surface or in the smelters, but not the good-paying underground jobs at the mines. The housing was segregated too. The Mexicans lived on Chihuahua Hill, the Irish on Laundry Hill, the Serbs raised goats in "Goat Grove," and the rest of the laborers and their families jostled for space in Old Bisbee or in the newer mining districts of Warren and Lowell.

I remembered that in New Mexico it didn't seem important what your skin tone was, as long as you could hammer an iron spike or lasso a calf. Blacks, Mexicans, Indians, and Anglos sat together in the train cars, but when they got within a few miles of the Texas border, folks had to get up and change seats because of the Jim Crow laws. In Bisbee, it appeared to be the same.

I started putting my hair up for work, trying to recall how Mama and Irene had effortlessly twisted theirs into Psyche knots. I was grateful to have Aunt JoJane's shirtwaist, but I needed a corset. I remembered that Mama had taken Irene and Ida to El Paso to be fitted for theirs. I was sorry to have missed that ritual. I bought a corset and cover at Woolworth's but longed for one embroidered by Mama's loving hand.

I didn't get to know the other maids well. They took their noon meal later than I and roomed at the hotel. They invited me to vaudeville shows, plays at the Orpheum, or the "flickering flicks," but I hurried home after work to make supper. Papa wouldn't let me go out at night. My family needed me.

5

While Papa and I worked, Charlie took care of Bethel and Sally. Stevie spent his days playing stickball and tag with a gaggle of boys in the schoolyard.

That summer, between cloudbursts that brought torrents of water down the winding streets, Charlie and Stevie worked on their pushmobile. Twice a year, the boys in town had competitions down the steep length of Main Street. Charlie and Stevie made theirs from planks and the wheels of a broken baby carriage. The Saturday of the race, Charlie steered and Stevie worked the brake, but halfway down the hill a wheel came off, and they skidded over the sidewalk into the side of a building. They arrived home with bruises and scrapes, already planning for the next race.

We didn't see a lot of Papa. When we woke up, he'd already left to tend his engine. After the copper ore was loaded onto the freight cars, Papa ran the ore to Douglas, twenty-two miles away, where it was processed at the company smelter. For the return trip, he hauled cars of coal for the power plant, timber from Washington state, or steel beams used for buttressing mine shafts. All supplies were brought in by train.

At first, Papa found the work challenging, but then he got restless. He didn't like cities, and Bisbee had a city's population packed into the acreage of a village "where all creation knows your business." Phelps Dodge owned the newspaper, built the parks, the schools, the YMCA, the hospital and dispensaries, supplied the stores, filled the hotels, and determined the wages and prices. Miners went to work, ate their lunches, and went home at the same time every day, regulated by the mine whistle. It made me feel safe, but Papa missed his freedom, missed Mama, and continued to drink.

Saturday nights he drank at the speakeasies that had replaced the saloons after Arizona went dry. When he returned, the scent of alcohol clung to his skin like bitter cologne. On Sundays, he slept in and then lay on the sofa and read the paper over a mug of strong coffee. In the afternoon, he pulled out the flask of whiskey he kept beneath his cot and had a few drinks before supper. He complained about conditions in the mines.

"There are accidents all the time," he told me as he lay on the sofa, the newspaper on his chest, his drawl stalled even more by drink. "The deeper they go, the riskier it gets. Makes my job look easy. The tales I've heard, Josie Belle, you wouldn't believe . . . cave-ins, fires, careless use of dynamite, gas asphyxiation, electrocution, underground floods, falls off rusty ladders into the shaft. The men have lung disease from breathing in the dust. They started the Safety First program last year, but it's not enough." He tossed the newspaper on the floor and sat up. "The men need to organize, like the railroad men did. I paid my dues and the Brotherhood took care of me."

It was all Papa got excited about. I looked at the miners differently after that. I noticed the sag of their shoulders, how slowly they lumbered up the steep walkways and stairs to their shacks, and the sallow tone of their skin from spending six days a week underground. It was their sweat and toil that brought the copper from the earth, but they'd neither the money nor the status to buy a cigar at the Copper Queen.

6

Our first months in Bisbee flew by like a speeding train. September arrived, and it was time to quit my job and go to school. Papa had a decent salary, but prices were high. And there were other expenses. Papa had to pay into the company hospital fund, and coal was still overpriced. The children had grown out of their clothes and needed shoes. A week before school was to begin, I approached Papa.

"I don't think I should go to school," I told him. "I want to work to help pay expenses. We can hire a neighbor to take care of Bethel and Sally while the boys are in school. I'll still make breakfast and supper and clean on weekends. I'll borrow books at the library and learn that way. Please, Papa."

He looked up from his newspaper. "That'd be fine, Josie Belle. You don't have to go to school."

I'd been prepared to argue. I was surprised and let down at how easily he gave up my education.

—

Charlie and Stevie attended Central School, a three-story brick building with a high middle tower. Charlie got an after-school job as a delivery boy for the Brown Brothers' Mercantile. He made friends and started talking to me like he used to. We played harmonica in the evenings and grew close again.

Stevie hated school but after classes came into his own. Quick on his feet, strong, and agile, he wrapped his fists in rags, pretending to be his hero, Jack Johnson, and boxed with other boys in the alley. He became the best stickball batter in his crowd, earning the nickname "Homer" Gore.

Papa found a widower to take care of Bethel and Sally until I returned from work. Men too old to bring in income were asked to run errands and take care of babies. Asa Borne watched the girls in exchange for spending money. He had a white beard, rotten teeth, and a stomach condition that gave him gas. He was dour but attentive. I felt bad leaving Bethel and Sally with smelly Asa but reminded myself that we needed my income.

On Saturdays, Asa stayed home, and I spent the morning boiling our wash, hanging it to dry, shopping, and preparing supper. Charlie watched the girls while I worked the late shift and came to the hotel to walk me home. On Sunday, my day off, I cleaned the house and bathed my little sisters, trying to make up for a week of neglect.

Bethel still asked questions about Mama. It seemed she couldn't get through her head what had happened. Was Mama an angel now? If we wished on a star, would she fly back to us? I tried to explain that only Jesus could come back from the dead, but it did no good. A four-year-old believes in miracles, and you can't talk her out of them.

One evening, as I stepped in the door, Asa rushed out, bumping my shoulder and knocking me against the frame of the door. The room smelled of flatulence.

"He was in the outhouse all day," Bethel said.

She shadowed me around the house. I changed Sally's diaper and rubbed calendula cream on her raging rash. The stove was cold. Papa would be home soon and if supper wasn't ready, he'd take out a bottle. I hurried to light the coals. Bethel followed so closely that I bumped into her turning around.

"Does Mama have wings?"

I tossed pinto beans into a pot of water and threw onions into a pan to fry. Grease splashed onto my shirtwaist. Then I burnt my finger.

"Why can't she fly back to us?"

"Bethel! I don't want to hear another word about Mama. She's never coming back. Do you understand? Not ever."

She turned away. I lit into the potatoes, chopping furiously, and dropped them into the pan. I found a tin of string beans, opened it, and tossed them in another pot. I glanced over my shoulder. Bethel was curled in a tight ball on the sofa, fiddling with threads of the frayed cover.

While the beans were simmering, I got a brush and gently began to untangle her hair. "It's true that Mama can't come back, but she's always watching over you. And I will be, too."

Bethel said nothing as she twisted the threads in her fingers. She finally rested her head against the arm of the sofa, and by the time Papa and the boys ambled in, she was asleep.

Bethel never spoke of Mama again. I sometimes found her alone, perched on our bed, looking out the only window that opened to the sky. She was looking for a star. I left her to her magic.

Sally was robust but had a quick temper. Only Charlie's antics could take the sour look off her pretty face. Papa called her ornery, but I believe she was simply unhappy. She had that temperament that turns disappointment in life into anger at the world. She needed a mother's lavish love, and I didn't have enough in me to meet her needs.

7

There were a lot of churches in Bisbee. I imagined Mama would be pleased if we attended one. I took Bethel and Stevie with me to try them out, while Charlie stayed home with Sally. I didn't venture into the Lutheran church because the services were in Finnish, or to St. Patrick's Catholic church, where they spoke Latin. But I tried others. Elegant Grace Presbyterian stood next to the Copper Queen Hotel. The usher told me that the mahogany interior was modeled after a European church. I felt too humble to worship there. The Reformed Christian church on Clawson Avenue was simpler. I went there twice and then tried First Methodist, which had the best music. I attended St. John's Episcopal one Sunday and then visited the Baptists, who met in a hall while they were waiting for their new church to be built on Main Street. I hoped I might feel at home there because Mama had been a Baptist. A young woman stepped to the front and loudly repented her sins, but I didn't have the courage to bare my soul before a crowd.

I liked the music at the churches but not the social hours that followed. Before I could find the door, churchwomen inquired where my mother and father were. I didn't want to tell the well-intentioned strangers that Mama had died and Papa drank on Sundays. I didn't want to be the subject of their head-to-toe inspections, or their pity, or their coffee-hour gossip. I no longer belonged in those tight circles of ambitious mothers and daughters with shiny ringlets, silk bows, and pressed white pinafores. Upon leaving those churches, I felt low for the rest of the day. After a while, I quit going. Instead, on Sunday nights, I read Bible stories to Stevie and the girls.

⁓

If Papa was ready to abandon my education, I was not. I returned to the library to figure out how to borrow a book. The librarian looked me over, typed out a card, and selected a volume for me. Though I can't recall the title, I admired the fine language in that book and tried to imitate it in my speech. I was determined to improve myself, as Mama would have wanted. In the ensuing months, I found novels that suited me better: *The Secret Garden*, *Anne of Green Gables*, *Rebecca of Sunnybrook Farm*, *The Wizard of Oz*, and *Jane Eyre*—all stories of motherless girls who'd journeyed to find happier lives. I gave up the idea of being a teacher and looked to those heroines for hope.

Later, I discovered the YWCA. On Sunday afternoons, it organized poetry readings, craft projects, cooking demonstrations, lessons on modern etiquette, debates on temperance or the war in Europe, or lectures on the wonders of electricity. Once a woman came from Providence, Rhode Island, and spoke about a woman's right to vote. I pursued my education with this group of inquiring women, though I often sat apart, free from the pressure to speak of things at home.

⁓

Ida wrote that she'd finished her secretarial studies and had gotten a job typing invoices but didn't like it. She wanted to move into her own place, but Aunt JoJane said she was too young to live on her own.

Irene wrote after the New Year:

The dam's finished, and last October 16th, we went to the dedication. It was quite a crowd, but there was a big mix-up and the important people didn't make it. Finally, the workers made the speeches. The water backs up for twenty miles to make a lake, and people can go boating.

There's no more work, and half the folks in Engle have moved on. We haven't been able to rent out the homestead in Cutter. I get lonesome, as Earl's often away. My Mona's three and a half, and little Joe just turned one. Bisbee must be an exciting place. Give the children bushels of my love. And Papa too.

In late January, the receptionist at the hotel explained that Germany had broken its pledge with the United States and threatened submarine attacks against ships to Britain. Then the US broke diplomatic relations. In Bisbee, the Cornish and Italian miners sided against the Austrians and Germans. The one thing everyone agreed on was that we would soon be entering the war. The talk frightened me, but Papa assured me that he was too old and had too many children to be a soldier.

"We've got our own battles here," he told me one night after he'd had a few drinks. "Copper prices have gone sky-high since the war started—they need it for gunmetal and for electric wiring. The company's raking in profits, but conditions haven't improved. The men are working around the clock. They're so overworked, they're making mistakes."

He rubbed his forehead, now scored with lines that had become permanent. "The cost of living has gotten so high that pay increases make no difference. The new immigrants are paid even less, and the Mexicans? They still won't let them work below for a decent wage. The Wobblies have signed on most of the Mexicans and scores of immigrants. The unions are agitating for a strike." He paused and looked me in the eye. "I'm a sympathizer. Do you know what that means? It means if they call a strike, I'll support them. We may see a battle in Bisbee before we see one in Europe."

8

I met him in March. A fresh breeze had blown down the canyon, purging the stench of the sewers. The cancer trees had just come into leaf, and wildflowers were blooming in the hills. As I was dusting the display case, I looked up and saw him standing in the lobby. He wore a pullover sweater and a derby cap and was studying a painting on the wall. Then he looked at me and approached the counter.

"Can you recommend a cigar?"

"It depends on what you're looking for."

He looked unsure. "The truth is I've never smoked."

I suggested a smooth blend.

"How do you know about cigars? You don't smoke, do you?"

"I just sell them. Some fellows prefer the new cigarettes."

He glanced at the advertisement for Lucky Strikes affixed to the side of the stand—"It's toasted!"

"I think I'll stick with a cigar."

I held out a White Owl. "This one's not too expensive."

"I'll take whatever you recommend."

He looked right at me and smiled. I smiled back. My cheeks grew warm.

He watched me closely as I wrapped his cigar. His fingers brushed against my palm as he handed me his dime. I gave him his change.

"Would you like me to cut the tip?"

"If you'd like to."

I slipped the cigar into the guillotine, sliced off a sliver, and handed it back to him. He stepped away and lit it, sucking in to fan the flame. The cigar smoked, and he started coughing. I looked down so he wouldn't see my smile. Then he gingerly put it to his lips and puffed again, this time barely inhaling. He strolled back up to my counter.

"You witnessed it. My first cigar. It's going to take getting used to."

He stayed around, and we talked. His name was George. He was nineteen. He had black hair, golden-brown skin, and cow eyes—big and dark with thick lashes. He lived back East, in Maryland. His father had invested in the mine and in oil exploration in Texas and had sent George to assess their prospects.

The next day, he returned to the counter.

"I'm sick," he groaned. "I smoked that whole cigar."

"Did you smoke it to the end?"

He nodded.

"Try stopping sooner. The end burns hot. At least, it's what I've been told."

"I'll remember that."

He visited every day. One day he sauntered into the lobby, stood in front of my counter, and recited,

Tobacco is a dirty weed. I like it.
It satisfies no normal need. I like it.
It makes you thin, it makes you lean,
It takes the hair right off your bean.
It's the worst darn stuff I've ever seen. I like it.

I laughed. "Did you make that up?"

"No, it's by a fellow named Hemminger. A college student. I thought you'd like it."

I liked everything about George.

Another day he pranced in waving a pamphlet in his hand.

"Have you seen this? It's called *The Case Against the Little White Slaver*, by Henry Ford. It says smoking's harmful to your physical and moral health. Even Edison agrees." He frowned. "I think I'll quit. I don't like the way my mouth tastes afterward and how my clothes smell. But I'll still come by to talk to you."

We discussed the price of copper. It was up to thirty-seven cents a pound, almost three times what it had been several years before. George predicted that America's entry into the war would be good for Bisbee and Phelps Dodge. Copper prices were bound to go higher. He told me about the Mary Pickford moving picture he'd seen in Baltimore. He wondered what her voice sounded like. He said he wanted to fight in the war but didn't think his father would let him. He'd been tapped to go into the family business. He told me he liked my hair.

I told him about the Jornada, but it sounded dull. I told him about Mama dying. He said he was sorry and meant it. I said my future was here now.

On a warm afternoon in late March, George told me that he had to leave for Texas to look into his father's oil interests. He'd be back in several months.

"Will you still be working here?"

"I plan to be."

He took my hand and placed a turquoise brooch in it. "Folks don't lay much store by these stones, but this one's the prettiest I've seen. It reminds me of the sky here."

I studied the blue stone. Its chocolate-brown edge looked like lace.

I looked up into his eyes. "My mother had a turquoise."

"Now you have your own. So you won't forget me."

He kissed my hand and walked to the lobby door, a suitcase in each hand. He turned around once, his eyes full of longing and a hint of a promise.

I wore his pin and missed him.

9

A month later, Congress declared war on Germany. General "Black Jack" Pershing, who'd fruitlessly chased Pancho Villa through Chihuahua, was to command the American Expeditionary Forces.

The hotel buzzed with excitement. Guests pulled out maps of France and discussed war strategy, predicting quick defeat for Kaiser Bill. Young men strutted around town bragging about signing up and fighting for the general. Women stood in tight groups on street corners and fretted. The bushy-browed librarian no longer had books to recommend. He worried over the newspapers spread across his desk.

Two days later, at a patriotic parade, stories circulated about spies, poison gas, and airplanes dropping bombs on civilians in their homes. I hoped we'd be safe in Bisbee. The town filled with gossip about the "Heinies" or "Krauts" in our midst, and neighbors became suspicious. A Bohemian man was beaten up in an alley, the assailant never found. Some of the boys who played stickball switched to war games, their sticks becoming rifles, their rubber balls, bombs. They wouldn't let the German and Austrian boys join in.

Posters went up. One showed a gorilla wearing a German helmet—"Destroy This Mad Brute: Enlist." Scores of young miners left their jobs to join up. Some headed south to Mexico to avoid the mandatory conscription that was sure to come. A wave of Southern European immigrants and untrained middle-aged men came to town to take their places. A Polish family with six children moved in next to us—the Dabrowskis. They were loud and friendly and brought us warm doughnuts that Mrs. D. made on Saturdays—a welcome peace offering in our agitated town.

One Sunday afternoon, I took Bethel and Sally with me to the YWCA to see a cooking demonstration for pound cake.

"With the war on and the rising price of sugar and butter, a cake like this will be a rare pleasure," our instructor began. She showed us how to whip the butter and eggs, grind the sugar, and sift the flour until it was powder fine. Then she lowered her voice and revealed that a secret ingredient made it particularly delectable—rum. The woman sitting next to me giggled. Our instructor pulled a cup from under the table and poured some into the batter.

"Whiskey will do if you can't find rum," she said. "But the rum imparts a richer flavor."

"Where do you find the alcohol?" asked a woman in the front row.

A tittering filled the room.

"If you can keep a secret, Brewery Gulch has a dry goods store named McAdam's. They sell alcohol—for medicinal purposes only."

She winked and passed around morsels of a baked sample cake. It was the most heavenly thing I'd ever tasted, moist and rich. Bethel and Sally gobbled theirs up.

"Bake us a cake," begged Bethel, looking up at me with her big gray eyes. "Pretty please, Josie?"

I decided to make one that afternoon. On the way home, I bought a half dozen eggs and a pound of butter. Papa kept a bottle of whiskey under his cot. I'd add the liquor to give it that special taste.

When I got out the ingredients, I was surprised that our sugar was nearly gone. Bethel told me that Stevie had been sneaking it. We had to go back to the mercantile for more. The price had doubled since the war started, and I cringed at having to pay so dearly. When we got home, it was time to start supper. I threw split peas into a pot of water, fried up salt pork and onions to add, then mixed up corn batter and made fritters.

I changed Sally's diaper, then mixed the cake batter while the soup simmered. I was running out of time to get the cake in the oven before Papa and the boys came home. I whipped the butter and eggs, ground the sugar until it was as fine as desert dust, sifted the flour three times, and mixed it in. I pulled the bottle of whiskey out from under Papa's cot, but it was empty. I didn't want this cake to be good—I wanted it to be delicious. I decided to buy rum.

Charlie and Stevie thundered into the house, hungry as always.

"I need to run out for an ingredient for this cake. Stir the soup a few times while I'm gone, Charlie. The fritters are in the warming oven. When Papa gets home, you can dish up for everyone. I'll be back soon."

I grabbed my shawl and handbag and headed toward Brewery Gulch. It was already twilight. Although the saloons and prostitute cribs had been closed, the Gulch was still a rough neighborhood at night. Besides the speakeasies where men drank and gambled, it was said there were secret rooms where opium could be had. I'd have to hurry.

The street was nearly empty. I passed Pythian Hall and continued up O.K. Street. McAdam's wasn't well marked. Finally, I located the door and stepped in. Boxes of hardtack and tins of fish and vegetables were scattered over dusty shelves. The store was empty. A dim gas lamp lit the counter.

"Hello?" I called. No one answered. "Is anyone here?"

The door behind the cash register opened. I heard men's laughter and the clink of glasses. A bent man came forward. His nose was bulbous in his sallow face, maroon veins branching out like jagged bolts of lightning. I knew the look of a drunkard.

He looked me over. "What do ya want?"

"I need a pint of rum, sir. For medicine."

He narrowed his eyes. "What the hell. You're the third damn dame asking for rum today. There must be some grippe going around. That'll be three bucks."

That was more than I'd planned, but I was embarrassed to leave. As he disappeared behind the narrow door, the smoke of cheap cigars filtered out. I waited a long time for him to return.

He came back with a pint bottle wrapped in newspaper. I handed him half a week's wage, set the package in my bag, and hurried away.

"Have fun, pretty girlie," he called.

Outside, it was already dark. The lamps were lit, but at this end of the street, they were sparse. If I cut through one of the side passageways, I could get home faster. I paused to look down one. It was a dead end. I went on. I heard a cry. A thin voice called from the narrow alley I was passing.

"Help me."

I hesitated.

"Over here, help," the voice begged.

I peered into the dark. A steel hand clutched my shoulder and pulled me into the alley. Before I could catch my balance, a set of fingers dug into my other shoulder. Shards of pain shot through my upper body. I smelled whiskey as a face drew near mine. I struggled to get away, but my attacker pulled me farther in. I kicked hard but was no match for the man. A heavy arm wrapped around my neck, cutting off my breath. I heard his heavy panting as he bent forward and pressed his weight against me. His foul breath filled my face as he forced his wet lips to the side of my mouth.

"German swine," he growled as he pulled back.

I reached up and clawed at his face. We fell onto the ground. He groaned. I scrambled up, kicked at his groping hands, and ran toward the light. I must have screamed. Two men standing near a streetlamp looked my way.

"Are you all right, girl?" called one of the men.

I put my hand to my face and to my hair, which had come undone. My shawl was torn. "Yes." My voice shook.

I looked back. The street was empty. He wasn't following me. I hurried toward home.

My neck and shoulders throbbed with pain. When I reached Main Street, I stepped into a shop doorway. I wanted to fix my hair, but my comb was missing. My hands trembled. My bag with the rum and my last two dollars was gone too.

It seemed as though I'd struggled for a long time against the man, but it couldn't have been much more than a minute. I started to run. I didn't care if people stared. I ran to our boardinghouse and burst through the door.

The family was sitting at the table. Papa froze as he brought a spoon to his lips. Charlie's mouth dropped. I stood dumbly at the door, not wanting to move.

Papa came toward me. "Josie Belle, what happened?"

"I don't know."

I couldn't talk. I retched. Charlie came running with an empty pot. My stomach empty, I shook with dry convulsions. When the nausea passed, Papa led me to the sofa and made me lie down.

"Charlie, heat up water and mop up that mess," he ordered. "Stevie, bring a blanket for your sister, then unfasten her shoes."

Papa went out back and returned with a shot glass and a flask of whiskey. I stared at the bottle in his hands.

He handed me a glass of whiskey.

"Drink this, Josie. It will help you relax."

I didn't want it. The smell made my stomach clench. But Charlie and the little girls looked worried, and Stevie fretted as he tried to unfasten the buttons on my shoes. I took a gulp. It scorched my throat. My nose burned.

"Another couple sips," Papa urged.

I drank half the glass. My face and chest flushed.

Papa sat next to me. "What in the Sam Hill happened, child?"

I was ashamed to admit I'd been in Brewery Gulch buying rum but told him the story.

"That's all he did? Grabbed you and kissed you?"

"All he did? It was horrible. I lost Mama's comb."

Papa didn't seem to hear me.

"It was dark, you said, and there was no one around?"

"Some men by the streetlight, but they couldn't see into the alley."

"There's no use reporting this. The gossip would only tarnish your reputation."

"People saw me running home."

"They don't know what for."

His eyes looked grave as he examined my neck and shoulders. It was nice to have him pay attention to me.

"You're just bruised. You're a fine girl, Josie. But you're growing up. You need to be more careful."

Charlie brought me chamomile tea, and Papa and the boys went back to the table to finish their cold supper. Papa told me I should stay home the next day and rest.

"You haven't missed a day of work. I'll tell Asa he doesn't have to come."

After Charlie had washed the dishes and put the babies down, I went into my room, gingerly undressed, and got into bed. Sally moaned and snuggled up to me, placing her pudgy hand on my breast. I smelled the sweetness of her hair, listened to her slow breathing, and tried to forget what had happened.

The shrill notes of starlings awakened me the next morning even before the roosters crowed on Chihuahua Hill. My shoulder hurt when I moved. In the mirror I saw the dark smudges of bruises on my neck. I was hungry. I tiptoed out to the kitchen. The bowl of cake batter sat on the table, a brown crust over the surface. I put it aside and started breakfast.

Charlie went to the hotel on the way to school and told them I was ill. On his way home that evening, he searched the alley for my handbag. It was gone.

I baked the pound cake that afternoon, after adding the recommended quarter cup of whiskey. The family was delighted to have dessert on a Monday. The cake was divine, but I never made pound cake again. Even the name was enough to make me shiver.

"You should quit your job," Papa told me as he finished his last bite. "I don't like you selling cigars. You should stay home where you're safe and take care of your family."

I loved my job. I loved the hotel. I defied Papa and kept on working. After supper I read library books and crocheted socks while I listened to Charlie tell jokes from his comic books. I recited Mother Goose rhymes to Sally and brushed Bethel's hair until it gleamed in the yellow lamplight.

The cancer trees were in full leaf, making welcome shade in the warm afternoons. Cigar prices rose—and the cost of everything else. Uniformed men roamed the streets. Liberty bonds were being sold at the banks. My bruises faded.

One Sunday evening, I prepared a fine supper of pork hock, cabbage, and Liberty potatoes. After a few bites, Papa set down his fork and knife.

"Josie Belle, you'll be sixteen in the fall. It's time you got married."

I laughed, figuring it to be one of his jokes. But from his stony look, I could see that it was not.

"I don't care to, Papa. I don't even have a suitor."

He took a bite of potatoes, chewed slowly, and cleared his throat. "I'm on the train all day. I can't protect you. I can't let anything else happen to you like what happened last month. A single woman, if she wants to be safe, she's gotta be good."

"I *am* good."

"Now hear me out. There's a gentleman I know. He's interested in settling down. He's seen you at the hotel. He spoke to me about you. Birch Fanner's his name. He's from Louisiana. He's well-to-do and would make a fine husband."

"I know him," Charlie blurted out. "He comes into the store. Birch Fanner's old, Papa."

"You shut pan and don't tell me what's what." He turned back to me. "I can't be watching over you, a pretty grown-up girl selling cigars and running all over town. He'll take care of you. Irene was married when she was your age."

I struggled to breathe.

"But I don't even know him."

"I'm telling you to get to know him."

I shook my head. "I don't want to."

"Now you're being impertinent."

My face grew hot. "I don't want to court that man."

"I won't tolerate your sass."

His face contorted. He stood, knocking his chair over, and raised his arm. I believed he was going to hit me, but he slammed his hand on the table instead. Plates rattled. Bethel spilled her water. He turned and stalked off to the shed.

I glanced at Charlie. He was staring at his plate. Sally started hitting her bowl with her spoon.

Stevie frowned. "Do you have to get married?"

I escaped to the bedroom and sat on the sagging bed. Through the thin wall I could hear the Dabrowskis laughing together. The front door slammed as Papa went out.

I surveyed the uneven walls, gray with the dinge of coal oil smoke, the crack in the mirror, and the shabby rug beneath my feet.

"We live in a dump," I seethed. "But he makes sure he's got money for his hooch."

I threw a pillow against the wall, lay on the bed, and cried.

After a while, I went out to the kitchen. Stevie lay snoring on the sofa. Charlie was washing up. I put the girls to bed and started drying the dishes.

"You did it now," Charlie said.

"I can't marry that man. I can't even tolerate the idea of meeting him. Can't you talk to Papa?"

"He's stubborn. You know it. I can try, but he's in a fine pucker now."

"You've got to help me, Charlie."

"Is there someone else you could marry? What about that George you told me about?"

George had left more than a month ago and wasn't due back for several more. I hadn't heard from him. There had been no promises made. Chances were he'd hightailed it back to Maryland to enlist. I might never see him again. I didn't even know his family name. A few other young men had been friendly, but the best of them had gone to fight.

"There's no one. I don't want to get married at all. I *won't* get married, no matter what Papa says."

12

The next day, Birch Fanner came into the hotel lobby. He was taller than Papa and heavily built. He had thick, chalky lips, a bushy mustache, and muttonchop sideburns. He was twice my age. I shuddered at the way he looked at me when he asked for a Cuban cigar, as if we were already courting. I looked down, but my cheeks burned hot. I refused to speak to him.

He laughed and puffed on his cigar. "You'll look pretty in white."

He swaggered off.

That Saturday, Charlie led me out back, behind the boardinghouse. "You can't marry that man."

"I don't plan to."

"He's got a pocketful of rocks, like Papa said, and he's used to having his way. I hear he's had lots of lady friends. And there's something else. Papa owes him money. From craps. Fanner's bothering him to pony up, but it's a lot. We don't got it."

I could feel the blood pounding in my head.

"How could Papa do this? He wants to get rid of me. He hates me!"

"He doesn't hate you. You're his favorite. Your attack scared him bad. All he knows is to get his girls married off. Ida beat him to the punch by leaving home."

"Oh, Charlie. He doesn't care if I'm happy."

"He's afraid he can't take care of you."

Charlie heaved a man-sized sigh that tore at my heart. I noticed how much taller he'd gotten in the past six months, as if he'd been stretched. Just thirteen, he was catching up to Papa. He wore his hair short now, like a man.

"Oh, I hate Papa," I hissed. "I'd sooner die than marry that old man."

I stopped talking to Papa. I'm not sure he noticed.

Birch Fanner came to the cigar counter every day. He leaned over the case as if he owned it. He didn't talk to me, just threw out remarks that got under my skin.

One night I dreamed that George galloped up to the hotel in a cavalry uniform, strode up to the cigar counter, and asked me to marry him—only to awaken to dismal reality. Most nights I lay in bed and worried. My stomach burned and milky tea gave little relief.

"I like your spirit," Birch Fanner told me as I left the counter on a Friday evening. "But I've never met a filly I couldn't break."

The next evening, after I'd put the girls to bed, Charlie dragged me out back again.

"You know Diego Sanchez, the Mexican who delivers vegetables from Tombstone?"

I shook my head. I'd never heard of the man.

"He owes me a favor. Me and some fellows at the store helped him out once after some hoodlums knocked over his cart. He can get you out of here. He said he'd hide you in the back of his vegetable wagon and take you up to Benson. You can take the train from there. You can trust him. That is, if you want to leave. And get out of marrying Fanner."

"Is this my only way out?"

"I reckon so. It's not Papa you need to worry about. It's Fanner."

"I can't run away. I can't leave Sally and Bethel."

"Stevie and I'll take care of them. We'll be real good to them. The neighbors can help out." Charlie sighed. "The thing is, Mr. Sanchez is going tonight. He said he won't be back for another month or so. I don't know how else to get you out of here. If you take the train out of Bisbee, Papa will find out where you went and go after you."

I nodded. A lump had stopped up my throat.

"So where do you want to go? To Ida May in St. Louis?"

"I don't have money for the ticket. I'll go back to Engle and stay with Irene. Maybe I can find work there."

"So I tell Mr. Sanchez that you're going?"

I hesitated, then nodded.

I felt dizzy. Things were changing too fast. Charlie left to take the message to Mr. Sanchez, and shortly after, Papa left for the speakeasy.

"Goodbye, Papa," I called as he stood at the open door. "I . . . I hope you have a good time."

These were the first words I'd spoken to him in weeks. He turned from the door and looked at me, a puzzled expression on his face.

"Good night, Josie Belle."

I heard the clomp of his boots on the front stairs and then only the complaint of house boards buffeted by the May wind blowing down the canyon.

Charlie returned and said Mr. Sanchez would wait for me across from the boardinghouse at four o'clock. I was to climb into the back of his vegetable wagon as quietly as possible. If we were caught, we'd be in a heap of trouble.

Charlie washed the supper dishes while I tucked Stevie into his bed on the sofa.

"I want you to know something, Stevie. Sometimes people have to do things they don't want to do because they have no other choice."

"What are you talking about?"

"I want you to know that I love you and think you're a marvelous boy."

"Sure you do."

He yawned and laid down his head. While I caressed his brow, he closed his eyes and fell asleep. I kissed his forehead and went into the bedroom, packed my clothes, and counted my money.

"I don't think I have enough to get to Engle," I told Charlie.

"I've got some money. I'll give it to you in the morning."

I clutched his forearm. "You'll watch over Sally and Bethel? And Stevie too?"

"They'll be all right. You gotta take care of yourself just now."

13

I lay in bed dressed for my journey, George's brooch pinned to my shirtwaist, my shoes laced. I couldn't sleep. About one in the morning, I heard Papa come home. He stumbled around, then plopped onto his cot and was quiet. A nearly full moon shone in the window, lighting my little sisters' faces. Bethel's skin appeared transparent in the white light. I could make out two blue veins running crookedly across her forehead. Sally slept peacefully, her round cheeks and rosebud mouth lax in slumber. If only she could be so tranquil the following day when she woke up crying, and I wouldn't be there to comfort her.

I climbed out of bed and laid Mama's turquoise on the table for Papa to keep. I would leave the sewing box too. Someone else would need to sew on the buttons.

I must have dozed. Charlie shook me awake.

"Josie," he hissed. "The cart's out there. It's time to go."

Careful not to wake my little sisters, I kissed their angel cheeks. Charlie picked up my bag, and we crept across the living room, past Papa on his cot, and out the door.

The vegetable wagon waited just outside the arc of the streetlight. A discarded page of newspaper, caught by a gust of wind, blew up and wrapped itself around my legs, as if to foil my escape. I peeled it off and hurried to the wagon. Charlie shoved some bills and our harmonica into my hand.

"Are you sure you want me to have it?" I whispered.

He nodded. "You can play the old tunes."

"Where'd you get the money?"

"Papa owes you."

He gave me a quick, rough hug. I rubbed his stubby hair and kissed his cheek.

"When I'm fourteen," he whispered, "I'll be going too."

"Charlie, you promised you'd stay!"

"Shh," he cautioned. "Don't worry. I'll stay."

I climbed into the back of the cart among the vegetables, and Charlie and Mr. Sanchez fastened canvas over the top.

"Don't forget us, Josie," I heard Charlie whisper. Then the clink of mule harnesses, clop of hooves, and rattle of wheels filled the night.

As we jostled over the rough road, I tried to get comfortable amid the bumpy squash, lost my balance, and fell onto a mound of Mexican parsley. The close air of the cart filled with its sharp scent. I felt the waxy forms of peppers and recognized their piquant smell. I put my hand to my eye. Pepper oil seeped in. I started to cry.

Who would remember to put cream on Sally's rash? Who would brush Bethel's hair? And what about Stevie? How would he survive being abandoned again?

I'd broken my promise to Mama. I hoped Charlie could explain to them why I'd left. I pined for George and my lost hope of deliverance.

I thought of all I was leaving. The Copper Queen had treated me well. I would miss its beautiful lobby. For an instant I believed I ought to turn back. What would it matter if I married that man? My promise to Mama was worth more. I could ask Mr. Sanchez to let me out at Tombstone and catch a wagon back to Bisbee. But then I pictured Birch Fanner, remembered his lecherous laugh, and knew I'd surely perish if I were to be his wife.

14

I dreamed I was in Old Mexico, riding el Cohete. We galloped over the golden grassland, then el Cohete stumbled, and we were falling to the ground. I woke up. The wagon was pitching wildly. It was daylight. We were far from Bisbee.

I pulled up a corner of canvas and looked out. Empty road wound behind us. The bare hills were brightened by flashes of wild phlox and yellow marigold. Purple creeper bloomed in the willow-shaded canyon.

A flycatcher skimmed through the morning air. As it spread its wings, I caught a glimpse of white against gray feathers. It flew straight up, then folded its wings and plummeted to the earth like a falling arrow. Just short of the ground, it made a sharp loop to the left and soared again. I felt as reckless as the diving bird, solely responsible for what followed—my ruin or safe landing.

I slept until a stifling heat awakened me. I stuck my head out the back. The desert spread behind me, the heat shimmering in waves upon never-ending brown. My body was damp with sweat.

Outside of Tombstone, Mr. Sanchez pulled behind a clump of trees, stopped the wagon, and came around.

"You all right?" He cocked his head and smiled.

"A bit stiff."

He pointed toward Tombstone. "Go to town and eat. I'll

deliver the vegetables. Meet me in two hours a quarter mile north of town."

He helped me out of the cart, and it rattled off. I walked to a restaurant and had a soft-boiled egg, a biscuit, and a cup of coffee. I sat near a window and looked across the dusty street to the row of false-fronted buildings in the sleepy town. Papa had told me that Tombstone had been a rough-and-ready mining town until the silver mines flooded. Like Cutter and so many others, the closing of the mines had brought slow death.

Diego Sanchez was waiting for me under a tree on the road to Benson. We made sure no one saw me climb into the empty cart. I made a bed out of burlap sacks, and the last twenty miles passed comfortably. When he let me off outside of Benson, I gave him two dollars and thanked him for his help. He refused the money.

"I did it for Charlie. He's a good boy."

"Yes, I know."

I missed my brother already.

I walked to the depot and studied the timetable. The Southern Pacific would put me in at Rincon at ten o'clock that night. The connecting northbound wouldn't get me into Engle until after midnight, too late for Irene to fetch me. I'd need to take a room at the Harvey House in Rincon and travel on to the Jornada in the morning.

After buying my ticket to Engle, I had just enough money for the hotel and to send Irene a telegram: ARRIVING ON THE MORNING TRAIN. What would she think? When I went to the toilet, I couldn't bear to look at myself in the mirror, for fear I'd see Mama's disappointed face. I was no longer her sweet lamb; I was a wily ewe, as stubborn as Papa.

15

The train screeched into the Benson depot, and I found my car. I clutched my cardboard ticket and stared out the window as we roared across the desert. We passed a cactus, seared by lightning. It stood hollow, its ribs splayed, bleached by the unforgiving sun. I felt as done in as that cactus. Would my heart ever be filled again?

I tried counting the glass ampoules atop the telegraph poles, but they were passing so quickly I got dizzy. I pulled the curtain and closed my eyes. A man passed, trailing the odor of cigar—a Manila or White Owl—the kind that George had once gagged on. I fingered my Bisbee turquoise. I wondered what had happened to George, whether he'd found those Texas oil wells or donned a uniform and gone to fight. Would he return to Bisbee, disappointed that I wasn't there? I should have left him a note at the hotel, but it was too late. Perhaps he'd forgotten me long ago. I would never know.

I awoke to someone shaking my shoulder. The train had stopped.

"Excuse me, miss," the conductor said. "Weren't you getting off in Rincon?"

I dusted the cinders off my shoulders and arms, gathered my bags, and tagged behind a group of travelers going to the Harvey House.

A Harvey girl showed me to my room. She wore a trim black

dress with a white collar, a snow-white apron, pinafore, and linen cap. She placed my bag on a chair, handed me fresh towels and a bar of soap, and turned down my bed. She left the room and returned with a pitcher of warm water for the washbasin.

"You're young to be traveling on your lonesome. My ma wouldn't let me go nowhere on my own till I was eighteen. Then I skedaddled to Topeka and got this job."

She promised to wake me for the early train.

If only I could be a Harvey girl. It seemed a perfect job for a girl on her own. But my eighteenth birthday was more than two years away. Those years loomed like a chasm I would somehow need to cross.

I washed the train grime from my face and neck. I fingered the handle of the pitcher, cold and foreign in my hand. The towel felt coarse on the skin of my face. I felt disconnected from everything I'd known. I lay in bed, pulled the starched sheet to my chin, and stared at the ceiling. As the smell of supper wafted in from the dining room, my stomach growled and cramped. I counted on my fingers. It had been ten hours since my meal in Tombstone. I closed my eyes and willed myself to sleep.

VII

CUTTER

(1917)

saw the children first. A toddler, new on his feet, stumbled after his nimble sister, who darted behind their mother's skirt. He took a large, clumsy step, teetered, and tumbled to the ground. He sat for a moment, surprised, while the dust whirled about him, laughed, and rolled to his knees. His mother hardly noticed. One arm clasping her floppy hat to her head, she peered up into the windows of the moving train, intent on locating someone within.

She turned her face in the direction of my car. It was Irene. I pulled closer to the window and waved. A look of uncertainty crossed her face, and then a lift of her chin and a smile. She'd seen me.

She picked up the boy, who'd spilled back onto the dirt, held him close so that his round, dusty cheek rested against hers, and pointed to my window. He stared at my car, uncomprehending. She blew me a kiss. The girl stood still, serious, and then lifted a hand for a tentative wave. A blast of wind hit them, and a flurry of sand blew into their faces. They turned away.

I pinned on my hat, grabbed my bag, and hurried to the door. The train screeched and jerked to a stop. I hopped down the steps.

"Josie Belle!" She was scuttling toward me, Mona on one arm, baby Joe bouncing in the other. She pulled me to her and hugged me. "Oh, little sister. You look all grown up."

"Are you surprised to see me?"

"Are you in trouble?"

I looked down. "I'm sorry, is all."

"Hush now. You can tell me about it on the way home."

We cowered against the gusts and made our way to the wagon, where Earl waited. When we'd settled under blankets in the back, he set off for the ranch. Out of the wind, our heads bent together, Irene took another long look at me.

"You've changed, Josie."

"Not me. Papa changed."

I told Irene about the attack, about George and Birch Fanner.

"It's one thing that I married so young. It's what Earl and I wanted. But to push a girl into marriage before she's ready . . . that's not right."

"Papa got this idea that I needed to go."

"He thinks a girl of fifteen is all grown up. Like Charlie told you, it's what he knows."

Then Irene started asking questions that were hard to answer.

"Couldn't you have bought some time? Told Papa you'd marry when you were seventeen? Maybe he'd feel differently then."

"I don't know."

"Maybe you could have told that man a white lie. Told him you were engaged to George and he was fighting in Europe. Any good man would leave a soldier's girl alone."

"He's not a good man. He's a rake."

Irene giggled. I laughed until tears stung my eyes.

Earl looked sideways at us, gave a wry smile, and shook his head.

"I couldn't reason with Papa. We weren't on speaking terms. And I couldn't fib. What if George came back? I'd be mortified."

"Oh, Josie, you were in a fix." She shook her head and re-arranged the blanket around baby Joe, who slept despite the jostle of the wagon. "Our poor babies."

That night, as I lay in Mona's bed, I couldn't clear my head of Irene's words. If I'd been more cunning or less stubborn, Papa might've let up. Maybe Birch Fanner would have left me alone if I'd made up a story. Perhaps I hadn't needed to leave.

I had a nightmare that Bethel was standing in her nightgown at the edge of a deep canyon. She was crying for water. I stood at the opposite side, unable to reach her.

I opened my eyes in the dark. The cries were real. It was baby Joe. Irene had told me he sometimes woke in the night, crying from earache. I heard someone stir, Irene most likely, a door open, and the creak of a rocker between Joe's shrieks. The baby's cries became whimpers, and he dropped off to sleep. The rocker stilled, and I was lulled to sleep by the brush of the breeze against the house.

2

Irene's home was neat and comfortable. It was odd seeing our furniture there—Mama's rocker and sewing machine, the night table that had been next to Mama and Papa's bed. I stood in the sitting room, my arms outstretched.

"All Mama's things. Even your clothes. That's Mama's skirt."

"We brought everything over from the homestead after you left. Does it bother you?"

I spied Mama's jade plant, bigger and glossier than I remembered. I knew I shouldn't covet things, but since losing Mama's comb and leaving her brooch for Papa, I had nothing of hers. I opened one of the little drawers of the sewing cabinet to see a rainbow of colored bobbins. Of course, Irene should have it. She needed to clothe her children. I couldn't even sew.

"It feels right, Irene. I'm glad Mama's things are in the family."

"It brings me comfort."

I stayed at Irene's for a week. I held Joe as she dripped garlic oil into his aching ear. I taught Mona to play pat-a-cake, something Irene had forgotten to do, and played her songs on my harmonica. While Irene knitted, I told her about Bisbee and the hotel, and Charlie and Stevie's pushmobile races. Mona sat next to me and drew stick figures of her adventurous uncles.

Irene told me all she'd learned about running a ranch. "I can repair a fence, milk a cow, and I've learned to ride quite well. Earl's going to buy a motorcar and teach me how to drive."

I commented on a streak of white in Irene's hair.

"Oh, it was a fright, Josie. I was lucky to survive. I was running the gas pump in the well house when my hair got caught in it, and it tore clean out. It grew back pure white. Earl reminds me to put my hair up when I go out there now."

"Is he good to you?"

"Yes, we do nearly everything together—he even helps with the dishes. He works hard and expects me to, as well."

She filled me in on news of family and friends. Uncle Stephen was renovating our grandparents' Austin home. Marv and Dora Fenton had sent a Christmas card from San Francisco. And roly-poly Mrs. Winston from Chihuahua had written. She was living back in Kentucky, still kept out of the sun, and had sent a recipe for western Kentucky burgoo, with a reminder to use only baby limas.

I laughed. "Did you try the recipe?"

She nodded. "It's as spicy as she was. She made Mama laugh. I had to write back and tell her about Mama's death."

We stopped our chatter, and our eyes met in a solemn gaze.

Despite our talks, the ranch was too quiet for me after Bisbee. One evening, as I watched Irene work the treadle on Mama's Singer, I told her I needed to find a job. She stilled her foot.

"Did you see how empty Engle was when you arrived?"

"I didn't notice anything but you and the wind."

"You didn't see all the FOR SALE and FOR LET signs? Everybody's moving out, now the dam's finished. The gold was a rumor. Not enough opportunity to keep people coming."

She shook her head and turned the fabric beneath the needle.

"It's going to be just ranchers left. I hope they can keep the school open for Mona. The teacher left last month, and they're looking for another."

"Is she that big?" I squeezed four-year-old Mona, who sat on my lap playing with my turquoise.

"You'd do best looking in Cutter. Some newcomers took a lease on the hotel and are fixing it up. It's been vacant since the Currys left. You know how the desert takes over."

The idea of working at a hotel again cheered me. I braided Mona's hair into two short braids and tied the ends with pink ribbon. With the hair back from her face, she looked like Bethel. An arrow of guilt pierced my heart. I gasped and pressed my hand to my chest.

"Are you all right, Josie Belle?"

"I feel so bad."

"I'm worried too. Oh, Sister, I hope you can go back. They need you. And you're Papa's favorite."

"That's not true anymore."

"You hurt most the ones you love the best." Irene pushed her foot to the treadle. "He'd be glad to have you back."

I couldn't return yet. It was because of his stubborn ways that I'd had to leave. And Birch Fanner was still waiting.

3

The next day, Earl gave me a ride to the depot. I made straight for the brick hotel when I reached Cutter. Several of the downstairs windows were broken, and others had been boarded up. The rail of the back porch where I'd first seen Earl courting Irene lay flat in the dust. A sign at the front read: UNDER NEW MANAGEMENT. CLOSED FOR REPAIR.

I stepped inside. A man in work overalls knelt on the dusty floor, hammering together a window frame. A young woman stood behind the front desk sorting a pile of keys. I asked if they were hiring.

"We're the new managers," the woman said, "but we won't be ready for business for at least a month. We're not in a position to hire."

She frowned as she looked down at the jumble on the desk.

I stepped toward the door.

"Wait a minute." She looked over at the man. "What do you think, Thomas? I could use help. It's daunting, all this work."

The man cocked his head and sized me up, as if I were a heifer for sale. He had to take the nails out of his mouth to answer. "She looks strong and smart. That would be fine."

"Wonderful! I'm Eliza Brown and this is my husband. We'll hire you on trial for a week. If we make a good team, we'll keep you on when the hotel's up and running. You can start by helping me organize these keys. We need to match and label them. Then we can open the rooms upstairs and gauge the damage."

She was hard to look at. Her cheeks were pocked by scars, as bumpy as chicken flesh. I'd seen smallpox scarring before, but her skin was more ravaged than most. Her eyes were pale green and lovely. In time, they were all I saw when I looked at her.

As we lined keys across the surface of the desk, I told her I was staying east of Engle but would be looking for a room in town.

"Hmm." She leaned toward me and spoke softly. "I'll have to ask Thomas, but you can possibly stay here. The wallpaper's peeling and there's dust everywhere, but you'd be comfortable."

Thomas started hammering again. She raised her voice. "We've leased the hotel as an investment. We'll fix it up and hire a day manager to operate it. Then Thomas wants to start a bus service up and down the Jornada and over to Hot Springs."

We sorted the keys and went upstairs, unlocking the stuffy rooms and propping open windows.

I found the two rooms that my family had stayed in. It seemed so long ago.

"I didn't realize you'd grown up here."

"Yes, though I've just come from Bisbee."

She pulled me down to sit on the bed.

"What made you come back? Bisbee's quite a town."

I hesitated. The room brought fresh memories of Mama. I choked up.

"It's all right. I'll tell you about myself."

She and Thomas came from Tucson. Eliza had an older sister, Susannah, who kept house for their father, and a younger brother, Joseph, who, the day he'd turned eighteen, had taken a train to Ottawa and enlisted.

"He's fighting in France. I worry about him constantly."

She fingered a pitted cheek as she told me about her mother, who'd died of typhoid while visiting a sister in Biloxi. Eliza had been fifteen at the time. Five years later, she'd married Thomas.

"So here we are." Eliza smiled and patted my thigh. "I think we're going to get along fine."

I nodded. We had something in common. She, too, had been a motherless girl.

"Listen," she said. "Thomas has stopped pounding."

We went downstairs. He was in the kitchen frying eggs while reading a book.

"Did you get things aired out?"

Eliza smiled. "The important things."

"Would you like eggs?"

We sat on the back porch and ate fried eggs, canned peaches, and bread and butter.

⁓

I moved into the room on the second floor where I'd stayed as a girl. At night, memories rushed back. I remembered Mama fixing my hair at the dressing table the afternoon of the Thanksgiving dance, the smell of roses when she leaned close, and Papa climbing the stairs singing "Betsy Brown." The name Brown again—perhaps it was a good omen. I lay in bed, listened to the distant howl of coyotes, and remembered.

Weekdays I worked alongside Eliza—sweeping, peeling wallpaper, scrubbing sinks and tubs. She chatted as she worked and laughed at little things. Thomas made our meals, but all he could cook were eggs and soup, throwing in herbs and spices and whatever else was at hand. Eliza and I sipped our soup with caution. Once we found raisins in a cream of potato soup, and another time, pickles in the vegetable stew.

"Don't you cook?" I said.

"I cooked for Father for years. Thomas enjoys it, so I let him."
She took a spoonful of corn chowder and pulled out a string
bean. Thomas had peculiarities, she explained. He was a noncon-
formist—a vegetarian and a pacifist.

One afternoon, as Eliza and I were washing grime from be-
hind the kitchen stove, I reminisced about our homestead and
Mama. She stopped and held my hand when I told her about
Mama's illness and death.

"You were lucky to be able to say goodbye. My mother was
far from home when she passed."

Yes, I thought, but at least Eliza couldn't be blamed for her
mother's death.

I described Bisbee, told her about Papa and Birch Fanner and
why I'd left.

"You poor thing. You certainly needed to leave. We're both
far from family. We'll have to stick together."

We returned to our scrubbing.

I began to think of Eliza as a sister, and better yet, a friend.

4

I spent Saturdays and Sundays with Irene and Earl at the ranch. Irene's cooking was a pleasant change from eggs and soup.

On Saturday nights, I washed the supper dishes while Irene and Earl bathed the children and put them to bed. Afterward, I carried Mama's rocking chair out onto the porch and listened to the gabble of chickens as they settled in and the final chirps of desert birds. The smell of juniper floated down from the foothills. I softly played the old songs from home on my Hohner. It seemed I'd been away for a long time. Some nights I lit an oil lamp and read one of Earl's Zane Grey adventures or one of Irene's novels— *Daddy-Long-Legs*, *Pollyanna*, or *Tarzan of the Apes*—more tales of orphans made good.

After the children were asleep, Irene and Earl joined me. Earl talked about his designs for the ranch, and Irene told me of her hopes for the children. During the week, I listened to Eliza's and Thomas's plans for the hotel. It was as though I were a character in a novel, stuck between chapters. Everyone but me was working on a dream.

"I got a letter from Charlie," Irene told me one night. "Yes, I let him know you were here. He says Papa's still sore enough to swallow a horny toad backwards." She chuckled and sobered. "There was quite a scene when Papa had to tell that man you'd run away. The fellow almost hit Papa. Charlie says to tell you that Asa's still taking care of the girls, and that they're fine."

I nodded. A lump stuck in my throat. I didn't know whether I could believe that.

"He says there's trouble in Bisbee. The union miners are threatening a strike, and Papa's on their side."

I recalled the miners trudging home like worn-out packhorses and wished them luck.

⸎

The next week at the hotel, Eliza and I hauled buckets of soapy water up the stairs and began washing the walls of the dirty hallways.

"The squatters did a lot of damage," I said.

Eliza kept on scrubbing.

"How long do you think they stayed here?"

She didn't respond. She seemed to be in a dream, rubbing the plaster with rhythmic motions.

"Eliza?"

She started. "Oh, I was pondering, or you might say, reflecting."

"Reflecting?"

"I suppose everyone's different. Some would call it prayer. I picture the people I care about and imagine them surrounded by pink-and-white light. The pink is for love and the white's for protection. It's all you can do if they're far away." She paused. "Thomas and I are Catholic. Lately, I've been praying to Mary for the end of the war." She dipped her soiled rag into the soapy water. "If you'd like, we can send our loving thoughts to your family."

Mama had taught me to say evening prayers, but I liked the idea of making images in my head to send positive thoughts.

"Yes, I'll try."

We moved to a new part of the wall. As I scrubbed in circles, I pictured Sally napping on the bed, her pudgy cheeks lax with sleep. I saw Bethel curled up in a corner of the sofa, whispering to her rag doll, Stevie lying at the other end, a comic book propped above his face. I could see Charlie standing at the sink, washing dishes. I tried to imagine them enveloped in a pink haze of love and protective white light. I felt a wave of comfort.

"I'll send my thoughts to your brother in France. What color should I send?"

"Send him white light for safety. I'll pray for him too."

For the next hour, we worked silently, each lost in meditation.

_⸎_

Some evenings after supper, I walked to the Cutter graveyard. Paint had already chipped off the fence around Mama's wooden cross. One night, Eliza joined me with a can of white paint and two brushes, and we put on a new coat.

"My mother's been gone so long, but I still pine for her touch," Eliza whispered. "I say she's passed *on*, not away. It makes her feel closer."

I yanked at a start of mesquite that had taken root a foot from her grave and sent Mama pink thoughts of love. The breeze whispered in the grasses. Overhead, a red-tailed hawk rode a current of the wind, so close that I could hear the ruffle of wing feathers.

5

Early one morning, Eliza and I started painting the window frames. Just as we finished a first coat, a gust of wind frosted the wet paint with sand. Eliza threw up her hands and suggested we take the train to Las Cruces. She needed to order wallpaper. Thomas needed plumbing fixtures and wanted to inquire about electric circuitry.

In Las Cruces, Eliza headed for the Manasse Brothers' store, where she ordered rolls of cream wallpaper with royal-blue stripes and made a large down payment. I agreed it would brighten up the rooms.

Thomas hobnobbed with the clerks at Ryan Drug and Emporium while Eliza and I meandered through town. We stepped into the lobbies of the Amador and Don Bernardo hotels, and Eliza checked the prices for lodging and food.

"If we had more time, we could see a movie at the Crystal."

Instead we window-shopped, admiring the fabrics and five-dollar dresses at Wilfinger's. We walked by a saloon and peered in the open doorway at the sparkling chandeliers, mahogany bar, and gaming tables. A bartender who stood at the door polishing a drinking glass with his apron whistled and winked at us. We hurried past.

We ended up at St. Genevieve church, a massive brick building with two tall spires. Eliza asked whether I wanted to come in with her. I looked up the wide stone steps to the arched doorways beneath stained-glass windows and nodded. She handed me a lace veil to pin on my head.

The inside of the church was cool and quiet and smelled of smoky perfume. Beneath the high beams, a swallow glided, like a bat through a cavern. A scattering of men and women sat in pews. In front of a life-size statue of Mary, candles flickered.

I followed Eliza to the figure, where she dropped a penny in a metal box, lit a candle, and crossed herself. We moved to one of the back pews.

"Are these people waiting for the service?" I whispered.

"No, they're praying."

Eliza knelt. I sat next to her and sent pink loving thoughts to my sisters and brothers. The swallow swooped and chirped. No one noticed.

An old woman entered the church and trudged up the center aisle. She wore broken sandals on dusty feet, a threadbare skirt, and a ragged shawl. Behind her waddled two scrawny dogs. They followed her to a pew and plopped down in the aisle next to her, groaning at the pleasure of the cool tile floor. I was glad that the woman could pray with her dogs.

I leaned toward Eliza. "Are they praying to the statues?"

"Not the statues. The holy souls they represent," she said under her breath. "Images and candlelight—they take us to a deeper place."

Church bells pealed above us. Eliza rose, and we headed out. She dipped her hand into a basin of water near the door. As she blessed herself, she spoke softly into my ear. "I prayed for your papa."

I stumbled on the doorsill. What a notion.

6

That Saturday, Earl washed the dishes while I helped Irene give Mona and Joe baths in a tin tub on the porch. I told Irene about the trip to Las Cruces and the visit to the church. I told her that Eliza was teaching me to do daily reflections.

Irene looked up from soaping Joe's back. "Those people have a lot of influence on you."

"They're not trying to change me."

"They're papists."

"Oh, Irene, you don't even know what one is. And neither do I."

"That's what I mean. You've no idea what you're getting into." She took the soap and started to wash behind Joe's ears. "It's because you never got baptized, like Ida May and me. I'll take you down to El Paso, and you can get blessed with the water too. Mama would have wanted it."

"I don't think I want that anymore."

She pursed her lips like Mama, turned away, and soaped Joe's front. "It's not the religion. I feel I'm losing you."

"You're not jealous of Eliza, are you?"

"How could I be? She's been so good to you."

Yet I could see hurt in her eyes. "You've got a nice home, Irene. And a husband and a family. I want something of my own."

"Just don't fall for the first thing that comes your way."

She rinsed Joe's pudgy belly. As she was lifting him out of

the tub, we heard the rapid clomp of horse hooves, and a rider approached. Earl came out to the porch. It was Cephus on a fast Morgan. He pulled up and held a telegram out to Irene.

"This came in this afternoon."

I took Joe and wrapped him in a towel.

Irene dried her hands and reached for the envelope. "Thank you, Cephus. Oh, I hope everyone's all right." Her hands shook as she ripped it open and read. Her face remained expressionless. "It's from Papa."

She handed me the paper and took Joe from my arms. I read the message: HALF OF BISBEE ON STRIKE SINCE JUNE 27. SEND MONEY.

"He must be broke." I handed the telegram to Earl.

He glanced at the paper and turned to Cephus. "We'll put you up for the night. It's too late for you to head back now. You're probably hungry too."

Cephus and Earl went into the house.

Irene and I didn't say anything while she dressed Joe. I helped Mona from the tub and dried her.

"What's the matter, Mama?"

Irene slipped a nightgown over the girl's wet head. "Nothing, dear. You take Joe into the house and play with him awhile."

Irene sat on the porch bench while I dribbled bathwater over her flowers.

"Miners don't get paid while they're on strike, do they?" she said. "Papa must owe money that someone needs now. I don't suppose he's been able to save anything."

"He drinks too much to save."

"So he's gotten worse."

"He's got debt from craps."

"Worse than I imagined. We'll have to help him."

This was my fault. Papa needed my earnings from the hotel.

On top of that, I'd taken his money for my train ticket. Now my actions were causing problems for Irene and Earl.

They wired Papa fifty dollars, and I threw in fifteen from my pay at the hotel. It was all I had to give.

7

From the outside, the hotel looked ready for business, but the walls inside were stripped naked. We were waiting for Eliza's wallpaper. Folks stepped off the train and found their way to the hotel, only to learn that it wouldn't be open for several more weeks. The temperatures soared into the nineties. We were losing our zeal. After a morning of sorting linens and a lunch of coddled eggs, we sprawled on the back porch.

I studied Thomas. "How can you think of so many ways to prepare an egg?"

"It's called creativity." He gave a smug smile, though I knew he had a recipe book.

Eliza and I counted the ways: soft-boiled, hard-boiled, coddled, fried, sautéed, scrambled, poached, and shirred.

We ended our meal with a bowl of black cherries, competing to see who could spit a pit as far as the rubbish heap. Eliza, who was losing, had called it quits when we heard someone behind us clear his throat. It was a delivery boy.

"Telegram for Mrs. Thomas Brown."

Eliza put her hand to her heart. "It's Joseph. Open it for me, will you, Thomas?"

He pulled out his penknife, sliced open the envelope, and handed her the sheet of yellow paper.

"It's not Joseph. It's Father. He's had a stroke." She began to cry. "He can't walk or talk. Susannah needs me home immediately. Oh, I need to pack."

She wiped her eyes and wet cheeks with her fruit-stained hands and hurried into the hotel with Thomas following.

I threw the last of the cherries onto the rubbish heap and washed the dishes. Eliza came into the kitchen as I was finishing.

"What are you going to do, Josie? We may not return for some time."

"I don't know. Look for other work."

"There isn't any other work. Thomas and I would like you to come to Tucson with us."

I set down the dishrag.

"Thomas's parents have a spare room where you could stay. You could go to school."

Thomas stepped into the kitchen. "You'll stagnate here."

"I'd like to go, but I'm not sure." I felt dizzy. "I need to think about it. I need to talk to Irene."

"Of course," Eliza said. "I'm sorry to rush you, but we'll be leaving on the first train tomorrow. Talk to your sister. If you're not on the morning train, we'll know you chose to stay." She paused. "I do hope you'll come."

I packed my bags. I felt as though I were being pulled into a river by a fast-moving current, when what I needed was more time on shore to think the journey through.

I made my decision on the ride to Irene's.

⁕

She was alarmed to see me.

"What's happened?"

I sat at the table and told her I wanted to go with Eliza and Thomas.

She was quiet for a minute. "So you won't be going back to Bisbee."

"I want to, but Papa's still cross, and Birch Fanner's still there, and now there's this strike. I'll find work and send Papa money."

Irene picked up a head of cabbage and Mama's grater. "And they'll give you someplace decent to stay and send you to school?"

"That's what they said."

She began to shred the cabbage into a bowl. "I can't tell you how nice it's been having you here. I get so lonely. And Mona adores you." She stopped grating and turned the bowl around. "But there's nothing for you here. I just never thought all my family would go away."

The cabbage had diminished to a small white lump. She handed it to Mona, who climbed onto my lap and began to gnaw it with her tiny front teeth.

"You don't want to stay and marry a cowhand. That's about all you'll find here, except for the section crew, who are mostly shiftless. You deserve better."

She opened the stove side door. The smell of sizzling meat filled the room. She kept her back to me as she poured water into a pot, tossed in the shredded cabbage, and set it on the stove. She turned around with tears in her eyes. I went to her and held her. My dear Irene. I would miss her so.

She pulled herself together and patted me on the cheek. "Go, Sister, and get that schooling Mama wanted for us. Maybe you can still be a teacher. But promise to come straight back if things don't work out."

❦

The next morning, Earl and Irene took me to catch the early train. The sun rose at our backs and colored the desert pink. In the still dawn, flycatchers chirruped, soared, and dove for insects. The light mellowed to new-morning yellow, its warmth evaporating the dew on the creosote. A ghost of a breeze crept in from the eastern ridge, carrying the residue of pine. I caught a whiff of burning mesquite. The scents of home.

No place ever smelled like home again.

I meant to tell Irene so many things—how glad I was that she had Earl, how beautiful her children were, what a good mother she was, how proud Mama would be, how much I loved her. But I disintegrated into a sobbing mess. We clung to each other at the door of the train until Earl pulled her away. As the locomotive carried me off, I waved until they disappeared from sight. That was the last time I saw Irene.

My life was a runaway train. Even when I wanted to slow down, it was as though someone kept throwing in coals to keep it moving full steam. Why was I always saying goodbye to the ones I loved?

Eliza and Thomas were waiting at the Cutter station. I leaned out the window. "I'm coming with you."

"Huzzah!" they cheered.

They settled into the seat across from me, and the train pulled out. I took a last look at Cutter, willing myself to preserve it in my memory—both the good and the bad—like residue in amber.

As we roared south, Eliza's clear eyes bored into me. "You're blue, aren't you?"

"I know you're upset too. I think I'll sleep."

I leaned back and closed my eyes.

"Do you think we did the right thing to bring her with us?" I heard her ask Thomas.

"Undoubtedly," he said.

I dozed and awoke as we were approaching Rincon. We changed trains and continued west on the Southern Pacific. My spirits improved.

Eliza moved to the seat next to me. "I keep wondering what's going to happen to all the wallpaper I ordered. I suppose it will wait."

We bought cherry lemonades, nibbled at Thomas's hard-boiled eggs, and Eliza and I devoured the roast beef and cabbage that Irene had packed for us.

"You'll love Ma Brown. She's like a mother to me."

"What's she like?"

"Um . . ." She glanced at Thomas reading his book. "She's like Thomas."

I didn't know what she meant. Was she tall and lanky with sleek black hair? Was she well-read and disturbingly quiet? Was she completely candid?

"Does she only cook eggs?"

Eliza let loose her effervescent laugh. "No." She flipped her wrist in frustration. "You'll just have to meet her."

"Will she meet us at the train?"

"That depends." Her eyes twinkled. "If the train's on time, I doubt she'll make it. If it's late, there's a high possibility."

Thomas swiveled his head from the pages of his book and shot her a look. She laughed again and peeled another egg. The train lurched on.

VIII

TUCSON
(1917–1918)

M rs. Brown wasn't what I expected. She looked perfectly ordinary. Her pewter hair was pulled on top of her head in a flat bun. I couldn't tell the color of her eyes. She was of average height and wide-hipped. On a man, her high, freckled forehead, beaked nose, and square jaw might be described as distinguished, but a woman with such features was called plain.

"Thomas! Eliza! Welcome home. And you must be Josie."

She threw her arms around us, led us to her Model T, and donned her goggles. She drove at breakneck speed, honking the Klaxon horn at every turn, frightening horses and children. I clutched the leather armrests so tightly, my hands hurt. When we finally reached Eliza's home, Susannah came out to meet us. Eliza took one look at her sister's drawn face and scrambled out.

"It's best if I see Father alone."

"I'll be back tonight," Thomas said, and we rattled off.

The Browns' house was an adobe in an older neighborhood just south of downtown. Thomas helped me carry my bags around the three-wheeled, doorless metal frame of a roadster resting in the dirt front yard, then into the wide entrance hall.

"Make yourselves comfortable," Mrs. Brown said as she moved newspapers off the sofa and removed dirty glasses from the table. "I'll fetch some refreshment."

"May I help you, ma'am?"

"No, you sit and rest. Call me 'Ma Brown' like Eliza does. Or 'Ma' suits me fine."

We sat on the sofa. Thomas plucked a newspaper off the floor and began to read. I looked around at the thick walls, recessed windows, and saguaro-ribbed ceiling. It reminded me of our casita in Chihuahua. Clay pots, baskets, and odd pieces of machinery crowded shelves that lined the walls. Colorful Indian blankets were piled in corners next to boxes of parts—crank handles and metal tubes, wires, valves, and various caps and knobs. A bucket of nuts and bolts sat next to the door, and above it someone had pinned a newspaper clipping, *Travel Hints for Motorists*. I read the list of important tips: the use of chewing gum to mend a gas line, oatmeal or dried horse manure for a radiator leak, sliced onion to clear a windshield.

A gilt frame displayed a picture of the Brown family—Ma, her mottled-faced husband, and two boys.

"Papago and Pima baskets and pots," Thomas finally muttered from behind the front page. "Ma collects them." He waved his arm in an effort to explain the rest of the room. "Father's crazy over motorcars. Loves his gadgets."

He lifted a triangular arrangement of thin metal rods and spikes from the end table.

"This is his invention. A bread toaster. I don't know what it's doing in the sitting room."

He handed the toaster to me and returned to his newspaper. I looked at the contraption and set it back down. Ma Brown had been a long time in the kitchen.

"Do you think your mother needs help?"

Thomas looked up at the clock above the mantel. It was late afternoon, but the clock read 11:20.

"I suppose the Mexicans have come. She's probably forgotten about us. Let's go see."

I followed him into the kitchen. A Mexican woman stood at

a table slicing oranges into quarters and heaping them onto a platter. A great pot of beans bubbled on the stove. I looked out the back door. Several dozen Mexicans, mostly children, sat at two long tables in the dirt of the fenced yard. Ma was serving tamales out of a basket.

"Ma and Rosita serve a meal every day at four," Thomas said. "It's for the women and children or anyone who comes. They're refugees from the revolution. They come into town half-starved. There's hardly a cow left in parts of Sonora."

Ma bustled into the kitchen. "Josie, can you fill these bowls with beans and bring them out?"

She spoke in rapid Spanish to Rosita, the woman slicing oranges. I was surprised I understood her. I brought out the bowls and greeted the children. I thought of my little brothers and sisters and hoped someone was feeding them. After everyone left, Thomas and I cleared the table.

"That was good of you to speak to the children in Spanish, Josie," Ma said. "It makes them more comfortable."

"I know what it is to be homesick."

She nodded. "Have some tamales and beans, you two. You're surely famished after your journey."

While Thomas and I ate, Ma motored into town for a meeting.

We'd just returned to the sitting room when Mr. Brown clomped into the entry hall, pulled off his cap, and groaned. Trickles of sweat ran down the back of his neck. He pulled out a handkerchief, wiped his face and neck, and turned around.

"Holy Moses! I thought you were due tomorrow."

I couldn't place his accent.

Thomas cracked a smile and stood. His father bounded up to him and thumped his back.

"Welcome home, Son. You look well. Real well."

"Great to see you, Pop."

Mr. Brown was a big man with a wide, crooked nose that looked as if it had been broken more than once, thick lips, and pendulant ears. He looked smart in his policeman's uniform.

"So this is the foundling?" His deep voice boomed in the tiled room. "Welcome, Josie. Eliza wrote us about you. Said you've been a great help at the hotel. We've got a room here for you."

"Thank you, sir."

He strolled over to the mantle and removed the watch from his wrist.

"Excuse me, please," he said as he unbuttoned his jacket. "I'll go change me clothes."

Thomas stood expressionless. "Pop's from Ireland. Arrived in New Orleans when he was fourteen, then hopped a boat to Galveston, where he met Ma. He hated the humidity, so they settled here, but he can't tolerate the heat either."

I could hear Mr. Brown rummaging in the kitchen. He emerged with a napkin tucked into a collarless work shirt, a plate of cold fried chicken, tamales, a mound of beans, and a quart jar of lemonade. He lowered himself into a high-backed wing chair, set his plate on his lap, and bit into a drumstick. He asked about Ma.

"Gone to a meeting," Thomas said. "Something for the war effort."

"The Liberty Club, probably. How's Eliza's father?"

"Don't know exactly."

"I haven't heard yet how it happened."

Thomas plunked down on the sofa. "We telephoned Susannah early this morning. He was cranking his motorcar when apoplexy hit him like a bolt of lightning. Keeled over. They just brought him home from the hospital. I'd like to motor over in a while."

"Of course." Mr. Brown took a gulp of lemonade. "So what are you going to do about the war, Son? Registration day was June fifth. It's illegal not to register."

"I don't want to fight. I know too much, Pop. It's carnage. That's why I went to the Jornada. Hard to find me there."

I sat up. So that was why Thomas and Eliza had leased the hotel in Cutter. They were running from the war.

"It's not wise to be a maverick just now."

"I don't want to serve as fodder for the fortunes of the munitions companies. You heard about the mustard gas?"

"Brutal."

"One whiff and your throat burns. Then you go into a stupor and can't fight. Your lungs fill with fluid and then . . ."

They stopped talking. Mr. Brown put down his fork.

"I could probably get you into the civil service."

"I could go back to the Jornada and get lost somewhere. Or I could head to Mexico."

"Nogales is a rough place. Full of out-of-work miners, a lot of no-good men too lazy to fight, and idealistic kids like you. The draft board will be making raids down there, sooner or later. And Mexico's still unstable." Mr. Brown put his large hands together and cracked his knuckles. "All I know is someone's going to check up on you now that you're in town. You put me in a bind, Son. Me an officer of the law, and you breaking it."

Thomas said nothing.

Mr. Brown took his plate into the kitchen and passed

through the sitting room again on his way to the door. "I want to get at that carburetor."

He disappeared behind the metal hulk in the yard.

Thomas stepped up to the mantle and read his father's watch. "It's past seven. Let's go see Eliza."

We took Mr. Brown's working motor buggy. The car sputtered along and then quit in the middle of the street. Thomas hopped out and adjusted some wires. Then he got back into the driver's seat and explained what he was doing as he placed the gas and spark levels even. He jumped out again, pulled the ring on the choke wire, and turned the crank. It didn't move. He swore.

"Hope I don't flood the carburetor."

He adjusted the choke again, cranked the engine, and it coughed to a start. He leaped into the driver's seat.

"Heap of junk, the Model H. Pop bought it from the Sears catalog. It's given him trouble since day one."

Something was still not right. As we jolted along, the car backfired. People stopped and stared as we jerked with each small explosion. We finally shimmied up to Eliza's house.

"I'm glad you've come." She showed us into the parlor. "Father's awake but hasn't spoken. We've been feeding him teaspoons of broth."

Susannah, a taller, clear-faced version of Eliza, popped her head into the room. "I'll stay with Father while you visit, Sister."

She disappeared behind the door.

Eliza looked my way. "Susannah's shy. I'll introduce you when she feels more comfortable."

She sat in the love seat, and Thomas squeezed in next to her. I found a chair.

"The doctor said it'll be some time before we know how much Father will recover."

She looked worried. Thomas put his arm around her. She rested her head against his shoulder and turned to me.

"What do you think of Ma Brown?"

"I haven't seen much of her."

Eliza laughed like a bell. "That doesn't surprise me. She's involved with the Liberty Club and the women's suffrage association." Eliza started counting on her fingers. "And she's a member of the National Women's Party, the Ladies' Guild at St. Augustine's, volunteers with the Red Cross, and has her four-o'-clock meals for the refugees. I don't know where she finds the time. Then again, she avoids chores that keep most women occupied at home." She glanced up at Thomas.

"She's not what you'd call domestic. She has difficulty serving a meal at a regular hour—except to the Mexicans. Thank goodness Rosita's well organized. Ma can't keep a schedule.."

Thomas nodded. "Mother's an eccentric gem."

"Josie, I'd love to show you around Tucson when things have settled. I'll take you to the cinema, and we have dances every month at the Knights of Columbus. But for now, I'm needed here. Susannah's worn out."

"Is there anything I can do to help?"

Eliza shook her head. Thomas leaned forward, kissed her forehead, and stroked her hair. Susannah tiptoed into the parlor.

"Excuse me, Eliza. We need to lift Father."

Eliza and Thomas jumped up.

"Can I help?" Thomas said.

"No, we can manage. He's light as a feather. You go home, but come see me tomorrow." Eliza gave him a peck on the cheek and hurried to help her sister.

We rattled home, slowed by only a few stalls.

Ma arrived back shortly after.

"The meeting went well. I would've been here sooner, but my motorcar had a flat, which, thankfully, the apothecary was able to repair. We've planned a bake sale for Saturday to raise funds for the troops. We've each pledged to use no more than a cup of sugar and two cups of wheat flour in our recipes. Now for supper."

She marched into the kitchen. I hurried after.

"I'll fry up some chops. Peel a couple carrots for me, will you, Josie? And there must be some tamales left from this afternoon. I'll warm them up."

It was ten o'clock by the time we sat down to supper. I had little appetite so late, but Thomas and Mr. Brown ate heartily.

By the time we were through, I was sleepy and retired to my room. Strains of heated conversation between Thomas and his parents filtered in from the sitting room—the words *war*, *conscription*, *Mexico*, and *Eliza* rising above others. I ran my hand over my harmonica's smooth cover plate and brushed my lips over its wooden comb, comforted to be holding something familiar. I played low notes softly while they talked on.

2

The next morning, Thomas fried eggs and sliced tomatoes for breakfast while Ma juiced grapefruits.

"They're rationing in earnest now," Ma said. "They're suggesting two wheatless days, two porkless days, and one beefless day a week. Of course, for the poor of this country, going meatless is nothing new. And sugar! Now *that* will be a sacrifice for your father and his sweet tooth."

She handed around glasses of juice.

"We're expected to plant a garden. Thomas, I'd like you to till up a plot in the side yard."

"I'll dig it today."

"This is the morning I help at the mission. Would you like to come, Josie? We can always use more hands."

I was glad to have something to do.

"Do you want a lift into town, Thomas?"

"No, I'll take the streetcar to Eliza's. I need to talk to her."

Ma gave him a piercing look.

"I imagine you do. You need to make plans, you two."

⚓

Before we left, Thomas and I picked lemons and oranges from the side yard while Ma packed several baskets with dried beans and tins of vegetables. We stopped at the mercantile to buy Ovaltine, canned milk, and coffee, and at the druggist's for cough elixir and fever powder.

As we shopped, she told me about the mission. "Health seekers, many with tuberculosis, have flocked to Tucson. 'The Land of New Lungs,' they advertise. 'Go west and breathe again!' Reverend Comstock ministers to the sick in Tent City—those too poor to pay for decent lodging or hospital care. His Adams Street Mission started with three tents, but now it's in a building."

She rummaged through her purse to pay.

"We members of the Red Cross and Ladies' Guild try to help the good reverend out. Some of the consumptives are weak from poor nutrition. Many are lonely."

We loaded our goods, stopped at Felix's station for gasoline, then left the paved streets for a dirt road. Ma handed me a handkerchief against the dust. She pointed out the bulky university building, and then past it, on a stretch of desert, a jumble of canvas shelters.

"That's it," Ma announced. "Tent City."

In the mission building, the reverend's plump nurse-assistant greeted us. Sweltering in her uniform and cap, flicking a fan with her thick wrist, she asked us to visit the residents in the back section who had been missed by the previous volunteers.

"There's been hardly a visitor of late, with this war on and everybody being asked to do so much. Our lungers are being forgotten."

"We'll be on our way, then," Ma said.

We chugged down a dusty tent-lined street. Most of the tents were one-room structures; the worst were makeshift hovels of canvas and boards. A few of the tent houses were substantial, with wooden sides and steel roofs above the canvas, some with front porches, kitchens, and faucets out back. Ma explained that they'd been improved over the years by a succession of tenants who'd moved on.

"Where do they move to?"

"Either recovery or death—occasionally by suicide."

I shuddered.

We stopped at the end of the complex. A dry tubercular cough sounded from the nearest tent, and from across the way, another lunger answered.

"They're always worse in the morning," Ma said.

We lugged a basket down a narrow path to the back row of tents.

"I'm glad you're strong. This is no work for weaklings."

She knocked on the splintered door of a one-room tent.

We heard a cough and a woman's voice. "Enter."

Ma pushed open the door. A puff of hot air hit us. I couldn't help but stare at the man lying on the bed before us. He was chalk white but for a flush of pink over prominent cheekbones. His sunken eyes glittered. The fleshy parts of his body had wasted away. His hands lay limp, his nails gray.

We set the basket down. A gaunt woman rose from a chair next to the bed.

"Thank you for coming." Her eyes darted to take in the basket. "He's still frightfully weak from the journey."

"We've brought you provisions," Ma said. "Josie, would you take them from the basket?"

I set beans, vegetables, oranges, and coffee on the table.

"I'm afraid I don't have anything to offer you. Not even a chair."

"Never mind," Ma said. "Tell us where you've journeyed from."

"We're from Ohio. My Burt got the consumption over a year ago. We believed he was improving, but last fall he started coughing to beat the dickens. We tried everything. Eggs and cream, honey oil, prussic acid. But not the gold treatment. Couldn't afford that. Doc finally told us we had to get him somewhere warm and dry."

The man began to cough again. She went to his side as the hacking racked his emaciated body. He gasped and closed his eyes. She repositioned his pillow.

"Hope we didn't get here too late."

"When he's rested, when he can get up again, it might do him good to sit in the sun outside," Ma said, "where there's more air."

The woman flung out her arms. "We had such a pretty little house in Akron. Thought we'd be able to find somewhere better to stay than this."

She looked ready to cry.

"Why don't you step out for a spell, and I'll watch over Burt," Ma suggested. "Josie will take a turn with you."

The woman shrugged. "Some air might do me good."

I walked next to her as she talked about the garden she'd left, her snapdragons and delphiniums. She sighed as we circled a row of tents and paused when we heard a brassy cough from behind a canvas wall.

"Sounds like a child."

Ma was singing when we returned. Burt was asleep. Ma moved toward the door.

"Perhaps after a few weeks in the dry air, your husband will be feeling better."

"Oh, he's not my husband," the woman said. "Burt's my son."

Ma blinked. "Bless you both. Will you help me with the basket, Josie?"

"Have you any elixir to spare?" the woman asked. "They say

it's the poppy flower in it that does wonders for Burt's cough at night."

Ma handed her a bottle.

"Oh, he's further gone than I thought," Ma whispered as we hauled our basket away from the tent. "So little hope now."

The heat was getting to me. The basket felt heavy.

The next tent was larger than the last, with a separate room for the young woman whose husband and three children attended to her. Sitting up in her bed, she looked healthier than Burt, with high-colored cheeks and meat on her bones. We left the family fever powder and food supplies.

We dropped into a dozen other tents that morning, each a variation of misfortune and despair.

"Aren't there hospitals they can go to?" I said as I set the empty basket in the car.

"There are. But for the soul who arrives with few resources expecting a quick cure, it's a sad affair." Ma shook her head. "And there are hundreds arriving every year."

"Is there a chance a volunteer might catch the disease?"

"A chance. Many are scared to get near this place. The afflicted are treated like lepers by some." She looked at my worried face. "Don't fret. Tucsonans rarely get the illness. They say it's the sunshine."

She pulled on her driving gloves.

"You're not going to catch this plague, Josie." She tilted her head and studied my face. "You'll have a different battle. Don't ask how I know. These things come to me."

It struck me that it was merely a wall of canvas and the goodness of others that could shield a person with little money from destitution. I was vulnerable, too.

Ma walked to the front of the vehicle and turned the crank.

The engine exploded, coughed smoke, and shook with life. She climbed in and adjusted her goggles. As we sped home, I looked over at Ma Brown, so strong and brave and set to take on the world. I clutched the dashboard and braced myself against the bumps on the road and those future troubles she seemed so sure of.

3

Ma Brown wasn't always on the go. Some mornings she stayed home and caught up on her letter writing. She cleared magazines off the table and set out a box of stationery, a bottle of ink, a fountain pen, and a stack of letters tied with ribbon. Reaching into her handbag, she pulled out a pair of horn-rimmed glasses. When she put them on, her eyes grew to twice their size.

"Do you write letters, Josie?"

"Sometimes."

"Thomas mentioned you come from a large family, but you've become separated. Mine has also dispersed to far corners, but we've been able to stay close through letters. I write weekly to my son in Portland and my sister in Los Angeles."

She placed a sheet of buff-colored stationery on the table and picked up her pen.

"If you want to stay connected, you'll have to become a writer. Tell your family the details of your life, and they'll feel part of it."

She opened the drawer of a side table and handed me a pen and ink. "Here you are."

She dipped the tip of her pen into the ink and pumped the silver handle until the reservoir filled. She placed her freckled hand squarely over her paper and began to pen her lines, stopping at the margin to blow on the ink. She paused now and then to reread a phrase, mouthing the words to herself in a breathy whisper.

Yes, letters were a way to keep us close. I started a letter to Irene. I thanked her for the beef and cabbage and asked whether she and Earl and the children were well.

Ma shifted in her seat, signed her name—Helena—with a flourish, slipped the folded sheets into an envelope, and picked up another.

"Thomas doesn't tell me much. I'm curious to know how you've become separated."

I hesitated. How much should I tell? Ma looked like a wise owl behind her round frames. I could trust her.

"My mother died a year ago last February."

I explained that Ida and Irene had already left home, and the rest of us moved to Bisbee.

"How did your mother die?"

I told her about Mama's illness. "It was my fault."

Ma looked up from her stationery. "How could that be?"

I hadn't gotten her to a hospital, I explained. I hadn't known she could be cured.

Ma removed her glasses, and her eyes shrank to normal size. "Glory be, child. Where was your father?"

"Running the train."

"Decisions about medical care are adult matters, not those of a girl. Who knows whether your mother would have lived, even if she'd made it to a hospital? She might not have survived the journey. She may have died on an operating table or in a room alone. Would you have wanted that for her? You may absolve yourself of blame, child." She shook her head. "And to think that you've been harboring such notions."

I told how I'd left my younger siblings.

She stood and placed her arm around my shoulders.

"Eliza did write me about that. Those were circumstances beyond your control. In leaving Bisbee, you safeguarded your own life, dear. It's time to forgive yourself and move forward."

She held me close. I leaned my head against her, soothed in her embrace.

"I'll bring us some iced tea. It's uncommonly hot today."

She went to the kitchen.

She was right. Nothing could have been done for Mama. And I'd been forced to leave my family. I wanted to believe that her words were true.

Ma Brown looked beautiful walking into the room with the tray. Lemon slices floated in two tall glasses of amber liquid. She settled herself to write again. I tried to think of what to tell Irene next.

The Browns have been good to me.

I finished my letter, and Ma mailed it on her way to the Ladies' Guild meeting. I would write to everyone. Perhaps I still had a role in my family.

4

The next morning, Thomas marched into the house with both Tucson newspapers under his arm.

"This news concerns your family." He plopped onto the sofa and opened the morning *Citizen.* "There's been trouble in Bisbee. They've run the strikers out of town."

All I could think of was Papa. I hoped he hadn't gotten mixed up in the strike.

Thomas threw down the paper and jumped to his feet. His face was red. I'd never seen him angry.

"What next? Hardworking men call a strike to improve their conditions, and they get forced out of town at gunpoint. The strikebreakers call the unions 'anti-American,' when all they want is a decent life."

Ma came out of the kitchen where she'd been making a cake for the bake sale.

"Thomas, what's this about?"

"Folks have gone crazy since this war began. If you dare question anything or venture an opinion contrary to the established line, you're branded a slacker, a German, or a communist sympathizer."

"Folks are frightened."

"Does that give them the right to stop thinking like rational human beings? They justify their brutality by saying it interferes with the war effort. Bull!"

"Calm down and tell me what's happened!"

"The strike in Bisbee was busted up by vigilantes with guns. They loaded the men into cattle cars and dumped them in the desert in New Mexico."

"Josie, your family's there. Is your father a member of the union? Was he on strike?"

"He's not a Wobbly. I believe he's still running the train, but I don't know. He's a sympathizer."

Thomas picked up the paper.

"Says here supporters were deported too."

If Papa were sent away, what would happen to my brothers and sisters? I went numb. I couldn't think.

Ma wiped her hands on her apron. "Is there a list of deportees?"

"They don't even know how many men were evacuated. Hundreds, it's alleged. It's all rather vague."

"Oh, those poor families." Ma went to find her glasses. She put them on and picked up the *Star*. As she read, her magnified eyes grew larger. Thomas threw down his paper and stomped out the door. I picked up the *Citizen* to read for myself.

Ma jumped up from her chair. "I'm going to call Jack at the police station to see if he can find out the status of your father. What's his given name?"

"He goes by Harry."

When I read the story, I felt sick to my stomach. The town described in the paper seemed a different Bisbee from the one I knew. How could the management treat the miners so badly after building them a library, a hospital, schools, and sponsoring their picnics? Especially now that copper prices were at an all-time high? Thomas was right. The world had lost its senses.

I could hear Ma dialing the telephone, and the crash of the earpiece.

"Oh, these confounded inventions meant to save time! The lines are all tied up. I'll stop by the station on my way to the bake sale. Oh, the cakes! I have to get them in the oven or they'll be late."

She dashed into the kitchen.

I walked to town and sent a telegram to Charlie. PAPA WITH YOU? EVERYONE OK? I wasn't sure that it would get through. I sent another to Irene: STRIKERS FORCED OUT OF BISBEE. WHERE ARE PAPA AND CHILDREN?

There was nothing more to do.

That afternoon Ma returned from the bake sale elated. All the cakes had sold, and the Red Cross had raised enough to buy cotton for bandages and wool for socks. We sat down to an early supper.

Mr. Brown told us that he wasn't able to learn the names of those deported.

"It's a mess down there. They've got armed guards surrounding the town and have closed it to reporters. No one's getting in or out."

I couldn't take another bite.

"Aren't you feeling well, Josie?" Ma said.

"I'm worried."

"If your father was sent out, surely someone's caring for your siblings."

I hoped our neighbor, Mrs. Dabrowski, or Asa had taken them in. If only I'd stayed in Bisbee. Oh, thoughtless me.

─✧─

Ma had baked an extra cake for us, a stack cake. It was five thin layers, unfrosted to save on sugar but dusted with powdered sugar. Thomas and Mr. Brown dug into the cake but stopped eating after the first taste. I took a cautious bite. It was the worst cake I'd ever had—dry as cardboard, with a bitter aftertaste. Ma looked at our faces.

"I was able to follow the recipe to a certain degree. I used a cup of molasses and a half cup of sugar. It should be sweet enough. I used oleo, but that shouldn't matter, and a cup and a half of corn flour and an equal part barley flour to substitute for white flour."

She chewed a forkful.

"Oh, my. I can taste the bicarbonate of soda. I was so disturbed by the news, I must have added it twice. Or did I leave out the baking powder altogether?"

Mr. Brown suggested that the next time she needed to conserve wheat flour and sugar, she should bake a smaller cake.

She agreed. "A fine suggestion, Jack."

I helped Ma clear the dishes and the uneaten cake.

"I wonder if the Mexicans would like it?" she muttered as she opened the spigot to collect water for the dishwashing. I imagined the reactions of the unfortunate family who'd bought Ma's other stack cake at the bake sale. I giggled. Ma caught my eye and laughed, too.

I lay in bed that night and fretted about my little brothers and sisters. I remembered the motherless girls I'd seen at the train station so long ago. I didn't want to think of what could happen. I tried to picture them surrounded by white, protective light.

5

On Sunday, the Browns went to church.

"Josie, you're welcome to come with us, or I can take you to Reverend Comstock's church. You mentioned your family was Baptist."

I didn't want to go to church. I wanted to be alone.

"I'll stay here."

"I understand. We'll pray for your family. And for Eliza's father, of course."

It was peaceful in the empty house. I washed my hair, wrote a letter to Ida, and read a story in *Scribner's*. I sent Sally, Bethel, Stevie, and Charlie all the pink love I could muster. I sent white thoughts to Eliza's father, to her soldier brother, and to Thomas, who didn't know what to do about the war. I sent protective energy to the sick people in Tent City. I even prayed for Papa.

⚜

When the Browns returned, they brought Eliza. Mr. Brown suggested we take an excursion out of town for relief from the heat and to help get our minds off our worries.

"There's little we can do, Josie, until we get word."

Eliza and Thomas headed into the kitchen to pack a picnic lunch.

We loaded into the runabout and headed northeast toward Mount Lemmon. About ten miles from town, in the lower reaches of the mountains, we reached Sabino Canyon, parked, and followed a path by the creek. Paloverde, mesquite, and acacia clustered along the streambed, making welcome shade. We found a cool spot under a desert willow. Thomas and Mr. Brown headed off to explore one of the trails heading into the hills. Eliza, Ma, and I settled in the grass, took out our handwork, and breathed in the fresh air. Bees hummed in the bushes, and hummingbirds buzzed our heads. A curve-billed thrasher called out to its mate. Eliza dropped her work and lay down.

"If only every day were this peaceful," she said. "If only the war were over, and Father were well. Thomas and I would settle down here in Tucson and start our family. I'd have a baby right now if it were a different world."

"To have children is to strengthen your bones," Ma said drowsily.

"I think of my little brother fighting in France." Eliza looked up between the leaves at the jagged fragments of sky. "Then I think of Thomas, who refuses to fight. Part of me wants to convince him to enlist because it's the right thing to do. Another part wants him to hide away because I couldn't bear it if something were to happen to him." She sighed. "We all know he'd make a dismal soldier."

"Thomas has always been stubborn. I couldn't even get him to take a nap when he was a toddler. These are hard times with difficult choices." Ma pulled herself up out of the grass. "How's your father doing?"

"He still hasn't spoken. He uses hand signals to tell us what he needs."

"Don't give up hope," Ma said. "I see Jack and Thomas heading back. You two relax. I'll set out the picnic."

I sat at the edge of the creek and bathed my feet. Crickets

ticked in the tall grass. Sparrows flitted in the trees. But their bright calls couldn't allay my fears.

-⚓-

The day after our excursion, I received a telegram: NO NEWS FROM BISBEE. WILL DO WHAT WE CAN. IRENE

"You'll need to keep busy," Ma advised. "It's all you can do."

I helped her serve meals to the refugees, accompanied her to Tent City, and began a scarf for a soldier. Some Tucson boys who'd been conscripted months before received postcards to report for military duty. The war was coming closer.

6

M r. Brown read the paper each night while sucking on pieces of horehound candy.

"The world's going to hell in a handbasket," he said. "Massacres of troops in Europe, and now this Bolshevik revolution in Russia. They didn't even have the decency to let the czar's children leave the country. They're still in prison."

He held out the paper with his trunk-like arms and told me about Bisbee.

"The town's under martial law. Hundreds of strikers deported. Sympathizers too. Two killed—a deputy and a miner. Tch, tch." The lilt of his voice softened the harshness of the news.

Another evening, Mr. Brown lifted his head from behind the print and groaned. "'Tis a shame. Another race riot in Houston. This time at Fort Logan." A look of disgust marred his usual kind demeanor. "A dozen white civilians killed, and dozens of Negro soldiers arrested. Says they'll be hanged if found guilty." He shook his head. "Oh, but the world is upside-down and surely."

"People are afraid," Ma said.

"Folks scared of change can be brutal," Mr. Brown tossed back from behind the page.

I considered those vigilantes in Bisbee and fumed at what their fear had made them do.

Finally, I received a three-page letter from Irene, with the news I'd been waiting for.

It's been wild as a bronco ride around here, but the children are safe with us. Papa appeared the afternoon of July 16th. He'd been on that train sent out of Bisbee. What a tale he told of the deportation.

Papa had described the militia with white armbands and guns who'd pounded on the neighbors' door the morning of the twelfth. Mr. Dabrowski had been on the picket line, and they had orders to arrest him. They roughed him up so badly that he twisted his ankle. Papa helped him limp to the post office and then the two miles to the Warren ball field.

A lady handed Papa a loaf of bread. Some wives shouted and threw stones at the militia, while a Wobbly organizer called for the strikers to stay strong. But those vigilantes formed a chute and forced the striking men onto a freight train. Papa helped Mr. D. up, and then they slammed the door, trapping them inside. The train didn't stop until the next day near Columbus. Papa knew a conductor at the depot, who got him on a train out.

Irene described how Earl had gone to Bisbee for the children, though he'd had a heck of a time getting in. Fortunately, Mrs. D. had cared for our little ones.

They arrived a week ago. Papa's gone back to work, since they're desperate for railroad men with this war on. Charlie's grown almost as tall as Earl and is a big help. My house is full to the brim.

I stared at the letter. It was hard to believe the strange and frightening tale. But my family was safe. I hoped they could stay with Irene for good.

⚜

That August brought blazing heat and mornings helping Ma with her volunteer work. Evenings when Ma didn't have a meeting to attend, we wrote letters or convened for "letter reading"—sharing our news from family and friends.

One warm evening, I crocheted while Ma wrote a letter to a soldier whose name she'd gotten off the Red Cross list. Some of the boys overseas had no mothers to write to them.

Ma lifted her pen and removed her glasses. "Do you have good memories of your mother, Josie?"

I unwound an arm's length of yarn from the ball on my lap. "I do."

She rested her forearm on the table. "What do you remember best?"

Oh, so many good things. Mama's soft hazel eyes, the scent of rose water, her husky hum to calm her babies, her dark head bent over her sewing, the warmth of her hand in mine, the creak of her rocker that lulled me to sleep . . .

"Mama was pretty and kind, and she baked the lightest biscuits ever. She was a fine seamstress too." I set down my crochet hook. "Before she died, she told me to remember to sew on the buttons. I don't know what she meant. She knew I didn't sew."

Ma Brown put a hand to her temple and pulled back a strand of hair.

"Sew on the buttons," she muttered, while staring at a spot on the coffee table. "A button seems like a small thing, but a missing button makes a suit look shabby. A top button fastened against a winter chill can prevent a child from getting ill." She placed her fingers on one of the plain buttons of her shirtwaist and looked up at me. "I'd venture to say she was asking you to mind the details, to take care of the little things and the little ones. The small things we do are surely as important as the others. They can make a difference."

I went back to my crocheting. Of course. Mama wanted me to take care of our family. And then guilt engulfed me, like a cloud. Overworked Irene was doing my job.

Ma picked up her pen to write but held it in the air.

"I suppose you've noticed that Thomas is no longer with us. If anyone asks you, you don't know where he is."

"Did he go to Mexico?"

"He went back to Cutter. He mentioned wallpaper he needed to claim. And he needs to find someone to sublease the hotel. I don't believe Eliza will be joining him." She looked me in the eye. "He's there to be out of the way, so to speak, perhaps until the end of the war. Thomas tells me the Jornada is a place where one can easily get lost. Is that true?"

Yes, the Jornada del Muerto was a place of loss—of vanished hopes and forgotten lives, of scarce water and fading towns, of outlaws on the lam, of scattered families, and of my lost mother. It seemed a good place for Thomas to hide.

"I believe so."

"Oh, a mother does worry."

Ma donned her glasses and repositioned her fountain pen.

"And what comforting words can I write," she said under her breath, "to an eighteen-year-old Nebraska farm boy who finds himself on a ship of war in a stormy sea?"

—✥—

On September 5, a crowd gathered at Armory Park to honor the first Tucson draftees preparing to leave for training at Camp Funston in Kansas. Important men gave speeches and folks cheered, and each of the soldiers received a wristwatch from the *Citizen* newspaper. Four days later, the same jubilant crowd gathered at Union Station to wave the soldiers goodbye, as though they were leaving for a picnic. I stood and watched but didn't shout or wave. Train departures had taken on a sad note for me. Out of respect for the superstition I still half believed, I didn't stay to watch the train go. I turned and hurried home.

A few days later, I celebrated my sixteenth birthday. Eliza and Susannah brought over a lemon chiffon cake that contained an unpatriotic amount of sugar and white flour. Shy Susannah smiled but hardly spoke a word. They gave me a painted paper fan, and Ma gifted me a new shirtwaist of thin lawn with lace at the collar and a practical linen skirt.

"That's for you to go to classes in."

I asked whether I shouldn't go to work instead. I wanted to pay my way. I wasn't sure of my position in her home now that Thomas had gone.

"Certainly not. You left your sister so you could return to school. Classes start soon. Eliza will take you to register."

Eliza and I took the streetcar a mile east of downtown to the university stop. The large brick building housed schools of agriculture and mining and offered classes in the liberal arts. Since there were so few high schools in Arizona, the university offered classes to prepare students for advanced classes. I chose typing and English grammar, skills that might be useful. Eliza paid my fees and bought me the textbooks. I promised to pay her back.

"Let's celebrate, Josie. We'll get an ice cream, and I'll show you around town."

We took the streetcar downtown and walked down Congress Street. As we enjoyed our cones, Eliza showed me the opera house, the Carnegie library, and the meeting house recently built for the Women's Club.

"I'm thinking of joining when Father's well. He's walking and talking. But queerly." She lowered her voice. "He only speaks German. He knew it as a boy but didn't speak it at home. The doctor says that can happen with brain injuries." She frowned. "We're afraid to take him out. With this war on, we don't want anyone to hear his German."

I laughed and then stopped myself. Poor Eliza.

We looked at the shoes at Drachman's and then stopped into Kress's, where I teased that I was going to buy her a German dictionary. I bought notebooks, pencils, a pen, and ink. Back at the Browns', I leafed through my books, keen to begin classes.

Every morning at eight, I took the streetcar to the university. The grammar class was boring, the typing more interesting. Our teacher taught us the parts of our Remingtons and how to change the ribbon. She pointed to a large diagram of the keyboard in the front of the classroom. Our homework was to memorize the placement of the letters.

The next day, our typewriters had hoods over the keys, so we couldn't see them. We opened our books, felt for the correct letters shown on the diagram, and typed what was on our page. The room filled with the clack of keys and the ring of carriage returns. I was terribly slow. I failed the first few typing tests, but after two weeks, I no longer needed to consult the chart.

I wrote Ida that I was learning to type. She replied that she was moving to San Diego. The city was booming, and she was sure to find work. Aunt JoJane had finally given her permission to leave St. Louis.

It was the violence last July that convinced her. A mob of white people on the East Side attacked the Negros— blameless men and their families. They hanged three, set fires, and drove thousands from their homes. I feel ashamed to be an Anglo here. I long for sun and dry heat. I'll be eighteen soon—ready to be on my own.

Write me, dear Sister, I replied. *Tell me all about California, the sea, and your new life at its edge.*

8

I read my grammar book from cover to cover, and Mama's corrections finally made sense. But sentence diagramming vexed me.

"Do you know Philip, Josie?" Mr. Brown asked one night at supper. "He's the boy next door with the clubfoot. He works at Western Union and says they're hiring. There's a test on Saturday. Those who pass will be trained to be telegraph operators. What do you think?"

"I doubt they'd hire me. I don't type well yet."

"It's an aptitude test to see if you can be taught."

"It would be a good job," said Ma. "You could work half-time and still attend school."

I decided to try. Mr. Brown brought home the application, and I took the test. Western Union sent me a telegram the next week. I'd qualified for the monthlong training program. The four-week full-day course was to begin on Monday.

"I'll have to quit school for the training," I told Ma.

"They'll teach you to type and pay you while you learn."

I dropped my courses. Those compound-complex sentences never got diagrammed, and I didn't care. I was thrilled to earn a salary. I would pay back Eliza and send money to Irene to help her care for our family.

Twenty girls trained together. We were taught to type using the university method. Soon we were given old telegrams to copy. This time, I was at the head of the class. When we were moved to the main room, we typed at long rows of machines. The room echoed with our tapping and clicking. The words came out on a piece of paper on a roller that I read and typed onto telegram paper. When I got quick at receiving, I learned to send. All employees worked eight-hour shifts. I was assigned the night shift.

I wanted to work days, but everyone wanted that shift. It would take a year or more before I would have a choice. I started on the Tucson–Phoenix wire and earned twelve dollars a week. Evenings, Mr. Brown drove me to work, and I returned by streetcar in the mornings.

My first night, I sent messages for an hour, received telegrams from the type wheel, and then took a ten-minute break. I sent for another hour, then received again. During my "lunch" at four in the morning, I sat at the break room table, put my head on my crossed arms, and closed my eyes. A girl tapped me on the shoulder, looked at my bleary eyes, and laughed.

"Oh, you've got it written all over you. You're new. You'll become a night owl soon enough, but be careful. If you make too many mistakes, they'll write up a report, and you'll be out the door."

She unscrewed the lid of her thermos and poured me coffee. I downed the bitter stuff and was able to stay awake for the rest of the shift, with only a few mistakes. I nearly fell asleep in the streetcar.

When I walked into the house, Mr. Brown was leaving for work. "Here's our working girl. How was your first night?"

"Long," I said, and fell into bed.

After that night, I was never so tired at work. The Browns' adobe was cool and dark, good for sleep during the warm days. I missed going with Ma on her volunteer missions but awoke in time to help her serve the refugees and eat supper with the Browns at odd hours.

⁓

In November, I received a letter from Irene.

> *The children have gone back to Bisbee. They opened the town after three months of martial law. Papa told me to send them—he wants the boys to go to school there.*
>
> *The war has been kind to the ranchers in the Jornada. Daddy Graham sold a thousand horses to the US Cavalry and bought himself a Ford. The beef prices have never been higher. We made a tidy profit after the fall cattle drive. We're saving for that automobile Earl has been wanting.*
>
> *P.S. Papa will take care of the children. Don't worry.*

But I did. Irene didn't understand that her partial attention was far better than Papa's benign neglect.

⁓

That night I had a nightmare. Stevie, Bethel, and Sally were wandering the streets of Bisbee. Sally had a rash on her hands, Bethel's hair was a mass of snarls, and Stevie was covered with bruises from alleyway boxing. Men with guns and armbands made them march to a canyon, where they found Charlie sleep-walking. Bethel stood at the edge, a hairbrush in her hand, calling my name. I awoke and cried in my pillow.

But I didn't want to go back. The "lightning wire" seemed a miracle to me, and I was a part of that modern marvel. I was good at my job and received approving nods from my supervisor. The tap of the machines reminded me of the beat of Mama's Singer. My life had a new rhythm.

9

I wasn't supposed to read the messages I sent or received but couldn't help myself. Many were mundane, but each day messages of sickness and loss spilled from the machines. To improve its reputation, WU started a campaign encouraging people to send good news messages and flowers by wire—a joy to transmit. Reading the wires informed me about the war. I began to read the papers and discussed the news with the Browns.

Before Christmas, I received a letter from Ida. She'd found work at the San Diego courthouse. She'd met a soldier named Teal, an aerial photographer. They'd gone to a movie together and to a picnic at Balboa Park. She believed she might be in love.

That Christmas of 1917, I wired my first savings to Papa, asking him to buy coal and a treat for the children. I'd crocheted wool scarves and sent one to everyone in my family. I went to Christmas Mass with the Browns. We took two cars, and when we stopped to pick up Eliza, Susannah, and their father, we were shocked to find Thomas at their house.

"He got in last night," Eliza gushed. "He's the best Christmas present ever."

"I'm only here for the holiday," Thomas said. "I don't think the law will corner me on Christmas."

I'd seen St. Augustine Cathedral from Stone Avenue but had never been inside. It was a lofty brick building with squared-off sections on either side of the arched doorway. Ma explained that the diocese had run out of money to complete the two French towers.

It felt good to be sitting in a pew with the Browns and Eliza's family. The yellow candlelight, incense, thrum of the organ, and drone of Latin carried me to another place. Mama seemed near. I joined the Browns in "Joy to the World," thankful for their kindness.

After Mass, we went to Eliza's for a goose supper. I asked Thomas what was new in the Jornada.

"I sold the lease on the hotel. The new owners are almost ready for business."

Eliza looked up. "And what about the wallpaper?"

Thomas squeezed her hand. "The man agreed to buy that too."

"We did all that work for nothing."

He gave her a steady look. "The world will be a different place when this war's over. What we wanted may have changed."

"Where are you living, Son?" Mr. Brown said.

"In a horse camp in the San Andres. This time of year, it's dead quiet up there and cold as heck. I'm studying up on electricity. I want to open an appliance store after the war."

"It's the way things are headed. You can sell washing machines and vacuum cleaners. And repair them too. I've heard they've electrified the ice box."

The men talked about machines, while we women discussed local efforts to win the vote for women. Ma Brown was active in that cause too.

Thomas returned to the Jornada the day after Christmas.

"He tells me it won't be long till the end of the war," Eliza complained the next week. "But nearly all the news is bad, especially now with Russia out. I can't stand having Thomas so far away. Sometimes I want to jump on that train and hide out with him. All day long I take care of Father and try to coax him to speak English. 'How do you do,' and 'I'm pleased to meet you.' Then he sleeps and forgets it. I still can't take him out for fear he'll be called a Hun." Eliza sighed. "I need some fun. Let's go dancing."

—⚜—

Several weeks later, we went to a dance at the Knights of Columbus. The hall was crowded with soldiers on leave, students from the university, town girls, and older couples. I'd hardly walked in when I was asked to dance. All evening, I never lacked a partner for jitneys, spotlight dances, and slow moonlight dances to romantic tunes—"At the Jazz Band Ball" and "Dallas Blues." Eliza and I found each other between songs to rest our feet and sip orangeade. The faces of all the young men in khaki brown and civilian white began to blur, but near the end of the evening, I realized I'd danced with one brown-eyed soldier three times.

He asked me to dance the last slow song, "After You've Gone," told me his name was Richard and that he had a week's leave before he'd be sent to Europe. He invited me to go to a movie.

"I'll have to ask Mr. Brown, my guardian," I said.

At work that night, I replayed the music in my head and thought about Richard, eager to see him again.

In the morning, Mr. Brown asked me how I'd liked my first dance at the hall.

"Wonderful. I met a soldier. He's invited me to a movie."

He shook his head. "We don't know the boy. You're just sixteen. You may go to the dances with Eliza, but as long as I'm responsible for you, you'll not be going on dates with soldiers."

I was crushed. When Richard telephoned, I declined the movie. He said it was all right, and we'd see each other at the next dance, but I knew he'd be gone before there would be another. I sat in bed, quietly played my Hohner, and thought about Richard and overprotective Mr. Brown. I decided to find another place to live.

At Western Union, messages came over the wires of battles and casualties in Alsace-Lorraine, Haute-Marne, and Meuse-Argonne. I learned to type the names but couldn't guess how to pronounce them. I read the list of the war dead and slowed when I saw the names "George" and "Richard," but I would never learn what happened to those dear boys.

As my bank account grew, my need for independence did too. I worried that I'd become a burden on the Browns. Like everyone, they scrimped to pay for food and gasoline. Mr. Brown dug a garden twice the size of the one they'd planted the year before. They canceled magazine subscriptions, went to bed early to save on electricity, and took the streetcar more often. My departure would free up money to feed the refugees and send to Thomas.

I found a boardinghouse for single women near WU. When I broke the news that I was leaving, the Browns protested but gave in when they learned I'd already paid my deposit.

"I expect you to be careful living on your own," Mr. Brown said as he drove me to the house with my bags. "We want you to spend Sundays with us, you and Eliza, like before." He placed his large hand on my shoulder. "You're family to us now, Josie. The daughter we never had. Helena's mighty fond of you."

Since I worked nights and slept during the day, I saw little of the other boarders, university students who kept normal hours. Eliza and Ma Brown remained my closest friends.

—❧—

I bought a new dress for Easter, of pale peach cotton with a bodice of white lawn. Below the vee of the neckline, I wore my Bisbee blue turquoise. I spent Easter Day with the Browns. Eliza's father, dressed in a well-pressed suit, looked like a new man. His eyes were clear and bright as he shook my hand and greeted me in slow, stilted English. Ma had splurged on a ham, but she wasn't in the frame of mind to put together a formal Easter meal. Spring had arrived with the last rain, and the desert was calling. We would picnic at Sabino Canyon.

Mr. Brown drove, and Eliza's father sat next to him, looking round-eyed, as if the world were new. Ma and Susannah sat in the back seat, and Eliza and I, goggled against the dust, perched on the pleated seatbacks. The desert bloomed, its sands splashed with orange poppy and blue lupine, as if bedecked for the holiday. I felt at peace with the world.

That night I wrote to Papa. I told him I regretted our fight over Mr. Fanner. I wired him ten dollars to buy clothes for the children.

We returned to our work and worries. We read in the papers that the Germans had launched an offensive on the river Lys. There had been terrible losses. Eliza feared for Joseph. I was grateful Charlie was too young to fight.

I was surprised to receive a response from Papa. He said he had a new job with the El Paso and Southwestern Railroad, running a freight train out of Douglas to the mines in Courtland. The children were being sent to Irene again. He enclosed a photo of the family in front of the boardinghouse. The children were handsome in new outfits, but not one looked happy. I slipped the picture in my dusty grammar book. I couldn't look at their sad faces.

Ida wrote that she and Teal were engaged. They would marry during his next leave. When the war was over, they planned to move to Los Angeles, where she would work and Teal would set up a photography studio. I was thrilled for Ida.

I'm worried about our babies, she added. *It's sad to see them passed from place to place like orphans.*

I read about more battles in France. The government set up an army school for radio operators at the fairground. More soldiers came to town.

Late one Friday afternoon, Eliza and I stopped by the Browns' to collect magazines for the Library Association's campaign. Thomas sprawled on the sofa, reading the paper. Eliza ran to him and fell onto his lap.

"Why didn't you tell me you'd come home?"

"I was going to come over after dark. I had to leave the Jornada." He held her close and kissed her cheek. "Some fellows in Cutter asked if I'd conscripted. I couldn't lie. I told them I was staying out of the war. I'm sure they were going to send the sheriff after me."

"He can't stay," Mr. Brown announced. "The One Hundred Percent American Club's planning to round up the slackers in Tucson. They're going to block the roads and ransack every pool hall, horseshoe pit, and men's club." He turned to Thomas. "You need to conscript or head to Nogales."

"A regular manhunt." Thomas reached for Eliza's hand. "I don't have a choice, baby. I've got to go." The muscles twitched in his taut jaw.

"I know, Thomas. Even if you joined up, you'd have to go."

"He needs to leave tonight," Ma said.

"Can't he stay a few days?" Eliza begged.

"No. I have this feeling . . . it must be tonight."

"One thing I've learned over the years is to pay attention to your feelings, Helena." Mr. Brown wiped perspiration from the rim of his upper lip. "It was you who insisted we leave Galveston the summer of aught-one, and we missed the hurricane, and you who kept us out of the arroyo the day of the flash flood. I'll drive you south tonight, Son."

Eliza held tighter to Thomas.

"It's tough for young folks in love," Ma mused. "It seems as though the whole world were conspiring against you. I remember my ma talking about how grieved she was when Pa left her for the Civil War. He came back a changed man—one blind eye and nerves gone to pieces."

"I'll need some money, Pop," Thomas said.

"Yes, after dinner. Be careful in Nogales, Son. They'll be making raids at the border."

"I'm certain the war's changed course. In less than a year, it'll be over." He looked down at Eliza. "Then we'll be together."

We went out to the kitchen, and Thomas baked eggs while Eliza and I put together a fruit salad.

"Take care of Eliza while I'm gone, Josie," Thomas said. "Take her to the movies or to a dance, but keep her away from those soldiers."

Eliza rolled her eyes. "And you stay away from those señoritas, Señor Brown."

After supper, I bundled the magazines and left the two together.

The next day, the One Hundred Percent American Club made its raid on the town. Several deserters were picked up and sent to prison. Dozens of men without papers were brought to City Hall and only released after they'd signed up or had their conscription papers delivered.

Thomas remained out of reach in Nogales.

12

In early June, I read about the German offensive on the Aisne River at a place called Chemin des Dames. When I went to see Eliza that week, I asked her to say the French words for me. It was difficult to believe that such bloodshed could occur in places with such lovely names.

She was finishing a letter to Joseph, who'd been on leave in Halifax but hadn't had time to come to Arizona to see his family. "It breaks my heart to think of my little brother returning to the battlefield. He's no longer romantic or ignorant about war. He's just terribly brave, and I'm awfully proud." She tucked her letter in an envelope, unsealed because of the censors. "There's going to be another dance at the Knights of Columbus. Shall we go?"

"It's what 'Señor Brown' recommended."

I wore my Easter dress. The hall was full of soldiers, most of them radio operators. The gramophone played the war songs we were hearing everywhere: "K-K-K-Katy" and "Pack Up Your Troubles," and sadder songs—"Till We Meet Again," and "The Rose of No Man's Land." Couples danced slowly, clung to each other like vines, and tried to forget about tomorrow. I looked for Richard but knew he'd been shipped to Europe.

I met another boy named Mack. He'd been attending the university when he received notice to report for duty in three weeks at Camp Funston in Kansas. He liked to talk, and I didn't mind listening. He wanted to be a pilot—his hero was the fighting ace Eddie Rickenbacker. He asked me out on a date. Eliza whispered that I shouldn't go, but I told him yes. I gave him my address, and he said he'd come by the next day.

Mack and I took the streetcar out to Elysian Grove to see a baseball game. He bought us hot dogs, Cracker Jacks, and colas, and we sat down to watch. He took a flask out of his pocket and, under the cover of my hat, poured whiskey into his drink and explained the plays. He took me back to the boardinghouse and asked whether he could see me again.

The next day, we took the streetcar to Speedway Boulevard and watched the "scorchers," the young men who raced their Fords and Buicks. Mack bought me a lemonade, then left me in the shade as he crossed the road to stand and cheer with a group of men when the racers roared past. From across the way, I could see him taking drinks from his flask. On the way home, he put his arm around me and talked of racing cars and bombers. He asked me to go to the cinema the next night.

That night at work, thinking about Mack gave me a queasy stomach. Eliza dropped by my room at the boardinghouse as I was waking up.

"Did you go out with Mack?"

"Yes, twice."

"What's he like?"

"He likes to gab, and he's excited about everything."

"Do I detect a girl who's falling in love?"

"Maybe." I couldn't help smiling.

That evening, Mack invited me to the moving picture at the Broadway Theatre. I could see from his swagger and slow speech that he'd been drinking. I told him I'd changed my mind and didn't want to go.

"You can't do that to me," he whined. "I'm a soldier boy

who's headed off to war. Who knows if I'll ever get back? Give me one more evening to remember."

I gave in. He would sober up during the picture, and anyway, I wanted to see the film version of the book I'd loved—*Rebecca of Sunnybrook Farm.* The girls at work had liked it.

As we walked to the cinema, Mack lit up a Player's and raved about Rickenbacker and an English pilot, Albert Ball. He spit through his loose lips as he imitated the roar of their bombers.

The usher seated us in the back of the stuffy theater. The organist played, and the movie started.

Mary Pickford was beautiful with her dimples and long ringlets. Mack put his arm around me and massaged my shoulder. Then he moved down my arm and touched my breast. I took hold of his hand and pulled it off. He placed it on my shoulder again. I ignored it. Then he leaned over and kissed me.

The alcohol on his breath and his wet lips on the side of my mouth repulsed me. I was back in the alley in Bisbee, reliving my attack. I jumped up and fumbled down the row to the aisle, past the uniformed ushers, and through the curtained doorway. I stood in the lobby, my heart pounding, waiting for Mack to come after me, wondering what I should say.

I waited for a quarter of an hour. Had he fallen asleep? Or was he angry? When he didn't come out, I left.

I walked home quickly, increasing my pace as I smoldered. What a louse. He didn't care for me. He was only looking for a good time.

When I reached home, I picked up my harmonica and stumbled through "El abandonado,"—the sorrowful love song Elias had played the night of Irene's wedding party. I played my anger and hurt until it was time to go to work.

—❦—

After church the following Sunday, Eliza asked whether I was still seeing Mack.

"I broke up with him."

"So soon?" Her eyes peered into mine.

"He drank too much."

"Let's go for a walk after supper."

After we finished Ma's pea soup and corn bread, Eliza asked for candles, and we excused ourselves. She said she wanted to take me "somewhere special."

"I was so embarrassed, standing in that lobby with the girl at the candy counter staring at me," I confessed. "I should've known he was too fast for me. Please don't tell the Browns."

"Of course not. I know about love gone wrong."

As we walked, she told me that Susannah had once had a beau, a charming salesman from Flagstaff, whom she'd met while she was working at Ferrin's store. He was away often, but when he was in town they went out—to the park, the theater, and the opera house. Susannah was planning her wedding—in her mind, leastways. But a fellow clerk visiting Flagstaff saw the salesman with a woman they later discovered to be his wife. The truth broke Susannah's heart. She quit her job. Fragile to begin with, she never fully recovered.

"She stays at home, writes poetry, quilts, bakes, and takes care of Father. I suppose she's contented," Eliza said. "After her tragedy, I brought her to El Tiradito, a sidewalk shrine. We're almost there."

When we'd reached the spot, I realized I'd passed by but never really looked. A Mexican woman in a black lace shawl knelt in prayer. Then she lit a candle and affixed it to the sidewalk with melted wax.

"It began as a site to remember a sinner but has become a place of prayer for any who've erred in love," Eliza said. "*Tiradito* means 'castaway.' They say if you light a candle and it burns all the way, your prayer will be answered. Most people come here at night."

"Who was the sinner?"

Eliza's voice dropped to a whisper. "He was a young shepherd, killed in this spot by his father-in-law for committing adultery with his mother-in-law. That was nearly forty years ago. He was buried where he fell because, with such a sin, he couldn't be placed in the cemetery. His family came here, lit candles, and prayed for his soul. Then other parents started coming, and now anyone who's lovelorn."

The woman stood and walked away. I wished her well.

I sent pink clouds of love to Susannah and her broken heart, and to Eliza and Thomas, torn apart by this war. I thought of Irene and Earl, so lucky in love, and Ida and her fiancé, Teal, hoping he'd be good to her. And I prayed for Papa because he'd lost the love of his life. I sent white protective thoughts to George and the promise of love that was never meant to be, to Richard, and even to Mack, that he wouldn't get killed in the war. Compared to real love stories, my time with him was only the misadventure of a foolish girl.

-&-

The next morning, I was awakened by a frantic knocking at my door. It was Eliza.

"I was awake all night."

"So was I." I yawned. "I worked, remember?"

She sat on my bed. "At the shrine yesterday, I realized that

I'm lovesick. Do you know what that means? It means that I can't eat or sleep or think. I need to be with Thomas."

"Do you know where he is?"

"He's in a town about fifty miles south of the border."

I rubbed my eyes. "Can you open the shade? I need to see you."

She lifted it to blinding sunlight. When my eyes adjusted, I saw that hers were swollen from crying. She rubbed a washboard cheek as she explained what she had to do.

"Father's well enough now, and Susannah will provide good care. I'm going to ask Mr. Brown to drive me to Nogales."

I didn't argue. I agreed that she should go to Thomas, no matter how much I would miss her. She left for Mexico the next day.

13

That summer, folks celebrated the Allied victory in the Second Battle of the Marne. Four hundred fifty tanks had crashed through the German lines and were advancing toward Germany. I hoped the war would soon end and Thomas and Eliza could return.

Irene wrote that she was pregnant, due in late fall.

I'm tuckered out taking care of six children with a seventh on the way. Earl told me to ask others in the family to help out. Aunt JoJane has agreed to take Sally after Christmas. I'm asking if you can take Bethel. She's six now and as gentle as a kitten. Stevie and Charlie can stay here and help out.

I was moved by Irene's plea and wrote to her to send my little sister. Dear Bethel! I longed to hear her soft voice. She could attend school in Tucson. I could work while she slept at night and sleep while she attended school. We would spend our afternoons together.

Then I realized that what Mama had most feared had happened. Our family had come apart—scattered to five different towns in four states.

Bethel arrived in late August on the El Paso and Southwestern line. As I waited on the platform, I worried. Was she angry that I'd left her? Did she want to come to me?

The conductor helped her down the stairs and began walking her toward the station house. When she saw me, she broke away. She crashed into my outstretched arms, then shyly looked up at me and smiled with the sweet, solemn expression I remembered. My little sister had so much to teach me about forgiveness. She took my hand and didn't let go.

Every night, I brushed Bethel's hair, played songs on my harmonica to help her get to sleep, and went to work. The widow proprietor kept an ear open for her while I was gone, and Susannah spent mornings with her while I slept. They got along well, those two gentle souls.

In September, Bethel started school. That weekend we joined the Browns at Susannah's to celebrate my seventeenth birthday. We shared an angel food cake that took all Susannah's sugar ration. Charlie sent me a birthday card with a note that he was quitting work at the ranch at the end of the year and would join us in Tucson. Oh, joy! I wrote that I would send him money toward his train ticket.

14

By the end of the month, folks knew the war was ending. Men stood on street corners and talked excitedly when they heard about the tens of thousands of German prisoners taken in one day but sobered at reports of thousands of American soldiers killed and wounded in those final battles.

Privy to news over the wires, I was one of the first to hear about the sickness in Boston. Soldiers were coming down with the flu and dying, and no one knew why. A telegram reported that thousands of men in US Army camps had been struck by the illness in just forty-eight hours, and another that almost three hundred soldiers had died. The break room hummed with talk about a terrible pneumonia that was killing our boys. Three days later, messages came in that a hundred thousand cases of the disease had been reported and the epidemic was moving westward. The telegraph office buzzed. I could feel tension in the air, fear growing, panic being held in check.

"They say it comes from germs spread on our troopships by the Germans," a wide-eyed typist whispered.

Others claimed that it was the Lord punishing us with a plague because of our participation in the war. Our supervisor told us it was a rare disease from China run amuck. Then reports came from back East with the facts: it was a new strain of influenza called the Spanish Flu that was highly contagious, and there was no sure cure.

The newspapers said one in four people who came down with the disease became seriously ill. I received a wire telling of its assault on Philadelphia. In the days following, we read about overrun hospitals, overworked medical staff, lack of supplies, and hundreds of deaths. The wide-eyed typist quit and returned to Philadelphia to care for her family.

"I'm glad we're far from those crowded cities," my supervisor said. "You wouldn't catch me dead on a train heading east right now. We're safe out here. The disease can't possibly travel through the plains, over the mountains, and across the Sonoran too."

I read the news with morbid fascination. Old people, little children, and babies were getting sick, but also young, healthy people. Robust soldiers were dying. It struck without warning. A person might leave for work feeling healthy as a horse and be dead by evening. All the army camps were under quarantine. The draft call was canceled. A wire came in on the first of October, saying that as many as twelve thousand soldiers and civilians may have died from complications in September.

The epidemic spread west. On October 4, two hundred cases were reported in Winslow, Arizona, and sixty in Flagstaff.

Rumors circulated, only to be proved wrong—about a vaccine to prevent the scourge, that camphor balls in your water would kill the germs, that the cure was kerosene in sugar or boneset tea, or that one would be safe in Mexico, where the epidemic had not yet hit. Shoppers crowded stores to stock up on food and bought up all the boneset and camphor in a day.

I worried that Bethel might catch the disease.

The soldiers at the university were quarantined. The schools, cinemas, YMCA, churches, and pool halls were closed. The liberty bond rally was canceled. The city began a campaign against sneezing, coughing, or spitting in public. Ma and her Red Cross volunteers gathered in the Browns' sitting room to stitch up masks of butter cloth and gauze to supplement those shipped to the stores. By law, we were required to wear the antiflu masks over our noses and mouths whenever we were out of the house. Bethel and her classmates chanted the rhyme:

> Obey the laws and wear the gauze.
> Protect your jaws from septic paws.

Frenzied talk filled the break room when, on October 8, the *Star* reported several thousand cases of the flu at Camp Funston. Many Tucson families had boys stationed there.

Irene telegrammed, asking me to take special care of Bethel. She was going to keep her children at home until the epidemic had passed.

The illness reached Tucson that week. Folks shut their businesses and locked their doors. I didn't want to go to work but had no choice. The wires were overloaded with death notices. I sent and received among a sea of tired eyes above thick masks, trying not to think about the grief of those receiving the news. Dozens of operators were taken ill, so we healthy ones were required to put in longer shifts. I was too tired to care for Bethel. I sent her across town to stay with Susannah.

The city was divided into Red Cross districts. Ma coordinated doctors' calls, transportation to hospitals, and requests for supplies, but she could only respond to half the calls. I stuffed my ears with cotton but was awakened by the sirens of ambulances taking flu victims to the hospital. Afternoons, I closed my shades but couldn't shield myself from the *clip-clop* of horses pulling funeral carriages followed by strings of mourners. Alone in my room, I wrote letters to Irene, Ida, and Charlie and tried to crochet or read. I played my harmonica to ward away the death that lurked outside my window.

Mrs. Myers, the butcher's wife, got ill yet survived, but her burly soldier son, stationed at Camp Funston, died. One of Mr. Brown's fellow police officers got sick and died in one day. Reverend Comstock's nurse-assistant at Tent City passed away, as did a six-year-old girl in Bethel's class at school. Many residents of Tent City succumbed, their ravaged lungs too weak to resist the pneumonia that followed. The hospitals were full. Vicks VapoRub was rationed. The stores sold out of elixir and masks. The mortuary ran out of caskets.

I missed Bethel and longed to see Susannah and the Browns, but social calls were prohibited.

Though citizens were still required to wear masks, in early November, church services resumed, held outdoors. The health authorities grudgingly allowed the Tucson-Phoenix exposition baseball game to take place. Mr. Brown invited me and Bethel to go with him. The men played in masks, and we spectators were subdued under muzzles of gauze, only our eyes registering excitement after a hit, stolen base, or run. Bethel moved back in with me and returned to half-day school. The law required a vacant seat between each child.

Irene wrote that they had stayed clear of the influenza. For once she was glad to be so isolated. Eliza telegrammed that she and Thomas were well in Mexico.

1" />

15

On November 9, I read on the wire that Kaiser Wilhelm would abdicate, followed by the message that the Allies and Germany had signed a truce. The workers at Western Union let out a muffled cry but kept working. It didn't take long for the news to spread. In the early hours of the morning, whistles, sirens, and church bells woke the rest of the town. The war was over.

That week, parades, picnics, and public gatherings were held. In the midst of it all, I received a telegram from Earl. Two days after the armistice, Irene had given birth to a baby boy. She'd named him Charles.

With the peace, everything changed. Rationing ended, but there still wasn't enough sugar to go around, and prices remained high. One morning I was awakened by a sustained siren—the signal that it was safe to remove our antiflu masks. Schools, businesses, and theaters returned to regular hours. I tossed my smelly mask in the trash can, relieved the epidemic was finally over.

Soldiers on leave or released from duty flocked to town. Within the month, every girl who'd been with WU for less than eighteen months was given notice—our jobs were needed by men back from the war. That included me. I was told I could stay with the company if I transferred to Denver or Los Angeles.

How cruel that I was being made to leave, just as things were improving—the flu epidemic nearly over, the war ended,

Bethel and I together, Charlie planning to join us, Eliza and Thomas soon to return from Mexico, the Browns like family. I wanted to stay. But I needed my job.

After a sleepless day, I went to see the Browns.

"I think you should go, Josie," Mr. Brown said. He was sitting in a corner of the sitting room, polishing a brass headlamp ring. "It's not easy now for a young girl to find work. There aren't enough jobs with the veterans returning." He put down his rag. "If I were you, I'd choose Los Angeles. It's a modern city. And the climate's fine, I'm told. You'll like the ocean. The sea is what I miss most about Ireland."

Ma lifted a hand to her forehead as if she had an ache. "I'm not as certain as you, Jack. My feelings aren't clear on this one. It makes me nervous, her setting off on her own. Do you know anyone in LA, Josie?"

"My sister Ida's planning to move there."

"You'll be near someone in your family, then. That's a comfort. I've a sister in Lincoln Heights. I'll give you her address."

Western Union wanted my decision soon. I knew I couldn't support Bethel, Charlie, and myself without work. And I couldn't expect the Browns to support us either. I accepted the position in Los Angeles. I was to report at the start of the new year.

I regretted having to send Bethel back to Irene's but couldn't bring her to a strange city. I'd had so little time to make up for my past failings, and here I was, abandoning my little sister again. I told her I'd send for her after I was settled. I bought her a harmonica, proposing that each time we played, we would think of each other. She solemnly accepted my gift.

I couldn't bear to see her off. I kissed her goodbye and had Susannah put her on the train. I wrote Charlie to tell him to change his plans. I wouldn't be in Tucson to welcome him.

The night before I left, I had my recurring dream. I saw Charlie and Bethel sleepwalking on the edge of the canyon, searching for water, their unbuttoned night-robes flapping in the wind. Bethel awoke and called to me to brush her hair. I shouted that I would untangle it later, but she couldn't hear me.

I awoke and softly played my harmonica—each note an apology.

The Browns drove me to the train on a cold morning in early January. We were running late, as usual.

"You must telegram when you've arrived," Ma said, breathing hard after our run to the platform. She fastened the top button of my sweater. "As soon as you find a place to live, send us the address. Right away, you hear? And contact my sister. Be careful, Josie. I have a feeling . . ." Her voice was drowned out by the hiss of air brakes.

She kissed me, pushed a lunch basket into my hands, and turned away. Mr. Brown was too choked up to speak. He patted my wet cheek and enfolded me in a mammoth hug.

Amid billows of smoke and ash, the locomotive slowly pulled out from the depot. I watched their backs as they crept toward the station house, their arms entangled.

I pulled the napkin from the basket and wiped my eyes. Ma had packed hard-boiled eggs and oranges, soda bread, and Mrs. Myers's sauerkraut, wrapped in a double layer of butcher paper.

Nestled in among the food was a card with her sister's address. And a rosary. I held it up to the window. The cut-glass beads glittered in the sunlight. I remembered Guadalupe and her beloved string of seeds. I clasped a bead and prayed for good fortune.

The train rushed out of Tucson and burst into the desert. I turned from the sun's glare and looked around me. Half of the car was filled with weary soldiers heading home or to new commissions at California military bases. Most of them dozed. A flush-faced soldier across the aisle slept fitfully, rousing himself now and then to mumble, cough, and drop off again. I stared out at a lone ridge of mountains rising from the sands.

I was adrift again, at the mercy of a current carrying me where it willed. I would need my wits to be ready for wherever I might land. I tried to think of the positives. I'd have steady work. I'd get to see the sea. And I'd be near Ida.

Finally, I slept, awakened once or twice by the rasp and cough of the ruddy soldier boy across from me. Then he, too, was lulled to sleep by the rhythmic rock of the locomotive.

IX

LOS ANGELES

(1919)

My train pulled into the Los Angeles depot in the late afternoon. The first thing I noticed was the salt in the air. Even in the station, amid the smoke, ash, and noise of the trains, I could smell what must be the sea.

I had to inquire at several boardinghouses before I found one with a vacancy. So many swarming into the city for work after the war had caused a shortage of rooms. By the time I found Mrs. Diamond's rooming house, my head hurt and my body ached.

"I just had a room vacated," the haggard proprietor told me. She took a puff from a stub of a cigarette held between two yellowed fingers. "The fellow was carted off to the hospital last week. They say he won't return."

I had to talk her into giving me the room right away. My first shift was that night. While she was having her girl clean it, I picked up a sandwich and an apple at the corner store and took the streetcar to the sea.

I heard it before I saw it, the gentle *swish-a-swish* of waves on sand, the screams of milk-bellied gulls, and the squeals of children. I crossed the street, passed under a row of palms, and there it was—a great blue carpet sparkling beneath the winter sun. It smelled of salt and fish and rotting debris. Dora Fenton had been right. The sea was pungent creation and death mixed together.

I pulled off my shoes and stockings and sank into the dry

sand, then strolled down to the moister, firmer beach and stepped into the water. The cold woke up my aching feet. They tingled and turned numb.

I lifted my skirt, waded in calf-high, passed my hand through the water, and lifted dripping fingers to my mouth. It was a salty-sweet mouthful of minerals. I laughed out loud. Had Ida felt such delight when she'd first tasted the Pacific? I patted my hot forehead with my cold hand and felt relief from the heat.

I found an empty bench on the boardwalk and ate my sandwich, hoping my fatigue would pass. As the sun lowered, a trail of gold reflected over never-ending water.

A man was swimming just beyond the break of the waves, dipping his arms in and out of the water in perfect rhythm. I watched until he was a mere speck and marveled at the courage it must take to swim through a murky sea.

The fiery sun dropped into the ocean, and a breeze picked up. I was quickly chilled. Shivering, I walked back to the streetcar and stepped onto the clanging vehicle.

found the Western Union office near the depot. Before I checked in, I sent a telegram telling Ma Brown my rooming house address, and that I was beginning work that night, despite a slight fever. I went to the personnel office and was taken to meet my supervisor, a slight man who darted around the room like a hummingbird. He finally stopped long enough to speak to me.

"It's a busy office. You'll need to work fast."

He assigned me to a line of new operators sent from other western towns. I sat at my machine and started sending. As I typed, my head began to throb with a force that made it hard to concentrate. The supervisor buzzed by and shook his head at my slow typing.

"Told them to send me experienced help."

"I'm tired from my travels," I began, but he'd dashed off. I gritted my teeth, begging coffee during breaks, but my headache stayed with me. I was glad when I was switched to receiving, which was easier, and relieved to finally see daylight and walk the five blocks to Mrs. Diamond's for some sleep.

My room was a tight, dark box on the north side of the building, next to an alley. It smelled of bleach. I opened the window and lay down on my bed. Breakfast was being served, but I was too tired to eat. My muscles ached. My head spun. I remember pulling the thin spread over my body, and no more.

I awoke to the smell of frying meat and made my way to the dining room.

"You almost missed supper, girl," Mrs. Diamond said as she set a plate of pork, boiled potatoes, and pale peas in front of me. I took a few bites and shoved my plate away. My limbs were lead. I laid my head on the table and closed my eyes.

"Not enough sleep?" The woman stood over me. "You working girls keep the oddest hours. Never know if you're coming or going or how much to cook. I don't want you snoozing at my table."

I pulled myself out of the chair, stumbled to my room, and fell into bed. I dreamed I was back in the Jornada, listening to the grate of a crosscut saw cutting fence posts. I awoke. The noise wasn't a saw but the sound of my breath passing through my aching lungs.

Then it struck me like the kick of a horse—I had the influenza. The word itself was terrifying. It seemed I'd fallen asleep in Los Angeles and woken up in a foreign country. I was lost.

It can't be, my head protested. *I survived the epidemic in Tucson. I'm one of the lucky ones.* I slept again and awoke to the wail of an ambulance far away.

I don't want to die alone in this room, my mind screamed.

I needed to get help, but my limbs were too heavy to lift. I coughed and floated away.

I was in a boat on the ocean, the wind whipping the waves into frothy peaks. The boat plunged into deep troughs, and all that I could see were walls of gray water. My teeth chattered. Someone told me to jump out, but I didn't know how to swim. Then a great wave threw me overboard with a terrific force and washed me onto land. I was in the Jornada, in a desolate place where no travelers passed. Skeletons of animals, dead from thirst, littered the sands.

I awoke in the dark. I knew I might die. Then I sat perched on the top of the chest of drawers across the room. I calmly observed the pale crumpled girl lying in her bed and listened to the rasp of air entering and leaving her lungs, her bark, and her battle to breathe. All went black.

3

I awoke in a white room. My head thudded with pain, my lungs stung, and I felt too tired to move.

A woman in a white gown and long wimple stood next to a white curtain, her back to me. A Red Cross volunteer. How did I get back to Tucson? She was saying words that sounded like gibberish. I wanted to speak to her, but the effort of bringing my lips together and my dry tongue into position was beyond my strength. I closed my eyes.

"She's dehydrated. Give her an infusion."

I felt an excruciating pain in the bone of my thigh. I tried to jerk away, but my legs were fastened to the bed. I felt like a bound calf being branded with a hot iron. I heard someone scream.

"Yes, it hurts, but this is for your own good," someone said.

I wondered whether those innocent calves believed so when they were roped, flung onto the ground, and marked for life. I slept and dreamed of Mama. I saw her sitting in the air near the ceiling of the room with Grandmother. They turned to look at me.

Mama, I want to be with you. She smiled sweetly and turned away. I heard someone sobbing.

"Wake her." Someone was shaking my shoulders and tapping my cheeks.

The woman in white stood before me. She was a pair of black eyes above her mask. "I have medicine for you."

She held out a spoonful of liquid. I opened my mouth and swallowed the bitter stuff.

"You have a chance to beat this, child. Your color's still good."

She filled another spoon. I took it in, gagged, and forced it down my throat. I closed my eyes.

"No, don't go to sleep yet. You must have water. Drink, child. This isn't a game. Do you want to live?"

Her words surprised me. I parted my lips as she dripped warm water into my mouth from a rag.

"Good girl," she crooned from behind the gauze.

I drifted in and out, waking to swallow medicine. I shivered and burned; and she was there with a damp cloth for my head and cool water for my lips.

One day I opened my eyes, and for the first time, my head didn't feel as though it were being twisted by a wrench. The woman in white sat in my room, writing on a piece of paper. Her hat wasn't a Red Cross wimple. The white cloth encircled her face and fell down her back. Gauze covered her mouth and nose. She looked up at me.

"Where am I?" My voice came out hoarse.

"You're in St. Vincent Hospital. I'm your nurse." Her eyes folded into black slits as she smiled. "I'm Sister Mary Carmel."

"Are you a Red Cross volunteer?"

"No, I'm a Daughter of Charity."

"How did I get here?"

"A woman brought you in."

I recalled Mrs. Diamond and wondered when she'd found me.

"You've had the influenza. This third round of the epidemic has taken us all by surprise. The hospital's nearly full." She brushed a strand of hair from my face. "And you're not out of the woods yet. You have pneumonia. I'll give you your medicine, and you must sleep."

I coughed and my chest burned. Then I slept.

She was there beside me when I awakened.

"You've been dreaming, Josie. You've been talking about a well. And about swimming. You seemed frightened. You were kicking and crying out. Do you like to swim?"

"I don't know how."

"You're afraid of drowning, then. It's your lungs. You must cough and spit out what comes up. I haven't seen any blood in your sputum yet. That's good. Now try to clear those bellows."

I tried, but mucus lodged in my throat, and I couldn't breathe. I panicked. She pushed me forward and thumped my back. Finally, I was able to take in a breath. I looked into her eyes, the only warmth in that cold, white room.

"How do you know my name?"

"The woman who brought you here told us. She was quite concerned about you. She was adamant that you be given a private room. She checks on you every day, but you're still too ill for visitors."

My heart warmed to think of Mrs. Diamond coming by.

"Sleep now," the nurse whispered, and I closed my eyes.

—❦—

It felt as though my head were being beaten with a stick. I opened my eyes, and she was leaning over me, jerking at my pillow. I looked up into Sister's eyes and was shocked to see that they'd paled and become red and watery. It was a different nun bending over me.

"Don't look so surprised," she said. "Your nurse has left for a while. Hadn't had a day off for months."

I started coughing, and she watched until I could pull air into my lungs again.

"If you start coughing up blood, it'll be the beginning of the end." She shoved a fresh pillow behind my neck and a thermometer into my mouth and picked up my arm to check my pulse. "My own sister survived the influenza but is still short of breath. She got her due. She was a sinner." She dropped my arm. "Your temperature's elevated. Pulse is thready." She turned to the table to get my medicine. "Don't mean to scare you, but I don't believe in sugarcoating the truth."

I was sick to my stomach. I tried to ask for a pan, but it was too late. I vomited onto the floor next to my bed.

She gave me a withering look and left the room. I coughed and my lungs burned. I lay back, exhausted. I didn't hear her return with the mop.

4

The hospital was dark when my barking woke me. I sounded like a sick coyote. Every bone in my body was aflame. I stared into the shadows and listened to the noises of the night. A clock ticked, a patient in another room moaned, a nurse clicked over the linoleum floor, the coughs of other patients echoed off the walls. Outside my window, an automobile backfired and rumbled by.

I ruminated about what the nurse had said. She'd told me what others were afraid to say—that I was dying of pneumonia. This was my punishment for leaving my family.

I listened to the wheeze of my lungs, like a seesaw, as constant as the winds of the Jornada.

I dreamed that I was alone in a black cave. No, it was a hole. Far above me shone a circle of light. I was holding on to something—a rope. I was inside the narrow well in the Jornada. Mama's head came into the light, and she was looking down at me.

"Hold on, Josie," she called. Her voice sounded airy, as if she were shouting into the wind.

"But the rope," I cried. "It's fraying."

It was coming apart in my hands, and I was falling into the black abyss. I woke up crying.

"What's wrong?" someone asked. I recognized her voice.

"I'm going to die. They told me."

"Oh, don't say that. We thought we might lose you a week

ago when they first brought you in, but you've made it this far. You can't give up now."

I looked up into the dark eyes of Sister Mary Carmel and was surprised at how lovely they were. She gently placed a hot water bottle on my chest and set a thermometer under my tongue.

"Who took care of you while I was gone? Was it the sister with the eye condition?"

I nodded.

"Sister Mary Dolorosa. Oh, she's a humorless soul. Don't you let anyone tell you when your end will be. Only God knows how many days you're destined to walk on Earth." She took the thermometer from my mouth and studied it. "A slight fever."

"How long were you gone?"

"Three days. I didn't want to leave you. I was ordered to take days off. I went to visit my mother."

"My lungs are bleeding."

I watched her eyes to see how she'd react. She glanced into the pan next to my bed.

"That bit of rust? That's normal."

I started to cough and couldn't breathe. Sister held me until the spasm ended. My chest felt as raw as freshly ground beef.

I held out my hands and showed her what frightened me. My fingernails had turned gray.

"That other sister said I brought this on because of my past. She's right."

Sister Mary fixed angry eyes on me.

"This isn't a punishment! Genghis Khan and Ivan the Terrible, two evil men, did not die of the influenza, and you won't either if I can help it. Now buck up and tell the grim reaper that we've got other ideas. I have a plan."

She lifted my head and adjusted my pillow.

"My mother comes from Italy. They have pneumonia there too. She told me about the old cures, and I'd like to try them. But you have to want to try."

I felt too tired to try. I closed my eyes.

"What do you want to live for, child? What would you miss? Your family? Are there parents or brothers or sisters you love? Do you have dear friends?"

I squeezed my eyes shut. She took hold of my hand.

"What about the man you may someday marry, or the children you may someday bear? Do you think they're worth living for? What of your lovely body . . . do you want to leave it so soon? And the world and all its beauties? Wouldn't you like to smell a rose again? See the world?"

I didn't answer.

"Hope is just a little four-letter word, Josie, but it's the most important weapon you have. When God gave you your life, he gave you hope. Without that, you wouldn't have taken that first breath. Pray for the courage you need to keep hope alive."

I kept my eyes closed to stop the tears from sliding down the sides of my face. She stroked my forehead and whispered into my ear, "You're a fragile butterfly with an injured wing. Don't give up on ever flying again. I won't leave you."

She didn't ask permission to heal me. She practiced her medicine, and I cooperated. She made me sip fruit juice and chicken broth with cayenne pepper—to loosen the phlegm, she told me. She gave me peppermint tea and a tonic of hyssop to keep the mucus flowing. She crushed garlic in a bowl and made a paste with cooking oil. She placed the paste on the sole of each foot and covered it with a bandage each evening.

I slept with the smell, and in the morning she unwrapped my

feet and washed them. She straightened my sheets, so the stiff, scratchy cotton had no wrinkles to bother me. When I complained that the rubber beneath my sheet made me sweat, she removed it.

"Are you named after the candy?"

She laughed. "No, that buttery treat's spelled differently. I'm named for a mountain in the Holy Land—a place of miracles."

I had lots of time to think. There were things to live for. I wanted to have enough breath to play the harmonica. I wanted to see the ocean again. I wanted to learn to swim. I longed to see my sisters and brothers. And someday I wanted to have children of my own.

I got better. When I could breathe without rasping, Sister helped me into a wheelchair. She encouraged me to walk from one end of the room to the other.

"How long have I been here?"

"Three weeks. It will be a little longer until we're able to release you. We wouldn't want you to have a relapse. So many have."

One afternoon she announced that I was to have a visitor. "The woman who brought you in."

I tried to remember Mrs. Diamond's face but drew a blank. All that I could see were her hands, dangling from thin arms like withered leaves.

"I'll help you fix your hair and give you cream for your face."

Without a mirror, I wondered how I looked.

"You look fine, considering what you've been through."

heard her before I saw her.

"Oh, where is she?"

Ma Brown bounded into the room and wrapped her arms around me.

"Josie, Josie! You've pulled through!"

Tears hurtled down her cheeks.

"Was it you?" I looked at her in disbelief. "I thought Mrs. Diamond brought me to the hospital."

"She didn't even know you were ill, that woman. But I had a feeling that something was wrong, and I was clear back in Tucson. I read and reread your telegram. You mentioned your fever. I've been called impetuous by some, but in this case my actions were justified."

She sat on the edge of my bed and held my hand.

"I telephoned my sister who lives in Lincoln Heights. She went to the boardinghouse, found you mad with fever, and called the ambulance. I took the first train I could get."

"But how could you know?"

"We've had another wave in Tucson—they believe it was brought in by soldiers. Our neighbor boy, Philip, died—the boy who told us about the opportunity at Western Union. And the coroner's son. Survived horrendous fighting at Belleau Wood, only to come home to die of pneumonia with a handful of others in a freak third round."

She unpinned and removed her hat.

"But you look well. Pale and thin, as I expected, but on the mend. You can't know how I've worried. I blame myself for letting you go away with no one to watch over you. I've been staying with my sister and checking every day to see how you're faring. Your nurses have given you excellent care, and we've been saying rosaries for you."

I thought how lucky I was to be in this hospital and not in a stifling canvas shelter like those we'd visited in Tent City.

"I wrote to your sisters. They know you're here, and when I leave, I'll telegram that you're over the worst."

Sister Mary stepped in the room. "Josie's still weak, Mrs. Brown. We wouldn't want to overtire her."

"Of course not. She needs her rest."

Ma got up from the bed and bent to hug me, and I held her close.

"Thank you," I whispered. She squeezed my hand and promised to return the next day.

I slept deeply until a sharp pain in my chest woke me in the night. I lay in the dark and listened to nurses talking about a death and a vacant room. I remembered Philip, the Western Union boy, and the coroner's soldier son, and those who'd died in the first round—Butcher Myers's boy, the nurse and so many poor souls in Tent City, and all those babies.

The next morning, Sister helped me to the wheelchair and began to change my bed.

"It's not fair."

She looked up. "What? That you got ill?"

"No. That I survived."

She tossed my soiled sheets onto the floor.

"It's not right that I'm alive and others didn't make it."

"It's a mystery, Josie, but perhaps I can put it in a way you'll understand. Imagine that we're all in a train station together, and everyone's train leaves at a different time. Some take an early train . . . and others take the late one, determined by a master timetable we're not privy to see. Because we can't know when the stationmaster will call out our departure, we must make the most of our time while we're in the depot."

She plopped a sheet on the bed and carefully unfolded it. She circled the bed, tucking it under the bare mattress and mitering the corners.

"I don't think there's a soul in these United States who hasn't lost someone to this epidemic. You're in a new club now. You're a survivor. There are millions of you out there who've had close calls but come out on the other side. Don't think you're alone."

"But it's not fair. I didn't even try, really."

"Your train hasn't come in yet. Live, dear. It's what you're meant to do."

She took a snow-white drawsheet and laid it over the other. She tucked it beneath the mattress on the left side, walked around the bed, and pulled the right side of the starched sheet as taut as a trampoline.

"There," she puffed as she pressed her thighs to the bed and tucked it in. "I used to think the most important part of my job was making a perfect bed. Shall we give it the test from nursing school?"

She brought a coin from a hidden pocket in her robe and dropped it onto the bed. It bounced twice.

"I passed." She laughed, bent to pick up the sheets, and left the room.

Ma returned the next day with my two bags in her hands.

"I checked you out of the rooming house. It was easy to gather your things—you'd hardly begun to unpack. You're not going back to that place. I took the liberty to go to the Western Union office to inquire about your job. They scarcely remembered you, given you'd only worked one shift. They figured you'd up and quit. I'm afraid they've given your job away, dear."

She stood before the window. In the winter light, her face shone white as parchment, her freckles like specks of brown ink.

She explained that there were no more openings in the Los Angeles office, but the supervisor had said I might have a position in San Francisco if I could begin by the first of March.

Ma left the window and settled herself in a chair. "There's another option, dear. You can come live with us in Tucson. Perhaps in time a position will open up with Western Union or the Postal Telegraph Company, or you can find another job. We'd love to have you back."

My head had begun to pound. I put my hand on my temple and closed my eyes. What a lot to think about.

"I see you're tired. Take your time to decide. For the time being, WU believes you'll be taking the job in San Francisco. And I can wait indefinitely."

She kissed me goodbye.

I lay in bed, willing the thrumming in my head to stop. I stared at my canvas bags, hunched on the floor like orphans, and watched a lone sparrow looking for food on the windowsill.

I coughed and rolled over to sleep. My chest hurt. Tomorrow I would decide what to do.

On Wednesday, the visiting hour was from three until four. Five minutes before the hour, Ma still hadn't arrived. Then she swept into my room, late as usual, kissed my cheek, and handed me a parcel.

"Letters from your sisters and Eliza."

I began to unwrap them. Sister Mary came into the room. "The visiting hour's nearly over."

"Oh, goodness." Ma wrung her hands. "Josie, I've something else to tell you. I'm needed at home. I've been away from Jack and the refugees for nearly a month. I leave tomorrow morning."

"You've already spent too much time waiting on me."

"Not at all. Remember that you're welcome in Tucson. Write to me and tell me what you decide."

When she'd reached the door, I called to her, "Ma, I want to go to Tucson to be with you!"

"Oh, that will be divine. We'll be waiting for you."

With one backward smile, she was gone.

took my time going through the letters. Reading tired me. Eliza wrote from Mexico. She was relieved to hear that I had improved. Thomas was sporadically employed as a mechanic for broken-down motorcars and other machines, but she was homesick and bored.

The locals stare at my face as if they've never seen a person with a scar. I'm tired of being poor and different and far from family. Now I understand how Ma's refugees feel.

Irene wrote a long letter with news of the family. Papa had taken a job the first of the year running a mine train in Ruth, Nevada. Charlie, Stevie, and Bethel remained with her. Sally was still with Aunt JoJane.

Now that the war was over and the men had returned to the ranches, Earl had fewer jobs to hire out for. Cash was scarce, and the bottom had fallen out of the horse market. Since the armistice, a rancher couldn't sell a horse for what it cost to ship it. Some were shooting the horses they couldn't afford to keep. Earl let a number of his go wild in the hills to fend for themselves. He was going to invest in more cattle, but not until the present drought ended. They were praying for spring rain.

Engle has shrunk, as if it's being slowly erased. Seems all the world's moving on. But you've been through so much. Grow strong so you can come back to us.

Your devoted sister, Irene.

At the bottom of the page was a postscript from Charlie: *I'm helping Earl out till I can enlist. Have been worried about you.*

Reading his scrawl, I could almost hear his voice. What would I give to listen to one of Charlie's funny stories? It had been so long since I'd had a good laugh. I missed him so much. Oh, I missed them all. I started to cry.

Sister Mary chided me for getting upset. My health was still fragile. She told me to put the letters away and rest.

I read Ida's letter the following day. Her pink envelope smelled of perfume, postmarked in San Diego.

Teal was to be discharged from the navy in March and had been offered work in a portrait studio in Oakland, California, a small town on the bay near San Francisco. He'd saved enough to buy a Model T and promised to buy her a little cottage with a garden of roses. They'd be driving north in March.

I yearned for Ida so much, my throat hurt. In that moment, I changed my mind. I would take the job in San Francisco and would visit her often in her rose-covered cottage.

I had a telegram sent to Ida that I was moving to San Francisco. I wrote to Ma Brown to say I'd be staying in California after all. Ida wrote back.

We plan to be in Oakland by the third week of March. Where shall we meet? Let's say the Conservatory of Flowers in Golden Gate Park on the twenty-fourth of March. At twelve noon? I'll be counting the days.

"You must walk," Sister said, "to strengthen your legs and build up your lungs. Now that it's warmer out, we'll open your window. Fresh air will do you good."

"I'm feeling stronger," I told her. "My lungs don't hurt. My fingernails aren't gray anymore. I'm hungry again."

At last it was time for me to leave the hospital. Sister Mary washed my silk stockings, mended my corset cover, pressed my dress, and brought me the train schedule.

"You've put on weight. You look lovely. One would never know your condition a month ago. You've time now to make things right with your family, dear, if that's what you want to do."

My hands shook as I buttoned my sweater.

"I don't know how I'll pay my bill."

"It's been taken care of. Mrs. Brown paid part of it, and the rest . . . well, we are the Daughters of Charity. We've some generous benefactors."

When I was ready to go, she stood back and looked at me.

"What a lucky girl you are to be young and well and heading out into the world."

I took her hand and held it tightly. "Thank you for everything, Sister."

"It's the Lord's work. I'm merely his assistant."

She handed me my bags. "Josie!" I saw longing in her eyes. "Live, child. Don't look back. Don't be afraid. Be happy."

"Yes, Sister."

By the time I'd reached the door, she was already stripping the bed.

I wasn't prepared for the shock of spring. The sun blinded me. The orange blossoms outside the door smelled so sweet, I grew dizzy. A delivery truck thundered by, then screeched its brakes to avoid a dog. Everything was louder, more fragrant, and more colorful than I remembered. By the time I'd reached the station, bought my ticket, and boarded the train, my legs ached and my head throbbed. I slept most of the way to San Francisco.

X

SAN FRANCISCO
(1919–1921)

A girl met me at the Alameda Station. She held a card with my name and gave me a wide smile.

"I'm Miriam Stein," she said as she reached for my bags. "Mrs. Tuttle sent me to fetch you. She's your new boss at Western Union."

Miriam was small and slim. She wore a loose, calf-length dress, with her belt at her hips, not her waist, and wore black pumps that left her ankles bare. Over her bobbed hair she wore a cloche-style hat. She had an air of easy sophistication. I was enthralled.

"She's asked me to take you to the boardinghouse where a lot of the WU girls stay. She's reserved a room for you. She takes care of her girls—the ones who work her night shift."

"Do you live in the boardinghouse too?"

"No, I live with my brother and sister in another part of town. But I'm one of her girls. I've worked for Mrs. Tuttle for two years now."

She led me from the train down the walk to the San Francisco passenger ferry and paid our fares. We found a spot at the rail on the upper deck.

"I'm afraid you won't get much of a view. It's been overcast all day."

But even under clouds, the city looked like a jewel in the hills. Miriam pointed out the different parts of town—Telegraph

Hill, Nob Hill, and Russian Hill downtown, and Fisherman's Wharf to the north. After the ferry docked, we caught a streetcar. "I'm glad you don't have more luggage." She huffed as she pulled one of my bags onto the car. "It's so hard to find space during the evening rush." We squeezed in against a wall of coats and hats and grabbed onto the handrail overhead. "Are you having the rest of your things sent?"

"It's all I have."

She smiled and looked sweet, despite her bold makeup.

The rooming house was on California Street, not far from the office. Sixteen Western Union girls lived there. Five worked the night shift, from midnight to eight.

Miriam showed me to my room, then left for home. I ate supper at a table full of girls my age and older. They wore variations of Miriam's dress and were bright and witty. I wanted to be like them. I glanced down at the peach lawn dress I'd loved so much in Tucson, already wanting a new outfit—something svelte and modern.

At eleven thirty, we night shift girls left for work together. As we walked quickly down the quiet, shuttered streets, the girls joked and laughed loudly—too loudly for that hour of the night. I felt tired by the time we reached the office.

One of the girls led me to the supervisor's office, then hurried off to her post. I stood before Mrs. Tuttle's desk and waited as she finished reading a memorandum. She finally looked up.

"Welcome, Miss Gore. Follow me."

I tagged her around the busy office where, in clipped phrases, she pointed out the cloakroom, the lunchroom, the sickroom, the area where they handled money transfers, the stock tickers' desks, the dispatch center for the uniformed messenger boys, and the administrative offices. It wasn't the first time I'd encountered a longtime employee of Western Union who spoke in telegraphese, as if even in everyday speech, she was being charged by the word.

"Been here twenty-five years. Work hard. Got to stay ahead of the competition." She folded her arms and turned to me. "During the war, we had an operator send seventy messages in an hour. Sixty-one in the next. He holds our record." Her eyes gleamed with pride.

"Frisco office burnt down in the quake and fire of oh-six. Lost every piece of equipment. The West Oakland wire chief climbed a thirty-foot pole and wired LA with news of the quake. Started the rescue effort. Saved lives."

She was getting wordy.

We stood on the main floor watching the senders type with controlled urgency and frenzied messengers rush between machines. I recognized the girls from the boardinghouse. A young man encountered a torn tape and signaled from the floor. Mrs. Tuttle marched across the room to assist him. She was tall and broad-shouldered, with massive hands and thick fingers with short, square nails. She reminded me of a ranch wife—sure of herself and up to any challenge. Having helped him replace the flawed roll of tape, she handed me a form and looked me over. She must have read my fatigue.

"Fill out your paperwork. I'll have a messenger walk you home. Get some sleep. Be here tomorrow night. On time."

She slowed long enough to send me a broad smile, then dashed off to assist another operator. From my first step off the train, I felt I belonged.

2

I slept until noon the next day, then unpacked and wrote postcards to Irene, Ma Brown, and Eliza, informing them of my
safe arrival and new address. There was no point writing to Ida
—she was already on the road.

I joined the WU girls for supper, where I was assigned a seat
between two sisters with brunette bobs whom I could hardly tell
apart. They shot comments back and forth as quickly as they
surely typed.

"Ready for your first night on the job?" said the one on my left.

"Mrs. Tuttle's swell," said the other.

"Takes a gang of us into the Marin Hills Sunday mornings
after our shift," the first one said.

I looked from one chatty sister to the other but couldn't get
a word in.

"Mount Tam's our favorite."

"You'll have to come with us."

"Yes." I smiled. "I'd love to."

※

At work Mrs. Tuttle had me sit next to Miriam Stein, who
checked my sending. I was rusty, having been away from the
machines for so long. But after a few days, my fingers limbered
up, and I worked up to my former speed.

"You're the calm type, aren't you?" Miriam said. "Some of

the girls panic and make mistakes when there's a lineup of messages. You'll do well."

She gave Mrs. Tuttle a nod and abandoned her role as watchdog. We took our breaks together.

"Some don't feel comfortable around me," she said, glancing toward a clump of girls at the next table.

"What do you mean?"

"I'm a Jew. Doesn't that mean anything to you?"

"I've met all kinds of girls—Methodist, Baptist, Catholic, Mormons in Mexico. It doesn't matter."

She gave me a sad little smile.

"Where did you say you're from?"

"New Mexico, mostly."

"People say things about us because we're different. Because we stick together. Help each other out."

"Where I grew up, what mattered most was how well you could ride or rope a steer."

She laughed. "I wish it could be that simple."

⁓

Miriam and I had the same night off. At the end of my third week, she invited me to her home for supper. She lived in the Fillmore District, in an apartment above a watch repair shop on Golden Gate Avenue.

I could tell as I took her sister's chubby hand that she was different. Maggie had Miriam's high coloring, but her face was broader, her nose pug, her eyes somehow void. She was Miriam gone awry. I remembered the little daughter of one of the mill workers in Cutter who had the same features and narrowed eyes. Maggie must be a slow thinker too.

Maggie hugged me when I handed her the daisies I'd brought for Miriam's table. She took them and danced around the room, while a young man sitting on a wicker chair laughed at her antics.

Miriam introduced me to her brother, Sam. He got up, took my hand, and began to sing the popular song "Come Josephine in My Flying Machine."

I blushed.

"Oh, Sam, quit that. Sit down and talk to Josie while Maggie and I finish preparing supper."

Sam let the song go. He told me he repaired watches in the shop downstairs. He'd learned the trade from his father. When he had died the year before, Sam was left the business.

"We haven't been lucky in that respect." His eyes went dark for a moment. "Mother died five years ago. We've Maggie to care for and can't leave her alone. That's why Miriam works nights."

He shifted in his chair. "Did you hear they're going to magnetize the rear axle of the Tin Lizzie? Do you want to know why?"

I nodded.

"So it will pick up all the parts that drop off."

Sam hooted, and I chuckled.

"Sam, are you boring Josie with your silly Ford jokes?" Miriam called from the kitchen. "Lucky for her, supper's ready."

Maggie led me to the table.

After supper, Sam's girlfriend, Rose, stopped by with an almond cake. Sam pulled out his banjo and we sang until late. Reluctantly, I excused myself to go home. Miriam pulled a tweed coat out of the closet and told me to wear it against the damp fog that had rolled in.

"Keep it. It was my mother's, and it's too large for me."

I didn't own a warm coat. I put it on, and Miriam and Sam walked me to the streetcar stop. A lighted arch extended from each of the four corners of the Fillmore intersection and met in the middle. Every intersection in the neighborhood was lit in such a way—a beautiful sight.

The car squealed to a stop. I jumped aboard and waved as it sped down the line.

It had felt good to be with a family again.

I visited them often. Sam greeted me with, "Come Josephine," and sometimes I brought my Hohner and played songs with him. He was funny and chatty but tense, like a rubber band pulled too tight.

"He's not suited for work in the shop," Miriam explained. "I'm the methodical one." She said Sam was dying to get into vaudeville and involved with the new wireless radios—he was certain there was a future there. But he was tied to the business until their lease ran out.

Miriam taught me the streetcar system and how to dodge the motorcars, cable cars, and horse carriages to get across Market Street. She took me to the wharf to buy fish, to Chinatown and Japantown, ordered my first pizza pie in a Little Italy restaurant, and showed me how to get to Golden Gate Park.

On work nights, we'd cram into Sam's Model T with his handmade sign on the window—DANGER! 10,000 JOLTS—and he'd drive us to work. He screeched around corners and threw us forward at stops. I wondered if he was angry at having to drive us so late, but Miriam said he was bored silly at the shop and looked for excitement at night. I giggled at the thrill but was always a bit shaken as we pulled up to the WU office.

꘎

To celebrate Maggie's fourteenth birthday, we met at the Cat and Fiddle Restaurant and had roast beef sandwiches and malts. Miriam wore a long, plush coat with a black wolf collar and short black galoshes, unbuckled, that flapped as she walked. Several men turned to look at her. I felt matronly in her mother's tweed coat.

Afterward, Sam treated us to a silent movie—a William S. Hart Western.

As we stood to leave, Maggie wrapped her arms around me in a long, exuberant hug. Her fierce show of affection reminded me of Bethel.

"She loves you, Josie," Miriam said. "She doesn't hug just anyone like that."

As we walked back to the apartment, Miriam linked her arm in mine, and we talked about the Western.

"Is that what it was like in New Mexico?"

"It looked like that—dry and brown much of the time. There were always cowhands around, but nobody's clothes looked so spanking new, and I never saw a gunfight." I tried to recall the qualities of my home. "It was peaceful. But things were harder for us."

In the film there were no droughts or windstorms, no stubborn mesquite or prickly pear. The film left out the nomadic families in search of opportunity—and the loneliness. The climate and a shifting world were our adversaries, not men with guns.

In bed that night, awakened by the clang and scream of a passing streetcar and the shouts of late-night revelers, I felt worlds away from that harsh but tranquil desert. I missed my family and yearned for a day when we could be together again in one place.

3

The third week of March, I went to meet Ida, as planned, at Golden Gate Park, where I made my way to the Conservatory of Flowers. I let myself through the double doors and was hit by a blast of warm, humid air. I looked around but didn't see her. I took off my coat and walked past towering ferns, succulents, and glossy vines crawling up the trunks of trees, each with an identifying label.

I looked at my watch. Where was she? Had she forgotten?

When I reached the end of the building, I heard the door open, and through a tangle of leaves, I saw a woman in a white hat—Ida May! She looked around, hesitated, then turned the other way. I was too far to call to her.

As I hurried toward her, my foot caught on a hose, and I was down on the ground. I picked myself up. I'd torn my stocking and my knee was bleeding. I spotted Ida's hat behind a fern and called out to her.

She turned as if on a spring. "Josie Belle!" We flew at each other and embraced. "I'm so sorry we're late. We missed the ferry. What happened to your leg?"

"I tripped. I'm all right."

She fished in her purse for a hanky. She looked the height of fashion in a loose white dress, fringed at the sleeves, and white gloves. Her once-straight hair waved softly around her face. Her lips were burgundy, her brows thin black lines.

"Ida May, you look like a city girl."

"I suppose I've become one. I've dropped the 'May.' Teal calls me Ida."

"I'm Josie now—no more Belle."

"Mama would cry if she knew that."

We laughed. She handed me her hanky, and I wiped my knee.

She turned to her husband, a stocky man carrying a bulky camera. "Teal, this is Josie, my long-lost younger sister."

"Delighted to meet you." He made a slight bow as a woman pushed past us. "Shall we clear this roadblock and go outside, ladies?"

"We arrived a week ago," Ida said as we walked, "but we'd no way to contact you. We've rented a house in Oakland. It has a garden with a lemon tree and an arbor with yellow roses. Come visit us."

"Can I come next weekend?"

"We'll be in Sacramento. Teal travels quite a bit, doing photography for the newspapers. How about the following Sunday?"

Teal suggested we take a drive to see more of the park.

We got into their Model T and drove to Stow Lake. Teal went to the concessionaire and brought back french fries and fried egg sandwiches for Ida and him, and a hamburger for me. I hadn't cared much for eggs since Thomas's cooking in Cutter. We ate on a blanket in the shade of an American elm. Then Teal got a tripod and another camera out of the car and set it up on the lawn. While Ida and I talked, he took photos of us.

"Don't mind him," Ida said. "He takes pictures all the time. It's his work, you know."

Although we'd written over the past three years, it wasn't like talking. I loved the sound of Ida's voice, more melodic than mine. She told me about San Diego and meeting Teal. Their wedding hadn't been much—a visit to the courthouse and dinner with friends—and then Teal had to go back to the war.

I described Irene and Earl's house and their sweet children. I told her about Eliza and Thomas and Tucson and how Ma Brown had been so good to me. I said my clearest memories of LA were a white hospital room and a white-clad nun. Ida laughed.

We walked down to the lake, and I tried to wash the blood-stain out of my stocking, but it was ruined because of the tear. We rented a pedal boat. Ida sat in back while Teal and I pedaled around Strawberry Hill Island. When we were halfway across, we switched places so Ida could pedal, and the boat nearly tipped.

"I can't swim," she squealed as she teetered forward and clumsily plunked herself onto the front seat.

"Neither can I."

"I'd rescue you both then," Teal said. "One in each arm."

I wasn't reassured.

We got into the car, and Teal drove us up to the Japanese Garden and tea house. A woman brought us a pot with little cups with no handles. While we drank the pale, steaming tea, Teal talked about his aerial photography in the war. Then he launched into politics.

"You'd think things would've improved by now, but with the shipyard contracts canceled, factories closing, and the rise in the cost of living, they're worse. With the general strike in Seattle and talk of others . . . it's downright anarchy. Some blame the communists, but I think they're looking for a scapegoat." He took a swig of tea. "Have you noticed how in bad economic times they've always got to drum up an enemy?"

I was figuring out that politics was Teal's favorite topic.

"I'm no communist, but I do think you've got to give folks a decent wage and a decent place to work." Teal finished the pot and ordered more. "Now, if a man was smart, he'd invest in medicinal alcohol. With prohibition on its way in, things are going to change."

"I'm looking forward to being able to vote in the next presidential election," Ida said. "They say women's suffrage is coming. Isn't that terrific, Josie?"

I nodded. But it would be three more years before I would be old enough to cast a vote.

"It means you'll have to learn something about politics, but I'll teach you girls what you need to know," Teal said.

I smiled. I could think for myself, but it wouldn't do to argue with my new brother-in-law on the day we met.

The woman brought fresh tea and three cookies on a plate. They were made of thin dough folded into two triangles and fried a delicate brown. Ida poured tea around, and Teal picked up a cookie and broke it in half. A scrap of paper fluttered onto the table.

"Fortune cookies. The Japanese fellow who runs this place came up with the idea. I had one back in fifteen, when I was here for the Panama–Pacific Expo. They're serving them in some Chinese restaurants now. Real popular."

"Read us your fortune," Ida said.

"No, it might be personal." He held the paper in one hand and looked at it.

Ida grabbed it and read it aloud. "'Your curiosity will take you many new places.' Why, it's perfect, Teal. As if they knew you."

She broke her cookie and silently read her own. "Mine's a good one. Shall I read it to you?"

We nodded.

"'You will have many husbands.'"

Teal blinked, frowned, and took a sip of tea.

I laughed. "No, it can't be. Let me see that." I plucked it out of her hand. "Why, yes, that's what it says. You'll be like Aunt Lucy. She's on her third husband."

Ida started to giggle.

Teal screwed up his eyes, took Ida's fortune from my hand, read it, and shook his head.

"I should've known you sisters would be in cahoots. This is much better: 'Loyalty will bring you a long and happy life.'" He shot us dirty looks and chuckled. "Now it's your turn, Josie."

I broke my cookie in two, pulled out the fortune, and read it aloud. "'One friend will pass through the door, and another will enter.'"

Ida looked puzzled. "If it's a false friend who leaves and a true friend who enters, that'd be good. But if it's a true friend who leaves, it's sad."

"It can't be true," I said. "It's chance which fortune you draw. Have you tasted a cookie yet? They're crisp but bland."

The sun was setting by the time we left the tearoom. Teal drove me to the boardinghouse, and Ida and I reluctantly parted.

I played my harmonica that night while contemplating the day and my fortune. It mustn't be true, that prediction of loss. I couldn't bear the thought of losing anyone else.

4

I woke early the day of my visit to Ida's, took the streetcar to the terminal, paid my nickel fare, and joined a crowd of passengers huddled in the damp station waiting for the Oakland ferry. At last its horn sounded, and the squat boat appeared from out of the fog. Passengers spilled from its decks for a Sunday in the city.

I stepped aboard and found a seat on the upper deck. Halfway across the bay, the fog lifted to reveal a gold-and-olive shore and a backdrop of hills awash in sunlight—the East Bay.

Ida and Teal met me at the dock and drove me to their home in a neighborhood of neat brick bungalows and orderly trees. Ida was excited to show me the house and garden and wanted my advice on decorating. After lunch she'd show me Oakland—a town that had taken off since the earthquake of 1906.

Teal dropped us at the house and drove off to photograph the annual cattle auction at the Mexican Catholic church. He promised to be back for lunch.

Ida's front door opened into a generous parlor she called the living room. Her kitchen had a gas stove, running water, an icebox, and shiny green linoleum flooring. In the spare room, she showed me her Underwood typewriter.

"I've made connections with an office here in Oakland. They'll be sending me work when their secretaries are behind, which seems to happen often."

She placed the dust cover over the machine and showed me the nook where Teal kept his photography equipment. In her bedroom she showed me the clothes in her wardrobe—four times what I owned—and her sewing machine.

"I do what Mama did. I study the newest fashions in the stores and make them up myself. You're a size larger than me. What a pity." She shook her head. "But this tunic and skirt fit me like sacks. You can have them. Try them on."

Ida sat on the bed and frowned at my worn, twice-repaired undergarments.

"You've got to throw out this old corset, Josie. Free yourself and wear the mini corsets everyone's got now. And a girdle with garters. No one's wearing petticoats anymore."

The tunic fit, but the skirt was tight.

"I'll make you a skirt. Something black. Crepe de chine with an attractive belt. You're built like Irene."

"I worry about Irene," I said as I wiggled out of the skirt. "She has so much work on the ranch, and with our three, she has six children to feed and care for. We should help her out—have the children here."

Ida traced the mosaic pattern of the bedspread. "I blame the war. It seems I couldn't plan for anything until it ended. And now with all our traveling, I'm still in no position to help."

She got up from the bed and showed me her newest pair of shoes—highheels with a lone strap. She was changing the subject.

"Mary Pickford wears shoes like these—we'll get you some too."

We sat in front of her vanity mirror.

"Look here. If you part your hair on the side, it'll bring out your cheekbones." She parted and combed my hair. "You have such a pretty forehead, you needn't cover it with fringe." She brought me lipstick and black eye paint. "You've already got the dark brows and lashes everyone wants, but the paint will accentuate your eyes."

She slipped a headband over my forehead and a string of beads around my neck. We admired my new image. I picked up the eyebrow brush and pretended to smoke it.

"Oh, Josie, you clown."

I pulled it from my mouth. "Seriously, what would Mama say if she saw us?"

"She was always fashion conscious, even in the Jornada. I think she'd understand that styles have changed."

"She'd tell us not to show our knees."

Ida laughed. We played around with her curling iron until we heard Teal walk into the house.

"Hey ladies, that auction made me hungry."

We jumped up and went to lunch.

On Sundays when Teal had to travel for work and Ida chose to stay home, I visited her. We painted her walls until the fumes drove us out to the garden, where we weeded her roses. One afternoon it rained, and we made pillow shams. I cut the paisley fabric, and Ida pieced together the fronts and backs while we talked of old times.

"Remember that July rain when the horny toads came out and crawled into the house?"

I laughed. "Mama raced from door to door sweeping them out with her broom."

"And the knitting minister who used to pass through on the

train? He knitted a complete layette for his granddaughter in two months' time. Oh, we had some odd preachers come through."

I handed her two squares of fabric to be sewn together. "Do you think you'll have a family, Ida?"

"I don't know if I'm cut out for it."

"What do you mean?"

"Teal travels for his living, and I like to go with him. I'd have to give that up." She looked out at the rainwater streaming from the gutters. "He doesn't want to leave me alone—like Papa left Mama."

"You're a perfect wife for him."

"I'm not a good person at all." She dropped the pieces onto her lap. "Papa wasn't the only one who left her. I left Mama too."

"No. I'm the one at fault."

"You?"

I set down my shears. "For letting Mama die. For leaving our little ones in Bisbee."

"Oh, Sister, where was I? Where was Papa when you needed him home? Where were Mama's sisters? I shouldn't have left you after her death."

"I thought I was the only one with regrets."

"Oh, I feel miserable. I can hardly speak of it."

She carefully positioned the fabric beneath the needle of the Singer. The tap of the treadle, whir of the needle, and patter of rain filled the room. I picked up the shears and studied the patterned fabric, trying to figure out where to cut next. I felt lighter knowing that I had a sister to share my burden with.

5

That summer, Ida and Teal were gone for weeks at a time for photography assignments in Yosemite Park, the redwoods, and Crater Lake in Oregon. They invited me to come along, but I had months to work before I would earn time off.

That same June, Miriam fell in love with Ben. I met him one evening when he escorted her to work in his shiny Dodge sedan. He was tall, soft-spoken, and kind. He was studying law at Stanford University. On Miriam's day off, they took drives to Half Moon Bay or visited his family in Palo Alto.

With Ida and Miriam gone, I missed my old friend Eliza. She wrote that she and Thomas had returned to Tucson and were renting a small adobe, not far from the Browns.

I supposed everything would be back to normal after the war ended, but we're a different family now.

Brother Joseph has returned to us. He left home a cheerful boy but is a stranger to me now. He rants about the gas, vermin, and barbed wire, or he broods. He's surely shell-shocked, and I hear there's no cure but time. Susannah's more of a recluse since the epidemic, and Father's still muttering half in German and cannot use one hand.

Only Ma Brown remains undaunted, but I wonder sometimes whether she's not simply deluded. Thomas tells me to cheer up. He's opening his electric appliance store and has bought a truck for deliveries. I think of all that wallpaper we left in Cutter. Oh, what I'd give to have it here, with the high cost of things.

I was troubled to hear Eliza so downhearted and sent back a gay letter, but I had to agree. The world had shifted, and we were all dizzy from it.

—❧—

I turned to the WU girls for company. They took me into their crowd. We were all orphans, of sorts, who'd flocked to the city from small towns and farms throughout the West. Everyone had left hard times—the war and the influenza. We didn't talk about it much. Mrs. Tuttle was our watchful mother hen at work, but in our hours off, we were on our own in the city. The future looked rosy to us. We wanted to live it up.

I got to know Naomi and Jimmie, the talky sisters I was sandwiched between at our rooming house meals.

"Are you going to join us in the parlor tonight?" asked Naomi, who'd gotten a permanent and had wavy hair now.

"What for?"

"To celebrate our suffrage, of course," Jimmie said. "Congress passed the Nineteenth Amendment yesterday—it only needs to be ratified."

"Jimmie's a progressive."

"I'm a communist."

"Please don't say that!" her sister said.

"This is a victory for women, and we're going to have a party."

Eight of us met that night. We had cherry pie and lemon beer, our housemother's homemade temperance drink, and Jimmie directed the conversation around adult topics such as the job shortage, the need for traffic controls for all the motorcars on the roads, and the future of Wilson's League of Nations. She talked about the candidates for the coming presidential election, Dewey and Harding, and the difference twenty-six million women voters might make. I realized I needed to start reading the news magazines again.

As I was walking back to my room, Jimmie and Naomi stopped me.

"We're going swimming at the Lurline Baths tomorrow. Do you want to come?"

I shook my head. "I don't swim."

"We'll teach you. Jimmie used to be on the girls' swim team."

"But I don't have a swimsuit," I said.

"Oh, they give you one."

"The lifeguards are dreamy."

"Naomi's got her eye on a tall blond named Erwin."

"You tease. I saw you looking at that brawny Italian."

We took the streetcar to the indoor pool on the corner of Bush and Larkin. For twenty-five cents we each received a towel, a locker, and a baggy gray cotton suit that covered us from knee to neck.

"It's the oldest public pool in town," Jimmie explained. She pointed out the hot and cold shower baths, the small tubs with fresh or salt water, the Russian steam bath, the barbershop, the special parlors for men and women, the boxing and fencing rooms, and the café.

The pool was crowded. Naomi dove into the deep end, surfaced, and floated on her back. Jimmie led me to the shallow end.

"First you need to get used to it." She waded in, plugged her nose, and lowered her body into the water. I bent my knees and dropped under the surface.

"It's salt water." I gasped. "And cold."

"Of course. They pipe it eight miles across the city from the ocean. But it's heated. A little, anyway."

I shivered.

She encouraged me to lie back into the water, close my eyes, and relax as she supported my back. In a half hour, I had learned to float by myself. I opened my eyes, and above me an immense chandelier glittered like a mass of stars. I floated in a liquid dream.

Then she led me to the edge of the pool and showed me how to kick with my legs straight.

"That's enough for today. You'll be swimming before long, and when you're solid, we'll take you to the Sutro Baths."

As we slunk past the lifeguards, our swimsuits stuck to our bodies like frog skins, and I wondered how those handsome boys could consider it work to spend the day watching nearly naked girls at play.

We swam twice a week that summer and fall. I learned the breaststroke, the new Australian crawl, and how to dive. As I coursed beneath the surface, noises muted, and I entered a sealed-off place. The tension of the hectic office, those blame-filled memories of Mama, fears for my little brothers and sisters and the crazy changing world receded. I left the water revived.

—&—

We went to the Sutro Baths, as promised.

Inside the bathhouse, Naomi and Jimmie led me past the amphitheater, with its rows of seats facing the ocean, to the promenade on the upper level. I looked down at the row of glimmering pools and up into the acres of paned glass. After sandwiches at the lunch bar, we wandered through the museum, past a suit of medieval armor, an Egyptian mummy, and a set of Tom Thumb's real clothing. I marveled at this strange and wonderful world.

We changed into droopy black suits and swam in all seven pools. We started at the largest, an L-shaped salt tank, then tried the others, ending in what Jimmie called "the soup bowl," a warm eighty degrees.

"Now let's take the plunge!" Naomi shouted.

We ran over to the icy freshwater pool, jumped in, and squealed at the shock. Then we did it all again.

As I left the baths that evening, I said a silent thank you to Mr. Sutro, the immigrant-become-millionaire who'd not forgotten that common folk, too, long for pleasure and beauty.

Mama would be proud that I'd learned the life skill of swimming and wouldn't drown like darling Clementine.

6

At work, I introduced Miriam to Jimmie and Naomi, who I learned had Jewish heritage too. They welcomed her into our group, and we spent breaks together at one noisy table. Every day was like another—eight hours of concentrated typing. We might have gotten careless, but Mrs. Tuttle was constantly at our backs.

That summer, Mrs. Tuttle posted a notice for the first excursion to Marin County. I joined a dozen other telegraph operators in the break room that Sunday morning after our shift. I was surprised to see that Jimmie and Naomi had changed into boots and breeches with laced leggings and carried army surplus canteens. They looked at my skirt and flats and promised to take me to buy my own gear.

I turned my attention to Mrs. Tuttle, who was giving a curt speech. She wore a brown wool skirt and jacket, a German-style hat with a feather in the band, and she carried a gnarled walking stick.

"We'll take the streetcar to the terminal, the nine o'clock ferry to Sausalito, the train to Mill Valley, and another up to West Point Inn on Mount Tam. Let's be off."

The crowd moved to the street, where we waited in the fog. We boarded the streetcar, handed our nickels to the conductor, and plunked down on the hard bench seats. The bell clanged, the car lurched, and we sped over the rails, zipping along the network of overhead wires.

Naomi rested her head on my shoulder and closed her eyes. She jerked awake when the conductor shouted at a scrawny boy who'd jumped aboard when we'd slowed around a corner.

"Oh, let him stay," a tall, dark-haired WU operator called out.

"If I let him on, I'll have every urchin in town hitching rides."

"All right, then." The fellow, named Frank, reached into his pocket and handed the conductor a nickel. "There's his fare."

The man scowled. Frank laughed. He looked at me, and his gray eyes sparkled. The boy grinned and settled into a seat at the front of the car.

The car raced through the clammy morning until the lights of the ferry tower shone before us. We traipsed past a couple of sailors slumped on a bench outside a saloon, crossed the railroad tracks, and climbed the stairs to the second floor of the ferry building. We slouched on benches in the crowded waiting room, until the *Ukiah* blew its horn—ten minutes late because of fog—and unloaded. Finally, we were able to board.

Crowded into a few booths, we shared our breakfasts of bread and cheese, sausage, and fruit, augmented by coffees, a few orders of toast, and slices of pie from the restaurant. When breakfast was done, Frank and his friends pulled down lapboards and started a round of pinochle.

Jimmie, Naomi, and I bought Saratoga chips and chocolate bars for the hike and walked out to the deck. The air smelled of salt and soot from coal-powered engines. Steamers bellowed, smaller boats sounded their horns, and the foghorn from Alcatraz blasted at regular intervals. Tugs, freighters, fishing sloops, ferries, and pleasure boats slid across the bay. A pack of gulls flew above the rail, matching our boat's speed, squawking for handouts. We went inside and joined the office crowd singing "Oh, How I Hate to Get Up in the Morning," and we docked.

Hilly Sausalito looked like a picture-book town. The rows of crooked houses perched above twisting roads reminded me of Bisbee, except this town wasn't crowded into a narrow valley surrounded by desert but was open to the world, with the sea on one side and the wide sky above.

We hurried down the ramp to the interurban that took us to Mill Valley, and from there we climbed into open cars of the Mount Tam train that would take us to West Point Inn, halfway up the mountain. We zigzagged up, slowing to a crawl in the steepest sections. By the time we'd reached the inn and gathered, the sky was a clear blue, the sun warm on our faces.

At the trailhead, Mrs. Tuttle pointed out the fir, laurel, and the largest trees, the redwoods.

"She's a frustrated botanist," Jimmie murmured as our supervisor educated us about the species of oak, madrone, spotty black huckleberry, and ceanothus up the mountain.

Mrs. Tuttle set a brisk pace, and we followed single file. We stopped to drink water, scrounge for walking sticks, and listen to more nature notes about wild geranium and poppies. Then the woods opened to golden meadows of long grass, punctuated by green thickets in the folds of the mountain. The air was the freshest I'd smelled since the Jornada.

Climbing up and up, we caught views of the sparkling bay, the city tumbling over its many hills, and the mountains ranging down the coast. We scattered like strewn pebbles over the grassy chaparral to eat our lunches, no longer tired but giddy to be away from the noise and bustle of the city. I lay on my back, inhaled the mellow scent of sun-warmed grass, and watched hawks ride the thermals.

We started up a steeper path and finally reached East Peak, where we crowded onto the observation tower. Frank loaned me his binoculars, and I took in clearer views of the city, East Bay, and of the distant Pacific. Perhaps it was the clean mountain air or those telescopic lenses in my hand, but my uncertain path since leaving Tucson was finally becoming clear. I felt as though this was where I was meant to be.

After a short stay, Mrs. Tuttle hurried us along. "Must go. Can't miss the train." Even miles from the office, her speech was abbreviated.

Approaching Sausalito at dusk, we passed a motionless line of motorcars that wound like a snake down the road into town waiting for the car ferries back to the city. We strolled to the front of the line and boarded the next boat.

My legs and feet ached. My flats were too thin-soled for the rough terrain, and my toes had been pinched from my first step. Supported on either side by Naomi and Jimmie, I limped from the streetcar to my room at the boardinghouse, peeled off my shoes and stockings, and without counting my blisters, fell into sleep.

That night I dreamed I was on top of a mountain, above miles of ocean. A small boat bobbed on the waves below. Someone handed me binoculars, and inside the boat I saw Stevie, Bethel, and Sally.

"You know how to swim," a voice said. "Save them." But I set aside the glasses and pretended I hadn't heard.

⚜

Twice a month I went with the hiking group on trips to Marin County. I invested in a pair of leggings and men's boots, pleased to find footwear to fit my size-10 feet, and Ida altered a pair of army trousers for me. We felt modern and adventurous in our men's shirts, neck ties, knapsacks, and canteens. Usually we hiked the flanks of Mount Tam, but if the mountain was clouded in, we stayed on the lowland walks in the Muir Woods. The beauty of the hills, the views from above, and the camaraderie of my WU friends were worth every blister.

7

Weeknights we gathered in the boardinghouse parlor, where one of the girls played the melodeon organ. We sang "Meet Me Tonight in Dreamland" and other favorites. Sometimes I brought out my Hohner and accompanied the group or played the Mexican songs I remembered.

We traded WU gossip and talked about prohibition and whether folks could stop drinking. One of the girls who'd grown up on a vineyard in the Santa Clara Valley feared the grape industry was going to collapse. She told us about a friend of the family, a vintner, who'd committed suicide.

We wondered whether Lenin was truly behind the strikes in Seattle and debated over the Reds being arrested and deported. Jimmie decided not to be a communist anymore.

I bought a sleek new dress, and Ida made me another. When I went to the dance halls on Saturday nights with the WU girls, we wore dresses that hung from our shoulders, fell loosely over our hips, and left our legs free to kick.

We bought strips of dance tickets at dime-a-dance ballrooms and twirled with tattooed sailors who came and went on the navy ships; with slick fellows with shiny hair; and with regular guys from the Western Union office—Ernie, Stan, Milt, and the dark-haired one with the sparkling eyes, Frank.

We abandoned the prewar ragtime and folk tunes and embraced the new sound of jazz. We mastered the foxtrot, Charleston, and tango—practicing to the Castles' dance guide in Jimmie and Naomi's large room in the boardinghouse. I bobbed my hair.

Jimmie took up smoking, refining over time the subtle twirl of the cigarette holder and tilt of the head as she exhaled blue smoke. I watched in admiration, knowing I could never pull it off. I grew to love that aromatic mix of floor wax, perfume, cigarette smoke, and sweat.

We were becoming brash. Once, I borrowed a bathing suit from a coworker, and Jimmie and I played hooky and caught the early train to Half Moon Bay, where we sunbathed and swam like seals. I felt as free as a man.

I hadn't felt such freedom since riding bareback over the sands of Chihuahua. I'd never dreamed that so many good times could be had in such a short while. I wanted to forget the past, as Sister Mary Carmel had prescribed.

≈

That same month, Eliza wrote that Thomas's appliance business was doing well. The previous month he'd sold ten washing machines.

> Life in Tucson is improving, even if the state of my family is not. There's little I can do but accept the changes that the Great War has brought. You write of the gay times you're having. San Francisco must be a lively place. I'm glad to hear of all your new friends. Ma sends fond regards. My news is that I'm carrying a child. I've been well, but tired—my excuse for not writing more.

Dear Eliza. I hoped a child would bring her joy.

8

rene sent me Dora and Marv Fenton's telephone number and urged me to visit them. They lived with Dora's daughter in the Richmond District.

When I phoned from the boardinghouse, her daughter answered.

"Josie Gore? I remember her speaking of the Gore family." Her voice was faint beneath the buzz of the telephone. "Mother died last November. Of the influenza."

I went cold. I didn't want to believe it.

"I'm so sorry."

"She'd been volunteering. At the military hospital."

"And Mr. Fenton?"

"He . . . he's gone downhill. He spends his days at the livery on Geary Boulevard."

"Might I visit him?"

"Yes, of course. It would do him good to see an old friend."

I went that afternoon. The livery was one of the few still in business downtown. It smelled of sweet hay, manure, and horsehide, an old familiar perfume.

I peered into the dark. The place looked empty but for the horses in their stalls. Then I saw a boy in the tack room, partially hidden behind the saddle he was cleaning. He didn't hear me approach over the carpet of wood shavings. He jumped when I asked him about Marv Fenton.

"Old Man Marv? Sure, miss. He's back near the office."

He pointed to the opposite end of the barn. I recognized him on a bench in a corner. He wore the old, creased Stetson I knew from the Jornada. As I approached, he lifted his head and gave me a crooked smile, but he didn't get up.

"Josie Belle Gore, I'd know you anywhere. Like a vision, you are."

His eyes were yellowed but soft with affection. I leaned down and gave him a hug. He smelled of camphor and chew and horse. He patted the bench next to him, and I sat down.

"You're all growed up."

His head shook as he studied me. He was the same Marv Fenton I remembered from those early days in Cutter before he'd met Dora—though thinner and more wrinkled. A couple days' worth of white stubble covered his chin. One cheek bulged with tobacco. His mouth was hidden by a shaggy walrus mustache.

"You're the image of your ma, you are." He cleared his throat and looked up into the rafters. "We was mighty sorry to hear about her passing. She was a good woman."

I remembered how much Marv Fenton had admired her. He was the first person I'd seen in a long time who'd known Mama.

"It's been three years now since she passed on."

He nodded gravely, then dropped his head and studied his boots.

"You heard about Dora?"

"Yes, sir. I'm awfully sorry. Mama loved her. We all did."

He kept his head down.

"They finally got their revenge. Took 'em twenty years since the war, but they got it. Sent in the Spanish Lady." He reached for my hand. "God takes the best for himself, but it's the living that suffer."

A wagon and team of four had pulled in at the other end of

THE WAYS OF WATER

the livery. The hostler and stable boy unhitched the horses and led them to their stalls. After a while, Marv Fenton let go of my hand and looked at me.

"What brings you all the way to Frisco?"

"I live here now. I have a job at Western Union."

"You're goin' somewhere, then." He scratched his chin. "What's that you got on your eyes?"

"It's eye paint."

"Makes you look like a showgirl."

He was out of step with the times.

"I'm not the same girl you knew in Cutter."

"Humph. And what's Charlie up to?"

I told him that he was working at Earl and Irene's and of his hopes to join the navy.

"That was some wedding party fer those two. I reckon that was . . . what was it? July of 1912."

I nodded and watched the stable boy saunter past, leading a gray mare with a white mane and tail. She was a beauty.

"So you help out here?"

He snorted. "Can't hardly move these days. They put up with me. This salt air's heck for the old bones."

"Do you like the city?"

"Can't tolerate the noise and the smell. 'Specially those stinkin' motorcars. Things changin' so fast, seems I can hardly keep up. This is the only place I can get peace. Here with the dumb beasts."

He leaned back, as if even the mention of it had worn him out. I sat with him and took in his piney camphor and his stillness. It was the longest I'd sat with anyone without talking since I'd come to the city. City people, it seemed, always wanted to fill in the gaps.

"And your papa and the young'uns? Who's taking care of them?"

I told him about Papa's job running the mine train in Nevada, that Ida was married and living in Oakland, and that the children were with Irene.

"It's a crying shame you all are so far apart."

He spit chew onto the ground in front of us. I watched it sink into a patch of freshly laid sawdust.

"I'd go back, but I'm too old now," he mumbled. "Never felt myself here. Tried to stay on that bronco, but I've been thrown off. Heck, I'm not even in the ring no more."

"Irene tells me it's all changed back there. Places have shut down. Everyone's moving out."

"Goin' back to what it was before the mining boom and the dam. I recall those days. They was quiet. A man could think."

He stopped talking. I glanced over at him. He was staring at a spot across the barn. He'd left me for his thoughts.

"Mr. Fenton, I've got to go. I work tonight. I'll come to see you again."

He raised his head, looking small under his big hat. "I'd be tickled to see you any time, Josie."

He reached for his cane and shifted forward to stand but grimaced and fell back onto the bench. I shook his hand, just loose skin and knobs for knuckles, kissed his rough cheek, and turned to go.

"You still playing that Hohner?"

"Yes. Charlie gave it to me."

"Good. Keep at it while you've got the breath. Next time, bring it along so you can play me a tune."

As I headed out of the livery, a man in a jaunty derby rushed past me.

"Does this barn rent motorcars?"

I shrugged.

I never went back to see Marv Fenton. I got busy with work, visits to Ida, and swimming, hiking, and dancing with my new friends.

Several months later, Irene wrote. She had little news except that Engle had dwindled to two hundred people, counting those living on the surrounding ranches. She added that the Fentons' daughter in San Francisco had written. Marv Fenton had died in his sleep.

Oh, what an inconsiderate girl I'd become, always wanting to be having fun. I couldn't even find time to play a tune for a lonely old friend. He was with Dora now. Surely they were happy together.

I received a letter from Papa a few weeks later. He'd fallen and broken his leg in three places. While in the hospital, he must have had time to think. He said he was sorry about the way things had turned out between us and understood that I needed to have my own life. He knew I was working hard, but he wanted to remind me of my duty. When I was able, he wanted me to help Irene out with the care of the children.

Perhaps Marv Fenton's passing softened my heart. I didn't want any more regrets. I wrote to Papa. I said I was sorry too, and that I missed him. I needed time to save money first, but I was planning to do my part. It felt good to write those words.

9

That December, folks went crazy over alcohol. Saloons hosted wild holiday parties, and people stocked up on liquor.

January 18 was Law and Order Sunday. The streets were quiet. While some slept off the previous night's binge, others were in church giving thanks for the new law.

My WU crowd didn't start drinking until after prohibition. We'd had little interest beforehand, but now it was the thing to do. Speakeasies opened in every quarter of the city. When we went dancing, we bought cola or ginger ale, and somebody would bring out a pint and covertly pour a round. Drinking made the conversation flow, the laughter ready, the dancing easy, and brought in a tolerance for lawbreaking.

In August, the Nineteenth Amendment was ratified by the final state—Tennessee, just three weeks before my nineteenth birthday. We had another party in the rooming house parlor on a night our housemother was out, but this time we toasted women's suffrage with glasses of California chardonnay our friend from Santa Clara had sneaked in.

The dancing and drinking all cost money. By fall, I had little saved for the apartment I would need when my siblings came to live with me.

One night at WU, Miriam and I escaped the busy clicking of the sending machines and shared a root beer during break. She invited me to dine at the Cliff House with her family to celebrate my birthday. I was touched. We talked often at work but had not been out together for some time. Miriam didn't drink.

They picked me up and we drove to Ocean Beach. It was low tide that Saturday afternoon. The air smelled of seaweed and iodine. Beachgoers, blankets, remnants of picnic lunches, and articles of clothing littered the sand. We removed our shoes and stockings and played in the surf.

At the Cliff House, we each ordered a different kind of fish and passed our plates around to sample each other's. Sam told us about the comedy routine he was developing and about the best vaudeville act he'd ever seen—a man named Al Jolson. Following the meal, the waiters brought out a chocolate cake with a white candle.

"Happy birthday to our dear Josie," Miriam said as she handed me a package.

I untied the ribbon. Inside the slender box was a pair of Shalimar gloves.

"A girl can always use an extra pair," she said as I admired them.

Maggie looked sad, so I removed my necklace, placed it in the box, and retied the ribbon. She was thrilled to open a present too. When she felt the string of glass beads around her generous neck, she squealed how pretty she was and wrapped her arms around me, refusing to let go.

"That's enough now, Maggie." Sam gently pried her arms from me. "Speaking of pretty girls . . . have you got a beau yet, Josie? There must be more than one fellow at the office with his eyes on you."

"There certainly are," Miriam said.

"No, they're all pals."

"Not even one that makes your heart go pitter-patter?" Sam asked.

"Maybe one."

"Do tell," Miriam said. "It won't go beyond us."

I looked down at the tablecloth, up into the inquisitive eyes of Miriam and Sam, and at Maggie, who was playing with the ribbon.

"Do you know Frank?"

"Frank? The one with the merry Irish eyes who works our shift?" Miriam said. "Oh, he's full of fun, isn't he? I'll tell him tomorrow that you've taken a shine to him."

"Don't you dare," I hissed.

She giggled. "I wouldn't dream of it, you goose. You're my best friend."

"But not your only best friend. How's Ben?"

"Busy with studies. I'd love for you to know him better. We'll take you with us sometime when we visit his family."

The waiter cleared our plates, and Sam excused himself to have a smoke on the observation deck.

"Sam worries me," Miriam said as she stirred sugar into her coffee. "He's been so unhappy lately. Always fancying being somewhere else—Chicago or New York. But he doesn't want to leave us. He's drinking more, and it makes him reckless."

Miriam reapplied her lipstick and pulled on her tight silk cap, and we joined him on the deck to search for seals near the crashing waves. Tendrils of fog crept in from the sea, slunk around us, and blanketed the land.

Back in the car, Sam turned around. "Want a drink, Josie?"

"All right. After all, it's my birthday."

Ignoring Miriam's frown, I took a swig of rum and handed it back. He drove fast over the rough roads.

"Golly, Sam," Miriam said, "can't you slow down? I don't know how you can see in this soup."

He took another sip from his flask, slowed for half a mile, and sped up again. I was worried he'd lose sight of the road or lose control of the shaking steering wheel. Miriam and I gripped our seats and peered nervously into the mist. We stopped talking. It was no longer fun.

I was relieved when we reached the WU building.

"Thanks for the dinner, Sam," I called, as Miriam and I crawled out of the car.

He smiled, started singing, "Come Josephine," and roared off with Maggie.

"I'm so sorry," Miriam said.

"We survived the drive, and the evening was wonderful. Thank you again, my dear friend."

But I worried about Maggie, racing with her brother over those slippery streets.

I n the spring of 1921, I received a letter from Irene. Drought had come to the Jornada. If they didn't get rain soon, they'd have to move their cattle or lose them. It meant leaving the ranch, maybe for another state. Earl was gone most of the time trying to find work to pay for hay, and Irene was running the ranch single-handedly. She sounded tired and discouraged.

> *I was wondering whether you and Ida May might be able to take Stevie and Bethel for the summer, she wrote. I know you working girls lead busy lives, but if you could find it in your hearts to help out, I would be grateful.*

Ida and Teal had received a similar plea from Irene. I met them at a speakeasy on Market Street. We drank beer and talked about the problem. Ida was hesitant about taking the children, but Teal was not. He assured us that it was time for us to relieve Irene's burden. We pooled our money and bought the children train tickets to California.

—⁂—

In mid-May, Stevie and Bethel arrived. Ida and Teal met the children and took them home. The following afternoon, Teal picked me up at the Oakland Pier, let me off in front of the house, then left to photograph an air balloon exhibition in Hayward. I walked up the front steps and peered in the living room window.

A sturdy suntanned boy sat on the sofa, his brown hair parted in the middle and slicked back. He wore slacks and a shirt and tie like a grown man, but the curve of his jaw was still that of a child. His head was bent as he studied the pictures in a comic book. His sister sat next to him, her neck craned to see the pages. She was plumper and prettier than when I'd left her two and a half years before in Tucson.

She looked up and saw me through the window. She jumped to her feet, opened the front door, and flew into my arms.

"Bethel," I choked. "I missed you so."

She was all softness and little girl sweetness. She clasped my hand as we entered the house.

Ida came into the room, an apron tied around her middle.

"Can you believe they're here, Josie? Our little ones? Can you believe we're together?"

The boy put down his book, slowly stood, and walked toward me.

"Oh, Stevie," I cried. He stood awkwardly as I embraced him. "It's been four years. You were a little boy when I saw you last. You remember me, don't you, Stevie?"

My eyes had flooded.

"Of course, he remembers his sister," Ida said.

"Yeah, I remember now." His voice was husky. He stiffly hugged me.

"Come into the kitchen," Ida said. "I promised the children we'd make popcorn balls. The syrup's ready."

As Ida and Bethel stirred the popped corn into the pot of thick syrup, Stevie sat next to me at the kitchen table and told us about the train ride out. Irene had sent them with a hamper of food. Daddy Graham had given the conductor money, and the man had checked on them often. They'd seen starving cattle in New Mexico, a pack of coyotes on a moonlit night in Arizona, and deer in the California mountains. We buttered our hands and began shaping the puffed corn into hot, sticky balls.

Stevie looked out the window. "There are so many houses here. Are there any animals in Oakland?"

"We have birds and dogs and cats. And horses," I said. "And the ocean's filled with fish and all sorts of creatures—seals, octopuses, and sea lions. And sometimes a whale swims by."

Stevie's eyes got wide.

"There's a zoological garden in the city. We'll take you there for sure." I placed a popcorn ball on waxed paper. "Oh, we're going to have a grand time this summer."

—⚹—

On weekends, we rode the streetcars all over the city—downtown to see the skyscrapers and Civic Center, to Fisherman's Wharf to ogle at the seafood and to take home a shiny silver salmon, to Land's End to play at the beach, and to Golden Gate Park to float model sailboats on Spreckels Lake. Stevie loved everything. He jumped the ocean waves, threw his rubber ball high into the air at every park we visited, and ate voraciously. Bethel said little but was always ready for the next adventure. Watching them take in the commotion of the city reminded me of how excited I'd been when I first arrived in Bisbee.

—⚹—

For Stevie's twelfth birthday, Teal managed to get free tickets to the Neptune Beach amusement park in Alameda, good for any day but the Fourth of July. We arrived early to be the first through the gates.

"I came to this park as a kid," Teal said. "We called it Neptune Gardens then."

At nine o'clock when the gates opened, Ida hustled us toward the sand "beach," a rectangle of white sand, and threw a flowered cloth on a picnic table. She set our basket on top and told us it was our gathering place for the day. Teal rented a striped beach umbrella, buried its pole, and laid a blanket next to it. Then he gave us our bearings.

"That's the main building, across from us." He clicked a photograph with his ever-present camera. "It's got a dance hall. Maybe Ida and Josie want to go dancing tonight?"

"If we stay long enough," Ida said.

"We'll stay until the fireworks," Teal replied, "since we have two birthdays to celebrate. I believe there's another coming up soon."

Bethel, soon to turn nine, giggled.

Teal pointed out the kiddie playground, the swimming pool, and beyond it, the natural beach. He indicated the fairway, with its game arcade and rides.

Ida turned to Stevie and Bethel. "What shall we do first?"

"I want to go in the pool," Stevie said.

Teal and Ida weren't swimmers, so I paid our quarters and handed the children towels, wool suits, and brass locker disks. I demonstrated the Australian crawl, but they were more interested in playing beneath the fountains. They ran in and out of the spouting salt water, shouting about rain, a wonder after the drought in the Jornada.

After wolfing down Ida's liverwurst sandwiches, we headed to the arcade where we spent a load of nickels playing games of chance. Stevie got frustrated, but Teal was lucky and spun the flashing, buzzing wheel to win a live canary. I was entranced with the tiny yellow bird and offered to carry the cage.

Teal and Stevie shot rifles at the shooting gallery where Stevie hit the bull's-eye and won a Kewpie doll he gave to Bethel. Sorry that Stevie had won a prize he didn't want, Teal bought him a toy airplane at the souvenir stand.

Bethel wanted to ride the merry-go-round. As we waited in the longest line of the park, Teal told us it was a Dentzel carousel, one of the finest in the world. He'd ridden this one at the 1915 Panama–Pacific Expo before it was moved to the park.

When the carousel slowed to a stop, we dashed from beast to beast, trying to decide which to ride. Bethel chose a galloping cat with a fish in its mouth, Stevie climbed onto a striped tiger with a frog saddle, Teal jumped onto a trotting ostrich, and Ida found a creature with a fish's tail and a horse's head. I settled on a wild-eyed stallion with a tiny fairy nestled in its mane. The music began, and we circled make-believe lands painted onto the center panels. I lost myself in a fantasy world, wishing I could ride this enchanted horse forever.

Stevie was thirsty, so Teal and the children headed off to the concessions to get Neptune Beach snow cones. Ida and I relaxed in the shade of the umbrella. I took a little flask of gin from my handbag, shielded it from view, and poured it into our drinks.

"Gin's so refreshing on a hot day, don't you think?"

"So true. Be sure to save some for Teal. He loves it. Oh, my feet are killing me." Ida slipped off her pumps and wiggled her toes in the warm sand.

I threw off my flats and buried my tired feet next to hers.

―❧―

In the early evening, while Teal and the children watched a tightrope walk above the sand, Ida and I went up to the dance hall. Lanterns lined the walls. A mirrored chandelier hung above the maple spring floor. Jazz played, couples danced, and waiters circled tables at the edge of the floor. We ordered sodas and sat down. Some fellows asked us to dance, and we joined the crowd of swinging, kicking couples.

We danced for the better part of an hour and then took our sodas and stepped outside. I brought out my flask and supplemented our drinks. A little gin remained, so I looked around, lifted the bottle to my lips, and finished it off.

"Did I tell you a couple of us girls are thinking of taking an apartment together? Our housemother's too strict. We want to do as we please."

"Come here for a minute, will you?" Ida said.

I joined her on the bench.

"I'm not sure it's a good idea, Josie. I'm worried about you. I think you drink too much."

"You drink too."

"Not as much as you. Even Teal has commented on it." She stared into her glass. "You run with a wild crowd. It can lead to bad habits—you know what drinking did to Papa. You're even carrying your own hooch now. You might get in trouble. And it's not a good example for Stevie and Bethel."

"Oh, Ida! I'm only having fun."

I stood and threw my empty bottle into the trash canister. Didn't I deserve to have a good time after all my hard work? Ida could talk. She had a man to look after her. I was on my own and could do as I pleased. Why did she need to pry into my life?

"Let's go back and dance."

But the music had slowed, and the dancing lost its appeal. We left the hall and returned to the picnic table. Bethel and Stevie were gobbling chocolate creams. They'd gone back to the arcade, and Teal had played a game of housey-housey and won the candy prize. While we waited for dark, Ida cuddled next to Teal while I fumed at my meddling older sister.

Without warning, shooting stars of red, white, and blue burst into the sky. Ida scooted next to me and took my hand, and I softened and took Bethel's.

At ten o'clock the park closed, and we walked with the crowd to the front gates. I carried the canary, Bethel clung to her Kewpie, and Stevie buzzed his mechanical airplane above his head. We were tired and broke, but we were together. We were a family again.

Back in my room, I reflected on our day. It had been perfect but for Ida's comments about my drinking. Alone in the dark, I couldn't deny that she was right. My crowd drank, not only on weekends but on weeknights too. I often awoke with a headache. I didn't like what I'd become.

―※―

In mid-September, Ida wanted Teal to see the place where we'd grown up and to meet Irene, so they decided to drive the children back to New Mexico. Teal planned to photograph the sites they would pass for a newspaper travelogue. I offered to keep the canary while they were gone.

They serviced the Model T and spent days preparing for the long drive and camping along the way. I was sorry to see Bethel and Stevie go but hoped to have them back the following summer.

Early on a Monday morning, I waved goodbye from the Oakland dock and, yellow bird in hand, walked onto the ferry. Canaries are meant to warn of danger, but that silly bird sang the whole ride back to the city.

The following week at work, Miriam and I shared a sandwich at break time and worked a newspaper word puzzle.

"It's been too long since we've had you to the apartment," she said. "I need a four-letter word for 'destiny.'"

I told her I'd been spending Sundays with Ida and the children.

"And weeknights you go out with your friends. We miss seeing you—especially Maggie."

She, Ben, and Sam were going to drive down to Palo Alto on Sunday, and she invited me to go with them. She and Ben had news, and they wanted me to be there.

"News? Oh, tell me now."

"No, I promised Ben not to. You're going to have to wait." She said she'd telephone Sunday to arrange my pickup.

"*Fate*," I said.

She placed the letters in their boxes, and we hurried back to our machines.

That Sunday morning, I waited but didn't receive a call. Naomi and Jimmie invited me to a matinee, but I declined. Miriam finally telephoned.

"I'm afraid we're a bit disorganized. It seems Sam had planned to take Rose all along, and now Maggie's having a conniption fit over staying with the neighbor. I've never seen her so unreasonable." She paused. I could tell she was beside herself. "I simply must bring Maggie. There won't be room for you, Josie. I apologize. We'll take you next time."

I was disappointed to be left out and frustrated to be missing the movie with Naomi and Jimmie. I considered going to join them, but it had begun to rain.

I stayed home and washed out my stockings, girdle, and underwear. I wrote a letter to Eliza and played a few songs on my harmonica, thinking of Bethel and Stevie. I'd forgotten to ask Miriam her news. I guessed that she and Ben were going to announce their engagement.

⸻

It wasn't until I got to work on Monday that I heard the news. As I was taking off my coat in the break room, Mrs. Tuttle told me that there had been an automobile accident. Miriam and her family had perished. I shook my head in disbelief.

No one knew quite what had happened. The roads had been slick with rain. Perhaps the brakes had failed, a wheel had come off, or maybe Sam had been driving too fast. The car had gone off the road and fallen down a ravine into a river.

No, I protested silently. *Miriam was going to get married, and Ben was going to be a lawyer. Sam was sure to become a vaudeville star after he married Rose. And Maggie. Poor Maggie.*

But I saw the tremor of Mrs. Tuttle's hands and her reddened eyes. It was true. How could they be gone?

Mrs. Tuttle took my coat, had me sit, and handed me coffee.

"I know you were close. I was fond of Miriam too." It was the slowest I'd heard her speak. "Stay here. I need to tell the others."

For once I was glad she didn't say more. I sat, stunned. Some of the operators came by.

"It's a tragedy," said a girl with tears streaming down her face. "She was so pretty."

I couldn't respond. I stirred my coffee.

Frank came up and squeezed my hand. "I'm sorry. I'll ask the nuns to say a rosary for her at St. Patrick's. I know she wasn't Catholic, but it's all I can think of."

I nodded in appreciation, too choked up to speak.

Naomi and Jimmie gave me hugs. "Let us know what we can do."

I didn't want to sit there any longer. I stumbled into the work room, where messages were being sent all over the world. I wondered whether a telegram had been sent announcing the death of the Stein family of San Francisco.

I sat at my switchboard and tried to work. I was too numb to think. My fellow workers, busy as they were, sent me sympathetic glances. Miriam's sending machine sat empty. An hour later, a girl I'd never seen sat in her chair and took over her wires.

At first daylight, Mrs. Tuttle came by and put her hand on my shoulder.

"I thought staying busy might do you good. I was wrong. Go home early. Times like this, you need time alone."

I left and walked down the nearly empty sidewalks past tall city buildings, until I could see the water of the bay. They'd died in the water. Had they even had the chance to swim?

I didn't know where to go. So many I'd loved had left me— Mama, Dora and Marv Fenton, and now Miriam. I longed for my sisters, but Ida was somewhere in the desert, and Irene had troubles of her own.

I wandered like a stray. An hour later, I found myself in front of St. Mary's Cathedral. I hadn't entered a church since I'd left Tucson.

I let myself in a side door and crept into a pew. I knelt on the hard wood and talked to Miriam. I told her how much I loved her and would miss her and how grateful I was for her friendship. I told her that she'd better know a good reason for this to have happened because I couldn't think of one. I could almost hear her laughter, as if she knew something I did not.

I talked to Ben and told him I was glad he was with Miriam. I greeted reckless Sam and his girlfriend, Rose. And then I thought of Maggie. I felt relieved in an odd, sad way. She would have been lost if they'd perished without her. She was with the people she loved.

I was alive because Maggie had made the trip in my place. She'd unwittingly sacrificed her life for me. Or did she insist on going that day because she knew it was a final excursion, in a way the innocent have of comprehending what others cannot?

Why was my life spared? What was it worth?

I looked up at the lifeless Jesus on the cross above the altar. His sacrifice was repeated when any person gave their life in an act of love.

I pondered Dora Fenton forfeiting hers to bring comfort to the soldiers with influenza. I thought of Mama and the life she'd given Sally, resulting in her own death, and the young men who'd died alone in trenches in France, while trying to defend people they would never know. Love for others ultimately resulted in sacrifice of self. Marv Fenton was right. God takes the best for himself.

They were all there with me.

I looked at the statue of Mary. I'd been saved by three

419

women who'd loved me. Ma Brown and Sister Mary Carmel had rescued me from the death grip of influenza, and now Maggie had spared me from the accident. So many people had been so good to me. My life was a gift. I rested my forehead on the wooden pew in front of me, too dazed to weep. It was my turn to take care of the ones I loved.

A calm settled over me like a dressing on a wound.

I heard steps on the marble floor, the creak of kneelers, and sighs. I lifted my head to see strangers kneeling around me in the half-light. Their silent petitions filled the church. Their pains might be as great as mine, or even harder to bear. I wished them healing strength.

I left the pew and pushed open the door. I stood for a moment, stunned by the glare and din of the street, and walked to my room. I pulled the blinds, took off my clothes, and lay down in the dark. I slept until late afternoon.

The canary's chirping woke me. I thought of Miriam, Ben, Sam, Rose, and Maggie and what had happened. It was strange that the canary should be so cheerful and the sun so bright.

I put out seed for the yellow bird and changed its water. It cocked its head, blinked its black eyes, and sang to me. I dressed for supper. Taking a cue from the caged bird, I penciled my eyes and painted my lips an unsuitable red. Miriam would want me to try to savor my precious life.

12

Ten days after the funeral at the Fillmore synagogue, I received a letter from Irene.

The summer rains have not come. My garden has withered, the cattle are skin and bones, and most of the wells have run dry. We're moving our cattle to grazing land in Arizona. We'll take Joe and baby Charles, while Mona boards at the Sisters of Loretto school in Las Cruces. We'll be in Arizona until the drought ends—a year or more.

I cannot bring Stevie and Bethel. They'll have to go to an orphanage, unless someone in the family can take them. Sally will need a place too, since Aunt JoJane can no longer keep her. I'll tell Ida May and Teal the same when they arrive. I'm asking for your help.

The time had come. I telegrammed Irene: SEND THE CHILDREN. I AM READY.

Two weeks later, I received a letter from Ida. They'd had a long journey, camping many nights in the desert, the children wrapped in blankets on the seats of the car, while she and Teal slept on army cots in a tent.

The ranch is in hard times. Papa walks with a limp now. Our old home's gone.

Irene told me you've offered to keep the children. We will care for them together. They can stay in my home since I have room—I wouldn't have it otherwise.

Sally will soon be here, and we'll all return to you. Charlie will be coming out too, to enlist in the navy in San Francisco. Even Papa talks of finding a train to run in California.

I'm helping Irene pack up the ranch. She's desolate. I'll bring Mama's jade plant and her sewing machine. Irene wants us to take it, since it may be years before they return. Teal complained, but I insisted, and it's tied to the back of the Model T. It will be yours. We'll be home by month's end.

By the time I received her letter, Ida was on the road again. She was bringing our family home. And Mama's Singer too. I might even learn to sew.

13

Several weeks later, Mrs. Tuttle led a final fall excursion to Mount Tam—a healthy diversion for our hiking group. We all had known Miriam.

It was a clear and flawless October day. As we ascended the hills, the air took on the sharp scent of dying leaves and flowers gone to seed. Mrs. Tuttle was all business as she led the group. I hiked behind her broad back, watching the muscles of her heavy calves expand and contract with each step. Ahead of us, Stevie, Bethel, and Sally scampered to the next bend, then stopped to sit and drink from their canteens until the group caught up with them. Naomi and I chatted about nothing at all.

We stopped for lunch on the dry flank of the mountain. I gave the children crackers, cheese, and apple wedges, lay back, and looked up into the blue. I wondered whether Mama and Miriam and Maggie were really up there, and whether they were watching us. Some of the girls sang a round of "Rose Red," and I could hear Bethel's and Sally's clear, high voices chime in. I closed my eyes and inhaled the fragrance of sunbaked earth and golden grass. Life can be a kettle of sadness. But along with it comes lumps of sweetness so exquisite, like this day, that they give a girl the courage to dream.

When we started up the mountain again, Frank, so kind after Miriam's death, fell into step beside me. He didn't say much but touched my elbow to show me a hawk gliding above. When I tripped over a root, he put out his hand to steady me. His eyes twinkled.

"Can you walk on your own, or do you need my hand?"

I gave him a look, laughed, and skipped on ahead with the children. He caught up, and we walked together, his step synchronized with mine, my heart aflutter.

In the late afternoon, we reached a spot where the whole world seemed to lie before us—tree-covered hills extending to hazy mountains and the glittering bay dotted with islands, ships, and boats. We sat to catch our breaths and take in the view. Someone had oranges, and the children set to peeling them.

I wandered down the ridge, where I sat alone. I looked toward the miniature city on the bay and thought of the far-off people going through the exercise of living. I sensed nobility in this venture of bravely embarking, like the ships below me, on an unknown voyage sure to include storms, but more often, swells of delight and gladness.

Above the distant hills, I saw a wisp of a cloud. Or was it smoke from the stack of an everlasting train? Oh, I'd come far from the desert of my childhood. Such twists and turns I had taken to arrive at this place at the edge of the sea. This must be the Promised Land Mama had spoken of, with its water, water everywhere. I wished she could see it too.

A fresh breeze blew up the side of the cliff and engulfed me. Mama was near.

"Look at the little ones," I told her. "They're here."

And she knew everything that had happened. She understood, and, yes, she'd forgiven me.

Happiness came out of nowhere and lifted me, as though I were again emerging from a well. A vortex of joy whirled around me at dizzying speed. I felt frighteningly light, as if I might fall to the rocks below or float over the cliff to glide with the gulls. I grabbed for a root and clung to it until the whirlwind subsided. When I felt steady, I stood and went back to the others.

"There you are, Josie," someone said, and held out a flask. "Join the party."

I walked past and sat next to Frank. The children ran to me, canteens clanging, their fists filled with fruit, and settled at my feet.

"I'll just sit here a moment in the sun."

AFTERWORD

This is a work of fiction, inspired by the life of my grandmother, Josie Belle Gore. I often asked her to tell me stories about her childhood, and by the time she passed away, I had compiled a collection of notes. Years later, after exploring the remains of the old Cutter cemetery in search of the graves of my great-grandparents, I realized that there was a larger story to be told.

Cutter and Engle are now ghost towns. Historic sections of Las Cruces and Tucson have been razed. Bisbee is a fraction of its former size. Few trains pass through the Jornada del Muerto these days. The hopes and sacrifices of my great-grandparents, and countless families who weathered the boom-and-bust cycles of the early-twentieth-century Southwest, risked being forgotten.

This story originated as fragments of family oral history, yet to sculpt a full narrative, I found it necessary to create fictional characters, situations, and conversations, change names, locations, and alter time.

The real Josie Belle remained close to her siblings throughout her life. She married Frank in 1925 at St. Mary's Cathedral in San Francisco. In 1929, they moved to Seattle to work for Western Union. Later, Josie worked nights at WU to support their four children. She retired in 1969 after nearly four decades with the company. Josie lived most of her adult life in Seattle with a view of the sea, on a hill named for a queen.

ACKNOWLEDGMENTS

I'm indebted to my grandmother, for leading a life of courage and sharing her stories, and to my father Frank, aunts Rita and Loretta, uncle Pat, and cousin Charles Graham, who shared family lore. Abundant thanks to the kind friends and mentors who read versions of the manuscript and responded—Debbie, Jerold, Gerald and many others; Todd Manza, insightful editor, and to my dear writing partner, Pat Wiggins, for counsel through early drafts. I thank *She Writes Press* Brooke Warner and Lauren Wise and their stellar team for empowering women authors to tell their stories, and Caitlin Hamilton Summie for bringing mine to a broader readership. I am grateful to my family—my husband Claus, children Stina, Nico, Lukas, and Britta—for their patience, love, and support, and especially to my mother, Maxine, whose unflagging encouragement has lifted me more times than I can count.

A proverb states that she who does not look back to her roots will not reach her destiny. In putting this to paper, I have journeyed to the well and back again.

ABOUT THE AUTHOR

TERESA H. JANSSEN is a career educator whose essays and fiction have appeared in a variety of literary journals. *The Ways of Water*, her debut novel, was inspired by her grandmother's girlhood in the American Southwest. She resides with her husband near Seattle on Washington state's Olympic Peninsula.

SELECTED TITLES FROM SHE WRITES PRESS

The Black Velvet Coat by Jill G. Hall. $16.95, 978-1-63152-009-9. When the current owner of a black velvet coat—a San Francisco artist in search of inspiration—and the original owner, a 1960s heiress who fled her affluent life fifty years earlier, cross paths, their lives are forever changed . . . for the better.

Mt. Moriah's Wake by Melissa Norton Carro. $16.95, 978-1-64742-138-0. A young woman returning home to her small southern town must face her past and the skeletons in her small community—and come to terms with her present life.

South of Everything by Audrey Taylor Gonzalez. $16.95, 978-1-63152-949-8. A powerful parable about the changing South after World War II, told through the eyes of young white woman whose friendship with her parents' black servant, Old Thomas, initiates her into a world of magic and spiritual richness.

Valeria Vose by Alice Bingham Gorman. $16.95, 978-1-63152-409-7. When privileged Southern woman Valeria Vose discovers her husband's infidelity through his lover's attempted suicide, she turns to an Episcopal priest for direction and solace—and spins into a clandestine, ill-fated love affair that forces her to confront all her preconceived values and expectations.

Lost in Oaxaca by Jessica Winters Mireles. $16.95, 978-1-63152-880-4. Thirty-seven-year-old piano teacher Camille Childs is a lost soul who is seeking recognition through her star student—so when her student unexpectedly leaves California to return to her village in Oaxaca, Mexico, Camille follows her. There, Camille meets Alejandro, a Zapotec man who helps her navigate the unfamiliar culture of Oaxaca and teaches her to view the world in a different light.